QUANTUM GIRL

BEING THE FIRST PART OF
THE QUANTUM GIRL TRILOGY

BY

DONALD KIERAN AUSTEN

AND

PEYTON ELISE HERRON

INNER SPACE MEDIA
2020

QUANTUM GIRL, Volume I of the Quantum Girl Trilogy
Copyright 2020 by Donald Kieran Austen and Peyton Elise Herron

Published by Inner Space Media
10325 Donna Avenue, Porter Ranch, California 91326

Quantum Girl / Donald Kieran Austen, Peyton Elise Herron
    p.   cm.

ISBN 978-1-7377812-0-2 (pbk. : acid-free paper)
ISBN 978-1-7377812-2-6 (kindle)

Library of Congress Control Number: 2023918195

1. Science *Fiction*[1]   2. Superheroes   3. Alien Civilizations
4. Time Travel   5. Parallel Dimensions   6. LGBTQ
7. Bullying   8. Teen Suicide   9. Self-Harm

303025

Cover images designed by Donald Kieran Austen

Printed in the United States of America

---

[1] So stated as science *fiction* for the sake of Library of Congress Card Catalog classification and search engine visibility, though, most assuredly it is not.

Quantum Girl

FORWARD

If you believe the story you are about to read is fiction, then you had better stop right here and now. Go to your Amazon orders page or wherever you bought this book, and request a prompt return. My name is Peyton Herron, and there are things that happened to me that no one else born on this planet will ever go through. Hardly anyone reading this for the first time will know who I am. What is written has long since been rewritten by what I call the fabric of time. Once there was a world called Rendenaaar. Once in some reality, there was a woman who was reborn. Once there was a girl, who became a superhero, and that girl was me. But time is not irrevocable, and what was, may not be what is now. I did what I had to, in order to survive; in order that this world, and the universe in which it exists, could *continue* to exist. My name is Peyton Herron, and I am Quantum Girl, and whether you choose to believe or not, the words that I have written are true.

Now and forever, through time and space,

PEYTON ELISE HERRON

CHAPTER I

My name is Peyton Herron—Peyton Elise Herron; Peyton from my great-grandmother on my mother's side, and Elise from my father's mother, who died during childbirth. When all that I am about to describe first occurred, I was fourteen years old. That is when I decided to take my own life and succeeded. No, I am not a ghost, nor am I a corpse floating face-down in a pool in a mansion on Sunset Blvd. I am Quantum Girl—at least, that is what I chose to name myself. I am the most powerful being in every universe throughout time. That has been a heavy cross to bear, especially from the start with only fourteen summers to have shone down upon my face.

I had decided to keep this journal, as a result of certain circumstances, which might seem incredible, if not unbelievable. Be that as it may, it is what happened, though certain events have been erased from memory, which shall all be explained in good time, for time itself is what much of this story is about.

The story—my story—began on September 14. 2024, the anniversary of my birth, nearly one and a half decades ago. I was officially fourteen years old, but what did that mean in the grand scheme of things? Did that one day make any difference? Was I somehow smarter because the sun set and rose one more time? I *still* had to go to school. I *still* had to deal with all the shit that went on. I was a freshman in high school. School had just started a few weeks before. I didn't know anyone there other than Phee and some girl who had plagued me since the semester began. Phee is my sister; my fraternal twin, which makes absolutely no sense from a linguistic point of view, as the adjective has to do with brothers, which, obviously, we're not. Phee is short for Ophelia, Ophelia Jane Herron, who was named after absolutely no one. My Mom was just a devotee of Shakespeare, and, as for Jane, I guess it just sounded right.

I was fairly tall for my age; five foot eight and, as I had erroneously thought, possibly still growing. Phee was around the same, give or take a smidge. I started modeling that past summer. I had always been told that I was pretty. So it was with Phee as well, though I thought that between the two of us, she was the prettier one. Phee woke me that morning, half an hour before the alarm on my iPhone went off, pushing hard against the edge of my bed and disrupting my blissful sleep.

"Hey!" she announced—this followed immediately with, "Happy Birthday!" exclaimed in enthusiastic Phee-like tones.

"Yeah, right. You too." I grumbled, smothering my head under the pillow that separated me from the woken world. "HBP," I mumbled through the feathers, though it probably came out as something indistinguishable to her ears.

"Huh?" came the reply.

Baring a space between the pillow and the bed, I elaborated, still only half-awake, "Happy Birthday, Phee," mumbling out afterward, "I thought HBO would be too confusing, dear Ophelia." Hours seemed to pass (though, relatively speaking, it was probably only seconds) I mumbled out the question that loomed foremost in my incoherent brain, "What time is it?"

"Five a.m.," she announced. *How,* I wondered, *could anyone be so chipper at this time of night?* I rolled over onto my back, stretched out my arms, and yawned, watching as the blurry white canopy that hung over my bed came into focus.

"You are a rooster," I said.

"I have your present!" she raged on. "I hope you like it!"

"What is it?" I yawned again. "What did you get me?"

"If I wanted it to be that obvious, I wouldn't have wrapped it, Dumb-dumb," she announced, shoving a small but noticeably heavy gift into my hands.

"No need to get all persnickety on me," I said back.

As consciousness dripped back into my brain, I observed what she had given me. There was a box about two inches in each direction that was wrapped in black paper, on which she had affixed a galaxy of gold and silver stars, like the ones the teacher gives you in kindergarten or first or second grade when you've been good. The box was neatly tied with gold and silver braided cord and topped with a small star-shaped crystal ornament, all of which rested on a metallic gold envelope.

"Read the card first!" she insisted in her joy-filled enthusiasm. The envelope had been sealed with a round metallic gold paper circle embossed with the face of a bear as I recall. I tried to pry it loose but wound up tearing it in half. I could sense Phee cringe as I did. The card inside was a thick sheet of handmade white, deckle-edged paper on which she had mounted a photo of the two of us at some happy moment in our past. We were wearing T-shirts with our names emblazoned on them. We were on a raft on a river. It was in Colorado from a summer trip we had taken with Mom and Dad the previous year. I think Mom was the one who had taken the picture, while Dad rested from all of his rowing, trying to keep up with us. On the back of the card, Phee had neatly written, "Happy Fourteen! To the best twin sister ever!" It was obvious this had taken a lot of thought and time.

"Thank you," came my unscripted reply.

"Open it! Open it!" came hers with brave excitement.

I undid the wrapping, opened the box, and gasped. Inside was what I knew to be a small meteorite.

"No *way*!" I exclaimed. I had been intrigued by astronomy ever since I was little. Trapped on this speck of dust in the universe we call the Earth, this was actually something from the asteroid belt 400 million miles away.

"Do you like it?" she asked with bated breath, awakening me from my reverie.

I reached out—lunged out—to hug her, inadvertently smacking

her on the side of her head with the meteorite.

"Oh, my God!" I said as a tear literally dripped from my eye. "I'm so sorry. I just wanted to hug you. This is the best present ever!"

Phee brought her hand up to rub the injured spot.

"You okay?" I asked with grave concern.

"I'll survive," she replied. "It's just that…"

"What?"

"No one will ever believe that I was hit in the head by a meteor."

We both burst out laughing. Our laughter was interrupted by Mom calling us from downstairs. "Peyton! Ophelia! Breakfast!"

It was Phee who yelled back, "Coming!" to which I added, "Mom! Phee just gave me a meteorite!"

"That's good dear!" Mom shouted in return. "Now, come downstairs!"

"It's millions of years old!" I added.

"Well, you don't want your breakfast to be millions of years cold!" she trumpeted back.

"No, Mom!" I shouted and then rolled my eyes at Phee. "Your present's in the closet, next to my change bag."

Phee eagerly went to get it, as I wearily swung my legs over the side of the bed.

"Found it!" she called back. A moment later, she emerged with the medium-large box I had wrapped in the handmade paper, cloth ribbon, and elaborate bow that I'd ordered off the Internet. Having sat back down on the bed, Phee quickly opened the envelope that I'd affixed to her gift, and read from the bejeweled card, where I had written, "Happy Birthday to my Phee-nominal sib." Careful hands undid the wrapping, so as not to damage it, a task that seemed to take forever.

"Come on!" I said through gritted teeth, "It's not like you're going to reuse it!"

"You never know," she replied.

"Ugh!" I shrugged.

Finally, the wrapping paper off, she sat holding a box that contained a realistic, hand-painted statue of Gal Gadot as Wonder Woman, sword and shield in hand, golden lasso at her side. I should mention that Phee had a thing for Wonder Woman. Anyway, she appeared to like it a lot, which was good, as it had cost close to $400. I don't know what the meteorite had cost, but it didn't matter if she had found it in the dirt on the side of the road. It was the most special gift I'd ever gotten—one of those things you keep with you all of your life and want to be buried with.

"Oh, my gosh!" she exclaimed. She looked at me with tears in her eyes. "Thank you so much!"

But then came Mom's voice again, echoing through the halls. "Peyton! Ophelia! Come down now!"

"We're on our way!" I echoed back.

Phee rose from my bed and laid the box down on hers. "I'll take it out later and set it on my nightstand so I can look at it every morning and every night."

"You'd better get downstairs," I said. "I wouldn't want the chickens to have to lay replacement eggs. I'll be there in a few. I need to get dressed."

"Better hurry before Mom has a conniption," came Phee's sisterly advice.

After dressing, I thrumped down the stairs to the kitchen, wearing my mandatories as Phee and I called our uniforms. Mom stood at the head of the table with Dad faithfully beside her. All those years together and they were still in love. I should be so lucky one day. Phee sat in a chair facing the door with her head resting on her palms, her elbows on the table, looking about as bored as a groundhog waiting for spring to begin. In the center of the table was a flaming cake that had "Happy Birthday, Ophelia and Peyton!" written in blue icing on the white frosting that was tinctured with pink roses around its circumference. More blue lines of icing up and down the sides in triangular slants gave it the appearance of the drum that Laura

Brandywine always carried in the marching band when we were in junior high. Mom and Dad sang Happy Birthday slightly off-key, cramming in "Peyton and Ophelia" at the end, and all I could think of at that moment was, *Thank God we weren't triplets*! Then Mom called for us both to blow out the candles and to each make our annual wish. I watched as Phee shut her eyelids tightly together as she made hers. Phee was always a sucker for those sorts of things. As for me, I skeptically hoped that a piano would fall on Theresa Martinez, who had been bullying me relentlessly ever since we first met when the semester began. Nothing painful. I'm not one to want anyone to suffer. Just a nice, clean splat, with her, flattened onto the pavement like Wylie Coyote, as Roadrunner speeds away.

"Sure took you long enough," Phee breathed at me, as we both extinguished the flames.

"I had to take a shower," I replied.

"Clean mind, clean body, take your pick," she said.

"At least I don't have sticky fingers in the morning," I quietly retorted back, at which point Phee gasped.

"What did you two wish for?" Dad asked.

"Now, James, the girls can't reveal their wishes or they won't come true!" That was Mom. She believed in such things. And the Bible and God and Jesus. Mom was a devout Presbyterian.

"Peypey wished for a bigger bra size!" Phee said, looking at me with a demonstrably evil glance.

"My breasts are a perfect size for my age!" I replied defensively.

"If you were ten!" Phee responded, at which point Mom threw her a stern glance.

"Phee wished for Bobby Galdran behind the bleachers at school!" That was the best comeback I could think of. Phee really did have a thing for Bobby Galdran and it was that which made her blush.

"Stinker!" she shot back.

"Dunkhead!" I proclaimed.

Mom threw sharp looks at us both. "Girls! Peace out! It's your birthday!"

I glared at Phee. "Well, she started it!" I insisted.

"I thought I was going to be ready for my old age pension by the time you finally came down!" Phee shot back.

"I give the two of you a ride to school?" Dad broke in. "I can play some John Denver and you can both calm down."

"John Denver?" Phee and I said as though with one voice, and then turned toward each other.

"I don't think their names are really James and Katherine," I said to Phee.

"Wilma and Fred?" Phee speculated.

"Definitely!" I assured her. "Hey, I need to get my backpack," I went on. "I left it upstairs."

"Would you get mine, too?" Phee called to me, as she headed upstairs.

"Sure," I said.

That was kind of how things were between us. Whatever difference we had between us, quickly faded with the love for each other we shared. Anyway, later that night, Mom and Dad would give Phee and me each a Saint-Gaudens double eagle gold coin on a gold chain from Dad's collection that he inherited from Pops after Pops died about six years ago. Pops was Dad's father. There weren't a lot of coins in what was there, and now there are two less. Sometimes I think Dad was a bit disappointed that Phee and I came out with girl parts, but he always loved us just the same.

School was uneventful except for the bullying. She—Theresa the Terrible—continued her endless rage against me, even on what was supposed to be my one special day, not that she would know or even care that it was. She slammed her shoulder into me, as we passed each other in the hallway. It hurt. It really did.

"Slut," whispered in my ear with the body slam. And that wasn't the end of it—not that day. There was gym class. It was basketball practice and the girls were separated into two teams. True to form,

Theresa was one and I was on the other. Our girls' basketball team was called the Phoenix. Our colors were the same as the uniforms and the other sports teams, red and blue with a white stripe. The practice teams wore different headbands for us to tell each other apart—red for the one I was one and blue for the other. Before I tread any further, I want to say a few words about Theresa Martinez—Theresa *Maria* Martinez to be exact. I learned her middle name when I stood behind her during enrollment. She had drawn it on the manilla folder that she was holding. From what I have already said, one might picture her as some sort of grotesque monster, but she was actually quite beautiful. The first day of school she showed up with thick black eyeliner that was painted past her eyes and outlined lips. Mrs. Caulderson, however, who was in charge of admissions quickly put an end to that, much to Theresa's dismay, as one could hear her—probably clear across the school—blasting out the f-word with a grandiose and virulent "What the fuck!" that immediately got her sent to the principal's office. Fortunately for her, since it was the first day, the outburst did not create a detention. Theresa had come from a poor background and lived alone with her mother. The word on the street was that she had gone through a lot growing up, all of which had fomented anger. She was more or less an outsider, and whether it was she who didn't like the world or the world that didn't like her remained to be seen. But for whatever reason that I could not figure out, she turned me into her punching bag. *Why me?* I kept asking myself, but there was no one there to answer. Anyway, as I said, Theresa was beautiful physically, but the rest left something to be desired. The tall lean figure with sun-streaked hair and hazel eyes attracted a lot of guys' attention, but she quickly gained a reputation among them as being stuck-up. The nickname, Theresa the Terrible, wasn't just something that Phee and I had invented. It was a name that was bantered around the school behind her back. I might have been sympathetic. I might even have tried to approach her as a friend, but from the start, it was like she was a fuse waiting for a match—at least where I was concerned. Had I known then what I know now, things might have been different, but things are what they are, or, rather, were what they were and, for the most part, there's no going back.

We were in a practice game, and, as I said, Theresa and I were playing opposite sides. I had control of the ball and she was trying to take it away from me. No matter which direction I tried to go, dribbling the ball as I went, she blocked me. When, at last, I tried to pass the ball to Kiki, whose last name I've forgotten or never knew, Theresa thrust out her leg and tripped me, causing me to fall to the floor. Coach Nolan blew her whistle, called a personal foul, and sent me to the free-throw line. The score was close, and, just as I sunk the basket, the class bell rang, which left my team the winner and the other team sneering at Theresa for losing the game for them where they had been one point ahead.

It was Kara Blakely who retrieved the ball. Theresa called out for her to toss it to her, which she did. As for me, after some pats on the back from my teammates, I started to head for the showers when Theresa called out to me.

"Hey, Herron! Heads up!"

As I turned in the direction of her voice, I was hit in the face really hard by the ball she had thrown—so hard that I collapsed to the floor. I don't know if I blacked out or not, but I was woozy as hell as I staggered to my feet.

"Are you all right?" Coach asked, having rushed up to me.

"I guess so," I said, pressing my eyelids tight for a second or two, and then shaking my head, trying to clear my brain. "I just wasn't prepared when she threw the ball."

Looking down at the floor, I saw drops of blood that had dripped from my face and were still dripping down from where the ball had hit. Coach stared at the wound.

"You head over to the nurse," she told me. "You can shower up later." Then she turned toward Theresa and yelled, "Martinez!"

Theresa looked up at her. "Here! Now!" Coach ordered her. I don't know what was said as I headed out, but, glancing back, Theresa did not look pleased. She had hit me with hard rubber, but apparently, Coach had struck her a hard emotional blow. It didn't matter, though. She wouldn't stop. Even after the nurse, at my locker, minding my own business, preparing to go home, she came up to me with anger on her breath.

"Coach demanded I apologize," she said, "so I am. I'm sorry I didn't hit you harder." Then she grabbed my left arm with her left hand and pushed my sleeve up with her right. There were cuts and scars up and down my forearm from where I'd self-harmed. It wasn't something I was proud of. I did it to focus on the pain. I had thought up until that moment that Phee was the only one who knew. How could she not have when we literally breathed each other's breath? But I'd made her promise not to tell. I'd always tried to keep my arm at my side or turned inward in the girls' showers. I guess I wasn't careful enough because Theresa knew. I suppose a lot of kids did as well but didn't say anything about it—at least not to my face.

She glared up at me. "I heard from girls in the locker room that there were scars," she raged on. "Maybe next time you can cut a little deeper! Then I could apologize at your grave!"

"Leave me alone!" I said.

"Never. *Blancucha!*[2]" she replied.

Suddenly, we both heard Phee call out, "Hey!" in a sharp voice.

Theresa saw her and fled down the hallway but I knew she would be back. She wouldn't stop. Nothing would stop her. It amazed me how someone as pretty as her could be filled with so much anger. But *that* didn't matter and *I* didn't care. I just couldn't take it anymore. It was at that moment that I made up my mind. It wasn't worth it. I just didn't want to go on.

Phee came over to me, glanced down the hall to make sure that Theresa was gone, and then turned back and stared at my now black

---

[2] Spanish slang for white trash

eye. "You okay?" she asked with an abundance of concern.

"I'm fine," I replied in a truly depressed voice.

"You don't *look* fine," she said. It was then that she noticed the bandage on my forehead. She reached out and touched it. There was a bruise surrounding the cut that was still swollen. However gentle her touch was, it caused me to wince. She quickly drew back her hand.

"Sorry," she said.

"Mom's coming to pick me up. You're gonna have to brave the walk back home alone," I replied.

"I'll survive," she said. "I'm just worried about you. How did it happen?"

"Theresa the Terrible whacked me in the head with a basketball," I replied.

"I hope she got detention," Phee said.

"She didn't even get flustered," I replied.

"Just say the word," Phee said, "and I'll go beat her ass."

"I'm *not* helpless, you know," I insisted.

"I know," she said. "You're just more," and she paused, searching for the right word. "Delicate."

I closed the door to my locker, as tears began to well up in my eyes—tears I tried to hide but couldn't.

"It's just that..." I started to say and then hesitated.

"What?" Phee asked.

"This is my birthday!" I said. "Our birthday. It was supposed to be balloons and magic and rainbows! I just feel so alone sometimes." I wept out the words.

Phee took my hands in hers.

"Well, you're not," she said. "You have Mom and Dad and you have me no matter what."

"I know, but..." I replied.

Phee stared hard into my eyes, trying to pull out more words.

"Theresa keeps sending me texts," I went on.

"Saying what?" Phee asked.

"They're not very kind," I said. I took out my cell phone and showed her. "She sent this to me on Snapchat." It was a photo of me totally naked.

"How did she get it?" Phee asked.

"Obviously," I replied, "when I just came out of the shower. I don't know how many others she sent it to."

I lowered my phone, looked at her, and began to cry again.

"Why is she doing it?" I sobbed. "Why does she hate me? I never did anything to *her*!"

"Maybe she didn't *send* it to anyone else," Phee replied.

"Brent Campbell passed me in the hall this morning," I told her "His only comment was, 'Nice nips!'"

"It'll all pass," Phee assured me. "People forget."

"*She* doesn't," I insisted. "She doesn't let *up*!"

"I will take care of her," Phee assured me. "I promise."

"How?" I asked. "I don't want you getting in trouble or, worse, getting hurt."

Phee smiled. "I'm Wonder Girl," she said, "remember? I'll deal with her."

"Who knows what she's capable of?" I insisted. "She could pull a knife on you."

"You worry too much," she said. "I should have gotten you a vibrator instead of some old meteor."

Hearing that, I couldn't help it. A laugh broke through my tears. "Shut up!" I replied.

Phee wiped the tears from my eyes with her thumbs.

"You always know how to make me laugh," I said.

"I'm always here for you," she replied. "You know that, don't you?"

"Yes," I said.

"I'll walk you out," she went on. "And I don't care how hungry you get, you be sure and save some of that cake for me. Remember, my name's on part of it. After dinner, we can all play Ouija and talk to spirits from the past."

We started to walk toward the door to the outside.

"You know I don't believe in any of that supernormal stuff," I said.

"It'll be fun!" she insisted. "Guaranteed!"

I just sighed, "Whatever!"

That night, with little appetite in me, I nibbled at the roast *beast*, as Phee used to call it, that Mom had labored over for our birthday. There were whipped potatoes and carrots and peas and pearl onions and malt shakes. Malts were Grandma Margaret's favorite when she was a teen. So she said. She was not that coherent at that time. But I guess taste can be inherited because both Phee and I preferred them over milkshakes. It was just, with the knowledge that this was going to be my last day on earth, I wasn't really in the mood. However much I managed to sip up through the straw, I did it for appearances' sake. I didn't want anyone asking, "Oh, what's wrong?" so I sipped a bit at a time and tried to make it seem like I enjoyed both it and the meal.

They say that the death of a child can devastate his or her parents, but mine would at least still have Phee—dear Phee. I know she'll miss me. She'll stare at the empty bed, and wonder why I did what I did. But I thought to myself, someday I'll tell her. Someday she'll know. But for her, Heaven will be a lifetime away. I can picture her as a mother. I can see her children. And then, in her later years, old and wrinkled and frail, with her family all around her. Perhaps she'll think of me even then and a tear might drip from her eye. "Peyton" she might wonder to herself, "why did you have to leave me?" "I just couldn't take life anymore," were words I couldn't say because all that would remain of me would be what the worms had left behind— my desiccated skull staring upward, through sockets of bone that once held eyes, laid in a dark and musty casket that smelled of death after all the bygone years. Those thoughts and more fled through my brain as my molars gnashed down on the small pearl onion that I had speared with my fork and brought mercilessly into my mouth. As I looked around at Mom and Dad and Phee, my eyes started to tear up. Dad was the one who noticed and said something, and so I awkwardly attributed it to the onions. But it wasn't the onions. It was the knowledge that I would never see them again—not in this life at least. I don't know which was more frightening, though—the thought of existing or the thought of not existing at all. After dinner, Phee announced to Mom and Dad as she had to me that she wanted us all to play Ouija. As I had told her, and then repeated, I thought it was all just a made-up board game, but as it was to be my last time with all of them, I went along with it, a fake smile painted on my face. As it turned out, the board (or the supposed spirits within the board) predicted that Phee would find love and wealth and that I would live to accomplish great things, at which suggestion I took a deep breath of air and exhaled what must have been a liter of irony. Then something really odd happened, at least in retrospect, which even you, dear reader, will later come to understand. With all of our hands on the planchette—the teardrop-shaped thing that players move around the board—Phee asked *the spirits,* "Who is Peyton's worst nemesis?"

"Ugh!" I groaned. "We all know that one."

Regardless, planchette began to move, presumably guided by *the Spirits.* Phee was our Ouija announcer.

"K - H - A - T..." she said as the pointer went from one letter to another. She glanced up at Mom.

"Oh my God, Mom. I think it's you!"

"Pardon me," Mom replied, "but the last time I checked, I didn't have an H in my name."

And so, we all watched as the planchette traveled this way and that until it spelled out the rest of the name.

"T - A - A - A - R – A," Phee went on. "Who the hell is Khattaaara?"

"Khattaaara," I repeated, with a guttural inflection in my voice.

Phee stopped, took her hands off the planchette, and glared at me.

"Wait!" she spouted. "You're correcting me on the pronunciation of a name you've never heard before?"

"She was just joking," Dad said as he looked at me. "Weren't you, Peanut?"

"Emphasis on the nut," came Phee's witty response, to which I stuck out my tongue at her, and after which Mom stood up.

"I think it's about time we all turn in," she said. "You two still have school tomorrow." She looked at me with concern. "Unless you don't feel up to it, Sweet Pea."

"I'll be all right," I said with a frown.

Ten minutes or so later found Phee and me back up in our room. Having changed into my nightgown and brushed both my hair and teeth, I pretended to go to sleep, all the while waiting until Phee actually did. I had it all planned. I'd even written a short note that I laid neatly on my pillow that just said, "Don't worry about me. I'm in God's hands." Then I went into our walk-in closet and shut myself in. We lived in an older house that was built a hundred years ago with ten-foot ceilings. Our bedroom used to be an upstairs parlor, and the closet was an adjacent pantry. When electricity came into vogue, steel pipes were run through the attic, but for some reason, the one that ran through the now-closet was left exposed, and near it hung a single light bulb that could be turned on and off by a pull chain. The pipe had been run through the joists so that it was weight-bearing, which is significant to what is to follow. Also there, beyond all of the scads of clothes that two teenage girls could and did amass, was my metal train case and some climbing rope that Phee and I had used on our vacation last summer. Oddly enough, I had learned how to tie a hangman's noose from my history class in sixth grade, as my teacher was a student of the Old West and we were all required to read *The Oxbow Incident* by Owen Wister, which was about two cowboys, faced with being lynched for a crime they didn't commit. Anyway, turning my case on its side, I sat down on it, and tied the knot that I required, and then stood up and slung the free end over the pipe, having cut off about twelve feet of rope from the coil to which it was attached. Climbing on the case and having secured the other end to the door handle, I left the noose to dangle about seven feet above the floor. I pulled the noose over my head, tightened it around my neck, and then kicked the case away, leaving it to fall flat. As that happened, the weight of my body, all 108 lb. of it, caused the noose to start to strangle me. I've seen movies where people are hanged, but this was nothing like that. In the movies, a trapdoor swings open and the person being hanged drops down and I guess we're supposed to assume that the fall breaks their neck and death is instantaneous. Perhaps that *was* the case when someone dropped through the trapdoor of a gallows, but for me, the fall was only about a foot. I had never felt anything like that before—the crushing pressure around my neck—not even in dreams. Regardless that I had decided to end my life, my instinct at that moment was to survive. My fingers clawed at the rope, trying to loosen it to no avail. I grabbed at the rope and tried to pull myself up to loosen the stranglehold it had on me, but there wasn't enough strength in my arms to lift me more than an inch or so—not the two-and-a-half feet it would take to reach the pipe and, even if I did, what then? Even if I could wrap my arms around the pipe, it would still only be a temporary reprieve. I wouldn't be able to call for help. The rope had already crushed my windpipe. I know because with that inch or so the rope had loosened and I tried. All that came out was a whisper inside a closet with a solid hardwood door. After just a minute, the blood fled from my arms and made me lose my grip. When it did, my body dropped again and caused the rope to clench around my neck even tighter. And while the eased tension had allowed me to take a couple of breaths. Now, I couldn't breathe again. I couldn't even exhale. Beyond the need for air, which was overwhelming, my lungs felt like they would burst. My larynx crushed, there was nowhere for the air to go. Instinctively, I began to kick my legs, which only made matters worse. It was unbearable. There was unimaginable pain. It was as though my lungs were bursting from within. Perhaps it was my imagination, but it was as though I could feel the tendons in my neck being ripped apart. I swung my legs to try to kick the door but the door was too far away and my legs could only scrape against it. To make matters worse, with each attempt, the rope tightened more, like a boa constrictor, crushing and suffocating its prey. A person can hold his or her breath underwater for two or three minutes, but, even as they drown, water fills their lungs, not this intense pressure. My face must have turned red. I tried to think of other things. I tried to picture Phee and Mom and Dad. I prayed for Phee to wake up and find me. I prayed for the pipe to break from my weight. I prayed for death to end it all. I wanted to cry, but the pressure was so terrible no tears would come. Over and over, again and again, I tried to pull the rope away from my neck, my fingernails gouging at my throat to try and ease it back just a little, just enough to let me take one final breath of air, but nothing I did would help. It must have been only three or four minutes until I finally passed out but it seemed like an eternity before I actually did. I must have died then. My heart must have stopped—brain function ending once and for all. Death came as a relief. It was what I had wanted— to end my existence—no more being bullied every day—no more Theresa the Terrible to torment me. No more of anything at all. But then came the afterlife—just not in the religious way.

The pain was gone. That's what happens when death takes hold. But this wasn't death. It was something else—something strange. I could breathe again, but I wasn't in the closet anymore. I wasn't hanging by my neck. I was lying on my back in the dark. It was pitch dark—oppressively so. I remember once when I was eight years old, Mom and Dad and Phee and I had gone spelunking, meaning we had driven to Carlsbad Caverns and taken the tour into one of the caves. Once deep inside, the tour guide switched off the lights and it was as though we were being smothered by the dark. This was the same, only this air was stale, with an underscent of something medicinal. I felt a pillow beneath my head. My arms were oddly folded across my chest. I tried to sit up, but my head struck against some ceiling only inches above me that was made of padded cloth. In a panic, I reached up and around. *My God*, I thought to myself, *I'm in a box. No, No! No! No! No! No! No! I'm in a casket!* I could not imagine how, but the apparent fact that I didn't die was the one thought that raced through my head. They say that sometimes people can go into some sort of cataleptic state that shows all the signs of death, where one's life signs—the breath, the heartbeat—all slow to virtually nothing. And, so it must have been with me, my heartbeat slowed so much that the doctors had been fooled and then they buried me alive. *But wait!* I heard something from outside. And then, so strange, for one brief second, a flash of purple light lit up my tomb. It was then that I heard the voice of a man, barely audible, so much so, that I needed to strain my ears to make out what he said.

"Peyton Elise Herron was only fourteen years old when the Lord took her in his arms and welcomed her into his fold—Peyton Herron, cherished daughter, treasured granddaughter, beloved sister. Peyton chose to take her own life, finding weakness in her human existence, but strength in Almighty God, who has already reserved her place in His Kingdom of Heaven. Forasmuch as it hath pleased Almighty God of His great mercy to take unto Himself the soul of our dear daughter here departed, whom we shall sadly miss, we, therefore, commit her body to the ground; earth to earth, ashes to ashes, dust to dust; in sure and certain hope of the Resurrection to eternal life."

"No, wait!" I tried to scream, but no sound emerged, my larynx crushed. Frantically, I tried to pound against the padded lid, but to no avail. My fingernails tried to tear into the silken cloth. Tears rippled down the sides of my face. I felt movement as the casket was lowered into the ground. There was a brief silence, followed by a small sound—handfuls of dirt being thrown down on the casket's lid. I could hear crying up above. It was my father. I could hear him sobbing bitterly. I had been his favorite. Phee was Mom's.

"James," Mom said. "We need to go."

There was silence after that. Half an hour must have passed. The air inside the casket was getting hot and thin but then there was a thud. At first, I thought someone was coming to rescue me—that they knew that I was still alive—but then I realized that it was just the sound of the lid of the concrete liner, sealing me in for all time. I could hear the shovelfuls of dirt as they fell onto the concrete lid. So, this is how I was really going to die—not by the thousand small cuts I had made on my wrists—not by the bottle of pills I had once taken that just had made me sick—not by the rope I had hung myself with—but deep underground in the company of a village of corpses, destined to rot with them all, once the air in my death trap gave out. And then it did, and the darkness became eternal, as eventually it must for us all.

Suddenly, though, I was awakened by a brilliant light, violet like before, but with the brilliance of the sun; a light that came from me, that radiated from my skin and shot out from my eyes. Yet even through the blinding light, I could see the padded dungeon in which I lay. My fingers tore at the cloth again and, all so strange, an instant later I was clawing at empty air and I heard myself scream.

"Huh?" I said to no one. The transition was both frightening and a relief. I was gone from the casket, *But how?* I asked myself, and where *was* this place?

I was now outdoors on a vast open plain. I had no idea whether it was dusk or dawn. The sky was pale and above me was what at first appeared to be three moons. As I looked closer, though, one was in fact a ringed planet that was so close that I could see the continents that divided its oceans. Meanwhile, the air around me was thick with the sound of a *taaakra*. *What the fuck is a taaakra*, I wondered, *and why did that name suddenly pop into my head? Where the hell am I and, more importantly, how did I get here?* Then, all at once, I felt something licking my face. Turning to look at it, my heart skipped a beat as I observed a dog-like creature about the size of a standard poodle or German shepherd with its tongue flagged out. The odd thing was that something in me knew not to be afraid of it despite how alien it seemed. The creature—the word *goraaag* came to mind—was covered in snakelike scales that formed a pattern of spots, and which, upon closer examination, looked more like some sort of evolved dinosaur than any breed of dog. There were no perceivable ears or nose. But there was an intelligence that shone from its eyes. It appeared friendly enough and the fact that it wore a collar around its neck eased my fears a bit, thinking to myself that it was probably someone's pet. *But where on earth would such a creature have come from?* I wondered. As the question raced through my brain, the irony came that this could not possibly *be* Earth. The thought that this might be Heaven crossed my mind but, being somewhat of an atheist, I scoffed at the idea that any afterworld would look like this. Slowly then, as I rose to my feet, the creature remained by my side. Glancing down at it, I stroked its head gently and then surveyed my surroundings. Around me was scattered vegetation, all of which glowed with a black light iridescence. To my right stood a tree that resembled a weeping willow but with what looked like tendrils for leaves, and in the distance the horizon was marked by what appeared to be some futuristic city. Then there was the fact that my ears were filled with hundreds of unfamiliar sounds—from alien creatures, I assumed. But all of that was suddenly broken by the voice of an older man with some foreign breath on his tongue.

"*Peyton*," it said, and then, all so odd, the sound of my name seemed to fade like a memory.

I turned this way and that, searching for its origin.

"Who's out there?" I demanded to know. "Where *are* you?"

I am in a place that underpins all existence, it said back.

"That's not much of an answer," I replied. "Where *is* this place?"

This was Rendenaaar, the voice said, *once the most beautiful world in our universe. It was where we both were born.*

"Um, I hate to break it to you," I said, "but I was not born on some planet called Rendenaaar. I was born exactly fourteen years ago on Earth."

The same planet, the voice went on, *on which four days ago you died.*

"Obviously *not*," I said. But perhaps my answer was a bit overly smug, for an instant later I was back in the closet again at that exact same moment as when my feet had kicked away my makeup box. My body fell again and the rope snapped tight once more around my neck. I was hanging again by my neck but there was no longer any pressure or pain. My eyes were open but unblinking, my gaze turned downward. Beneath me danced the shadow of my corpse, as it interfered with the light from the bulb, breaking it up like dead planets must as they hurtle around their stars, unable to reason or wonder or escape. How long my body hung there I did not know. But, then, it must have not been more than minutes at best or all of the inertia from my death throes would have ceased long ago. Nor was there any light coming from under the door. Then a thought raced through my head. I was facing the door. My eyes were open and transfixed. What was the continence of death? Is that why hoods were pulled over those about to be hanged? Not so that they might know peace but so that those looking on would not have to bear witness to the contortions that their executions would graft upon their features. *Dear God*, I thought. *What of Ophelia, when, come morning, she would open the door and find me? How that would scar her forever. How could I have been so thoughtless in my quest to find an exit from my sordid life? But what could I do now, all the life gone from me forever?* And, as I had those thoughts of remorse, there I was again, erect on that plain, though less fearful than I had been only moments before. I could still hear the words I had said—the question I had asked. And then it repeated three more times—the hanging, the death, the tragic end of *me.*

I realized at that moment that the voice had come, not from any direction—for there was no one near me but the *goraaag*, if that's what it was called—but from inside my head. *Is this what death is like*, I pondered, *some phantasmagorical hell that derives from the heart of our fear and rides us alone and helpless through the river of*

21

eternity? No, I reassured myself. That cannot be. I am—I was— always a good person or at least I tried to be. I never did anything wrong. I never tried to hurt anyone—not deliberately. "So, what *is* this place? Where *am* I?" I shrieked so loud that my words scraped at my throat like sandpaper; so loud that the *goraaag* sprang to its feet, apparently frightened by the grating sound I had unleashed from my lungs.

You are everywhere and nowhere, came the reply. It was *his* voice again—he who was nowhere to be seen—he who knew my name.

"Who *are* you?" I screamed out. I felt my heart pounding in my chest, all the while my body trembled. It was fear that now gripped me. I had gone in minutes from wanting death to being afraid of it. I felt my breath become rapid and labored and then I just shut my eyes, hoping it would all go away. I clapped my hands hard against my ears, but it accomplished nothing.

I am Dhraaal, he said, *once mortal, now like unto a god.*

I let my hands drop. "Yeah, right," I replied. "You wish. You just sound old."

I am old, he went on. *Trillions upon trillions of years old. And as for where I am, be it enough to say that I am somewhere else.*

I looked around but there was no one in sight—just empty air.

"Then how come I can hear you?" I asked.

I believe your people call it telepathy, he replied.

"So, what do you want with *me*?" I asked.

Only to protect you, Dhraaal said.

"From what?" I wanted to know. "Why me?"

Because in your former existence, He went on, *you were my wife.*

"I don't think so," I replied. "I think you're just some perverted old man with a hidden microphone who wants to fuck some fourteen-year-old girl."

And then once more, I was back in the closet, repeating that moment when my body fell, but now I could feel everything. *The pain! Can't breathe. Can't exhale. Oh, my God! Oh, my God! Oh, my*

God! Not again! My hands clawed once more at the rope around my neck. I had made the noose too well. My cheeks were wet from tears that could no longer flow. My face seemed to swell from the pressure of indigo blood that fought for a way to turn red once more.

Phee, please, help me! Please wake up! Please, please come here! I don't want to die! It hurts. It hurts so bad, the pain! And then it repeated, all of it—the tightening rope, the lungs that couldn't breathe!

Stop it! I screamed, but the words didn't come from my mouth. The words formed in my head. I thought in my pain that if he were truly telepathic he would be able to hear me and he did and just like that I was back on the plain I rubbed my neck. I inhaled the air. I believed. Strange as it was, beyond reason and logic, I believed!

Your name was Khattaaara, he said, *and you were the most radiant woman I had ever known.*

Suddenly, the image of Khattaaara stood before me, standing in some ancient doorway, sunlight at her back. She looked a lot like me, though she was decidedly older, perhaps twenty-five by our measure of time, but with violet eyes and without eyebrows, but with pointed ears. She stood there naked in front of me, barely a breath away, with two pairs of beasts, one beneath the other. Then, as my eye traced down her form, I saw that she lacked both a navel and the delineation of her sex. Instead, to my great astonishment, was what I perceived to be a tail, though afterward, I learned that in *Gaaalthaaaran*[3], the language of her people, such was called a *yaaargh* and was the reproductive organ in both their women and men (if I may call them such) that was tipped in hair or fur. But whoever or whatever she was, she mirrored me like an alien reflection. When I lifted my right arm, she lifted her left. When I blinked, she blinked as well. Her lips moved with mine. And when I finally sneered at her, she instantly sneered back.

"And so how do you intend to protect me?" I asked after the image

---

[3] Pronounced *Gaaa' thaaa ran* with the emphasis on the first syllable.

23

of Khattaaara disappeared. "And protect me from what?"

Not from what, but from whom? Dhraaal replied. *Her name is Thara-Klo, and she most assuredly wants you dead.*

"Apparently, I already *was*," I stated, "before you brought me here, wherever here is."

I have brought you nowhere, he said. *You are still in your casket, buried beneath the soil. But I will take you back in time, so that you may rethink your decision to end your life. It would be a shame if you repeated your mistake, and I will tell you that those you love will suffer immeasurably if you do. I have already placed a god-stone in your head.*

"What's that?" I asked.

It's a kind of gem, he explained, *the size of a seed that will give you powers over quantum reality. Once I send you back, our minds will disconnect. You will be on your own. May the forgotten gods of Rendenaaar guide you on your path. Farewell.*

"Wait!" I cried out, but it was too late. All at once, I was back in the closet, standing on my makeup case, the rope in my hands, the soft but deadly braiding, now held captive in my clenched fists, blue as the blood that it had suffocated in my veins. A thought crossed my mind for a moment. I had read of people who were schizophrenic, who heard voices that weren't real, and then I wondered. *What if none of this is real? What if my having hanged myself was an illusion? What if my family—Mom, Dad, Phee, Grams, even Theresa Martinez—what if none of them existed? What if*, I thought, *I'm really a middle-aged woman in some mental asylum in a catatonic state, imagining all of this?* How could I know? How could I convince myself that *this* reality was the one I needed to believe?

It was instinctual—or perhaps it was fear—that caused my fingers to splay open and let the hangman's noose drop with a soft thud to the carpeted floor. It was no longer a rope in my mind. It was the serpent in the Garden of Eden that had tempted me to taste the fruit of death. I stepped down from the case, went to the door, and untied the knot I had made. I gathered up the rope and put it back where I had found it. Then, reaching up, I pulled the chain that hung from the light and immersed myself in darkness.

My hand reached forward until my fingertips met the wooden door, and then slid down until I felt the doorknob. I turned it counterclockwise and then pushed the door out into the bedroom. The room was dark as I had left it, with Phee still asleep in her bed. All the minutes or hours or days that had passed in the closet and the grave and on that foreign soil had crept back up the faucet. Somehow, I had been sent backward in time to just before it all began. Rather than return to my bed, though, I went over to Phee's as she slept on her side and climbed into her bed alongside her.

"What's wrong?" she asked half-asleep.

"Scooch over," I said in a voice that was like a whisper.

She moved a foot or so and I spooned up next to her and placed one arm around her.

"You okay?" she whispered.

"I miss being in the womb with you," I replied.

"I was having a sex dream," she insisted.

"Didn't mean to interrupt," I softly apologized. Then I asked, "Who with?"

"Don't know," she answered. "Blond guy. Totally cute." Suddenly, she appeared wide away. "Shit!" she announced.

"What?" I said.

"I have a book report due in sixth period," she replied, "and I haven't read it yet."

"Which book?" I asked.

"The 49th Parallel," she said. "John Dos Pasos."

"Not to worry," I told her in a most assuring tone. "I've read *it* and the other two. I'll help you write your report during lunch."

She reached up and interlaced our fingers. Then she brought both our hands to her lips and kissed mine. That was her way of saying thanks. And it was my way of knowing that life is worth living for as long as we can.

CHAPTER II

Morning reawakened the life in me—so much so that the world around me seemed different—resurrected. It was as though *it* had changed and *I* had stayed the same, but I knew deep down that it was the other way around. Death had given me a different perspective on life and on being alive. Theresa Martinez could no longer hurt me with her shoves or her words. It was as though I had been reborn—not in a spiritual way but in such a manner that I wasn't afraid of life anymore. Dhraaal had said that I was she who had been called Khattaaara, a woman as it were from some universe before this one, but how was that possible and how could anyone have explained how her name had been spelled out on the game the night before? A million thoughts raced through my head all at once, including the fact that six-dimension quantum physics proved that motion relative to quantum space coupled with particle field compression to a critical size would result in spontaneous expansion to a distance of twenty lightyears with a Q-effect equivalent to 56.8 quants to the billionth power. That in turn would cause the over-formation of stellar systems and galaxies from the residue, spread out through that terrain without the necessity of some imagined dark energy. *How do I know this?* That thought burst into my mind as quickly as the explanation I had just spontaneously propounded on the death, creation, and primordial expansion of a universe. I suddenly understood the mechanics of gravity and could explain not only how special relativity works, but why. My mind grasped the inescapability of parallel dimensions and even time travel. These were not things I had learned in school. This was beyond all the theories of Einstein and Hawking and even Roecort, who had and has yet to be born. What to them remained unexplainable events were all simplistic truths to me. Briefly, I pondered the idea of God and wondered on how many other worlds the abstract of an omnipotent being had been fostered. But now I knew that while such thoughts often gave beings comfort, terrified by the finality of eventual death, no such personage had ever existed. The quantum thread, the ambit that underlays the fabric of each universe, was no deity, and neither intelligence, nor even sentience, and needed neither time nor space to function. To demand that it conform to either time or space, when it did not exist in either, conjured images of a moth flitting itself into a flame that it believes in its insect brain to be an exit from the dark. All of those thoughts ended, however, as the scent of breakfast wafted from the kitchen to the room wherein I stood drawing liner on the upper lids of my eyes.

As I sat at the kitchen table, sipping from the glass of orange juice that my diligent mother had just squeezed (we have an orange tree just outside the front door), as random thoughts butterflied through my head, I stared at Phee, as she attacked the yolk of her sunny side up egg with a torn off piece of toast. It is truly odd and somewhat disgusting when one closely observes the eating habits of human beings—quite unlike how adorably cute it appears when small animals devour human food as though they were living typewriters hammering out a novel. Having brought the yellow and brown conglomeration to her mouth, the hungry blonde bit off a portion of it with her teeth, chomped at it till it was gnashed to smithereens, and then sent it helplessly down her slender throat to an ever-patient, ever-waiting stomach, where it would be dissolved into a gastric goo by hydrochloric acid. *Oh*, I thought silently as I watched her jaw's machinations, *how the chicken might have felt had it known the fate of its might-have-been child!* All that aside, however, I chose to engage her in casual conversation.

"I had a really weird dream last night," I said to her.

"I had a great one that you interrupted," she spouted back, chomping on another mouthful of eggs.

"You know," she went on, as her teeth gnashed at the bottom half of one of the sausages that had been on her plate, "it amazes me how I can have a sex dream when I'm still a virgin and have it feel so real."

She pushed the remaining half of the sausage into her mouth and then leaned forward toward me. "I could totally feel his dick inside me," she whispered.

As for me, I just stared off toward the far wall. "Lucky you," I replied.

Phee once again shoveled in another glob of toast and eggs, and once again spoke with her mouth full. "And then just as I was about to…" she began, glancing over toward Mom to make sure she wasn't listening, "*you* know," she went on, "you woke me up. But honestly, it was okay. Your climbing in bed with me reminded me of when we were little and you used to get all freaked about a thunderstorm."

She took a sip of hot chocolate.

"You okay?" she asked.

"Yeah, I guess," I replied.

She stared at me with concern. "You just seem more down than usual." She polished off the remaining eggs and then stuffed the last bit of sausage into her mouth. "You know I love you, don't you? If you want to talk about anything I'm here for you."

"I'm fine," I said. "I just had this bizarre dream where I was on another planet and there was some alien old guy talking inside my head, who insisted that he put some kind of quantum seed in my brain that would give me superpowers."

Phee wiped her mouth with her cloth napkin.

"Sounds creepy," she replied then she turned her attention. "Mom?"

"Yes, Dear?"

"Are there any more eggs?"

"She's eating for two," I added ever so nonchalantly, my chin resting on my hands, my elbows on the table, all so Phee-like.

Phee turned her head back and sneered at me.

"Those were the last," Mom said, "but I can make you more if you're still hungry."

"Yes, please. And another sausage if that's possible."

"Good thing you have a high metabolism," I added, "or you'd

29

wind up looking like a blimp."

"Shut up!" she said. "I'm on my period."

"Seems more like you're on an eating quest," I replied.

Phee grimaced and then said in consolatory words, "I wouldn't worry about the dream you had. As with mine, it was all just that. *I'm* not going to get pregnant and *you're* not going to get superpowers."

"It just seemed so real," I replied.

"So did mine," she moaned and then smiled broadly, at which point I wadded up then threw my napkin at her. "My guess," she went on, "is that you dreamt all that because of your subconscious desire to be able to retaliate against Theresa the Terrible."

"Thank you, Dr. Herron," I replied.

"Just sayin,'" she said. She shrugged and then stared at me. "Just say the word and I'll kick the fucking shit out of her." She lifted her cup with both hands and sipped her hot chocolate. It was at that moment that Mom, who had been as silent as the moon, tending to the pan on the stove, suddenly broke in with scolding words.

"Ophelia Jane Herron, I have warned you repeatedly about your language."

As I already had said, Mom was a Christian, though I do not wish to convey the impression that she is no longer with us. Mom always was what I like to refer to as a Bible-thumper, lacking neither pulse nor heartbeat. How strange it seems that I grew up in such a parochial environment, only to find for myself absolute proof of the nonexistence of God. But to her good grace, my mother indoctrinated me with a set of morals that transcend any deism. Whatever her spiritual beliefs may have been, she owned an abiding conscience, which she transferred through rule or rote to me.

"Sorry, Mom," came the genuinely apologetic response from Phee.

"And the thought of such violence! We are a Christian family and I do not condone such things!"

Right or wrong, Phee knew Mom's attitude toward profanity and she respected it, especially in the home that she, as our mother, had built for us. Mom had studied in college to be a nurse, but when Phee and I came along she sacrificed all of that to raise us. She might have been able to have juggled her schedule to take care of *one* child, but not two. I wouldn't say that it was with any reluctance on her part, but she was willing to sacrifice one dream for another—that of being in the medical profession versus the challenge of raising two little girls. Phee and I both realize that her decision was based on her love for us and that is something we can never forget. Anyway, my mental reverie was broken as more words were hurled at *me*.

"And that goes for you, too, Peyton!" she said in a stern voice.

"What did _I_ do?" I said.

Ten minutes later found my sister and me on foot to school, wearing our backpacks, walking up or down Elm Street, depending on one's perspective. It seemed an odd phrase either way, though, walking up or down, when the fact of the matter is that it was neither. Our school, Braxton High, was roughly six and a half blocks from our house. The walk was fine except when it rained or when cold winds would blow gusts up our skirts when winter sparked the air. Braxton was a private school. Uniforms were mandatory—dark navy trousers and pocket-emblemed jackets over white shirts with navy Windsor-knotted ties for the boys, with similar jackets, blue plaid skirts with red striping beneath white blouses crowned with navy crossover ties for the girls. Bows in girls' hair were permitted, so long as they were conservative and matched the rest of the attire. No jewelry of any kind other than a conservative necklace or pendant with a small cross or star of David or a simple ring were permitted and not more than one of each. Regardless of sex, socks were white, though the girls had to wear theirs folded over at the tops. Shoes were to be black leather. No sneakers were allowed, other than for gymnastics class or intramurals. Teachers were to be referred to as mister, missus, or miss, or sometimes, sir, or ma'am. Good or bad, declaring oneself as transgender was not allowed and there were no arbitrary pronouns permitted to be used. Your sex was determined by your birth certificate and your chromosomes and that was that. No critical race theory. We were all considered equal per the Declaration of Independence and most everything else that followed. We were taught reading and writing, history and science, but most of all to respect our fellow students and the sanctity of our lives, though, per my previous narration of what I had endured with Theresa Martinez, that didn't always go as it should. At that precise moment, however, my thoughts were not focused on Terrible Theresa, but, rather, upon what I had experienced only hours before.

Phee was the first to break the silence. "You know I'm mad at you, don't you?"

"Mad at me." I repeated the words, wondering what she was talking about.

"You thought about killing yourself," she replied.

"I didn't *think* about it," I said. "I did it."

"And then you were whisked off to some planet," she raged on, "where some alien put a quantum seed in your head to give you superpowers."

"It happened," I insisted.

"I'm getting rid of the rope and any sharp objects," she announced, "and I'm emptying all the medicine cabinets."

She stopped and turned to me in front of a large oak tree.

"Do you have any idea what effect your dying would have had on us?" she went on. "Not to mention Dad. You *are* his favorite. You *do* realize that."

"Sorry. I wasn't thinking," I replied.

"You know, God gave you more than good looks," she said in a lecturing tone. "He gave you a heart and a brain, which didn't include some quantum seed." She paused and then went on again. "Okay, you say that drag guy..."

"Dhraaal," I said, correcting her.

"Whatever," she shrugged. "Gave you powers. Show me one."

"They didn't come with a manual!"

"Oh, *that's* a great excuse," she replied. She paused, then, with a heavy, impatient sigh said, "I'm waiting!" Fifteen seconds later, she announced, "Nothing. I thought as much."

Suddenly, I noticed a red car barreling toward us.

"Oh my God!" I exclaimed.

As Phee glanced back it was only a few feet away. Instinctively, without there even being time to jump out of its path, she wrapped her arms around me.

"I won't let you die!" she said.

As the car was literally upon us, I closed my eyes, expecting that my life would end again but it didn't. Instead, Phee and I found ourselves back in the kitchen with our breakfasts before us, with Mom once again at the stove, her words drowning out any thoughts we might have had.

"Ophelia Jane Herron, I have warned you repeatedly about your language!"

Phee stared at me, wide-eyed and pale.

"I'm waiting for an answer, young lady," Mom went on, breaking the silence that had ensued.

"Yes, Ma'am. I'm sorry." Phee stammered out the words, visibly shaken, as was I.

"The very thought of such violence! We are a proud Christian family! Neither your father nor I condone such things! [4] That goes for you, too, Peyton!"

"Yes ma'am," I said this time. I glanced with obeisance toward her and then turned back to Phee, who might as well have been staring put laser beams from her eyes.

"*What* just happened?" Barely voiceless, her lips shaped the whisper of her words.

"I don't know," I mouthed back.

---

[4] She always pronounced the "I" in neither, being a refined woman of devout Christian upbringing and faith.

Phee leaned in toward me just a bit. "If what just happened, happened, maybe you *did* die."

"I *told* you," I said.

A sudden thought rushed into her head. "Wait!" she whispered. Then she reached across the table with her left hand and cupped it over the cell that I'd laid down beside me. "I need your phone," she said. "I left mine upstairs." She picked it up, stared down at it, and then attacked it with her index finger. Three tones rang audibly in the quiet room.

"911. What's the nature of your emergency?" came the voice from the other end of the call.

"I'd like to report an accident. A red car. Late model."

"What's the location?"

From the expression on my face, Phee must have thought I was about to interrupt. Preemptively, she held out her free hand, signaling me to wait.

"Elm. The north side. I think." There was a short pause. Amazingly, I could hear what the operator was saying, even though Phee had brought the phone directly up against her ear.

"Yeah. Yeah, definitely the north side," Phee went on. "Between 2nd and 3rd." And then she said something else that I didn't quite get, distracted by the sound of the sausage sizzling in the pan on the stove.

"Is anyone injured?" I heard the operator ask.

"I'm not sure, but I believe so. It looks pretty bad."

"We'll send an ambulance."

Phee ended the call, slid the phone back to me, and rose to her feet with one motion.

"Come on," she said, but come on where?

We both got up to leave.

"Pumpkin?" Mom called out to Phee. "What about the sausages and eggs?"

"Give them to the dog!" Phee yelled back. "Gotta jam! Love you!"

"Love you, too, Mom!" I yelled back as well.

Our backpacks were on the floor by the door, but Phee had to race upstairs to get her phone.

"Since when do we have a dog?" I said to myself.

I grabbed my backpack and put it on as Phee charged back down the stairs, grabbed the straps of her backpack, and flew out the door, with me close on her tail. She broke into a run once outside, heading back down the path that had led us to that fateful moment that hadn't happened yet. We stood there, out of harm's way, but with a clear sight of what was about to occur. At least it *should* have happened, and then it *did*. The red car had three teenage girls in it. The driver appeared to be texting. Phee shouted at them to stop. We both did, but to no avail as the windows to the car were closed, and, being teenagers, they probably had the radio turned up several decibels too loud.

The crash was enormous, the red deathtrap slamming into the oak like a meteor into the moon. The girl in the back seat flew through the windshield and hurled headlong into the left headlight and grill of a parked car. The one in the passenger seat, it afterward turned out, had her neck broken by the airbag as it burst out from the dash. The driver was the only one to survive, though replete with internal injuries from having her body slammed into the steering wheel. Some of this we witnessed firsthand. The rest we learned word-of-mouth at school. A memorial service was held in the auditorium several days later, with counseling being offered to any student who felt the need. Neither Phee nor I were friends with any of them, though I must confess that I threw up my breakfast after my brain imbibed the horror of the ejected girl's head split open, her bulged-out eyes lifeless, her tongue dangling out from a crushed lower jaw. The image, so unforgettable, remains with me to this day.

After regaining a bit of my stomach, I turned back to Phee. There were tears streaming from her eyes, as her voice resonated with tearful sounds.

"The driver," she sobbed. "That's Jenny Aragon. She's on my swim team. Life is fragile. That's why you need to fight to hold onto as much of it as you can."

"You did what you could for them," I said, trying to reassure her. "At least one of them might survive thanks to you."

"You and I are alive because of what *you* did," she said.

"Yes, but it's not something I can control," I replied. I stared at her with uncertainty in my eyes. She stared back with a tearful look.

"Not yet," she said. "Not yet."

CHAPTER III

School let out early that day. Phee and I were back home by ten a.m. The accident rattled both of us so much that the subject of my having *special* abilities didn't even come up for another twelve hours when we were alone together in our bedroom. The two of us share one room. It had been that way since we were brought home from the hospital after we were born. There were two twin beds with about eight feet between them and a window that faced the street. Phee occupied the one on the right, as perceived from entering the door. We live in an upscale part of Santa Monica. That's in California, bordering Los Angeles and the Pacific Ocean for those who might not know. Our bedroom is on the second floor, as is Mom and Dad's. The house, being more than a century old, included quite a bit of history, much of which involved the Mexican wars. There were no ghosts, but the Santa Ana winds that would blow in from September through May often play tricks with sound, and the floorboards are wont to creak, especially in wintertime.

Phee was sitting on the edge of her bed facing me as I stood looking out the window at the distant stars. She was wearing her blue silk PJs while I was clad in one of my short nightgowns.

"So, what else can you do besides travel through time and space and hear unhearable things?" Phee asked. My sister never wasted breath asking questions.

"No clue," I replied.

"Do you think you can fly?" she went on. "That would be so cool."

"No idea," came my response.

"Go take a running start," she suggested, "and try and fly out the window."

I turned and stared at her with a furrowed expression. "You *are* kidding?" I said.

"Yeah. Duh!" came her reply. "But come on. Try. Think, like, zero gravity."

All right, I thought to myself. *Maybe she's onto something. Maybe there are other powers I've been given.* I pressed my eyelids tightly together and tried to imagine that I was floating through the air.

"Nothing," I said.

"Really," Phee replied. "Try looking down."

Cautiously, I opened my eyes to find myself hovering about six inches above the floor.

"How did I..." I began to ask.

"I don't know," Phee said. "It was like you vanished and then reappeared half a foot above the floor."

Eyes shut, I thought as hard as I could about where I wanted to be. When I opened them again, I was back on solid ground.

"Can you project yourself sideways instead of up and down?" Phee asked.

I tried. When I looked this time, Phee was over to my right or, rather, I was over to her left.

"What's it like?" she asked, filled with curiosity.

"I really didn't feel anything," I replied. "I just thought about it and when I looked again, there I was."

"And yet I saw you in phases," Phee said, "when you teleported from one place to the next." She paused in thought for a moment and then said, "I wonder what else can you do."

"Like what?" I asked.

"I don't know. How about X-ray vision? Try and look *through* me."

I focused on her and concentrated. First, only her skin became transparent, revealing her muscles. Then her skeleton and organs appeared, as though everything else had been peeled away. Phee lifted her arms and stared at them in amazement. Obviously, I wasn't only able to just see *through* things, but I had the ability to create a see-through view of whatever I chose. I witnessed her heart beating and her lungs expand and then contract with each breath. Phee stared down at herself, amazement on her face.

"So, you can see it, too," I said. I needed to know.

"Totally." Her voice was filled with amazement. She looked up at me again. "You can turn it off now."

Incredibly, this was more than just X-ray vision. It was X-ray projection if that's the proper term to use. How many other powers there were I had no idea. I had grown up in a world where those with extraordinary abilities were the grist of comic books and film. None of them were real until now—until me.

"My sister the superhero," Phee extolled with widened eyes. Then she smiled. "But you definitely need a costume. And a mask. I can try and sew them for you."

"I still remember last Halloween," I replied. "No one at school will ever look at Wonder Woman the same way." I remember I had slightly squinted in order to focus my thoughts, but then, suddenly, I appeared in what would become my trademark uniform. All at once, my nightgown had turned into a short, long-sleeve tunic, strapped at the waist by a glittering silver belt. The *fabric*, if one were to call it that, was nothing less than a window into outer space, replete with stars, nebulae, and galaxies. I sported a cape of similar material that touched the hem of my skirt. Shallow silver metallic heelless shoes were on my feet. Meanwhile, my head was covered by a cowl, which, like my cape, mimicked the space effect of my dress. It hid the top half of my face, though my hair flowed freely where it ended at the nape of my neck. Meanwhile, I had caused my skin to become, well, solarized, irradiating a soft violet light, while the tips of my hair glowed as though made of optical fiber. No one would ever recognize me as Peyton Herron. Nothing so lame as a pair of eyeglasses to try and accomplish *that*.

"All right," I asked, "How's this?"

"That is *so* cool!" Phee said, totally impressed. "And the star patterns change as you move! Okay, okay, okay! You still need a name. How about Dream Girl?"

"What does anything I do have to do with dreams?" I asked.

"Time Girl? Gravity Girl? X-ray Vision Girl? How about Peyton Girl?" she ran on.

I flashed off the cowl and the glowing effect and glared at her. "If I'm calling myself Peyton Girl, why am I wearing a mask?"

"You're right. You're right," she admitted. "Wait! What did that Dhraaal guy say he put in your head?"

"A quantum seed, I think."

"That's it," she announced. "Problem solved. You're Quantum Girl."

And that was how I got my superhero costume and my superhero name. I remember having looked down over my shoulder, admiring my new cape. It was all so empowering.

That was the beginning but it took another year for me to fully realize and master what I was able to do. There was no instruction manual, no online guide. Everything I learned, I learned on my own. Painfully, I found that I was not invulnerable, though I could project force fields to protect myself from harm. I could not fly, but I could hover and phase[5] myself anywhere I chose, whether on Earth, in the sky, or in outer space. By the twelfth month, the furthest I had ventured was one of the five planets in the Alpha Centauri star system. I was afraid to go farther for fear of getting lost. It's a big universe out there. I named the planet Achilles. Why not? I was the first human there and astronomers hadn't even discovered it yet. The air was a bit thin and the temperature somewhat chill; but what surprised me was the fact that there were oceans and there was life, both animal and plant. They were different from life on earth in the way that a giraffe is different from a brachiosaurus or like a rhinoceros is different from a triceratops, but life evolves randomly to fill whatever niche it finds itself in. So, how was it that I was able to travel faster than light? Light moves at a rate of 299,792 kilometers or 186,287 miles per second, depending on which continent you're

---

[5] It was Phee who coined the term.

on, but that's light traveling through space. All right—quantum brain at work here for an explanation—light doesn't actually travel through space. The fact is that nothing does. When it appears to, it's an illusion similar to advertising signs made up of hundreds of lightbulbs where the words appear to move across the sign but really don't. In reality, the lights are programmed to turn on and off in succession, giving the illusion of motion. Well, it's the same with what we perceive as matter. Every instant, a new version of us is created as the old one vanishes. It doesn't disappear from existence but is left back in time. We do not notice this because the thread of our consciousness travels with the progression. Nor can we communicate with our former selves because as we move through space we are also traveling through time, which means that each version of us has a slightly different temporal variance. Anyway, when I decided to travel to Achilles I did so by traveling through the quantum thread, a realm of existence which underpins all universes and all dimensions. But by now, I've probably confused you enough, so back to my story.

My name is Peyton Elise Herron and I am Quantum Girl. By the time my fifteenth birthday had rolled around, I had pretty much mastered the bulk of my superpowers and it was all under wraps. The only other person who knew was my sister. One of my powers, not previously mentioned, was an ability to create a seemingly infinite number of duplicates of myself, each able to act on her own, but all connected by a single mind. I wondered with a trace of humor if that would prove the ultimate fantasy or the ultimate nightmare for any prospective future husband.

There were other questions, too. Would I age like everyone else or was I now immortal? Was I really the reincarnation of Khattaaara? Who was she? Who was she to Dhraaal? And where *was* Dhraaal? He had not made contact with me since saving my life. What was life like on Rendenaaar? And were there any others like me or was I the only one of my kind? These remained questions without answers, for there was no one there for me to ask.

41

CHAPTER IV

School began at eight a.m. the next morning with math class being heralded (as were all throughout the day) by the ever-annoying bell that rang out through the P.A. system. But where I had struggled before, solving quadratic equations now was like an artist from the Renaissance being *challenged* by fingerpaints. And then there was physics, taught with footnotes in science fiction, by Mr. Aarush Chatterjee, originally from New Delhi, who believed in his rote with the same fervor that a zealot in a wheelchair holds fast that prayer will heal his legs. It took forty years for him to attain his pinnacle of opinion. Poor Mr. Chatterjee, ever so convinced in the gospel of his beliefs; always standing as though he were waiting for someone to carve out a statue in his honor. Straight dark hair cut wildly across his umber-colored skin. A simple gold band encircled the third finger of his left hand, which would suggest to any onlooker that there was a Mrs. Chatterjee, waiting to serve some hot meal at home upon his arrival, desperate for his affection, eager to bear him however many offspring to perpetuate his ancestral line; but there was not and the Chatterjee lineage would one day end with him. The fact was that Mrs. Chatterjee had left him years ago, in part for his arrogance and in part for a pale Mr. Arbuthnot who had promised her and shown her all those things that her husband had failed to provide.

Mr. Chatterjee's lectures were generally insipid and could easily have been substituted with a page or two from an equally insipid textbook. That day's sermon involved the creation of our universe. So odd that we have given a name to our star system and our galaxy, but not to that which encompasses all of our existence. In that no one has ever even made an attempt, I chose to call it Sarah after my great-grandmother. Little did I know at the time the irony of that decision, but that will become clear later on. For the moment, though, there I was, stuck in a cauldron of nonsense, peppered with fallacious ideas that he spoke of as truths but salted with historical facts.

"In 1927," he began, "a Belgian Catholic priest named Georges Lemaître proposed the Big Bang theory, propounding that the entire universe was created from the explosion of a single super-atom. Two years later, an astronomer named Edwin Hubble— that's the man the Hubble telescope is named after—made a discovery that led him to theorize that the universe is expanding. Scientists now recognize the validity of those two postulates."

It was all too much for me to bear. I raised my hand to speak.

"Yes, Ms. Herron," he said.

"Wouldn't the same effects as seen by the red shift of distant stars be true," I asked, "if all matter in the universe were gradually shrinking?"

I sensed the hint of a disparaging smile and a restrained head shake at my words. Regardless, I went on.

"That being the case," I insisted, "might we not consider that eventually, when the subatomic fields are forced into critical proximity, a fusion-like reaction might occur, causing the quantum fabric that underlies space, to cascade outward, generating a new universe? That would mean that the birth and death of universes are cyclic, rather than, like Ptolemy, pompously believing that where *we* exist lies the center of everything. Krotaaarak," I said, "posited that matter and space are both anomalies of time. Therefore, the creation of a new universe, having no yardstick by which to measure anything, would appear to have happened in an instant. And since the explosions all occurred simultaneously, there would be no center, no one 'super-atom.' This would also eliminate the necessity for the existence of any supposed dark energy, which no one has ever detected, as some sort of dynamic engine."

"That's very," he said and then hesitated just a bit, "interesting, although I've never heard of this person, Krotaaarak. As I recall, and please correct me if I'm wrong, but didn't you get a rather unexplosive D in physics last year?"

I could hear a number of the students snickering to themselves at

43

his remark. Some of the girls thought that Phee and I were stuck up. Some of the boys were upset that we'd turned down their advances. Just then, though, Daisy McKenzie broke into the room with a note for Mr. Chatterjee. Daisy, who was the school's Barbie lookalike, had become notorious for wearing skirts that came within millimeters of being illegal, till Mrs. Markham, the principal cracked down on the school dress code, declaring that all of the girl's uniforms needed to be, well, uniform and that included the hemline, which was to fall no less than two and no more than three inches above the knee. Furthermore, blouses, even on warm days when it was permitted to remove one's tie, could not be unbuttoned past the collar, again preventing Miss McKenzie from flaunting her recently-acquired ample bosom. The day the edict was handed down was a sad day for most of the boys at the school who had all viewed Daisy Mae McKenzie as Miss August, September, and October all rolled into one. But as Marie Antoinette might have uttered had her head not gone the way of all cabbages, *C'est la vie!*

His head unmoved, Mr. Chatterjee raised his eyes from the paper to stare at me. "Miss Herron," he said in a tone that offered more than a hint of superiority, "this appears to be your lucky day. Counselor Andrews would like to see you in her office. 'Light speed.' Those were her words, not mine. That being said, both you and your extraordinary theories may immediately leave the classroom."

And so, I did. Bobby Applegate grinned and clapped silently when he saw me glance in his direction. Mycroft De Winter, whose parents must have been ardent Sherlock Holmes fans to have strapped him with such a name, tried to lift the hem of my skirt as I passed, though I quickly slapped down his hand. And Myra Kartinova, who modeled with the same agency as I did, and who was an on-again-off-again rival when it came to us vying for photoshoots, stuck out her tongue at me. It was rather like running the gauntlet but in no short time, I was out of the classroom and in the abandoned corridor, immersed in antiseptic quiet, having shut the door behind me as I left.

QUANTUM GIRL

There isn't a whole lot to say about the halls in that *institution*, which, in times such as those, was a fitting word. The hallways tended not to be the most brightly lit. The floors were all checkered in black and white decades-old linoleum tiles and the walls were lined with gray student lockers, though Daisy had painted hers bright pink, much to the chagrin of Mr. Kowalski. Mr. Kowalski was the school janitor, long since retired from the Queen's Navy, who liked his hallways kept Bristol fashion, though the Mattel doll did placate his ire a bit by informing him that the paint was, in fact, tempera, and would easily wash off once she graduated, which, I was convinced at the time, would be never. My own locker was next to Phee's, both of which were located just outside room 134, Mr. Trent's calculus class. Mr. Trent prided himself in his ability to impart unbounded mathematical wisdom to all those who entered his domain.

Back on track, though, this having been my first time to visit any counselor, I had neither an opinion nor a concern. What did cause me to wonder, though, was why I had been summoned to her office at all, for while neither Phee nor I live under the wire, we did not wrestle the boundaries of what those our seniors defined as proper decorum. Simply put, we never tried to rock the boat, and now especially, with my transformation into Quantum Girl, we recognized that we both needed to keep a somewhat low profile.

The door to Mrs. Andrews' office was, as were most in the building, made of heavy oak on which there were no markings save for a horizontal bronze plaque that read, "Laurel Andrews, Counselor." As the building itself was built in the 1930s, there was an oak-framed glass transom overhead. Such was the case with the majority of the doors at the school, though, with the advent of air conditioning, most had remained in their closed positions from long before I was born—at least, long before I had been born into this incarnation. Having knocked and received an invitation to enter, I opened the door and stood in the presence of her, whom I assumed to be Mrs. Andrews.

Mrs. Andrews' room was near the counseling office, which faced the north side of the building. Within it sat the presumptive Mrs. Andrews, Mrs. Laurel Elizabeth Andrews to be precise, a somewhat thick-set, middle-aged woman who might have been attractive at some time in the past before time crept up on her. Nor did the heavy-framed eyeglasses or the bangs, probably a carry-over from her teens help to embody the slightest measure of the youth that women at that age often so desperately try to regain. Whether or not there was or had ever been a Mr. Andrews had been the subject of debate among those students who had occasion to meet her, but she did sport a rather sparse diamond ring on the wedding finger of her left hand. High school students, myself included back then, considered all sorts of scenarios when assessing those whom they consider to be *ancient*.

"You wanted to see me?" I asked innocently enough. "What's this all about?"

"Please. Close the door," came the chilly reply.

"Am I supposed to have done something?" I asked.

She stared at me. Her gaze traveled down my form and then up again until her eyes met mine.

"You exist." She nearly spat out the words. "Again!"

"Ex*cuse* me?" I said.

I would have said more but my words were interrupted as bright white light burst from her eyes like a star gone nova. All at once, it as was though my entire body was hit by an explosion and I was thrown backward into the door, smashing the planks that had stood the test of time for nearly a century, and causing the transom glass to rain down on me like razor-sharp icicles from the gutter of a winter roof. It must have been the quantum seed that saved me because the blast from her seemed unending. It pushed my face to one side hard against the door. It was as though I was caught up in the brute force of a hurricane but I wasn't injured—not by the impact nor by the falling glass shards. I tried to turn my head to look at her but I couldn't budge. And then there was a deafening sound from the wave of energy that had thrown

46

me back and pinned me against the door.

"What does it take to destroy you?" Andrews' voice shouted at me, competing with the sound.

"Who *are* you?" I said. I don't even know if she could hear my words above the sound, as I struggled to break free. I clenched my fists and closed my eyes. I thought of Mom and Dad and Phee. I had been through death and been reborn and the seed was in my head that Dhraaal had said could protect me. With those thoughts, I became Quantum Girl. I could feel the cowl back over my face and the cape at my back. Peyton couldn't fight her but perhaps Quantum Girl could. I was able to turn my head toward her. Purple light blazed from my eyes, canceling out the light that came from hers. I felt myself floating once more. I could see the terror as it grew in her eyes and, with one single thought, I hurled her into and through the wall behind her and into the adjoining vacant room, leaving her to crumple into a heap of bones and flesh on that room's floor.

The wall now harbored a chasm that reached down to the basement. Regaining my footing, I phased into the other room to stare down at her—she who had just tried to murder me. But her figure, at first turning transparent, became a ghost that vanished beneath me.

"You didn't think it would be that easy to get rid of me, did you?" A girl's voice with a Russian accent came at me from the corridor outside the other room. I turned around to see Myra Kartinova, a devious smile on her face. But it wasn't Myra Kartinova. It was *her*, Thara-Klo, her eyes starting to glow once more.

"I've survived a lot worse," she said, gloating.

The only thought that raced through my head was that I wished I could have known what was about to happen before it did, and with that thought, I found myself back in class ten minutes before any of this had occurred.

"Miss Herron. This appears to be your lucky day." The words echoed in my brain, for there was Mr. Chatterjee, and there was Daisy McKenzie, so Lolita-like beside him. One just had to wonder how many of the male faculty had undressed her with their eyes and lusted over her unmapped flesh, regardless of whatever families or doting wives they had left at home.

"Counselor Andrews would like to see me in her office," I said. Mr. Chatterjee's right eyebrow raised at my words. His curiosity had suddenly peaked. How could I have known? I didn't need to be able to read his thoughts to know that that was what went through his mind. His eyes met mine and then stared down at the note he was holding.

"I believe her words, the ones on the paper in your hands, are, 'light speed,'" I said. And with that, the man's jaw nearly dropped to the floor, if I may invoke the use of hyperbole. I rose, went to the door, and then half glanced back.

"By the way," I said, "remember last week when you explained quantum entanglement, as caused by some invisible 'spooky' force that travels faster than light to move the entangled particle the same as its pair? Not quite. The effect on the one travels backward in time like a wave to the moment of entanglement and then forward to affect the other, though from a single frame of reference, it all appears quite instantaneous."

And then I left, headed down the corridor as before, but this time walked past that fate-filled room, opting instead to make my way to the swimming pool. It was an indoor pool, almost Olympic-length, allowing for practice regardless of the weather outside. If I haven't already mentioned it, Phee was a swim enthusiast, and quite good at it. She could beat out most of the other girls and some of the boys as well, though the sexes didn't intermingle when it came to aquatic sports. The official word was that competition between males and females was too unbalanced, but I believed that part of it was it there would have been too much flesh revealed and too much temptation. After all, Gina Gillespie, who was the star high diver, did become pregnant and started to show three weeks prior to the interschool competitions. It was shortly after it was discovered that she was on the nest so to speak, that the rule as to the segregation of the sexes was put into effect. And for those inclined to curiosity, four months later, she gave birth to a girl, whom she named Ariel, though all of this was before my time—at the school, I mean.

The air in the pool room was filled with the scent of chlorine and the sound of splashing water. About a dozen or so girls were making their way toward the farthest end of the pool, while others talked or watched. All of them wore one-piece bathing suits that were Persian blue with a wide vertical red stripe down the middle, edged with white pinstripes, as well as white swim caps. Emersed in the water, kicking, reaching, and splashing, they all looked pretty much the same. The swim instructor, a not-so-unattractive woman in her late thirties, whose name presently escapes me, stood near the end where I was, watching as the swim team made it to the far end, to perform an open turn to face the opposite direction and push off from that further wall. Walking over to her, I explained that I urgently needed to talk with Phee. Miss Windrows—that was it—pointed to the swimmer in the lane second from the left, who was making her way back. Miss Windrows, it later turned out, was having a dalliance with a very pretty freshman named Shelby Kine—that is until the girl's parents found out and went to the authorities, whereupon Miss Windrows was taken away in handcuffs by two uniformed policemen, sobbing out more tears than the pool could hold. At least, that's how the story later went.

But at that moment—the one I allude to now—Miss Windrows, yet to be caught, blew into the chrome whistle that hung from a chain around her neck and then yelled out, "Herron!" at the top of her lungs as Phee made it to the edge of the pool near us. In the wake of that shrill bleating sound and the contralto of Miss Windrow's lungs, I walked over to where Phee had surfaced in her breathless attempt to beat out the competition.

As I stood at the water's edge, Phee stared up at me and then grabbed hold of the rounded, smoothly glazed tiles that formed the circumference of the swimming pool.

"What's up?" she said, water beading down her face. She pushed herself up to waist height, lobbed her left leg up to the deck, and then thrust herself up to a standing position.

"We need to get out of here. Fast," I said. My tone was insistent.

As Phee pulled off her bathing cap and shook out her hair, I did a quantum thing and moved both of us through time. What had been, dissolved into what would be. Around us were images of total destruction. No longer were there walls around the once indoor swimming pool but only the remnants of mortar and brick. The pool stood drained except for some shallow water at the bottom at the deep end that had been polluted by time and neglect. The once reality of a swim team dissolved into an oblivion of manmade devastation. And yet one skeleton, at the bottom of the dry end, stared upward with hollow eyes at the stars that remained oblivious to the poverty that had been wrought.

Phee looked around, gasping at the world upon which she now stood. "Where are we?" she asked. Her voice fought against the wind that chilled her to her core.

"One year from now," I said. My words seemed to echo in her brain.

"Oh my God!" she exclaimed and took a step back over the edge of the pool so that I had to freeze the moment to keep her from falling headlong to her death.

Immune to time itself, I grabbed her wrists, pulled her back, and held her in my arms. As I started up time again, I could feel her tremble. Instinctively, I had become Quantum Girl. It had become my failsafe whenever I used my powers in moments of alarm.

"What happened?" It was barely a whisper that bore out from her.

"Thara-Klo," I answered in my Quantum Girl voice, which, to describe without hearing it, had somewhat of a hollow sound.

"What's that?" she asked. The words came as a pale breath to my ears.

I pulled back a bit to look her in the eye. "Not *what* but *who*," I said. "Hell hath no fury. Different universe. Different time. I'll fill you in when I can." I broke off and looked at her. There were goosebumps all over her flesh. "You need some clothes," I said and then I gave them to her. In an instant, she was wearing her street clothes again. I backed up a bit and looked at my work. Not only was she dressed but there was not a trace of wetness on her anywhere. I smiled at her and she smiled back. And then I split. No, I didn't abandon her. I literally became two Quantum Girls.

"Thanks, Sis," Phee said, feeling her sleeves. "Sis," she repeated, thanking the other me.

"I need to go," one of me said.

"I'll stay with you," said the other.

"Can you do that?" That was Phee.

"Seriously?" both of me echoed at once.

"We are, after all, Quantum Girl," said the Quantum Girl on her left.

"You're unreal," Phee replied.

I remember one of me having a somewhat smug expression on my face as the other of me pondered what she had just said.

"I may or may not be," said the me to her right.

"Sort of like Schrödinger's cat," said the me to her left and it was that one of me that took Phee's hand while the other started to fade away.

"More like the *Cheshire* cat, if you ask me," Phee replied as that one became barely a whisp of a girl. "Are you still linked to her?" she asked the one who held her hand.

"I *am* her," I replied. "I see everything she sees, hear everything she hears, think every one of her thoughts. I'm just in two places at once."

"Gotta jam," the Cheshire one of me said in a voice that was barely a sound before vanishing entirely.

"Damn!" said Phee. This was all so new to her.

51

The one of me that remained just smiled.

"What say we get out of here?" I said. And so we did.

CHAPTER V

With Phee safely under the wing of my second self, I stood my ground, so to speak, ten thousand feet above Cape Canaveral. It had become a favorite place of mine to be able to think as I observed the rockets take off with their spacecraft attached, watching brave men defy the gravity of the planet that had for untold ages bred their kind.

It was fascinating to view the missile-like thing, as it blasted off, surrounded at first by its water vapor exhaust and followed by billowing white smoke that rose from the tarmac like a cumulous cloud in the atmosphere. One by one, its stages dropped off as their fuel became expended, finally pushing the capsule into a weightless orbit. Then, suddenly, *she* appeared—Thara-Klo!

A trillion universes come and gone, and you still remember, she voiced into my head. There was smugness in her words.

Enough to know that you're the evil one, I thought back at her. *Of all those born in all of time, how could the quantum fabric have granted this woman immortality?* I wondered.

So, that's how your memory works? She telepathed. *You should look in a mirror.*

This was just banter—or was it? All I had to go on was what Dhraaal—the being who had brought me back to life—had said. But there she was, angered at me who had done nothing to earn such ire. It was very strange—her appearance I mean. It struck me as odd that somehow this woman from trillions upon trillions of eons ago, who had managed to survive the death and rebirth of countless universes, bore a strange, uncanny resemblance to me. Her hair was dark though, and her eyes violet, tinged with green. She wore a knee-length dress made of an amazingly thin metallic cloth that continuously changed color and clung to her body as the wind blew at her revealing two pairs of breasts, neither exceedingly large—perhaps what I would describe as a B-cup—one beneath the other to the lower extent of her rib cage. Stranger still was that she possessed a tail that was capped with the same long dark hair that streamed from her head. Meanwhile, a sudden gust of wind revealed two pointed ears. Other than that, and the fact that there were no eyebrows, she appeared no different than any human being, though all of that was a lot. Fortunately for her, she had learned how to morph herself, which allowed her to blend in. But there she was, not a stone's throw before me, an intense glare in her eyes as she appeared to contemplate me or, rather, Quantum Girl. And in that split second my own thoughts reflected back to Dhraaal's warning. *So, this is my immortal enemy*, I pondered in that instant. This was the woman from so long ago, who, for some reason unknown to me, wanted to do me harm or, worse, wanted me dead. No longer disguised as some middle-aged woman or some teenage girl, this is how she really appeared—an alien, not just from another planet or even another galaxy, but from another universe that existed long before the Earth or even God! I decided to divide into dozens of me.

What's that supposed to mean? I thought back at her.

The alien woman looked this way and that as if trying to discern which one of me had projected the thought. The fact was that we all did.

You were such a bitter woman, acrid and obsessed. The words dripped from her brain like acid from a flask. *For an eternity, I've waited for that woman and all I find is a girl in a silly costume.* She paused and then went on, *I see Dhraaal gave you his god-stone.*

What do you mean his? I thought back.

You truly don't remember everything, do you? The god-stones are the only things that allow us to survive the end of one universe and the beginning of the next—us being Dhraaal and me. There were only seven of them. I have the one that once was yours. Dhraaal had to wait for you to be reborn after I made you go away. She hesitated, and then added, *so to speak. Men are so imbecilic; slaves to their emotions—wading through a trillion universes for you to be reborn and then he gives up his immortality for you, a skin-and-bones, barely pubescent teenage girl.* She shook her head at the irony. *You may have even loved me once,* she said with her mind, *and I you, but that's far behind us. Things change. Times change. I want to put an end to you now, once and for all.*

With those words, I transformed into hundreds.

She smiled a wicked smile. *That's impressive,* she said, *but can you top this?* Then, with her palms held out, her eyes glowing as they had before, she crossed her arms and then whipped them apart. An intense burst of white light encircled her and then pushed out in all directions. It bathed me. It weakened me. It took all of my strength, all of me—each of me—to fight against it. I clenched my fists, I tried to retreat; tried to find some refuge somewhere.

Oh, no! she cried out into my head. Her *voice* was like thunder to my brain. *No time travel escape for you this go-round.* Her arms pointed at me faster than thought. It was as though frames had been deleted from a film, the move was so abrupt. A split second later, a flash of white light burst from her hands. It shot toward me and pushed against the force field that gave me air and protected me. I held strong, but the shockwave felt like when Dad was in an accident and I was in the front seat and the airbag went off. Instinctively, I retaliated with a blast of purple light, though it seemed to have little effect. That's when I chose to turn myself into thousands of Quantum Girls, surrounding her from every direction. *Call me legion for we are many.* The words ran through my head from something my mother had once read to me. I thought that would work—all of us, all of me, against her one. But could she do the same I wondered? Ten thousand blasts hurled *at* her all at once—not to destroy her but to encapsulate her. Regardless, she pushed out her light again, this time causing it to grow to such intensity it was like an exploding star, blinding me with its brightness, burning me with cold white flames.

Into orbit with you! All of you! came her telepathic scream. I can still hear her voice, as all of me, each one, was hurled out into space. *Damn you to oblivion, Khattaaara!* was the last thing I heard before every one of me passed out.

When I—when we—awakened, the earth lay beneath us, swollen with its cloud-filled atmosphere. Some of me stared down at it; some at the veil of stars that had cast out their light perhaps billions of years ago. How long it had taken mankind to reach just this far, and yet here I had come in but an instant, only to find myself alone in outer space.

Only, I wasn't alone. As I looked around, still too weak to move, some of me caught sight of the Space-X craft nearby. There was an astronaut staring out of its window. To this day, I wonder what had gone through his mind, seeing thousands of Quantum Girls floating in orbit without so much as a breathing mask. And then there was *her*, Thara-Klo, flying upward from the surface of the planet, half-morphed into a dragon from the legends of long ago. The gray-white hulk of a creature flapped its batlike wings, beating the breathless air like an eagle in pursuit of a hawk, though the head and face were still that of the ancient woman, who admittedly wanted me dead. The one of me, closest to the spacecraft, phased the hundred or so meters that it took to grab hold of it. And so, there I was, face to face with the astronaut, each of us staring at the other through the inch-thick pane of glass. I saw both fear and awe in his eyes as he watched half of my selves absorbed back into the me that was clinging to his ship and the others to another of my selves who floated half a league away. The end result, though, was to strengthen me, both of me, for some had already recovered from the effects of the white light that had hurled us out so far. The me who had clung to the ship rephased my position like the liquid metal Terminator so that my back was now to the spacecraft and not a moment too soon. Looking downward, I witnessed the finality of Thara-Klo's transformation. The Arthurian creature, its silver scales glistening from the rising sun, drew ever more near, breathing out white icy flames as it continued to advance toward its kill. I was now on both sides of the end mark of her trajectory. As I at the craft and I some thousand yards away stared at the mythic creature, both of me at once, as with a single motion threw out our arms and faced out our palms so as to project a force field that encapsulated the reptile in a giant energy sphere. Inside, the dragon struggled to free itself, its wings being crushed into its hideous, armored body as the sphere began to contract. Then, all at once, the beast was no more and it was Thara-Klo, who was trapped within. I, who was once again clinging to the ship, for all of this had exhausted me, watched in horrific apprehension as the ancient woman pitted all of her quantum strength against the barrier I had created to entrap her.

There were no words—there *are* no words in space—and the barrier barred her thoughts. She glared at me with the eyes of a woman who had not known peace for an ocean and more of time. She glared at me from within her jail, filled with insurmountable hatred, and yet I remembered nothing of her past other than a sense of familiarity. At last, she regained her feet and stood upright in her tomb as though, even in the vacuum of weightless space there was gravity beneath her. She, too, possessed a seed within her head. She, too, owned powers, different from mine but with a mastery that spanned universes of existence—and she sought my end!

What came next was like an explosion. The force field just burst open, the energy I myself had created pushing up against and hurling the spacecraft on a collision course with the planet below, with me clinging onto it for dear life. I lost awareness of my other self—gone, I sadly thought, for as that explosion came, I saw through my other eyes—a blinding flash and then nothing—only black. My other self, it seemed, had been too close to survive. That was all I could believe. What then would be the result, as clearly half of me had met oblivion? Would I still be able to exist? Just a year of being Quantum Girl, I was still new to this—my powers and the workings of the quantum fabric. But as I had that thought, I had no time to think. The capsule was in no danger. Its heat shield faced the friction of the burning atmosphere, but I, even as Quantum Girl, clung to it unprotected. I projected what force fields I could to save me but it was not enough. My flesh was being singed away; the hair that fell past my cowl burned up like tinder. I screamed uncontrollably from the unbearable heat though the sound of the flames that engulfed the capsule drowned it out. It was beyond what I had felt when I had hanged myself, and at least that was over in a few minutes. This went on for nearly half an hour. I did everything I could to stave off the effects of the reentry but still, my flesh was set on fire, charred, and burned off. Gone were my eyelids and then my eyes, leaving me blind to it all. If either of the astronauts were looking out their window I must have seemed like some corpse exhumed from a grave. I don't even know how I held on. After just five minutes, I could no longer scream, my lungs having been incinerated from the inside. *Why did Dhraaal have to resurrect me?* I thought to myself. *What did I ever do to deserve this end?* And then, at last, I felt the tug of the parachutes. The capsule was yanked briefly upward and then it splashed into the ocean. The force of the impact dislodged me and threw me some short distance away to land face down like a sailor hurled from a burning ship as its boiler room explodes. The cold salt water sent ribbons of agony throughout what was left of me. And then, miraculously, my body began to heal. Cell by cell, whatever was in my head was causing me to be restored. My eyes grew back as did my organs and muscle and skin—even my hair. I could see again and hear the splashing of the ocean waves that defined the water that buoyed me while from above came an unnatural sound. It was a helicopter, chopping the sea of air as it descended toward the Space-X crew whose mission had been cut short. But most of the life was gone from me. The act of regeneration had taken its toll and I was little more than flotsam on an endless sea.

CHAPTER VI

So, there we were, Phee and I, once again in our bedroom and it was nighttime. Actually, there were four of me as Quantum Girl and one of her. As I recall with regard to myself, one was staring out the window. Another was leaning back on the dresser. The third was bent over, fidgeting with something or other that I had picked up from my nightstand. And number four was lying *on* my bed, staring up at the ceiling. Phee had left the bedroom door open a crack, looking out into the hall with a watchful eye. It was so odd, even now as I think about it, that as I spoke, each one of me completed the thought in turn.

"She just came out of nowhere," said the first.

"The strange thing is that," the second went on.

"I sort of remember her," added the third.

"from uncounted universes ago," the fourth thought back.

"Shhhh!" Phee whispered, closing the door. "You'll wake Mom and Dad!" Then she turned and shook her head at the macabre scene. "Do there really need to be four of you?" she went on. "And you don't need to wear that costume—not in here!" Her voice was soft but scolding.

"It's who I am," the one of me at the window shot back.

"And I can think better when there are more of me," declared the one of me on the bed.

Phee ran the fingers of both hands through her hair.

"Argh!" she breathed out, exasperated, trying to imitate someone who is slowly being driven insane.

In a reciprocated, frustrated response I merged back into a single me in the persona of my un-super self, meaning Peyton, into the one of me who was lying on the bed.

"Happy?" I said as I breathed out more than a dollop of frustration.

Phee stared at the long black t-shirt I sported that drew past my now raised knees. Blazoned across my chest, were flashing words that alternately read, "Peyton's All-Powerful" and "Quantum Girl Rules."

"You're impossible," she groaned and her eyes rolled up toward Heaven.

I turned to her, leaning on my left elbow. The words on my shirt now read, "Blah! Blah! Blah!" Although often unappreciated, I do have a great sense of humor. "Honestly, you are such a stick in the mud!" I proclaimed.

"You need to be more careful." Her words were filled with both scolding and concern. "That... *woman* killed you once. The other you." There came a pause and then she sighed out in Phee-filled exasperation, "Whatever!"

"We don't even know if she's corporeal," I replied.

"Corporeal?" she repeated. "Who fed *you* a dictionary?"

"This quantum seed didn't just give my body powers," I replied. "It's enhanced my neural capacity."

"You mean your brain," she said.

I raised my right hand, palm turned inward, curled my fingers, and stared at my fingernails. The reentry had burned off my nail polish. They needed to be done. Pink or beige or maybe French.

"Not just my brain," I told her. "I can hear your heartbeat. I can feel the spider on the windowsill."

"Well, then," she replied, "what are *you*... what are *we* going to do?" She stared hard at me. This was my twin sister. Our souls were intertwined. In her heart, she was willing to sacrifice her life if necessary to stand beside me no matter what, though I had no intention of allowing that to ever happen.

"Don't know," I said. "But what I *do* know, Sis is that Quantum Girl needs her sleep." That said, I rolled over to turn off the lamp on my nightstand.

Phee climbed into *her* bed and pulled her blanket over her. "Some superhero!" she muttered, half to me, half to herself.

"Heard that!" I whispered back.

Okay, here's where it might get a bit confusing, and we need to backtrack to the future where the world had been reduced to ashes, where one of me went off to eventually do battle with Thara-Klo, while the other stayed with Phee to protect her from harm, and that is the me that this thread of the story now unwinds.

I had brought Phee to our bedroom but back about a year, it having been my belief, which was later confirmed, that Thara-Klo could not follow us through time. We sat there then and we talked.—as though a year of questions was not enough, Phee's sense of wonder never found its end. *What did it feel like?* she wanted to know. *Might there be other powers I possessed that I had yet to discover? Had I ever visited her in the future? What was her future, which is probably a misstatement, since the future had yet to happen—or had it? When one changes the past, does it rewrite the present or does the altered past then split off into another quantum reality?* And on and on. But truth be told, how many other superheroes had a twin sister? And those were just in comic books. I was real. I mean, for fourteen years we had grown up pretty much the same. We weren't identical but we were razor's edge close and then suddenly we were like carrots and bananas. That's what we used to say. Oh, we belonged together but now there were worlds of differences between us. The question, however, that had never entered her mind, was, *How will I age? Will I age? Had the quantum seed granted me immunity to death?* Apparently, it had for Dhraaal if he had come from a world so many universes in the past. But then, what would it be like to watch everyone I knew grow old and die and turn to dust? How ironic that I who had actually died might never see the end of my life unless it was taken from me by the likes of Thara-Klo. *And who was she really? Why was I the focus of all of her anger? What could I possibly have done as Khattaaara to have inspired such hatred that would span eternities? Was there no peace to be brokered with her?* Beyond all else, she had wanted me dead for something I couldn't even remember that had breathed its breath in another life. Life was never fair, I realized. *But, then,* I thought, *what is?*

CHAPTER VII

When I divide into many, each of us (meaning each of me) shares our (meaning my) thoughts with each other. What one of me sees or hears or tastes or smells, each of us does. It is quantum entanglement of the mind. Each of us (each of me), is connected, and yet whichever one I am, I can focus my thoughts on what that particular body needs to do. To those who are spiritual and think of God as connected to each of us, so I am to each of me. And while the quantum seed exists in each, there is only one of it in the quantum fabric, connected to all by quantum threads that cannot be seen or felt or even breathed upon in *normal* space and time. And so it happened that I knew that I was needed—that my other self was weakened to the point that I couldn't create others to fight off Thara-Klo.

"You'll be safe here. I have to go," I told Phee.

"Why?" she asked. "What's wrong?" A look of grave concern appeared on her face.

"I'm in trouble," I said. "I sensed it before I brought you here."

"What if something happens to you?" she asked. "What if you're hurt? What do I tell Mom and Dad?"

I split off into a pajamaed Peyton. "Don't worry. I won't leave your side," my Peyton self reassured her.

"…even if *I* do," I added from the Quantum Girl me.

"Fuck, this is confusing!" Phee said as she threw up her hands.

"Take care, Sis," I said from my quantum self. "Gotta go now. Be back soon." And then that one of me phased out of spacetime to offer an assist to the other one of me floating helplessly in the Pacific. I saw a tear, though, drip from Phee's right eye, which she smeared with the back of her right hand.

"Come on," I said, trying my best. "I'm not leaving you."

"I hope not," came the tearful response. "Anyway, I'm starved. Let's head downstairs and grab some lunch." I then went to the door and opened it, but, to my chagrin, there on the other side stood Phee, another Phee, the Phee from the past we were in. "Oops," I said, the word falling out from my mouth. In my haste to escape through time, the possibility of us encountering our former selves had totally slipped my mind. The question was, how might this affect the timeline?

CHAPTER VIII

I saw myself floating in the ocean nearly lifeless as I arrived from the past. The helicopter that had come to meet the astronauts hovered directly over the capsule and there were grappling lines tethered to it. The spacecraft hatch open, the first of the two-man crew was being hoisted to the whirlybird by a chair that had been lowered for him to climb into. The focus of all involved was on the recovery. Thus it was that no one noticed as I merged into my other self and then disappeared.

CHAPTER IX

What is time? It cannot be seen or touched or smelled or tasted or heard. It has no color. It is neither living nor dead. Yet all of us are trapped in the current of its motion, thrown in but one direction toward some distant, unknown shore. None can navigate its depths. None can escape its effects. No one. No one but me, Quantum Girl.

It was about a year before the battle in outer space that I had taken Phee a year back in time—two sisters about to become three. I had brought Phee back into the past to protect her from Thara-Klo, but I really hadn't thought things through. I was still rattled by my encounter with the Mrs. Andrews who really wasn't Mrs. Andrews only moments before. Thus, I made my three time travel escapes— first to the past, next to the future, and then to the past again. It was when I opened the bedroom door to go downstairs to the kitchen that I realized the gravity of what I had done. I had brought us back too far. The fourteen-year-old Phee glanced into the room and saw her year-older-self sitting on my bed.

"Peyton?" she said, her eyes transfixed on the face of her doppelganger. "Who is she? What the hell's going on?"

"I'm you," Fifteen answered.

"Shut up!" Fourteen said back to future her. "Who the hell *is* she and why does she look like me?"

I could see both confusion and fear on her face—she, who didn't realize that I wasn't the same Peyton she had awakened with earlier that day.

Fifteen glanced at me. "How far did you take us back?" Her gaze shifted once more to the Phee who stood at the door.

"I'm not sure." My voice was hesitant. "I haven't got this all quite down yet."

"She looks enough like me to *be* me," Fourteen said, her eyes still glued to the other.

"That's because I *am* you," Fifteen chimed back, and, poised in her stare like some statue, said to me, "I don't think she knows about Quantum Girl. She *does* look a bit younger. And I think shorter by an inch."

"Grrrr." That was Fourteen again. "This is driving me insane! Who is Quantum Girl?"

Fifteen broke form to look in my direction. My head was glancing back and forth like a spectator at a tennis match.

"Might as well tell her. You've already messed up the timeline," Fifteen said.

"*I'm* Quantum Girl," I told Fourteen.

And so, I explained, not in words, but visually. I became Quantum Girl, right before her eyes, as they say. And then she fainted. Well, actually, if memory serves, it was like "I... I... Ohhhh..." out of her mouth. And *then* she fainted.

Phee and I crouched down to check the condition of Phee's now-unconscious younger self.

"Can't you just undo all of this?" Phee asked as she felt for a pulse in Fourteen's neck.

"I don't know how," I replied. My quantum body tensed from the anxiety caused by what I had done.

Phee looked hard at me. "Maybe we should just leave."

"We've changed things," I said back. "*I've* changed things. I need to warn her not to say anything to me—to the other me—the one from this time."

After I phased Fourteen onto her bed, I sat down on the edge facing her then turned to Phee. "Get a cold wet rag for her, please," I asked and so Phee went to the bathroom to bring back a damp washrag that I might daub her forehead with.

But how does one deal with an altered past? How does one reweave the threads of time into the precise pattern they had previously been woven? The Ophelia, who lay unconscious on her bed had yet to learn who I really was. The quantum seed had yet to be placed in me back then—the me who had not yet tried to end her own existence. My younger self still knew the torment of being bullied. She was filled with self-doubt and still trembled at the thought of each tomorrow. At this moment in time, this sister was the strongest of the two. To her, there were no fears—only challenges. I stared at both of them, past and present or perhaps present and future depending on whose point of view.

"I've never had anyone faint in front of me before," I said. This was a new experience and, I must admit, somewhat unnerving.

"I don't remember myself ever fainting," came the reply.

"That could present a problem," I said.

"How so?" Phee asked, returning with the washcloth.

As she handed it to me, I explained. "The creation of an alternate timeline. When we go back, will you remember *our* past or *this* one? And will this incursion cause *our* reality to be erased?"

"You said there were an infinite number of dimensions," she said. "Maybe this one will just split off from our own."

I took a deep breath. "I sincerely hope so. I would hate to think that if she changes too much with what she knows, you and I, with all that we have done since I became Quantum Girl, would cease to exist, or perhaps the world as we know it will."

"Look, she's me and I *know* me," Phee insisted. "As long as we explain things, she'll hold her tongue just like when she accidentally dropped your toothbrush in the toilet when we were ten."

My stomach churned at the thought, but as my immediate concerns were still focused on Fourteen, I ignored the revelation and patted her forehead with the dampened cloth. Remarkably, and with a sigh of relief from both me and Fifteen, she slowly opened her eyes.

"Hey, there," I said to her in the most comforting voice I could muster.

"Hey," came the wearied response.

When Fourteen regained herself at last and the gravity of what had happened diluted her sense of fear, she saw me as Peyton again—her Peyton. I had changed back into myself because she needed something—someone—familiar to hold onto as the wave of *what might be* crashed sideways into her brain.

In another moment, she was pulling herself up to a sitting position, but as she stared at me with an occasional glance toward Fifteen, I could visibly discern her trembling. I suppose that was to be expected. Seriously, how often does one come in contact with one's future self? It took an entire year for Phee and me to arrive at the point of I don't even know what to call it (realization?) where we have half-heartedly accepted who I am and this was all splashed on Fourteen in an instant without warning. Regardless that she was from a year gone past, Fourteen was as much my sister as her year-aged counterpart and I could do nothing less than love her just as much. So, sitting facing her on the bed I held her in my arms and pressed my cheek against hers. I could feel the pounding of her heart and her body trembling like someone caught in a freezing draught as one's body tries to ward off the bitter cold. *Dear Phee. Dear innocent Phee. I'll hold you till it stops. I'll love you throughout time, no matter which version you are.*

"Am I awake?" she said. The words dropped from her lips like silent snow from a winter cloud.

I rubbed her back with my hands as I pulled her close to me. "I sort of took it the same way when it happened, when I first became..."

"Quantum Girl?" Fourteen filled in the name that had suddenly become so hard for me to say.

"We both did." That was Fifteen, who chimed in. I paused for a moment and then went on. "You know about Theresa."

"The Terrible," she whispered.

"The Terrible," I whispered back. "Well, it was all too much for me."

"You never showed it. I never knew."

"Inside it was a hurt that wouldn't disappear. So, one night I decided to *make* it go away."

"Oh, no," she said. "How?"

"You know that climbing rope from last summer?"

"The blue one?"

"I used it on myself. One night I pretended to go to sleep and I went into the closet and I ended it all."

Fourteen pulled back and stared me in the eye. "But you're here," she said. "I don't understand."

"I'm here because someone rescued me."

"Dad?"

I shook my head. "A man named Dhraaal. A man from long ago. He brought me back to life and told me that I was the reincarnation of a woman from an ancient past—a woman named Khattaaara. Then he placed what he called a quantum seed in my head, which gave me all sorts of powers in order to protect me from another woman from the back then named Thara-Klo. And so, when things went bad, where and when we were, you and I—the future you and I—escaped back to here. Only I, being such a birdbrain, didn't stop to think that we might run into you or Peypey from the past. I just want you to know that past, present, or future, I would never let anything happen to you. You are the one great love in my life." And with that, I kissed her on her forehead, hugged her close again, and she hugged me back so tight I could feel that the trembling had stopped.

"You must promise me something, though," I said.

"Of course," she replied, staring straight into my eyes.

"You must keep this to yourself," I said. "You need to let things happen the way they did before. Phee and I have interfered with the timeline and I don't want a paradox to occur. You need to let me hang myself. You need to let me die. It may be the only way I become who I was meant to be."

"I understand," she replied.

"I know it's hard," I told her. "I know you love me, too. But if you change the future there may come a time that I take my life and Dhraaal won't be around."

"I promise," she said. "I won't tell anyone."

I smiled at her and then rose from the bed. Fifteen looked at me and smiled then turned to Fourteen. "She's great, *isn't* she?"

"The best," came the reply.

Then I took Fifteen's hand, morphed into Quantum Girl and we phased from the room, probably leaving Fourteen with an even greater moment of astonishment.

When the two of us returned to our present, the me that I'd left behind was now literally beside herself.

"Oh my God, where *were* you two?" she exclaimed. "I've been worried sick." One could see the anxiety in her—in my—face.

Phee looked at her with questions in her eyes.

"I thought you shared thoughts?" she said.

"Not through," the Peyton me said.

"time," I finished with her as I merged back into my Peyton self.

"I managed to survive…" I said with a brief pause. "this time." My thoughts glanced back to the moment I had done battle with Thara-Klo. "She's hella powerful. I don't know if I can withstand another attack. She turned herself into an energy-breathing dragon."

"Damn!" came the response. "What if she goes after Mom and Dad?"

"I've already thought of that," I said. "I've placed quantum fields around both of them. As long as they don't try to have sex, everything will be fine."

"Ewww!" Phee replied, "Way TMI!"

"And I placed one around *you*," I replied.

"No worries there," Phee said as a sad frown twisted her lips. "Unfortunately." That from the picture-perfect girl whose relationships to date had been anything but.

"I was joking about the sex," I replied.

"Oh," Phee said. "Okay."

Poor Phee, I thought. If only there was something I could do in that regard. I wished her every happiness, but for whatever reason whichever guys she hooked up with nothing seemed to click. I shook my head to myself to wake myself from my reverie. There were more pressing issues at the moment. My focus had to change.

"She *must* have a weakness," I said. "You know, I've been thinking. What if twenty years from now I make it a point to come back in time to here and now to tell me what to do?"

And then it was that it happened, I guess because I had planned it to. There before us, out of thin air, stood a thirty-five-year-old version of me. No longer Quantum Girl, a haggard-looking Quantum Woman reflected all that I must have gone through over the coming score of years. It is difficult to imagine the ravages of time upon ourselves, but seeing it up close welcomed me to the harsh burden of reality. Apparently, my future held little but hardship as measured by the weary look in her eyes and from the quantum effect trying to sustain itself, her very presence flickering and revealing flashes of the prematurely aged Peyton two decades hence.

"They're all gone," she said. "I couldn't stop her in time." Her voice phased in and out as did spoke. It was as though only part of her had made the journey back.

"Who are *they*? Whom do you mean?" It was Phee. Her face had turned pale.

"Everyone," my older self replied. "Every human being on the planet. I'm the only one left." Her voice grew echoey and weak. "I don't have much time," she said. "There's not much left of the quantum seed but it was the only way for me to escape. It took everything in me to come here." She stared at me. "You know my thoughts," she said. "You know what not to do. You know who she is. Don't make the same mistakes."

"I won't," I replied.

"Go back in time to Rendenaaar," she urged, as her voice and her very presence grew dim. "Find the source of the quantum seeds. It's the only hope there is." And with that, she faded away.

So, there and then was to be the end of me. More than that, the fate of humanity and so much more pivoted on my existence. I looked at Phee. I thought of Dad and Mom and I wondered to myself how the fate of the world could have been laid on my shoulders. Better perhaps, I thought, that my life would have ended that night so that none of what Quantum Woman had foretold would ever have occurred. How ironic that every moment on this earth people prayed to a silent god for hope and salvation, pledging their souls when their lives rested, not on some supreme deity, but on some fifteen-year-old girl who hadn't the slightest idea what she should do. But I needed to try. I knew that much. And with that thought, I became Quantum Girl again and turned to Phee.

"I need to go," I said, "back to Rendenaaar."

"I'm coming with," she replied. Her voice was insistent.

In an instant, my quantum brain considered all the possibilities and all too many of them placed her life at odds. "I can't risk you," I said.

"Thara-Klo won't have her powers," she railed on.

"How can you know?" I asked.

"There must be a time," Phee replied, "before she had the quantum seed. Besides, her younger self won't even know we're coming. I can't let you do this all by yourself. We shared a womb for nine whole months. We share our lives forever."

I just let it go. Nothing more was discussed and Phee went to bed with the fervid belief that she had somehow convinced me to acquiesce.

I remember standing over Phee the next morning as she lay still asleep in bed. I was already dressed, my backpack already strapped on.

"It's time," I said, my left hand reaching out to rouse her, nudging her shoulder.

"I haven't had breakfast," she yawned, which was followed by a reaching stretch of her arms over her head. "Breakfast is the most important meal of the day."

She stared at me through the slits that guarded her newly

awakened eyes.

"I've adjusted your potassium and sugar levels," I told her. "Besides. You could stand to lose a couple of pounds."

She snapped to life somewhat quickly, having somehow become infected with my recently acquired ability to instantly shake off sleep, her eyes bursting open like window shades gone mad. Then her arm reached up to shield them from the sudden light.

"Are you inferring that I'm *fat*?" she demanded to know.

For myself, I said nothing, though I fear my mouth may have twisted just a bit.

"Do I get my own costume?" she asked, this foremost on her newly awakened brain.

"We'll see," I said, trying to appease her. "Now get up."

"I mean, I wouldn't want to embarrass you with layers of flab bulging out all over the place!"

"Shut up!" I replied. "You know you're gorgeous!"

Phee propped herself up on her forearms and smiled.

"Just needed to hear it said out loud," she replied. "Johnny Mayfield told Barry Kendall that I have the best-looking legs in the entire school!"

"And who told *you* that?" I asked.

"No one," she replied. "I was standing at my locker with my back to theirs and I overheard them talking." And with that, she raised up one of her legs to gaze upon it. "I *do* have the best legs, don't I?"

"And the best ego," I said, at which point she frowned at me.

"You're just jealous," she shot back.

"The bus will be here in five," I warned, ignoring her remark.

"We're taking a bus to the other universe?" she asked.

"To school, Dunkhead." I replied.

"But I thought…" she muttered as she sat up, sliding her legs over the edge of the bed.

"I already left," came my terse response. "I'm not risking you."

A frown darkened her face. "I guess I'm just not good enough," she said.

"You're the most important thing in the world to me. That's why I can't risk your being hurt," I replied, "or worse."

"Fine, fine. Just don't expect me not to grumble." In another second, she was out of bed and climbing into her school attire.

CHAPTER X

I was in outer space one minute before the Big Bang, though time at that point was pretty much irrelevant. It was as far back as I was able to go. I could time travel, but crossing into the universe that had preceded ours was a trick I had yet to learn. The moment before the last creation was as far back as I could manage. There are minute variances between universes but without knowing how to use a quantum seed, the physical matter from one to the other cannot or will not interact.

But in that past, I was like Gulliver among the Lilliputians, only so much more. What I at first perceived as tiny points of light, my quantum senses eventually discerned what they really were—entire galaxies! There were trillions of them, mostly reddish in hue. Such is how one universe must look when it is about to die and give birth to another. I tried to go back further. I tried to will myself farther back into that alien realm, but try as I might nothing came of it and time began to move forward. It was fear that struck me then as I realized that I was about to be caught in the biggest maelstrom the universe had ever known. And then it happened, with me in the midst of it all. It was what Krotaaarak had theorized and what Mr. Chatterjee had scoffed at. The shrunken universe that I was now in was about to explode—all of it—everywhere at once. The microscopic stars within their pinpoints of galaxies were about to burst into a new creation, each with the force of a quadrillion atom bombs as both they and the fabric of spacetime hurled outwards thousands of lightyears in but an instant. And then it happened—kaboom!

Blinding light surrounded me as the darkness lit up like the surface of the sun. But it was more than just light. The matter that had been part and parcel of the previous universe had been dissected into pure energy. Then, forming into matter, it was ripped apart by gravitational shockwaves again and again. Eventually, the tempestuous cosmic soup calmed a bit and gave rise to *quants*, the building blocks of matter, some of which in turn organized into leptons and gluons and quarks. This was all fueled by endless annihilations of matter and antimatter until pools of one or the other coalesced to form vast nebulae that eventually became stars that merged to form galaxies. As all of this was taking shape, only seconds to my mind, I was bombarded by the newly-created matter. I tried to shield myself from it all but the seed refused to protect me to the extent that I needed it to. The pain was excruciating—even more so than that which I had felt when clinging to the capsule. I screamed, but there was nothing there to make a sound. As matter particles were bombarding me their antimatter counterparts were ripping me apart. I tried to phase forward in time to escape but all of this had rendered me so weak that I wondered if I would even survive.

I watched in agony as the universe grew around me. My quantum vision saw atoms being born out of the primordial soup—saw how a tiny electron encircling a single proton would crash into its mass and be swallowed up, only to be spat back out into its orbit, the scene repeating a billion times in the blink of an eye, so fast that the nucleus appeared to be surrounded by a colorless cloud. Poor Heisenberg, who one day would believe that the imagined cloud was some quantum effect. Poor me, now trapped in this hell, where what might as well have been fire and brimstone ripped through my flesh, my heart, and my head. The formation of atoms took place at what on earth would have been reckoned at more than half a million years. That is how long I endured this—long enough to drive anyone insane—the unrelenting agony, the inescapable hours and days and months and years and centuries and eons by my yardstick, and, in all that time, I was alone. I wondered how Dhraaal and Thara-Klo had endured it. I wondered, how could I.

CHAPTER XI

Back that day, the morning I had left, Phee and I had boarded the school bus as there was a heavy rain—a downpour no less. And so, where we would normally have walked, we hailed it as it came. Nothing seemed out of the ordinary. The bus was filled with other students talking and laughing or focused on their tablets or laptops or cellphones. But as Phee and I were in the aisle walking back, looking for a place to sit, the agony that the other me was going through hit me all at once. I could feel her need though it had taken so many eons for my other half to connect with me. Afterward, Phee told me I screamed so loud that the driver slammed on his brakes. And then I passed out. Both of me did as my now ages-old quantum self merged back into the 15-year-old Peyton me in what must have looked like a blur if anyone was watching.

I awoke in a hospital room two days after the incident. Phee sat asleep in what looked like an uncomfortable chair, her head resting on folded arms on the bed I was on. Lifting my arm, I gently stroked her hair.

Dear Phee, I thought to myself, *always by my side.*

Suddenly, Phee sprung up and stared at me wide-eyed. "You're awake!" she exclaimed.

"I am," I said in a weak voice, with what must have been the hint of a smile. "I only made it to the Big Bang. It ripped me to shreds. I was trapped while the universe formed for hundreds of millions of years."

"Oh my God!" came the response.

"The quantum seed protected me," I said, "but to be perfectly honest, I wished I could have died."

"Don't say that!" she scolded. "Don't *ever* say that!"

"You can't imagine what it was like," I said. "It was an eternity of pain. I couldn't move or speak. And there was the endlessness of being alone. I may be Quantum Girl, but I'm human, too!"

I began to sob bitterly.

"Move over," Phee said.

I did and then she climbed onto the bed next to me and held me.

"My beautiful Peypey," she went on, "I wanted to go with you."

"You wouldn't have survived," I said. "I just wonder what would have happened to the me that stayed here if the other one had been destroyed?"

My body still unstable, I briefly phased into my Quantum Girl self and then phased back.

"I'll be fine," I reassured her, my cheeks wet with tears. I had no doubt she could feel me trembling. "Up and at 'em sooner than you think. But I have a really big favor to ask."

"Anything," she replied, and she meant it.

"I've heard all the rumors about hospital food," I lamented. "So, would you please go out and get me a cheeseburger? One of those slobbery ones. Extra pickles. And a chocolate shake. Part of me hasn't eaten in nearly fourteen billion years."

"Consider it done," she said, rising from her chair. She went to the door and then turned back. "Mom's at home. Dad's at work. You need to call them." She paused and then said, "You know, it's strange. Dad's been the one to cry his eyes out since you collapsed."

"And yet *you* stayed *here*," I said, sniffing in my tears.

"Hey, you'd do the same," she replied. "You and I, we're carrots and peas, remember?"

"Which one are you?" I asked. "I forget."

"Whichever you're not," she replied and then left for my junk food meal. I looked around the room. It was antiseptic and plain. There were no pictures on the walls or decorations of any kind. The ceiling was made of acoustic tiles with pinhole patterns that gave rise to embedded fluorescent lights. To anyone else with any sense of the aesthetic it would have seemed garish and devoid of good taste; but to me, someone who had lived through an epoch of hell, it was about the most welcoming sight I could ever imagine.

It was shortly after Phee returned with my meal that all hell broke loose. I had only taken a few bites of my burger when four men and a woman all wearing hazmat suits appeared at the door wheeling in a gurney. Phee turned and stared at them.

"Hey," she demanded. "Who *are* you?"

The woman stared back at her as she and the others entered the room.

"Please get up and step away from the subject," she ordered, an authoritarian almost military tone to her voice.

I surveyed them, one then another. "What's going on?" I said.

The woman again leveled words at Phee. "Miss," she demanded. "I need you to move back."

Phee bounded up from the chair she had sat down in with a resounding, "No!"

The woman, who appeared to be in charge, stared at Phee and then gave orders to two of her companions. "Restrain her."

In response, two of the men each grabbed one of Phee's arms.

"Why are you doing this?" she sobbed. She virtually wept the words and then looked toward me. "Peyton, you need to escape!"

I tried. I really did. I saw the skin on my arms turn the glowing violet that comes with my becoming Quantum Girl. I assume the rest of me changed, too, but there was no costume and the effect faded after a few short seconds.

"I can't," I told Phee. "I'm still too weak!"

Despite my struggles, the other men managed to lift me up onto the gurney. Those men and the woman wheeled it and me out of the room. I could hear Phee screaming for the men who held her to let her go as the gurney was rolled down the strangely deserted corridor. I assumed that those who came to take me had some sort of government clearance to empty out the halls. Once out of the room, still hearing Phee's cries, I began to struggle again, which prompted the woman to order the men to handcuff both my wrists and ankles to the gurney's rails. I felt helpless and I feared for my sister. How ironic, I thought to myself. Part of me had been trapped in the early universe for hundreds of millions of years, only to be trapped again, a prisoner of some woman, whose face I could barely see through the visor that was attached to the hood she wore. I lay there helpless, being taken to some unknown place. The ceiling blurred as I traveled past it. I could hear the woman's footsteps padding down on the linoleum, one and then the other, as she pushed the wheeled stretcher toward what turned out to be the service elevator. The corridor smelled antiseptic or was that just the scent of death? How many had died on the mattress on which I had laid? How many had screamed out in pain? How many held the hands of loved ones as they bid out those last moments of existence, a priest beside them to dole out comfort and hope? *Yea, though I walk through the valley of the shadow of death, I will fear no evil* and all that rot. And then their life bled out of them and they were gone forever from the trail of human existence, extinguished in the present as proof that the future was not just for them.

The reverie of my thoughts ended as the end of the gurney closest to my head bumped into the back wall of the elevator, followed by the sound of the doors sliding shut. Another moment gone and I felt the jar of movement as the room began to descend. Half a minute or so later, I felt a soft thud as we reached whatever level the button had been pressed for. In all of that time, none of my captors had uttered a word, nor did they break their silence as they pushed the gurney out the doors and into the garage where a fifth man also clad in a hazmat suit stood waiting. The silence continued as I was loaded into an ambulance or similar sort of truck. The woman and the two men entered with me while the other took to the driver's seat, started the engine, and drove the vehicle out of the structure.

"Where are you taking me?" I asked. It was the first time I had spoken since I had been kidnapped from my hospital room. "I have my rights! You can't just do this! I'm a living human being!."

The woman broke her silence. "That remains to be seen," she said matter-of-factly, and there the conversation found its end. What had they learned about me while I was unconscious? Had they detected the seed that was in my head? Did I become Quantum Girl in my comatose state? What did they think I was? Surely, they would have gone through my school records, viewed my medical history, and gotten a copy of my birth certificate. Or might they just have believed that I was some sort of invader, who had possessed or taken the shape of me? My heart pounded at the thought. I could, of course, explain to them the truth about what had happened, how I had committed suicide and been brought back to life by a being from another universe and been given the quantum seed, but who in their right mind would believe it? It would be so much easier for them to assume that I was part of an advance force from some other world determined to conquer the planet. That would be how anyone from the government would think, because, given the opportunity on some alien soil that they themselves had discovered, that's what *they* would probably do.

The ride took more than two hours as near as I could tell, not having a watch or clock to reference. Sometime close to that mark, I made it known that I had an extreme need to urinate. My pleas were met with stoic disapproval and I was simply told to "Hold it in until we get to where we're going." When we finally reached our destination roughly ten minutes later, our conveyance backed up into a building whereupon the gurney I was on was then unloaded and then wheeled into a large freight elevator that, once the gate was closed, began lowering us what must have been ten stories underground, stopping abruptly at what I assumed was the bottom of the shaft. That gate hoisted up, I and my gurney were escorted up to a metal door with a small window where I was unshackled and, after being allowed to briefly use the toilet, made to go into what turned out to be a padded cell.

Once inside, I turned my attention to my surroundings. The room was slightly oblong, the walls padded with what appeared to be square, flattened pillows, the fabric of which was comprised of the same sort of rubberized material from which gym mats are made. This, too, made up the covering of the door that held a small window. There were four overhead lights, one at the center of each wall, and cameras recessed in the ceiling at each corner. There were also four rectangular vents high up and from two of them a draught could be felt. The floor was built on the same principle as the walls except that, rather than numerous squares[6] traversed the length of the room. Meanwhile, in one of the farther corners, there was a mattress on which lay a folded blue woolen blanket, four plastic water bottles, and four tubes of paste-like food that tasted, respectively, of beef, ham, chicken, and potatoes. Still too weak to do much of anything, I laid down on the bed, covered myself with the blanket, and promptly fell asleep.

I dreamt that I was on Rendenaaar, trillions of universes ago. Only it was not me who stood in some oddly futuristic room so far in that buried past. Indeed, I was Khattaaara. I saw Thara-Klo standing nude at a replicator that was creating some sort of drink, her tail held high, poised over her right shoulder as though it had eyes, and was curious at what was in her hand. It was strange to see her as she then turned to face me. Her hair dripped water as though she had just come from a shower or a bath. It clung to her head revealing the pointed ears I had seen when we did battle. My eyes glanced downward then, to see her double pair of breasts. No, it was neither a shower nor a bath that had gotten her wet. It was the pool that she had just come from. That was it—the pool just outside that was fed by the waterfall at its edge. But how could I have known such things? I was *not* Khattaaara—or *was* I? Whoever I was, I sat on some sort of couch that appeared to be made of white light though how that could be possible I cannot imagine. My right leg bent, my knee raised, my foot rested on the farther arm of the couch. My left leg hung down. My body was draped in a loose-fitting chemise while on the floor at my side, just docile or asleep, was what appeared to be the same *goraaag* that I had met

---

[6] Perhaps pillows is a better term for them.

during my resurrection. My left hand held an almost invisible goblet that was filled with a glowing liquid that churned out a rainbow of colors. Meanwhile, a nude servant girl who had just entered the room scurried up to me and, after a nod in her direction, parted the hair on my tail and inserted her tongue into the exposed orifice with pleasurable results, decidedly sexual in nature. This was further evidenced by the fact that all four of my nipples became erect and turned a dark shade of blue.

The conversation that afterward took place must have been spoken in Rendenaaaran or whatever the language back then was called, but in my dream, the words in my head were in English—sort of.

"I fail to understand thee," I said as Khattaaara, "thou and thy one-life philosophy; just like all the rest of thy generation, content with growing old and frail when the god-stone could course immortality through thy veins."

"Death makes life special," came the stern reply, "and the fear of its inevitability makes us appreciate every moment."

It was then that I or rather Khattaaara caught a glimpse of herself in the reflection that the goblet threw back at her. She appeared much the same as the image of her that Dhraaal had shown me, though somewhat older, perhaps by ten or fifteen years— roughly the same age as the Thara-Klo who stood talking with her. Her violet eyes, though, reminded me of how mine appeared whenever I became Quantum Girl.

The image blurred as I brought the goblet to my lips and imbibed a mouthful of the liquid, letting it roll around my tongue before choosing to swallow. The beverage, whatever it was, was soothing and tasted somewhat like chocolate, but it created a rush through my veins and stimulated me sexually to such a level as I myself as Peyton had never felt. My heart beat faster, my tail began to convulse and then thrash around, spraying a bluish liquid in every direction. Thara-Klo, had moved across the room, apparently to avoid the results of my orgasm. The girl, who was kneeling on the ground all this time, had taken hold of my tail again and began licking off the *graaam,* as I believe it was called but I shooed her away.

It was then that a bitter conversation ensued between myself and Thara-Klo.

"Thou art such a fool," I scolded mercilessly. "That's what everyone says. They say, 'Khattaaara, thy daughter is such a fool!'"

"Daughter!" The word seemed to echo in my brain. So, this was Thara-Klo. No wonder she bore so close a resemblance to me. *But what must I have done to have inspired such hatred that would span immeasurable time?* I wondered.

"Trust me," she went on, "I will not mourn when thy body has fed the earth." This was the motherly sense or lack thereof that lay harbored in Khattaaara or me as Khattaaara in what may or may not have been my former life. *But what an awful thing to say!* I thought

"Thou *wilt* miss me, Mother," came the hollow response.

"I would miss the drink in my hand," heralded the reply. "I would miss the liquid that warms my desires. I would miss the *goraaag* that grovels at my side. I would miss all of them more than I would miss the abomination of thee that bringeth shame to the Royal House of the Gaaalthaaara," and with that, she or I polished off what remained in the goblet and then closed our eyes as we felt the rush of a thousand more orgasms all at once. *Oh, dear God. Is that what sex is like?* I thought to myself.

"And what wilt thou do with forever?" said Thara-Klo.

"I will own eternity," I as Khattaaara replied, "and as for those that refuse to kneel, dust be the scourge of their fate."

In my restless sleep, this dream or memory or whatever it was gave birth to another, years before when Thara-Klo was no older than I was at that time. There was neither the anger nor the fire in her eyes back then but only sadness and pain. She lay fallen onto the floor in a heap of sorrow, the robe she wore bloodied beneath the waist.

"He raped me," she breathed out in a voice that would not have been audible to any but Rendenaaaran ears.

Yet there I was, her mother, unmoved by it all.

"He joined with thee," I said with Khattaaara's breath. "That is the way of our kind."

"I do not want him. I want Saaahgra-Ræ! Saaahgra-Ræ and I are in love!" Her voice wept out the words.

"The joining in wedlock of females is not permitted under our law," came the dispassionate response.

"I care not what the law permits!" Thara-Klo wailed. "It is *my* life." She paused for a moment to swallow her tears. "Kaaaragar, hast always been cruel to *me* but ever held *thy* heart."

"He is thy cousin," I announced, unmoved, "and it is the way. Thou shalt bear his sons or thou shalt bear his wrath and mine as well! As for Saaahrah-Ræ, put all thoughts of her from thy mind. She was put to death last night on my command."

"No, oh, no!" Thara sobbed. "No! No! No!"

And then I awoke. I was back in the cell. I remember how the scene of young Thara-Klo had pierced my very heart and I remember how a tear had dripped down from my eye.

I'm so sorry, Thara, were my thoughts, *but whoever that was, whoever I was, it isn't me. Not now. Not anymore.*

In this universe—it was later on—Phee told me that she had been let go once I had been driven off hospital grounds. Meanwhile, Dad was beyond enraged at both the hospital and the police for what had happened to me. Of course, big businesses and the authorities being what they are there was little he could do.

The next morning, which I can only assume was in fact morning as there were no windows either in my padded cell or anywhere else, the complex being underground, I was gassed. Apparently, those in charge felt it was the safest way, at least for them, me being an unknown with some energy bead they had inadvertently discovered while performing an electroencephalogram that produced spikes off the chart. Meanwhile, their attempt to X-ray my head revealed nothing as the X-rays couldn't penetrate the barrier created by the quantum seed. *Well*, I thought to myself, *Phee always said I had a thick skull!* Anyway, apparently having watched too many Terminator movies, those in charge, medically speaking, determined that I was either a cyborg or an extraterrestrial, which led to numerous phone calls to the FBI, the CIA, Homeland Security, S.E.T.I., and probably James Cameron. Here I was, the oldest human being to ever exist, having been trapped in oblivion for a literal eternity and this was the reception I received—suspicion and fear. I just thanked God I wasn't yet old enough to have registered as a Republican or all of the hypocritical DEI proponents would have had me shot on the spot.

The gas had knocked me out for an indeterminable length of time. When I awoke, half-conscious and unable to move which left me to wonder if they had given me something to paralyze me while I was out. From what I could tell, I was strapped to the table of an MRI, my head locked in place by a helmet-like device. There were two others in the room with me, both men. My guess was, though, that I was no longer considered a biohazard because neither of them wore hazmat suits.

"What are we supposed to be looking for?" one asked the other.

"Don't know," the other replied. "Talk is, she might be some kind of robot."

"No shit!" said the first. "Looks human."

"What are you doing?" said the other.

"Just want to find out," the first said.

"You better not get caught," the other said, "or we'll both get in trouble."

"She's out like a light," the first said. "What's going to know?"

Suddenly, I felt a sharp pain in my vag, I was being penetrated by the man's finger but I couldn't move. I couldn't scream out. I couldn't cry. I couldn't protest. I couldn't move an inch! And, because of him, I wasn't a virgin anymore!

"Taste's human," the first said.

"You're fucking sick," the other replied. "You know that, don't you? Come on. Let's get this thing over with."

I could hear when they left the room and closed the door behind them. The machine was then started up and I felt myself moving forward. There was a humming sound coming from the machine that grew louder as the electromagnets began to spin. It was at that moment that I felt something strange. It was the quantum seed. Somehow, the MRI fields had strengthened it or perhaps fixed that part that had been damaged by the Big Bang, causing it to work sometimes and not others. At any rate, I felt like me again, or, rather, Quantum Girl. My old strength radiated throughout every fiber of my being. I sensed the cowl over my face and the cape beneath me. My hospital gown had turned into my costume. I focused on phasing away from there. The quantum seed did the rest.

A moment later I was back at home in our room, Phee's and mine. Phee was in bed, curled up in an almost fetal position, her eyes wet with tears. The room had been pitch dark, but now it was bathed in a faint purple glow. Phee appeared to sense it and turned her head a bit in my direction.

"Hey, Dunkhead. You miss me?" I said quietly in my Quantum Girl voice.

Phee now saw me standing beside her. "Oh my God..." she sobbed out as she burst into tears. Then she sprang up from the bed, wrapped her arms around me, and hugged me with all her might. "I was so afraid I'd never see you again!"

"I don't know which was worse," I spoke quietly into her ear, "getting ripped apart by all creation or being abducted by the government."

Phee pulled back just a bit and looked at me. "You seem..." she started to say.

"Fine? Healed?" I finished where she couldn't. "It must have been the MRI they put me in," I said. "It fixed whatever was wrong with the seed in my head."

Phee stared at me with great seriousness. "We need to tell Mom and Dad you're all right." She wiped her eyes with the back of her hand. "Dad's been in tears. Mom's bitten her lip, but I know it's been tearing her to shreds."

I frowned. "Look," I said firmly. "Sit down. We need to talk."

And so, she sat, never taking her eyes from mine.

"I need to go back," I said.

"Go back where?" she asked

"Not where," I said, "When."

"You mean before you went back in time?" Her eyes looked searchingly into mine for an answer.

"No," I said with a hint of remorse in my voice. "Back to the beginning. There are too many paradoxes that need to be undone. You meeting yourself, a defeated Quantum Woman who doesn't have to be. Whatever dangers lay ahead, I can't risk you anymore. Or Mom or Dad. I'll be fourteen again and so will you; but as far as you're concerned, I'll just be Peyton, nothing more."

"You mean, I won't remember?" Her face took on a pouting expression. "That's so unfair!" She broke off her words and then took hold of my hands. "Promise me you'll tell me," she insisted. "Promise."

I looked at her and shrugged. "When the time is right," I said "With all your memories restored. I can do that, you know. I *will* do that. For you."

CHAPTER XII

And so I went back, a year and a week to be precise. Oh, no one need wonder why there should not have been two of me. All that I needed to do was to merge into my former self, which gave her all of my memories as we became one.

I was fourteen again, but this time with full command of my powers and with the foresight of what could go wrong. This was my do-over, not based on some wish or magic dust but grounded in the fabric of quantum reality. I was back in time, back in my former self with the ability to fix what had gone wrong. As for Thara-Klo, my Thara, my daughter from time immemorial, I now knew in my heart that no matter what she tried to do to me I needed to protect her and heal her damaged soul. But for the moment, I had another dilemma at hand. Today was our birthday, Phee's and mine. I remember that after she had awakened me I had given her the Wonder Woman statute that she was all stoked up about, but now I had a chance to do so much more. The thought of *what* raced through my mind as I dressed to go downstairs to breakfast. How odd, I mused, to be back in a training bra, remembering how envious I had been of all of those other girls who had developed ahead of me.

At breakfast, Mom was again at the sink, washing the same dishes she had washed the last time around. Phee and I sat across from each other as before; as we always did. Phee, between gouging herself with sausages and eggs, was staring down at her cocoa, blowing waves onto its surface to cool it enough to drink. Our conversation, though, became far different from what it had been the first go-round. She seemed to sense my stare as it bore into her.

"What?" she asked.

"Supergirl or Wonder Woman?" I replied under my breath, knowing the answer.

"Wonder Woman," came the unhesitant response, with a *Why are you asking me that; you already know?* sort of look.

"Because?" I pressed on.

Phee's eyes poked over the cup she was holding with both hands.

"A," she replied, "her powers came from the gods. B, she can't ever get hurt. And C, totally awesome costume."

"Unlike Supergirl's?" I quietly shot back.

"Yeah, right," she breathed out, her sarcasm echoing volumes, as she stared back at her brew, "with a big red S on her chest in case anyone ever forgets who she is."

"It's not an S."

Her gaze went up again to pierce my own. "For forty years it was an S. Then it was some Kryptonian symbol for the House of El. Now it means hope. Jesus Christ, people, make up your minds!"

"Ophelia Jane Herron, I have warned you repeatedly about using the Lord's name in vain!" That was Mom, eavesdropping, listening in, or, perhaps just born with hearing that could rival that of Quantum Girl.

Phee's eyes moved sideways in the direction of the reprimand.

"Sorry, Mom," came the apologetic response.

"It is blasphemous! We are a Christian family and I do not condone such things! That goes for you, too, Peyton!"

"Praise Jesus," I replied, "for He is our Lord and Savior," though I meant Quantum Girl.

I could sense Mom smiling at my words, even with her back turned to me. I often wonder what became of the Phee I had left when I had traveled back to reset time. Did she cease to exist? Did time run backward for her? Or did she continue in an alternate timeline where I simply vanished from her world? I had no mentor. There was no one I could ask. Regardless, I now phased back through time from the kitchen table to before when Mom and Dad were even born.

It was October the 21st, 1941. America had yet to enter into World War II. Few homes had air conditioning. Television would not become truly popular for another ten years. The top hit *song* was *Piano Concerto 1 in B Flat Minor* by Tchaikovsky, which was a far,

far cry from *WAP* by Cardi B, seventy-nine years later. There were no shopping malls or supermarkets. Mothers pushed baby carriages up and down the sidewalks to visit their local clothier or butcher shop or grocer. Shielded from the atrocities being committed in Germany, these were simpler times for those who proudly called themselves Americans.

I had attired myself in the clothing of the day in a white blouse, a blue wool cardigan, a navy wool skirt that draped just below my knees, bobby socks, and blue and white saddle shoes. As for my hair, well, it was a bit too long and straight for the period, but it was now pulled back with a dark blue ribbon that matched my skirt. I had to assume that all was fine as one neatly dressed man in his mid-twenties, getting out of his red Packard, threw me a long wolf whistle as I casually walked by. I suppressed a smile as best I could. A little boy passed me on his tricycle, ringing the bell on the handlebars as he peddled frantically down the sidewalk. A woman in a brown tweed suit and felt wool hat, carrying a sack of groceries, walked past in the other direction. This was all a Norman Rockwell painting come to life. But how it would all end when, in just forty-six days, the Japanese would launch an attack on Pearl Harbor, shaking the nation to its core.

Across the street, though, was my destination. It was a small Rexall drug store—red brick with a large picture window and a long orange and blue sign above it all. I pushed the door to enter—no electric doors—not yet—just a silver bell to let the staff know that a potential customer had come in. The inside looked like an antique store. To the left was a long glass counter filled with the necessities of the day. The counter itself held up an old brass cash register, side by side with a display for Life Savers and Wrigley, Beech-Nut, and Black Jack chewing gum, while open boxes of cigars, emblazoned with pictures reminiscent of Cuba, surrounded by images of shiny gold coins, decorated the surface of the glass cabinet beneath. Cartons and packs of cigarettes lay stacked in abundance on the shelves on the wall behind—Camel, Phillip Morris, Lucky Strike, and Chesterfield. Meanwhile, to the right was a long counter, behind which stood an older male teen, who back then was called a soda jerk, though there was nothing considered derogatory about the term—not back then. A row of red upholstered barstools for the customers to sit on lined the bar's front, though they were unoccupied just then. Above it all hung a horizontal poster—a painting of some beautiful, smiling woman, wearing a beige aviator's cap and goggles, standing in front of a single prop-engine plane. In her hand was a soft drink bottle and there were words that read, "Coca-Cola, Delicious and Refreshing. Your thirst takes wings."

At the moment, the soda jerk was busily involved in polishing the jadeite green triple milkshake mixer (the pride of any drugstore back then), which stood prominently on the counter behind the bar and next to the sink. But none of this was my mission. My focus was drawn to a turning wire rack, which was filled with ten-cent comic books. A few young boys were at it, selecting this one or that. I picked out one, which none of them seemed to care about—All Star Comics, number 8. What ten-year-old boy wanted a comic book about a woman anyway? There were five of the same issue. I pulled them all out, selected the one in the best condition, and then, putting the others back, walked to where the cash register and the pharmacist both stood, handed the man the Liberty dime that Pops had given me when I was ten, and went on my way, hoping that no one would notice that it had been minted in 1942. For the next two or so months, it would be the most valuable coin in existence. After that, it would be worth only ten cents again. Once outside, I walked into an alley, made certain that no one was around, and vanished from that nostalgic time.

Having phased into my former self an hour and a half before I had left, I rose from bed and quietly went into our bedroom closet with the chilling memory of what I had done in there which for me had been more than fourteen billion years ago but was now refreshed in my mind. Regardless, I had purpose in being in there once more.

Searching around, I found the remainder of the gift wrap paper I had previously bought for the Wonder Woman statue that I could use instead to wrap the comic book. I didn't bother to change into my school clothes but rather went over to Phee's bed in an iteration of when she had gone over to mine. Phee was fast asleep. The alarm on her phone had yet to ring for her plan to get up before me and give me my gift. In my hands was her new present. The Gal Gadot statute could wait until Christmas.

"Wake up, wake up, wake up!" I called out to her, heralding in the new day, which had yet to break.

Phee rolled over, blinking hard to focus on me.

There was sleep still in her voice as she questioned, "What's going on?" she asked.

"Happy birthday, Dunkhead!" I exclaimed.

She sat up and rubbed her eyes.

"I was hoping to get up first to surprise you," she said, yawning.

"Well, I beat you to the punch," I replied. I paused and then went on, excitement in my voice, "Just open it!"

Phee switched on the lamp on her nightstand, read my card, uttered, "Aw!" then carefully unwrapped what I'd handed her, at last revealing the comic book I had purchased roughly eighty-four years ago.

"Oh my God!" There were tears in her eyes. "This is the first appearance of Wonder Woman. December 1941."

"October 21st, actually," I said it definitively, because, well, I was there. "That's when it hit the stands."

Phee examined it with gingered hands.

"It looks like it was printed yesterday." She stared up at me. "It can't be real."

"It is," I whispered out the words.

Phee's eyes grew large as cabbages. "It's worth millions," she whispered back. "Where? How?" she stammered out.

"I found it at a thrift store," I said, crossing my fingers behind my back. "The man only charged me a dime." That was the truth. "Well, the fact is I had to trade him the 1942 Liberty dime from my collection."

"You loved that dime," she bemoaned. "Peypey, this is too much. I mean, this could pay for your home someday."

"Or yours if something ever happened to me," I replied.

"Nothing's going to happen to you," she insisted, "not while *I'm* around."

"You never know," I shrugged. "I'm not Wonder Woman."

Phee stared hard at me. "If that Terrible Theresa ever bothers you again," she said, "I'll kick her ass."

"I've got things covered," I said with great confidence in my voice.

"Really," she replied. Phee looked at me as though she almost believed.

"I've got a pretty good idea as to how I can deal with her," I said, and indeed I had.

Incidentally, I did not forget about the three teenage girls in the car that had crashed the day I'd discovered my powers. This time, at the last moment, I phased each of them out of the car and onto a nearby lawn. The car still crashed into the tree, but they were all safe. Meanwhile, I caused the home screen on each of their phones to read, "Don't text and drive, morons!" and made it so that nothing they did to their phones could ever erase it—a small price for the alternative. My only regret was that the tree would never be the same.

CHAPTER XIII

How *does* one deal with a bully? There is no simple solution. Reason seldom works. Threats of retaliation are often laughed at or ignored. The bully tends to view its victim as helpless and it feeds on its victim's fear. Because of all of that, any resolution comes with great difficulty if there is any resolution at all—unless, of course, one has superpowers. So, there I was later that day about to head out to the showers when I heard Theresa call out to me… again!

"Hey, Herron! Heads up!" she yelled.

Only this time I knew what was coming. Without so much as turning my head, I reached up with my right hand over my shoulder and caught the ball that she had thrown so hard at me. Then I turned around to face her and bounced the ball several times, my eyes never leaving hers.

"Fuck me!" I could hear her say, even though her words were no louder than a whisper.'

I tossed the ball high up into the air but before it could descend I phased the two of us out of the gym.

Suddenly, Terrible Theresa found herself and me hovering over a live volcano, its fiery hot lava splashing, its sulfuric fumes filling her nostrils like the rotten egg she was. And there she was, screaming in terror.

"Don't drop me. Please don't drop me" she cried out with tears streaming down her face.

As for myself, I remained as calm as a sailboat in the doldrums. I looked at her and spread my arms. "I can't drop," I said, "what I'm not holding onto."

Theresa looked at me then looked down again at the fiery volcano and its molten rock beneath her feet. The realization that there was nothing holding onto her caused her to scream hysterically.

Then, suddenly, we were, floating in orbit above the earth, both of us in space suits. Still screaming her lungs out within her suit, fogging up her visor, I held up a large placard that caught her attention. On it was printed, "In space, no one can hear you scream."

Then on to Mars. No longer in a spacesuit on Martian soil, she clutched her throat.

"Kinda hard to breathe here," I lectured, as the fierce Aresian wind blew crimson sand at her back. "I guess that's why there are no more Martians."

But soon, there we were, back to earth, only seventy million years ago in the midst of a tropical jungle. The heat was sweltering. There were coniferous trees and giant ferns, the air filled with the voices of a thousand dinosaurs, both terrible and tame. And there she was with me in the midst of it all, her feet planted firmly on the ground, staring into the wide-open jaws of a T-Rex as it hungrily stared at *her*. She could hear the thunder of its roar. She could smell its reptilian breath. She could see its teeth glistening from the light that poked down through the canopy of trees. And again, Theresa Martinez, proud bully of a once helpless girl, screamed as tears fled down her cheeks and a trail of urine ran down her legs.

After that, we were back in the gym at that moment when the ball had dropped down to the floor and bounced back into my hands. Meanwhile, Theresa trembled. She stared at me, mortal fear in her eyes as her hand reached down to feel the liquid terror that had bled down the insides of her thighs, not to mention her gym shorts, which were soaked.

"So, anyway," I asked ever so casually, "you were saying?"

The girl, whom Phee and I had christened Theresa the Terrible now appeared more like Theresa the Timid. "I don't know who or what you are," she said with trembling words, "but I swear I will never say anything or do anything to you again. I swear to Jesus, the Holy Mother, and any Martians who might be listening."

Theresa Martinez never bullied me or anyone else again after that. There even came about a strange turn of events about a year afterward, but that's for later on.

CHAPTER XIV

In 1907, Albert Einstein, following the work of Antoine Lavoisier in 1785 and Julius Robert Mayer in 1842, came up with his equation, $E=mc^2$, which was eventually all merged into the Law of Conservation of Mass-Energy, meaning that while matter may be converted into energy and vice-versa, the whole of them can neither be created nor destroyed. The theory, however, failed to determine if such is limited to one frame of time or to the universe from beginning to end; nor does it consider previous or future universes, which are built successively from the matter and energies of one to the other. There is also the issue of parallel dimensions that share quantum existence. Add to that the fact that all of them—past, future, and parallel—are essentially confined to a comparatively minuscule pocket of quantum reality, allowing for an infinite number of other universes. Physical laws in each of them may be so different that an individual can pass from one to another without being affected by the laws of the other. In addition, to think that our universe is unique unto itself or that the time we are in is the only one there is, is Ptolemaic. Laregaaar, who was a student of Krotaaarak on Rendenaaar, described all of this in his treatise on the Quantum Fabric Theory that he had entitled, *Brukadaaan*, which loosely translates to "Coexistence." It was from his and Krotaaarak's works that Kostrikaaala-Ri, while experimenting with the seven quantum seeds, learned the potential consequences of their power when it caused her assistant to vanish before her eyes.[7]

All that aside, it must be noted that when Dhraaal gave me his quantum seed there was no mention of what it could or could not do. My attempt to go back to Rendenaaar had been met with disastrous

---

[7] From her journals, it was revealed that her assistant, Moograaas-Jen, did not merely vanish but was in fact uncreated, which had the effect of not only erasing her existence but that of her children as well. Kostrikaaala-Ri concluded afterward that her memory of Moograaas-Jen had been preserved because she herself had been in contact with one of the stones when the unfortunate incident occurred.

results. And I still had not figured out how to travel to other dimensions, let alone other universes that were separate and distinct from our own. I did not even know if I could. I needed help and as this was not the sort of thing a girl can go to her parents for advice, I decided to travel back in time just a bit. And so I split apart, determined to leave one of me behind as I had done before, just in case something went wrong… again.

It was November 29, 1904, 4:30 in the afternoon local time. I stood before a two-story brick building on *Stauffacherstrasse* in the downtown part of Bern, which is and was the capital of Switzerland. I was dressed appropriately for the time, wearing a long woolen coat, under which was a white cotton blouse and a woolen skirt that draped almost to the ground. A feathered winter hat nested upon my head, while a cashmere scarf wrapped around my neck, descending to my waist. The streets were filled with horse-drawn carriages and men and women—some returning home from work, others tending to the errands of their day-to-day lives. I entered through the wooden door that guarded the entrance, checked the office listings on the wall to my left, and then ascended the narrow flight of stairs that had grown somewhat dark, as day waned into night. There were newly installed electric lamps, which attended the hallways and stairs, fed by wires within the steel pipes to which they were attached, which in turn were bracketed onto the plaster walls near the ceiling. But, alas, they had not been turned on, as most in the building had already left their work and were either traveling to (or else were already comfortably back) home. My right hand gripped the wooden railing out of habit more than anything else. I could have just as easily phased myself to the upper landing but I didn't want to risk anyone remaining seeing me if I did. The light was somewhat better on the second floor. There were windows to the rear that looked toward the backs of other buildings on the adjacent street. But the cold, gray sky showed just enough light to reveal a clear path down the hall to the door that marked my destination. Words in gold, outlined in black on a partially frosted glass pane read, *"Bundesamt für geistiges Eigentum,"* which translated to "Federal Office for Intellectual Property." This was the patent office, where the man I wanted to question had worked. I could see from the sliver of light that bled through to the hall from beneath the door that someone was still inside. Had this not been the case I would have simply phased back an hour or so.

Cautiously, I turned the glass door knob, opening the door to reveal a man in his mid-twenties seated at a wooden desk. The man, who seemed (or pretended) not to notice me, had dark, wavy hair, a sizable mustache, and wore a brown plaid woolen jacket and vest over a white shirt with thin jacquard stripes. Meanwhile, around his neck was a maroon silk tie with a large Windsor knot that boasted a gold stickpin into which was set a reddish, gemstone, probably a garnet.

I cleared my throat to try and capture his attention, but there came not the slightest indication that my presence was known. *"Entschuldigen Sie. Ich heiße Peyton Herron. Ich suche Herrn Einstein,"* I announced, indicating that I was looking for Mr. Einstein, for historically this was said to have been his place of work as a patent clerk early in his career.

For the first time, the man looked up at me. *"Das bin ich. Wie kann ich Ihnen helfen?"* he replied, acknowledging that this was indeed him and wanting to know how he could help.

"Ich möchte mit Ihnen über die Quantentheorie und die Beziehung zwischen Zeit und Raum diskutieren," I told him with my best German accent. I wanted to discuss quantum theory with him as pertained to the relationship between time and space.

"Ach so," he answered with the hint of a smile. *"Ein Schulmädchen möchte die Natur des Universums diskutieren."* A school girl wishes to discuss the nature of the universe.

"Bitte schau nicht auf mich herab," I said politely, asking that he not look down on me. *"Mein Großvater ist Max Planck. Ich mag jung sein, aber er hat mir solche Dinge gut beigebracht. Ich bin das, was manche ein Wunderkind nennen würden."* My grandfather is Max

Planck, I told him. I may be young, but he taught me well about such things. I am what some would call a child prodigy.

The man looked puzzled. *"Aber wenn Sie Max Plancks Enkelin sind, warum sollten Sie dann mit mir über Physik sprechen? Wie Sie sehen, bin ich nur ein geringer Patentangestellter,"* he pondered out loud, wanting to know why, if I were the granddaughter of such a renowned physicist as Max Planck, would I want to talk physics with a lowly patent clerk.

"Aus irgendeinem Grund glaubt mein Großvater, dass Sie einer der großen Köpfe der theoretischen Physik sind," I told him, putting forth the lie that my supposed grandfather believed him to be one of the great minds in theoretical physics.

"Ich fühle mich geehrt, aber immer noch erstaunt," he replied as he disclaimed his worth. *"Bitte setzen sie sich. Und dann kannst du mich fragen, was du willst,"* he went on, inviting me to sit down and ask him whatever I liked.

And so, we talked, long into the night. We spoke of time and space, motion and gravity. He had yet to come up with his famous theories, and while I explained to him the mechanics of both general and special relativity, both of which he absorbed in an instant, his mind gave me insight into how I might use the quantum fabric to bridge parallel dimensions, though to be honest, *his* mind at the time was not capable of understanding the mechanics of that. Having briefly sojourned to a late cafe for coffee and hot cocoa respectively, we bid our farewells, him asking me to express his esteemed gratitude to Herr Planck for introducing him to his so beautiful and so intelligent granddaughter. I blushed out a thank you, stood up, and left, leaving him to ponder all that had transpired, his elbow on the table and his hand on his chin with a glazed-over stare that for the moment contemplated and one day would behold a pathway through eternity.

Far from tired, I went forward twenty-one years to Princeton University to a room where the now *Dr.* Einstein, forty-five years old, stood before a blackboard, carving out mathematical formulas with chalk. My clothes had changed, at least the illusion of them. Thus, I appeared to be dressed in a simple white blouse and a plain brown skirt that ended mid-calf.

"*Herr Einstein*," I said.

"Yes?" he replied, turning toward me. "May I help you?"

"It's Peyton," I told him.

He stared at me in amazement. "Peyton?" he said in English with a thick German accent on his tongue. "But how can this be? Oh, you must be joking. You are her daughter."

"*Nein, mein Freund,*" I insisted. "It's me. I've traveled through time. I'm from the year 2025."

"*Mein Gott!*" he exclaimed.

He leaned forward, his hands bearing his weight on the desktop, staring at me with glazed eyes.

"I once theorized that subatomic particles could travel through time," he said, "but never anything larger. To imagine that your people built a time machine..."

"No, Doctor," I replied. "No time machine. Just me. Quantum Girl." And right before his eyes, I changed into my alter ego. "I don't understand many things," I said. "How I can do what I do. How I can travel through time and space. How I can defy gravity or create matter from what seems to be nothing? I'm hoping you can help me find answers."

And so, we talked, again for hours on end. He admitted to me that from our meeting years ago had come the seeds of relativity. But then a question entered my head. I had learned about relativity from Einstein's works. But he had learned it from me, so where was its point of origin? It was one of those chicken and egg sort of things, only which was I and which was he? So, there I was, caught up in a paradoxical loop with Albert Einstein, who by my reckoning, had been dead for seventy years.[8]

---

[8] I later resolved that my knowledge of relativity had come, not from Einstein's published works, which, to be honest, I had not read, but from, instead, my knowledge on the subject that I had apparently learned on Rendenaaar as Khattaaara.

CHAPTER XV

From Princeton, 1925, I phased the hundred years it took to bring me back home. The truth is that I was exhausted after my excursion into the past. Phee was fast asleep, but as tired as my body was, my mind was charged with thought. Not wanting to make a sound, I phased into the guest bathroom, filled the tub with warm water, stripped off my clothes, and immersed myself in a lavender bubble bath.

Having gone through all that I did, I had become so different from everyone else that I felt as though I were an outcast from humanity. Although I was in the body of a fourteen-year-old, I had matured so much in my mind. Phee was as I remembered her. *Dear Phee.* She was worth more to me than the heart that beat in my chest but I had erased all of the memories that she had about the powers that I had. My life as Quantum Girl was something that I needed to figure out on my own before I brought her back in. Eventually, I fell asleep only to awaken at half-past noon covered in goosebumps from the now freezing water. Everyone must have gone mad wondering where I had gone off to. By now, I thought, they must have phoned the police or some missing children center. I quickly phased on my nightgown and phased myself back into my bed six hours into the past, just as both of the alarms on our phones went off to wake us up for school.

It was just before fifth period when I stood at my locker that Theresa Martinez approached me.

"Hey, Herron," she said. "How'd you do all that stuff to me?"

"What stuff?" I asked, innocently enough.

"You know," she said. "All that weird shit."

"No idea what you mean," I replied.

Books in hand, I shut my locker and turned away to walk down the hall.

"I won't tell anyone," she said beseechingly. "I just want to know."

She paused, waiting for a response, and then added, "Hey, I'll see you at lunch. We can sit together. I'm buying."

Hours later, as I was going through the cafeteria line, I found that Theresa had edged beside me.

"I'd stay away from the salad," she warned. "My cousin, Michelle—she got food poisoning from it last week. Seriously, she thought she was gonna die."

I took her advice and opted for a hotdog along with an apple and a Coke. She paid, which somewhat made up for the time she bumped into me and sent my tray of food crashing to the floor. I made my way to one of the deserted tables. Theresa sat down across from me and stared at me, even as she ate.

"Back to what happened," she continued, unrelenting. "I figure you must of hypnotized me or something like that." She broke off and then went all soft. "I just want to apologize for all the shit I put you through. The fact is I think you're probably the prettiest girl in the entire school. No cap. My therapist says I have anger issues and communication problems plus low self-esteem. I mean, I don't speak all proper like you or your sister, not that I'm not smart. I'm just not whachu might call airtight. I don't read a lot. I never found books all that interesting. Plus, I got bounced around from foster home to foster home after my uncle, well, he did a lotta shit to me when I was younger, and my mom, she never noticed and I blamed her for that. Anyway, he got sent to prison and my mom and me, we recently kinda straightened things out between us. Getting sent here, to Braxton, I mean, was more or less her way of apologizing. She took on a second job so we could afford it and I appreciate her for that. The thing is, seein' how you and your sister were perfect little white girls and all, it sorta made me feel like shit, which is basically the reason I did what I did."

As I sat there chewing without comment, she placed one hand on her chest.

"Whether you believe it or not, my apology comes from in here.

So, um, Herron, I mean Peyton, could you maybe find it in your heart to forgive me?"

"I can," I said, glancing up from my tray to look at her. *Why not?* I thought to myself. From my perspective, it had happened more than hundreds of millions of years ago.

"One more thing," she went on. "Do you think that maybe you could find the time to teach me to be more like you?"

I just stared at her, chewed, and then swallowed.

"We'll see," I replied.

That afternoon, as I was waiting to meet up with Phee to walk home with her, Theresa came up to me again.

"So, will you teach me?" she begged. "It's important to me. I don't have a lot of feelings of—what do you call it—self-worth. It makes me feel inferior."

"You're not," I insisted.

Her eyes brightened. "I look around at everyone else. Everything seems so easy for them. That's why I try and act so tough all the time."

"You just need to apply yourself more," I said. "Besides, you have an edge over most of the other girls here."

"How so?" she asked

"If you haven't already noticed," I said, "you're quite beautiful."

"You're not just saying that to be polite?" she said, begging for an answer.

"Ask any of the boys here," I replied.

"I don't want any of the boys here," she protested.

"Why not?" I asked.

"Because I only want *you*," came her reply.

It came in one quick act that I was in no way prepared for. Without warning, Theresa suddenly moved in toward me, threw her arms around my neck, and began to kiss me passionately on the lips, her tongue going into my partially open mouth. It seemed that the girl who had tortured me for so long was in fact really into me, so much so that my quantum senses heard her heart pounding like a hammer and could smell the scent of her sex as it wafted up and into my nose. But it was she who suddenly stopped as she felt no response from me. My arms did not embrace her. My lips did not pull at hers. And my tongue was flaccid in my mouth. She pulled back just a bit and stared into my eyes. Then hers seemed to try and hold back tears. Her whole body trembled. She looked embarrassed and rejected. Then she turned and ran off toward the street.

"Theresa, wait!" I shouted after her but it was to no avail. She continued to run and then disappeared around the corner. I hesitated as to whether or not to go after her. I thought perhaps to phase close to her but that would be opening a whole new can of worms. She had attributed her recent terror to a hallucination, but there would be no explaining my being able to materialize right next to her. When Phee showed up, just seconds later, I had already decided that I would keep what had happened to myself.

Three days had passed without my seeing neither hide nor hair of Theresa, which filled me with both relief and concern. I could have wished bad things on someone who was just plain mean, but not on someone who it turned out was in love with me.

It was one *week* later that Phee and I decided to take an Uber to go visit Grandma Margaret in the retirement home. She was ninety years old and was having trouble getting around and taking care of herself in general, especially with dementia starting to have set in. We sat with her in her room.

"Mom told us you were at Pearl Harbor on the morning of the attack," Phee said to her.

"I was six years old," Grandma Margaret replied. "The building we were in just exploded all around us. One of the timbers fell on Mama and killed her instantly. A couple of days later, I learned that my Papa had been lost at sea after the battleship he was on was sunk by the Japanese."

"I don't understand," Phee went on. "Mom said you were raised by her—Great Grandma, I mean."

"Oh, no," Grandma Margaret shook her head. "My mother was laid to rest at the National Memorial Cemetery. I was raised by my aunt. Her name was Sarah. I have a picture of her in my handbag." She indicated where the bag was with a motion of her head. I went over to where it sat on her dresser and got it then handed it to her. She opened it and then began to search inside.

"Ah, here it is," she said. "She was a beautiful woman. Died while I was off at Smith College. I miss her so much."

She handed me the photo, staring at me.

"She looked very much like you, Peyton," she said. "So very *much* like you."

"Funny," she went on. "I remember how hard it was for me when I was small to pronounce her name. Instead of Sarah, I would say Thara."

"Oh my God!" I said out loud, staring at the photo. "It can't *be*!"

"What's wrong?" Phee asked with sudden concern.

"Nothing," I replied. But it wasn't nothing. It was everything. The photograph was of Thara-Klo!

CHAPTER XVI

The universe is all around us. It is what we see and feel and hear and smell and taste. It stretches billions of times farther than the naked eye can take in. Yet humankind—all of us—are trapped on that infinitesimal speck we call the Earth. But there is more. There are universes, infinite in number, that lie outside our own—infinite realms in parallel dimensions—infinite possibilities of existence and life. *Am I alone in all of that?* I wondered. *Am I the only Quantum Girl?*

It may seem odd but the first time I tried interdimensional travel was in the nude. Well, actually, I didn't *travel* in the nude. That's just how I emerged and there was a reason. I wanted her to have no doubt as to who I was and who I was to her.

I appeared next to her in the girls' shower. She stared back at me as though frozen while the water from above continued to bead down on her face. Then her eyes glanced down as though to confirm I was her twin.

"Who *are* you?" she demanded. "What do you want?"

"I'm you from another—a parallel—dimension," I said, my demeanor most serious as I stared her in the eye. "You're in grave danger," I went on. "I need to take you somewhere where we can talk."

I phased us out of there and in an instant we were both in her bedroom. I went into the bathroom and grabbed a white robe from the same hook where I always leave mine. I had assumed there would be a second hanging next to it but there wasn't. That being the case, I put on the robe, took the one bath towel that was hanging on the opposite wall near the tub, and then returned to her. As I tossed her the towel, I noticed that there was only one bed in the room. *Curious*, I thought to myself. *Where does her Phee sleep?*

"Question," I said to her. "Why aren't you in hysterics right now? Personally, situations reversed, I'd be freaking out."

"Because I know I'm still asleep," she said, "and all of this is just a dream or a nightmare depending on how it all turns out. Besides, it's interesting, the thought of having a twin *sister*."

Having dried herself a bit, my interdimensional double dropped the towel and then went into the closet stark naked and unashamed to pick out some clothes. I must make mention of the fact that, as I found out later, she spells Peyton with an *a* rather than an *e*.

"What about Phee?" I asked.

"Who?"

"Your twin sister. Ophelia Jane Herron. In my dimension, she's my not-so-identical twin."

"Liam," she replied, as her fingers slid the clothes hangers along the rod. "He's *my* Phee, I guess, only he's a she—not unless he's been holding out on me." She glanced in my direction. "Mind grabbing me some panties and a bra?" she asked. "Top left dresser drawer, though…" and she paused.

"What?" I replied.

"I just don't know if things are where they *should* be in a dream." She said.

I opened the drawer, took out her underwear, walked over, and handed them to her. The ability to throw undergarments across the room and have them land where I've aimed was decidedly not my forte, even as Quantum Girl.

"This isn't a dream," I insisted.

"Uh, oh," she sighed.

"Uh, oh?" I repeated.

"Nightmare, then. Thanks," she said, as she looked at the unmentionables in her hands. "Gods, I hate them—training bras, I mean. They're all about becoming a woman, but a clear reminder that you're not yet there. A pox upon girls like Daisy McKenzie and their ample bosoms!"

"You have a Daisy, too?" I asked.

"Wraps all the girls around her little finger," she replied.

"Girls?" I repeated, astonished. "Not in *my* dimension."

She stared at me as she was putting on the bra.

"Don't tell me she's a sparrow," she said, wide-eyed, looking at me.

"Sparrow?" I asked.

"Straight as an arrow," she replied. "Sparrow. Heterosexual. *I'm* certainly not."

"That's not all you're not," I said.

"What do you mean?" she asked—this as the panties went on.

"Not asleep," I replied. "This isn't a nightmare. To be honest, I've never been to another dimension. I could never figure out how till I went back in time and met with Einstein."

"Ilse Einstein?" she said, taking a red dress off the rod, and holding it up against herself. "How's this?" She asked.

"Albert. You know, E=mc^2 and all. I prefer the blue one."

"You *do* come from a strange dream world," she said then continued to stare down at herself. "I don't know. The red one just seems to cry out, 'Girl, I'm yours for the taking.'" That was when I pinched her arm.

"Ow!" she cried out. "Why'd you do *that*?"

"To prove you're not asleep," I replied.

"Thanks so much," she said, rubbing her arm where it hurt.

"In my dimension, I'm not just Peyton. I'm also Quantum Girl."

"And that *is*?" she asked then began to put on the dress she had selected.

"This," I said, and I turned into my other self.

"Holy crap!" she exclaimed.

"Long story," I replied. "But I was given," I paused and then went on, "powers."

"Superpowers..." she said, "like being able to abduct girls in the nude. Cool!"

"I figured if you were naked in the girls' shower," I replied, "you wouldn't run."

"Oh, I'm hell on wheels on a wet floor," she said, "naked or not. Besides, I could have screamed. I'd wanted to. And I really, really wanted to."

"But you didn't," I said.

"As I said," she replied, "I thought it was all a bad wet dream if there is such a thing."

"Anyway…" I said and took a deep breath, "I've had to do battle with this woman from a previous universe and I wanted to make sure that her version here didn't do you in."

"I appreciate that," she replied, "but I don't know if she exists in this universe. Apparently, not everything is the same." She turned her back to me. "Help me with the zipper, would you please, Miss Quantum Girl." And I did.

"So, what powers do you have if I may be so bold as to ask?" she said, turning back to face me.

"Well," I replied, "I can instantly travel through space."

"I think you already proved *that*," she said.

"Right," I replied. "And time, and, obviously, parallel dimensions."

"Which *I* never knew existed," she interjected.

Undaunted, I went on. "I can project force fields and do X-ray projection," the latter of which I demonstrated on her hand, revealing all of its bones, as she flexed it in amazement. "And I can create as many duplicates of myself as I want," and all at once, there were three more of me in the room.

"Shit, shit, shit!" she stammered out, as I pulled them all back into me. "That is so sick. It puts a whole new spin on masturbation."

"That's disgusting," I said back.

"Well, they're *all you!*" she insisted. "Oh, my Gods! Where did I go wrong that I missed out on all this? Fuck! Don't you have any girl-girl desires?"

"I admit to it once," I confessed.

"What happened?" came the all too excited response.

"I kissed a girl when I was twelve." I said, "Gina Motagliano."

"No way!" she exclaimed. "Gina Vagina?"

"I got shamed for it," I said. "I wanted to crawl in a hole."

"*With* her?" she replied. "Me, too, girl. In it and on top of her or her on top of me. We did math homework together. Our favorite number was sixty-eight plus one!"

Her remark, none too subtle, I gave her a disapproving look. "Then just the other day," I said, "Theresa really laid one on me."

"Martinez? She's a diehard sparrow on *this* plane of existence. Pretty hot, though." She sighed. "Too bad not a thriver here."

"I hate to ask," I said.

"Muff diver," she replied, "Thriver." She looked at me like I should have guessed.

"*Uh*, huh," I shrugged.

She stood there for a moment then looked me in the eye. "So, tell me, Quantum Girl," she said, "why did you pick *this* dimension?"

"As I said," I replied, "interdimensional travel is all new to me."

"So. I'm your first," she said.

"Sort of," I stammered out. A short laugh burst from my lips. "You *are* actually. Definitely," I assured her. "I was an interdimensional virgin until I met you."

"Cool," she replied.

After that, going back into the bedroom I phased back into myself and we talked for hours on end. At first, I thought that her previously exclaiming, "Oh, my Gods!" as in the plural meant that somehow the ancient Roman religion had persisted, but it was just her reference to the Trinity. Still, I wondered how it was that things were just slightly off; how most of their history was the same as my own but then diverged ever so slightly Then I realized it must have been something Thara-Klo had done in my universe that had somehow affected it. Perhaps this was the way my world would have been had she not come to my Earth. How odd that I might have been a lesbian had she not interfered with our timeline, and Phee might never have been born. At least some small bits of light appear in the darkness. This universe had fortunately avoided her—Thara-Klo—and this Payton as well. That being the case, I knew that I needed to go back and fight my battle. Daughter or not, I had to stop her.

But before I left, I gave my doppelganger a "silent" whistle on a chain and placed it around her neck. "I don't know how safe you are or if there is a Thara-Klo you need to fear," I told her, "but I will hear this if you call me with it and I will come. Keep it with you always. I'm serious."

"Yes, Ma'am," she said. "But will you still come if I'm safe?"

I smiled and nodded then vanished from her sight.

Occasionally, I made other trips to other dimensions. Most of the other Peytons were safe, but in one, in that same shower, there was a Thara-Klo, who shot her through the heart just as I came. I froze time but could do nothing to save her, not being able to travel back through *her* time. There she was with a hole in her chest, the bullet hanging midair, with *that* Thara-Klo frozen as well, a wicked smile painted on her face. Oh, Daughter, I thought, what must I have done to have provoked such hate? After that, I never ventured out to a random dimension again. The image of what had happened had ingrained itself too harshly in my mind. My sleep was filled with nightmares that repeated that dreadful scene and I would awaken in a cold sweat, mindful of the fact that Quantum Girl was not a god, that death was inevitable, and that sometimes death came sooner than we wished it to come. I did make trips occasionally to the Payton I'd just left despite her repeated insistence that she and I have sex together, which I adamantly refused, except for one time when I was about to concede. Her excuse was wanting to see me naked again, "for comparison," though I knew it was more, and willingly undressed in front of her, while she did the same. Then, unexpectedly, her brother opened the door to come in. Embarrassed and filled with moral guilt, before he had time to see me, I phased back to my dimension, only to appear totally starkers in front of Phee, who thankfully didn't bother asking any questions. It was apparently one of those "whatever" moments for her.

CHAPTER XVII

It was a year later. It was night and both Phee and I were in our beds in an already dark room. Phee was sitting up reading a paperback copy of *Paradise Lost* for a school assignment with the aid of a small LED lamp that bent around her neck. As for myself, I was on my back, propped up by a couple of pillows, blowing bubbles from a plastic loop without any liquid.

"You *do* know that's just for little children?" Phee said to me without taking her eyes from the page she was focused on.

"Says who?" came my apathetic response.

I blew a bubble that looked just like Phee. The bubble scowled at me. Then I touched it and it burst.

"Mr. Bubble," she said without emotion.

"Well, Mr. Bubble can take his rules and go fuck himself," I said back.

She turned her head to stare at me.

"Seriously?" she replied.

Then she ripped off the light and rolled over onto her side to face me, propping herself up on her elbow.

"You've been acting all day like the world is coming to an end," she said.

"It is," I said. There was bitterness in my voice. "Eventually. All matter will collapse to critical mass and then boom. It all begins again."

"Who fed *you* the red pill?" she replied.

I blew another bubble that I caused to look like Rendenaaar, then Rendenaaar on fire, then *pop.*

"Apparently, I was not a good person in my former life," I said. Those were hard words to speak. "Funny, I never believed in karma, but there it is now, staring me in the face. I just feel so alone."

"Well, *that's* about to change." It was my voice, but it wasn't coming from me. I looked toward the source, past the foot of my bed, and there stood Quantum Girl, only not exactly as she was supposed to be and slightly older, perhaps twenty or twenty-one. Her costume was silver. The top was close-fitting, and long-sleeved but ended just beneath her breasts, which were somewhat larger than mine leaving her midriff bare. Rather than a skirt, she wore bikini briefs. Rather than shoes, there were boots that ascended to mid-thigh. The cowl was different as well. It didn't fit over her head as did mine but wrapped around it more like a mask leaving the top of her head exposed. On her chest was the quantum symbol, a single particle surrounded by three oval orbits with much smaller particles that encircled it at dizzying speeds. It was hypnotic and I had to break off my attention from it to look back at her face—same nose, same eyes, same mouth and chin, but with a touch more age than the image of myself back then. Oh, and as for the cape; it flowed down to the floor.

"Who *are* you?" I demanded to know. "You're not some version of me or we'd share our thoughts." A little harsh perhaps, but I was apprehensive. After all, Thara-Klo was a shape-shifter. For all I knew this could have been her. But then again, I considered the fact that I was not presently under attack.

"I'm the Peyton you saw killed; the one that Thara-Klo blasted a hole in; the one you couldn't save. Dhraaal did though—*my* Dhraaal." Everything about her tone was deadly serious. "For me, that happened more than sixty years ago." She glanced over at Phee, who was motionless. "Don't worry about your sister. I've frozen time for her."

"How…" I started to ask, but the question just hung in my throat.

"I merged into my younger self," she replied guessing what I was about to ask. "Just as you did, though forty-some years back, not one."

"What happened to Thara?" I asked. "Why couldn't *your* Dhraaal have just destroyed her?"

"Because he loved *me* more than he hated *her*. In order to *save* me he had to give me his god-stone." Her voice paused. "She killed him. I went back thousands of times to try and save him but the outcome was always the same."

116

"How many others like us are there?" I asked. The question had been hanging on my lips ever since I found out there were other dimensions but there had been no one for me to ask.

"There are an infinite number of Peyton Herrons," she explained, "Some became Quantum Girls—others did not. But of all the dimensions, you and I were the only surviving ones; at least in the time I'm from. In every other universe where there was a Thara-Klo, she prevailed. The more than one hundred billion other Quantum Girls were killed or, more precisely, are destined to be killed by her and that includes your lesbian interdimensional self."

"But she's not…"I started to say.

"Not yet," the older version of me said, "but there *will* come a time."

She paused and then went on. "It took me more than forty years to find you."

"What about *your* world?" I asked. "Why come *here*?"

"Because there's nothing left of mine. After the last battle, I lost consciousness for years. When I woke up everything was gone—destroyed. The Earth was a burnt-out cinder—my mother, my father, my daughter, my family. The charred remains of all that I loved were all that was left. She destroyed the entire planet trying to destroy *me*. Daughter or not, I hated her after that. There was no forgiveness to be had—at least not from me."

"I'm so sorry," I said. I stared at Phee and thought, *How I would feel if something happened to her?*

"I'm here to help," the other me went on. "You can't take her on alone—your Thara—but together," and she paused to take a deep breath, "perhaps."

My apprehensions got the better of me. "How can I be sure she isn't you?" I said.

"Because you know she can't do this," came the reply, and in an instant the room was filled with Quantum Girls. They all spoke as one. "We need to merge," they said in chorus but with a single mind.

"Become one Quantum Girl. Are you willing to *do* that?"

"Why can't we fight her as a team?" I asked, questioning her plan. "Why do we have to combine?"

The roomful of Quantum Girls now began to reintegrate with the first.

"Could you defeat her when there were many of you?" they said, as the process of realignment went on. "We need to combine the power of two quantum seeds." She stared at me with eyes that were a reflection of my own but with the accumulated wisdom of sixty-some years.

"What about our minds? I asked. Will I still be me?" Hell, I'd watched the Invasion of the Body Snatchers. I did not want to become a pod person.

"We're not that different, you and I," said the (now one) other me in the room. "There'll just be more memories."

"I suppose then I don't have much choice," I replied. I stared at Phee, still frozen in time. "I need to protect her," I went on, as I looked back at the other Quantum Girl. "What do I need to do?"

Quantum reality is separate and distinct from the laws that govern time and space in our and similar universes. I make the distinction that not all universes are alike in terms of how they work. Ours and those dimensions where I have encountered my counterparts and even those where I have not all subscribe to a physical reality where there are molecules and atoms and subatomic particles, and where *movement* through spacetime is linear and limited by a transmission rate of roughly 186,000 miles per second. Other universes and their accompanying dimensions may be globular (made up of cohesive energy), temporal, or an infinite number of other, often unimaginable forms, at least to our ability to understand. Underpinning all of these, however, is the science of quantum apportionment. Without delving into the voluminous works of Krotaaarak let me just say that the machinations of the quantum substrate are able to rewrite whatever laws there are in any and all universes. This is how I can split into an infinite number of quantum selves without being bound to this universe's law that neither matter nor energy, viewed as a cohesive dependency, can be created or destroyed. That being said, despite that our combined weight would have been on the order of 225 lb. when she and I merged, our integrated mass became reduced by half, which, despite her having owned an additional four and a half pounds and somewhat more robust-sized breasts, slightly fuller hips, and legs with somewhat respectable curves as well as being somewhat older, we managed to combine into my fifteen-year-old proportions. As for my mind, I still felt the same, though there were more memories as she said there would be, and I think that emotionally I had matured. One might have thought that having existed in primordial space for more than 300 million years would have endowed me with the wisdom of the ages, but that would be like believing that a newborn would emerge into the breathing world with percipience from the nine months it had spent in the womb. While it was true that afterward I had visited other worlds in this and other galaxies, searching for my home planet, it was never the same as the interaction on Earth that made me grow as a human.

Other-dimensional-me was right, though. I was still myself but I was also her. We were mostly the same person to start with, with only slight variations. Other me was never bullied, nor had she ever tried to end her own life, but then I was never murdered by Thara-Klo in an act of what must ultimately be called matricide. The fact is that there are now two versions of me packed into my head along with two quantum seeds or god-stones as she called them. But other me had lived well into her eighties, had married a truly kind man named Mark when she was twenty-two, but kept her quantum identity a secret from him through the day he grew old and died, and nothing she could do, despite all of her powers, could breathe life back into him. But from that union, when she was nearly thirty-five, came a precious little girl she named Giovanna, Vanna for short; Vanna with the *a* spoken out like the *o* in blonde, like the color of her hair. And then came

Ragnarök, the twilight of the gods, which brought forth Fimbulvetr, the end of days, the devastation, which tore all life from the earth, including that of her other daughter, that other Thara-Klo—a death that came about through a freakish accident by her own hand but which, in all the other dimensions, had never happened. Apparently, turning into a dragon with two heads that might accidentally breathe out cold fire at each other was not a good idea.

It is strange to think as a fifteen-year-old, just how glorious marriage to one's soulmate could be—to feel the pains of childbirth, filled with screams that could shake Methuselah from his grave but then to see those little eyes as they gazed upon the universe for the very first time, to hear the infant that grew in your belly cry, as she is thrown out from the comfort of her embryonic sac to then inhale the vacant air. How then comes love so quick and unconditional until just past her fifteenth birthday when she had grown to my age now and was swept from the province of existence, never to laugh or cry or breathe again?

Beautiful Vanna, the love of her life, the soft pale hair, the deep blue eyes, the smile that would make her heart melt, and those tears when they came that would make her cry, murdered with so many others by the wrath of her half-sister from so many universes ago. All of those memories were now etched into my brain as though I had lived them myself. And yet it was as though I had for she is now me and I am now her. I have lived two separate lives, which have come together as one single soul. She became my wisdom and I her strength and now we are one and the same. I had no regrets. Sadly, in retrospect, I should have. Anyway, after the merging and an hour or so of reflection and taking it all in, I restarted time and eventually went to sleep.

When I finally woke up, Phee was already downstairs, at breakfast. I had dreamt throughout the night but they're a curious departure, dreams. They seem so real while they're going on but once we awaken, they melt like snowflakes on a warm windowpane. I remember, though, being on Rendenaaar. And I remember some awful destruction but all of this came to me just in small bits, an aftertaste if you will from the projections of my previous self. Sadly though, the one thing that still stood fresh were the images of that dying little girl whom we held in our arms, who with her final breath said, "Mother, Mother, why?"

When I finally made it down, Phee and Dad were at the table, waiting for their meal, while Mom, unwavering as ever, stood soldiering what must have been the exordium of breakfast at the stove.

"Well, look who the cat dragged in," Phee purred softly at me. "I thought you were dead to the world."

"I didn't get much sleep," I announced. "I was restless most of the night."

Mom turned her head toward me as Dad read his Wall Street Journal and Phee diligently chewed on a strip of bacon.

I walked over to my usual place opposite Phee. I think Dad was too engrossed in the climate of some hedge fund he had recently invested in to notice. Such was not ever the case with the peripherally-visioned Katherine Herron.

"You just sit down and eat your breakfast," she said.

And so I sat, laying down the textbook I had brought with me, bookmarked to a chapter on Special Relativity.

It was then that she, my own mother, walked over and set down a plate in front of me, disgustingly garnished with fried eggs and sausages.

"Oh my God," I exclaimed. "What part of I'm a vegan don't you understand?"

"And just *when* did *that* occur?" Mom retorted back.

"I distinctly remember telling you just before my…" I broke off, as I glanced at Phee, and then continued, "our twentieth birthday when you asked me what I wanted on the menu for the party you had planned."

"I don't know about *you* Peypey," Phee shot back, "but *I'm* only fifteen."

"What I meant was..." I began to say, suddenly realizing it was the other dimensional me that had proclaimed that four years from now.

"Maybe she was calculating her age in dog years," came Phee's smarmy reply.

I just pushed away the plate.

"Anyway," I shrugged. "I'm not really hungry." I turned to Mom with half a frown. "May I be excused? I need to get to school early. I have a physics test and I need to memorize what the teacher thinks are the right answers."

"I'll pack some lunch," came the reply. Mom knew my moods and knew, too, that it would do no good to insist that I stay.

"Make sure there are no bum nuggets," Phee railed in.

"Sprout salad with avocado. No eggs. Box of orange juice and Oreos," Mom chimed in with a smile. Dad looked up from his paper for the first time—he who had apparently been paying attention all along.

"It's a sad world where Oreos take the place of sandwiches," he said. He looked for my reaction to his words. "I see the hint of a smile," he said cheerfully. "I knew there had to be a spark of brightness under all that doom and gloom."

I tried to hide whatever smile might have shown.

"You're interfering with her moroseness," Phee proclaimed.

"I'm not morose," I replied defensively. "I'm just trying to focus."

"Come on, Peypey," Phee insisted. "At least eat your sausages. Some poor ungulate died so you could live."

"Shut up," I said matter-of-factly. Then I rose and left the room.

CHAPTER XVIII

Seated in class later that day, biting down on the end of the pencil in my hand with the test laid flatly on my desk, I immersed myself in thought pondering all that had gone on. It is one thing to be told that you're the reincarnation of a woman dead for trillions upon trillions of years. It is quite another when you learn that the woman you were was the epitome of evil.

Imagine that it's 1959. You're a 70-year-old painter living a quiet life by yourself. Then one day out of the blue you learn that before you awoke in that hospital in Berlin, a hopeless amnesiac, it turns out that you were Adolf Hitler. How would you feel, you who had met and fallen in love with and married Hanna Grossmaier, a beautiful Jewish woman who loves you to this day? In fact, you loved her so much that ten years ago you converted to Judaism just for her. Now, you look at yourself in the mirror imagining the shaved-off mustache once more on your upper lip, and wondering who you really are. That's how I felt when I looked at myself in the mirror and saw the reflection of Khattaaara staring back.

Add to that the fact that my presumably immortal soul was now admixed with that of someone else—someone who while in many ways was identical to me but in others quite different, separate and distinct, but separate no more because now she was a part of me and I a part of her and there was no going back. Perhaps this is what it really means to be Quantum Girl—shared thoughts, shared heart, and with them both a shared responsibility to save eternity from the Gorgon who once sprang from your womb. Or are *you* the Gorgon and *she* Perseus? Who decides?

As I turned my attention back to the test paper, I noticed two men in suits talking to Mr. Chatterjee who had risen to greet them. Uncomfortably then, both of them began staring at me, following the direction of the outstretched arm of my ever-complacent instructor. Others in the room also took notice and in no short time, I became the focal point of nearly everyone with vision and breath in their lungs.

"Miss Herron, would you please stand up?" issued the command from the man who truly believed that the world spun on its axis just for him. I slowly rose from my seat as the agents approached.

"What's this all about?" I said to them.

"We're with the FBI. We need you to come with us." Which one of them said that I don't recall. I just remember being unnerved. I wondered whether my identity as Quantum Girl had somehow been discovered. *What was going on?* was the one thought that rang through my head like a church bell as one of the agents handcuffed my wrists behind my back.

"What am I being accused of?" I asked but my question went unanswered. I tried to phase out through time but I couldn't. Regardless that I now had two quantum seeds in my head my powers were simply gone.

"Everyone calm yourselves," Chatterjee said in a commanding voice. "I'm sure there is a simple explanation that will all be revealed in time."

I could hear the other students murmuring amongst themselves. as I was led from the room.

I was walked in silence down the hall out the front entrance to the school and into the back seat of a dark car with one of the agents. Without my powers, I was just like anyone else. The metal from the handcuffs pressed hard against my wrists. I could see the other agent who was driving, talking on his cellphone, but my hearing was no longer heightened by the quantum seeds and so I could only make out a word or two here and there, which was better than not being able to hear anything at all. The trip brought us to the airport where I was boarded onto a private jet at which point one of the cuffs was briefly unlocked so my wrists could be handcuffed in front of me. Once we were in the air I turned to the agent who sat beside me.

"I need to pee," I said and I really did have to.

The agent frowned to himself, unlocked the cuff that was attached to his wrist, got up, and moved into the aisle to allow me to pass. I walked to the stall, closed the door behind me, did what I had come there to do then still sitting there began to cry. It didn't matter to me how long I had lived or how many souls were combined with mine, I just felt so helpless at that moment—alone and scared. Regardless of all the wisdom or genius that I had had inculcated into my head, physically I was now just a fifteen-year-old girl with all the emotions that rage through a fifteen-year-old's brain. For whatever reason, all the powers had been bled out of me. Meanwhile, as I sat there, my flesh trembled at the thought of what would happen next.

In the midst of my tears, there was a knock on the hollow door. "You need to come out," the voice of the agent ordered.

"I need to call my Dad," I called out from within. I stood up, pulled up my panties, brushed down my skirt, and briefly closed my eyes. I brought my right hand up as I opened them, wiping away just some of my tears. Then I turned and opened the door. The agent stood just outside of it, blocking my path as he snapped the handcuff back onto his wrist.

"My family will be worried sick," I said, my voice trembling. "I need to let them know what's going on."

"They've been taken into custody as well," he said with noticeable dispassion in his tone.

"Why are you *doing* this?" I said tearfully. I wanted to be strong. I wanted to be arrogant. I wanted to be what I was when I was Quantum Girl, but I wasn't—not anymore—and so I just wept out the words.

The rest of the flight was met with silence. The plane landed on an airstrip in a city called Constance. I knew that because there were signs all around. Constance, Arizona, a dusty outgrowth of better, more peaceful times—population just over twenty-eight thousand. Here were people who lived ordinary lives—farmers and store owners and women who worked at the diner or the restaurant or the drive-in or at home. Imagine, people who lived their lives, day in and day out, without depending on the Internet or social media to dictate the course of their lives—people who didn't need the newest mode of everything but were content to drive their rusted cars—people who worried about their children and made love to each other as husbands and wives without having to worry about the political or environmental consequences to the world. This appeared to be such a community but the fact that we had landed here made me wonder whether there were ghosts beneath the soil. If the government had learned that I was different, I wondered, in what ways would they try to dissect me? Here I was in the shadow of a town I knew nothing about, captured by men who hid their affiliations at least to me. My rights were seemingly nonexistent. But they appeared to work for the government, and if the government owns any welcome mats, rest assured there are trap doors beneath them. And so, I sat there by a man who was part of it all, a prisoner on a world that had spun out of control without shame.

We stopped at a diner for something to eat. We sat at a booth with me near the window. I wore both handcuffs again; once more in front of me so that I could eat. I ordered a hamburger. I just didn't care. This wasn't the place for vegan meals. The old me may have battled my other self over that but I hadn't had lunch and I was hungry and too scared to worry about the slaughter of innocent cows. But what of Mom and Dad and Phee? What each of them must have been going through—they who knew nothing of Quantum Girl. That was foremost in my mind beyond all personal fear. As I sipped my Coke through a plastic straw I suddenly began to choke and then threw up on the agent who sat there next to me. The agent did not look pleased.

Outside on the sidewalk, some little boys about eight years old were playing robbers and cops. One feigned shooting the other and the make-believe victim pretended to fall down dead. A moment later, the supposed corpse was back on his feet, gun back in hand. How innocent is our childhood, our greatest upsets being cuts and scrapes and the toys we cannot have? And then we grow up and, as with a dream upon awakening, our childhood disappears.

"Let's go," said the other agent as a napkin wiped his lips, as my jailer in turn with a scowl on his face wiped the vomit from his suit with the damp cloth the waitress had brought him. When he had accomplished as best he could in ridding himself of the half-digested meal he cuffed himself to me once again and just like that we were out the door and back in the car—black and foreboding with government-issued plates.

The ride took less than ten minutes with the end result that the vehicle was parked in an open lot that gave berth to an older building, perhaps from the sixties, that stood nine or ten stories tall, looking like a relic from days gone by, concrete and glass, function before form, breathing out the same sort of cold indifference that seemed to emanate from my two captors. We entered through the front to a security desk, behind which sat a middle-aged man who offered an air of indifference as the agent who held me acknowledged his authority with a casual nod. The wall behind him was polished brown granite, on which was mounted a large dark bronze seal comprised of a shield with vertical stripes that were positioned beneath a balance scale and surrounded by a laurel wreath and thirteen stars. "Fidelity, Bravery, Integrity," boasted the words on the scroll beneath. This was all encircled by raised letters, which read, "Department of Justice, Federal Bureau of Investigation." *So, this is justice!* I thought to myself, as I was led into a somewhat claustrophobic elevator that took us to the seventh floor. What puzzled me most though was why was this here? What was an FBI building doing in some dry gulch town in the middle of nowhere? If Constance, Arizona was on any maps it certainly wasn't on any that I had ever seen. It was all too out of place, but then so was I in this world.

My final destination, it turned out, was a small room in which, dead center, stood a square table with two chairs facing each other. I was sat down in one and handcuffed to a thick steel loop, which projected from the tabletop near where I now sat.

"I want a lawyer," I insisted, and then I demanded it a second time much louder as the agent left the room.

A large mirror stood embedded in the wall where he had disappeared. I assumed they were watching me. I pictured them talking to each other, perhaps wondering whether or not I might turn into the threat they apparently perceived me to be. I jerked on the handcuffs but succeeded only in bruising my wrists. The Quantum Girl in me was gone, perhaps forever, and I didn't know why, yet here they were, the FBI, the most powerful law enforcement agency in the world, presumably in fear of a fifteen-year-old girl.

My thoughts harkened back to my family. What were they being put through as I sat there? I wondered. Dad was strong emotionally but he had a mild form of epilepsy that could be triggered by too much stress. Mom stood fast to her Godly belief. But what about Phee? She was my strength and my protector, but each of us has our breaking points. My thoughts were interrupted, however, as the door reopened and Quantum Girl walked into the room.

At first, I thought it might have been a quantum me or a self from another dimension having come to my rescue, but my rise to hope quickly vanished as the figure morphed into Thara-Klo. I hadn't ever had a chance to really look at her before—not in normal light and not up close. Now, though, having seen myself older I could see the strong resemblance. She looked more like me than my sister.

"Mother," she calmly said, her amber eyes boring into mine. "Long time, no sea. That *is* where you crash-landed, isn't it? The Caribbean? That must've hurt like hell."

Did that mean that the agent I had been handcuffed to all that time was her? How smug she must have felt to have sat right next to me without me ever suspecting. But what did she want? Why not kill me when she had the chance? Why not simply destroy the whole school with me in it? That seemed to be her style. I pulled hard on my handcuffs in anger.

"I'll bet you're wondering what happened to your powers," she said, and there was mocking in her voice. "I embedded an anti-quantum particle in the handcuffs. It nullifies the power of the god-stone when it's within a meter or so. Once removed, the stone needs to… How would these primitives describe it? Reboot I believe would be the operative word."

My eyes fixed hard on hers. "Aren't you just a bit concerned that whoever's out there's going to be listening in?"

"Not in the least," came the smug reply.

"I assume you told them that I'm Quantum Girl."

"So, that's what you're calling yourself." She broke off but then continued. "What I *did* tell them," she said, "was that you're part of an invasion force from another galaxy. Normally, that would sound insane but I have videos of you. You should really be more careful, *Quantum Girl*," and she emphasized the name.

"What is *wrong* with you?" I said in a tone meant to admonish this unremembered daughter of mine.

"That certainly is the pot asking the kettle," she purred back. Then she tossed me the key to unlock myself.

"Just to let you know," she went on with indifference, "the agent who brought you in with me is lying dead in the other room."

"And?" I asked.

"The video will show you turning into Quantum Girl and then burning him alive."

Unlocking the handcuffs, I questioned her actions. "My powers are gone. Why don't you just kill me?"

She spewed out hatred. Her eyes turned wild like a hungry tiger about to pounce on its prey. "I could have killed you in the classroom in front of all of your friends," she growled. "I want you to suffer. I want you to feel for just one moment the hurt that *you* caused *me*." She hesitated for a moment as her calm returned and then she moved off to one side.

"Feel free to leave," she said. "Go ahead. There's nothing in your way." Then she flicked her head toward the door.

I rose from my chair and then went to leave, my eyes ever on her as I did. My hand took hold of the doorknob with the caution of a man on a tightrope in the wind. The knob turned in my hand. The door broke inward and with guarded steps, I walked into the observation room.

There was a stench there that smelled like rancid pork. But what I saw before me caused my gorge to rise as Hamlet said. There on the floor lay what was left of the agent who had brought me here with Thara-Klo, looking as though he had been roasted on a spit. My gut began to heave uncontrollably wanting to throw up, but since there was nothing left in my stomach, I merely gagged again and again.

"They'll know you killed him!" Thara-Klo called to me from the other room. "They'll consider you a threat! There's nowhere you can go! There's nowhere you can hide! You'll be on your own, Quantum Girl, just as I have been—just as you left me so long ago on our world!"

At last, I caught my breath, then wiped the saliva away from my mouth with the back of my hand. I looked for the exit and left the room. As I did, I could still hear Thara-Klo.

"Run, Quantum Girl, run!" she called after me and then yelled one more word at the top of her lungs, reverberating and deafening, echoing through the halls, like a harpy gone insane, "Run!" So loud was it I had to pause, my back to the wall, my hands to my ears, till the deafening madness faded like thunder's past. Then, all at once, an alarm came on, pulsing and unrelenting. There was no question in my mind as to who had set it off. This was all just part of her plan. Two guards rushed past through the adjacent hall. Cautiously then, I made my escape from the building.

Removed from the effects of the particle, my powers starting to return, I became Quantum Girl, though the Quantum Girl of the other dimension. But neither of the seeds in me had yet totally regained their ability to fully link to the quantum substrate and so my costume flickered in the sunlit air. Mustering every bit of strength within me I pressed my eyelids tight and tried to phase back to yesterday but found myself only a moment before. I saw myself exit the building, and change into Quantum Girl. Apparently, I had not recovered enough to travel farther back in time, which meant that I had to escape some other way.

I tried to phase back home but found I could only get ten, and then twenty, and then fifty feet in the air. And then came another sound—a military helicopter in the distance was approaching fast. Again and again, I tried to phase myself back home or at least somewhere else but no matter how hard I tried I only managed each time to place myself a little bit higher in the air. The helicopter grew closer every second that passed. I could see a soldier with a rifle at the starboard door. And then it happened. A bullet entered the right side of my chest and exited my back, billowing my cape. I lost all control and began to plummet to the ground. Instinctively, I grabbed hold of the silver flapping cloth as though it were a parachute. Then just as I was about to hit the ground, I managed to vanish from the scene, to phase from this dimension to that other one—the one in which Payton lived—the one where I subsequently died.

CHAPTER XIX

By all reasonable explanations, the story should have ended here and now because of the events that transpired after Peyton had been fatally shot. To set matters straight as it were, my name is Payton—Payton Alise Herron—and my Quantum Girl story adventure began when I was fifteen years old. I am the mirror image of her whom you have come to know in the previous chapters—Peyton *Elise* Herron. When I say the mirror image I mean precisely that. She and I are from parallel worlds that coexist in the same space and time but have different quantum signatures. For whatever reason, our universes are the reverse of each other, meaning left and right are right and left. My heart and liver are on my right side, whereas hers were on her left, though to be perfectly honest, most people have absolutely no idea which side their liver is on; nor did I until I looked it up in the encyclopedia. I must add that on my world there is no World Wide Web, no Internet or social media, and no cell phones, all for the simple reason that solid-state technology was never invented or discovered there. That may or may not have been a good thing but in my dimension, companies like Microsoft and Apple and Google and Facebook and Twitter and Instagram and TikTok and Snapchat and all the rest simply do not exist. Bill Gates became a lawyer like his father. Steve Jobs, who is still alive, owns and operates a McDonald's franchise with this daughter in Cupertino, California, while Mark Zuckerberg sits in prison for having swindled numerous elderly women out of their life savings in a Lonely Hearts Club scheme. Other differences include my having a twin brother, Liam, instead of a twin sister, Ophelia, and my not being the reincarnation of Khattaaara or Maleficent, or any other evil person. Oh, and I'm gay—diehard, muff-divingly gay—lipstick lesbian if you will, but truth be told, I only ever use clear balm. I like boys, but not in that way. My family and friends are perfectly fine with it. There is no prejudice of that on my world. Everyone accepts the fact that love is a difficult find, and however it comes (no pun intended) it is a blessing and not a curse, and that one should be appreciative and grateful for its arrival.

That being said, I was naked in my bedroom bath, water raining down on me from the nozzle up above, and having just turned off the valve when Peyton appeared just behind me in full Quantum Girl attire.

"Jesus Christ!" I blurted out as I glanced back and saw her behind me. "You scared the crap out of me! And what *is* it with you and showers?"

I wrung the water from my hair and turned around to face her. It seemed to me that her costume was different but I had only a second's glance before she changed back into Peyton in her schoolgirl clothes. There was a scared-to-death expression on her face as she held her left hand tightly to her chest, her right hand gripping the shower curtains to try and support herself. One by one the curtain rings ripped under her weight. I grabbed her under her arms and pulled her tightly against me. Looking down, I viewed with horror, the sight of her blood mixed with the water at our feet. And then I saw her blouse was drenched and stained with red as her life bled away.

"You're hurt," I said.

She was shivering and coughing up blood.

"I was shot," she replied or tried to as she was having trouble talking. Her breath was labored. She was gasping for air.

"I'll call 911," I said.

"They won't get here in time. I've already lost too much blood."

Her legs began to buckle under her. I used all of my strength to lower her as gently as I could to lay her down in the bathtub. The tub was still wet and probably cold but what else could I do? I didn't have enough strength to carry her to the bedroom and lift her onto my bed. Worse, it was night, and there wasn't anyone else at home. Mom and Dad were at a drive-in and Liam was at the skateboard park with a couple of his friends. I reached up and grabbed the towel that was hanging on a hook on the wall just outside the bathtub to put around myself but as I looked at her, wet and in so much pain, I used it instead to put over her. I could feel her trembling and shivering and cold from loss of blood.

"I just wasn't prepared for it," she said. Her voice was barely a whisper as she desperately tried to speak. "I've tried to avoid her. I've gone back more than a thousand times each with the same result. A battle in space. A burn through the atmosphere. This time, though, it was different. I think things changed when I merged with the other Quantum Girl."

I wiped her cheeks with my hands. I couldn't tell if it was water or tears.

"You could have fled to any of a billion dimensions," I said as my own tears began to flow. "Why here?"

"I see more of me in you," she replied, "than in any of the others. And I don't just mean a reflection."

"But I'm *not* you," I insisted.

She coughed up more blood.

"I think we share one soul," she said, and her words just melted my heart.

"You're insane!" I cried. "You know that? You're insane! You just need to hang on!"

Her hand reached up. Her fingers touched the whistle that dangled toward her from the chain around my neck. It was the only thing I now wore—the one thing always next to my heart since she had given it to me.

"I'll live on through you," she said.

"No! Oh, no!" I sobbed. "If you die, a part of *me* dies, too!"

"But a part of *me* will live," she said, as she choked out the words.

"No, no, no! You can't die!" I cried. "I won't let you! I have to get some help!"

I started to get up, but she grabbed hold of my wrist.

"There's nothing they can do," she said. "My body's... different now. No one can save me. The bullet should have been deflected, but

I was still weak from what Thara-Klo had done. She put handcuffs on me, coated with something that took my powers away." She paused to gather strength and then went on. "I'm going to place my quantum seed in you. It'll take you back…" she started to say and then coughed up more blood. "Back to my dimension," she went on. "Thara-Klo will probably be watching the house. Find Ophelia. You can trust her. You just need to convince her. She doesn't know about Quantum Girl. I erased the timeline where she *did*. I'm counting on you. You're the only one who can set things right." Her words were garbled as blood began to fill her mouth.

"But how?" I asked.

The words came in pieces, each phrase said with labored breath. "My cellphone. In my locker. At school. Video app. Everything's on it. From when I was thirteen."

Then her arm that had held my hair let go and touched my forehead. It was like God's finger touching Adam's on the ceiling of the Sistine Chapel; the fresco painting by Michelangelo. Her arm glowed violet and for a moment I thought I saw a pulse of light travel up toward her fingers. And then I felt something electric touch and then enter my head.

"Don't think I'm not scared," she muttered, her words garbled by the blood that filled her mouth. "But I'm counting on you," she went on. "I just hope that my Mom was right about God." Those were the last words I heard her say. Her head slumped over past the edge of the bathtub, her eyes stared sightlessly and despite whatever disbelief I might have had I knew that she was dead. Then, suddenly, she was gone. *But wait!* I thought to myself. *Where's all the blood?* More than that, the shower curtains were intact. My heart skipped a beat as I heard a voice behind me.

"What happened?" the voice said—the voice of a teenage girl. "Some of the kids at school said you'd been arrested—taken away in handcuffs."

I wheeled around, startled. It was her sister. This wasn't my world anymore. It was hers. This was *her* house, *her* bathtub, *her* room, or *theirs!*

"Ophelia?" I assumed it was her. She looked like she could be my sister and not just a friend who just happened to walk in.

"Why are you crouching there naked? And why is there blood on you? Are you hurt?" There was genuine concern in her voice.

So, this was her, the sister I never had. Despite the fact that I had Liam, I was envious. *What would it have been like*, I wondered, *to have grown up with a sibling who was a girl instead of a bo—to have had that special bond of a common gender—to be able to share dolls and clothes and dreams?*

"It's not my blood," I said reassuringly then turned to look at myself in the mirror of the medicine cabinet that hung over the sink. There was blood all over me from when I had held Peyton and even some on my face from when I wiped away my tears. I must have looked like Chloë Grace Moretz in that Stephen King film. I immediately took one of the washcloth, that were lying on the sink, wet it, and began to wipe off the blood. But it hit me so hard that this was Peyton's blood—Peyton, whom I would never see again. I stared hard at my reflection, only thinking of her.

"Where's my robe?" I asked, hoping that there was one.

"It's on the hook behind you as always," she said with a thread of irritation in her voice.

I turned and looked. There were two robes hanging side by side— one pink, one blue. I grabbed the blue.

"That one's mine," she said, definitely vexed.

I hung it back on its hook then took the pink one and began to put it on.

"What's going on?" she asked. "You're acting strange." She glanced toward the toilet, which stood right next to the sink. "Move over," she ordered. "I need to pee."

She pulled down her panties and hiked up her skirt as she sat down. This was followed by the sound of a loud stream of urine splashing into the water in the bowl. As for me, I had positioned myself in the doorway, staring out into the bedroom that was similar but different from mine, especially in that there were twin beds and not just one.

"I needed to pee half an hour ago," Ophelia said. Amazing, this Quantum Girl stuff, I thought. I could hear her tear off the sheet of toilet paper. I could hear her wipe herself. I could hear her panties rub against her legs, as she slid them back on and as they were adjusted back in place. "What's going on?" she persisted. "Whose blood was that? You didn't get into another fight with Theresa, did you?"

"If I tell you," I said, "you're not going to believe me."

"I always believe you," she replied.

She stood up. I could hear the fabric of her skirt as it fell back and brushed against her legs.

"I'm not Peyton," I said. "I mean, I *am* Peyton, only I'm not your Peyton."

Then I heard the toilet flush.

"What are you talking about?" she said and then turned on the faucet and began to wash her hands.

"Peyton, your sister. The Peyton you grew up with—she's dead."

The water stopped, and there was the soft rustle of her drying her hands on the terrycloth towel.

"And this is your idea of some sort of a joke?" she said with a touch of anger in her voice. "I suppose you have a camera hidden somewhere." She paused and then went on. "If you have a video of me peeing that you're going to post on the Internet, I'll never forgive you!"

"I'm serious," I insisted. "Dead serious." I thought a moment about what she had just said.

"Wait," I interjected. "What's the *Internet*?"

She pushed past me to go and sit down on her bed and then picked up a book that was lying on her nightstand.

"Stop being a goof," she said.

"I'm not," I said back. "Look at me."

What she saw was the original Quantum Girl, with glowing violet skin, in a costume that danced with moving galaxies and stars.

"Oh my God!" she exclaimed. "What the fuck!"

"Don't be afraid," I said.

"Stay away!" she cried out, terrified, backing up on the bed. "What happened to Peyton?"

This was all too much for her to handle. No words could fix this.

Back in time, Quantum Girl, I thought to myself. *Gotta undo this. Back in time. Back in time. Back in time.* And I pressed my eyelids tight.

When I opened my eyes, still barefoot and in the robe, I found myself in a place that had been the target of a bombing attack. In fact, it was still going on. There were prop-driven planes overhead—Japanese Zeros from my history class—that were dropping bombs. There were bodies scattered all around—some under the rubble from the buildings that had collapsed. A half-fallen sign read, *Pearl Harbor Canteen.*

So, this was Pearl Harbor, December 7, 1941. How or why I had found my way here bewildered me until I saw *her.* She was as tall as I was and appeared to be in her late twenties. Her hair was dark and shoulder-length, but the ends curled under and she wore bangs under the small green pillbox hat that matched the jacket and skirt she had on. Most striking, though, was that she resembled both Peyton and me—enough for anyone who looked hard enough to notice. Then it hit me like an atom bomb. This was Thara-Klo, Peyton's daughter and mortal enemy, who was now giving comfort to a six-year-old child—a little girl who was clinging to her, seemingly filled with terror and tears. A moment later our eyes had met, Thara-Klo's and mine.

"Mother?" she spoke in a questioning tone. "Mother," she repeated, as though deciding that her first conclusion was correct. With that, she set the girl down on her feet next to her, and with her arms half extended, her palms faced outward toward me, hurled a blast of cold flames in my direction as her eyes glowed icy blue.

Instinctively, the seed in my head created a force field to protect me, but before the flames even reached me, I phased away from there.

CHAPTER XX

After several time jumps, I managed to materialize back in Peyton and Ophelia's bathroom earlier that day, which allowed me sufficient time to change into some clothes and head over to school where I realized Peyton's absence would be felt. Having dressed and having phased enough for one day I walked the several blocks it took to get to the high school. It was just after first period and the halls were crowded with students, many of whom I recognized from their counterparts in my dimension. And then I saw *her*, Theresa Martinez, whom I had had an intense crush on, on my world, but there she was totally straight, unlike here where she was a thriver like me. She was standing at her locker, the door open, exchanging books for her next class. She appeared to see me through the corner of her eye but pretended she had not and focused her attention on whatever contents her locker held. I walked over to her, not saying a word.

"What do you *want*?" she said sadly. "I made a fool of myself."

"Why do you say that?" I asked.

"You know why. Because I kissed you," she said. It was as though tears dripped from her words.

"And?" I said back. "Look at me, Theresa."

She turned toward me like a child expecting a reprimand, staring down at the floor. Ever so gently, I took hold of her shoulders.

"Look at me," I said again, though quieter now.

Slowly, she lifted her head and her eyes met mine. I pulled her close and kissed her as though she were the one great love of my life. And she kissed me back as though for her it was the same. Her cheek was wet as she laid it against my chest. As I looked up, I saw a lot of other students staring at us, sardonic smiles on their faces. I glared back at them.

"What are all of you staring at?" I shouted out. "Go back to whatever lives you think you have!"

"I'm so sorry for everything I ever said or did," she wept. "The truth is," and her voice broke, "I think I'm in love with you."

"Did anyone ever tell you that you're beautiful?" I said back.

"My mother…" she shrugged.

"Well, you *are*," I said. "You really *are*." I paused and then took a deep breath. "I have a question."

"What?" she replied, her voice as timid as a mouse.

"Will you be my girlfriend?" I asked.

"You're serious," she said, doubtful.

I smiled at her and nodded.

"Oh my God! Yes!" she exclaimed.

And that was how my relationship with her began.

A little while later found me at the administration office where I came face to face with a woman who seriously resembled a hippopotamus, vastly overweight with very, very thick, dark-rimmed glasses. I shall not go into further detail but shall leave it up to the reader's imagination to envision. And while I have never seen nor heard a hippopotamus in person it brought to my mind the Island of Dr. Moreau. Thus, do I stand both remorseful and apologetic but those were my thoughts at the time.

"Can I help you?" the hippo woman asked.

"I need a copy of my class schedule," I replied as I had absolutely no clue where I was supposed to be or when.

The ungulated woman stared at me over her glasses.

"You *do* know it's on your portal on the Internet," she said.

There went that word again.

"I know," I said, "but my portal got stolen."

"Name?" she scowled.

"Payton Herron," I replied.

"Spelling?" she asked. She glanced up from what appeared to me to be some sort of board.

"P-a-y-t-o-n H-e-r-r-o-n," I replied.

"They have you listed as P-e," she said as she continued to look at the board, which must have had some notes on it, I thought. "We'll need to change that," she went on in an emotionless contralto. My mind distracted, I didn't notice that she had picked up a phone and was quietly talking into it... about me! Looking around, I noticed two men dark suits headed in my direction. Entering the office where I stood, one of them pulled put an FBI badge and brandished it in my face.

"Peyton Herron?" he said. "We have a warrant for your arrest."

Panic took hold of me. I realized they were coming for Peyton, but I couldn't very well explain that I wasn't her. I closed my eyes once more, focused as best I could, and went back ten minutes in time.

I was once more at the locker with Theresa in my arms. She was staring at me in disbelief.

"You're serious," she said again.

"We need to get out of here," I told her. "I'll explain later."

And with that, we hurried down the hallways ignoring the whistles and jeers that followed us halfway through our flight. Outside one of the side doors, Theresa turned to me.

"Where are we going?" she asked.

"I don't know," I said, as I looked around. The building gave way to a parking lot and football and baseball fields. Beyond them were ordinary homes. There was nowhere we could disappear and I didn't want to risk phasing again. This last time I was lucky but I still didn't have enough control, especially as I was so anxious, my heart racing in my chest. I didn't want to wind up phased into the middle of a wall, and I didn't want to leave *her*. I couldn't risk losing what it had taken all my life to find. "Somewhere safe," I told her. "Can we go to your home?"

"I supposed," she offered. "My mom's at work. She won't be back till five."

We took side streets and back alleys to her house. It was about a mile from the school in a low-income part of town. There was graffiti on building walls and trash along the curbs. Looking at the street signs though, I realized how difficult life on this parallel world would be for me as everything was written backwards. It was like being dyslexic. I had to take time to figure out what things said. Perhaps the quantum seed had the ability to fix that for me, but I was still operating in the dark where it was concerned.

Theresa's home was a small, one-story wood-frame ranch-style tract house with a chain-link fence around the front. The yard was unkept, the bushes untrimmed but, not to complain, this was a place of refuge, at least for a while, and it was her sanctuary. We wound up in her bedroom. She sat down on her bed as I peered out the window.

"Okay," she said. "So, could you please tell me what's going on? My mom will have my ass for missing school."

"You said you love me," I said back, and I turned to face her. "I need you to not freak out."

"I do," she replied. "I won't. Just tell me."

"Do you believe in superheroes?" I said. I looked at her with all seriousness.

"In comic books and movies," she replied. It was one of those, *Why are we going there?* sort of responses.

My answer was to become Quantum Girl.

"Holy fucking crap!" she exclaimed. "That is so dope. How are you able to do that?"

"I just think about being Quantum Girl," I replied, "and I am."

"So, I wasn't hallucinating when all that shit happened," she blurted out. "The volcano, outer space, being on Mars, the giant tyrannosaurus?"

I was about to explain that wasn't me but all I got out was, "That wasn't…" when she interrupted, filled with excitement.

"Show me." She insisted. "Show me the time travel again. Only no dinosaurs this time."

I had calmed down by now, so I believed I had the hang of it.

"Turn around," I told her.

"What? Why?" she questioned.

"Just turn around," I insisted. "Trust me."

And so, she did. I wrapped my arms around her from behind.

"I like this already," she said, falling back against me.

"Don't be afraid," I cautioned. "You're going to hear a pop."

I closed my eyes again, pressed my eyelids tight like before, and then phased us six hours into the future. The room was still the same but it was dark both outside and in as the lights in the bedroom were off.

"Fuck me!" Theresa exclaimed.

"I thought I just had," I said from just a few feet away. Only it was future me who had said it, who had assumed that it had come from the Theresa she lay naked in bed with.

"Shhhh!" I whispered in my Theresa's ear. We were just a foot away from where she and I in our future states were fervidly making love. Suddenly, an older woman's voice broke through the quiet air.

"Theresa!" it called from the kitchen or dining room. I don't and didn't know which one it was. "Supper's on!" it announced and then silence once more filled the room.

Future Theresa sat up just a bit. Future me continued to kiss the nape of her neck while one of her hands, meaning one of my hands, meandered somewhere else.

"Coming!" Future T called out and that is when the one I held returned with me to our time.

In an instant, we were back in the sunlit room. The bed was undisturbed other than the dent on the bedspread where Theresa had just sat down. Theresa looked at me filled with wonder.

"What else can you do?" she eagerly asked.

"I'm not sure," I replied. "I need to get a hold of," and I paused as I thought. "I need to get something from my locker at school that will tell me but I can't go back."

"How come?" she asked.

"I don't know why but the police are after me."

Her eyes stared hard and then she shook her head.

"You don't look like a bank robber or anything," she replied. "I don't know. Maybe there's something on the Internet."

"Oh, my Gods!" I exclaimed. "*What* is the Internet?"

And so, she explained. But it was when we stood watching the news that my heart stopped. "Authorities are searching for the fifteen-year-old girl who had murdered FBI Agent, Richard Balmoral," the newscaster said. "Graphic footage shows the murder as it took place. The suspect, Peyton Elise Herron, remains at large. Herron is considered armed and dangerous."

Theresa turned toward me. She didn't look at me but just stared off.

"Did you *do* it?" she asked.

"I wasn't even there," I said. "And I'm sure she didn't do it either."

Theresa turned around and looked at me. "Who is *she*?"

"Peyton. The other Peyton." I said. "I'm not from this universe."

"Oh, I have to sit down for this," she replied.

I explained as best I could all that had happened from the moment that Peyton and I first met. Then I told her about me and my world, my thoughts and my fears, and how I questioned whether I could fill the shoes, so to speak, of my counterpart from this dimension.

By the time I had said all that I had in me to say, we were lying on the bed together, naked and in each other's arms. Theresa lay on top of me, gently kissing my lips with little pecks of love. I could feel the warmth of her body. I could smell the scent of her want. Yes, we were both only fifteen years old but, I thought, if Peyton owned an ancient soul why not the same for me or for this girl who owned my heart? She rested her head against my breast, gently caressing my arm with the tips of her fingernails.

"So, the other Peyton that I kissed yesterday wasn't into girls, but you are?" she asked. It was half a question.

"Exactly," I replied.

"Fuck me!" I heard her say.

"I thought I just had," I said and then I remembered and I turned my head to look, just as my former self and—I don't want to say my former love—my *endless* love vanished into the past with a short burst of light and a pop.

An instant later, the sound of a woman's voice broke the quiet of the room.

"Theresa!" it said. "Supper's on!"

Theresa lifted her head just a bit. "Coming!" she called back.

"I think our selves from the past just came." I paused, then added, "and left."

"I love it when you talk like that," Theresa said. She had propped herself up above me, her arms extended, her face just inches from mine. She kissed me ever so gently on the lips and then stared into my eyes.

"Like what?" I asked, and then it dawned on me what she meant. "Oh," I said.

"So, do you like *frijoles*?" she asked.

"What's that?" I replied.

She sat up to a kneeling position and then wriggled herself so that the seat of her passion sat directly on mine.

"It's Mexican pinto beans with bacon and chilies," she said as she ground herself down onto me.

"It sounds very unhealthy," I replied as my heart began to pound once again.

"*Oye güera, necesitas probar cosas nuevas*," she said. Her Spanish was as impeccable as her ability to turn me on.

"What does that mean?" I asked, trying to focus on her face.

"It means," she replied, "*mi hermosa chica blanca*, that you need to have new experiences."

I smiled at her and remarked, "I thought that was what *this* was all about?"

She jumped up off of me and the bed.

"Come on," she said and smiled. "We need to go eat and put some *curvas* on your skinny bones."

"What about your mother?" I asked. "What if she recognizes me from the news?"

"No worries," Theresa replied. "She only watches Mexican soap operas and cooking shows."

After getting dressed, we went to the dining room where Mrs. Martinez had dinner set up. Most of the food I had never tasted before. It was different and a bit too spicy for my taste but I did my best to show that I enjoyed it. Needless to say, I drank a lot of water to try and assuage the burn[9]. As Mrs. Martinez dished out some *frijoles* into my plate from where she sat, she commented, "Theresa says that you two are in sports together."

"Basketball. Mama," Theresa answered for me. "Basketball."

"When I was your age," Rosita Martinez went on, "only the boys played such sports. The girls learned to cook and to sew."

"And play with the dinosaurs," Theresa answered back.

"No, that was in my mother's time. I had a—how do you say—a wooly mammoth." Then she turned to me. "Do you have any brothers or sisters..." and she hesitated.

"Payton, Mama," Theresa said, rolling her eyes. "Her name's Payton"

"Payton," Mrs. Martinez replied. "Oh, yes, Payton. That's such a pretty name."

"Thank you," I answered with a mouth full of food. I swallowed and then said, "I have a brother. Liam."

"Liam. Like William. Perhaps you can introduce him to my Theresa," she said, looking at her daughter, my new and forever love, whose elbows rested on the table, as she slapped her own forehead with both hands. "She will make a good wife one day."

Theresa's eyes glared up at her mother from under her hands in frustration. "Mama, I told you a million times, I'm only into girls."

---

[9] I later learned that only milk will work as it contains a protein called casein that breaks down something called capsaicin, which is a neuropeptide found in chili peppers.

"Your father," her mother said as she began to eat, "rest his soul, is turning in his grave." She swallowed and then looked at me. "What about you, Payton? Do you have a boyfriend?"

"No, Ma'am," I replied.

"Ugh! Mama," Theresa tried to explain. "I told you! Payton is a lesbian, too!"

"How can such a pretty girl not like boys?" Mrs. Martinez commented, staring at me as she lifted her glass to drink.

"Would it be all right if Payton spent the night?" Theresa asked, trying desperately to appear nonchalant.

"If she lets her mother know," came the maternal response, "and she sleeps on the sofa."

"Really?" Theresa exclaimed. with an exasperated sigh.

"I don't want any—how do they say here—hanky-panky going on." Then, to herself, under her breath, "*Gracias a Dios que no te puede embarazada*," which means, "Thank God, she can't get you pregnant."[10]

---

[10] Just to be clear, unlike Peyton, I took Spanish in middle school.

CHAPTER XXI

When morning came (a reprieve from that uncomfortable couch), I used Theresa's phone to call Ophelia and have her meet us behind the school. She was already there, impatiently waiting, when we finally arrived.

"What's going on?" Ophelia said, nervously glancing this way and that to make certain no one was around. "You're all over the news. The FBI has been to our house. They have a car parked outside. Seriously, I was even followed to school. They say you killed someone."

"It wasn't me," I told her. "It was Thara-Klo."

"Who the hell is Thara-Klo?" Ophelia stood there, waiting for an explanation.

Theresa broke in. "She's her daughter from a previous universe."

Ophelia looked at Theresa with a scowl. "Was I even *talking* to you?" she said.

"Just saying..." came the reply.

"Why is she *even* here?" railed Ophelia. "I thought she was your tormentor?"

"White girl," Theresa came back at her. "She's not your sister. Your sister *fue y murió* in another dimension."

"Theresa, please..." I tried to insist.

"She needs to know," Theresa replied. "It's only right."

"Know what?" Ophelia asked.

"Look, bro," Theresa said without a whole lot of regard. "*Your* Peyton got shot when she was Quantum Girl. Before she died she put some quantum seed shit into *my* Payton's head so that *she* became Quantum Girl. Only *my* Payton doesn't know how to use her powers, which is why we need you to get *your* Peyton's cell phone from her locker 'cause *your* Peyton left a video diary on it with instructions."

Ophelia turned to me. "Is she fucking insane?" she asked.

"Ophelia," I begged, "would you please just get the cell phone?"

"Fine," she relented. "And why are you calling me Ophelia?"

"Because it's your name?" I replied.

"What happened to Phee?" she said.

I didn't have a response. All I offered back was an awkward shrug. This wasn't really my sister and so I didn't have a lot of intel on her or her relationship with my deceased dimensional twin. All I knew was that we didn't have a lot of time which in retrospect seems somewhat ironic.

I waited outside as Ophelia (pardon me) *Phee* and Theresa went to Peyton's locker. Less than five minutes later—though it seemed like an eternity—they returned.

"How did it go?" I asked.

"Dude!" Theresa said to me excitedly, "We were accosted by a pair of *federales*. They had a fucking search warrant but your sorta sister here is a *totalmente brava*. She totally whipped their asses."

"She beat them?" I asked astonished as I stared at Phee.

"No," she explained, "it was like 'I'm just here to get my sports bra. Maybe the two of you pervs would like to follow me to the girls' locker room and watch me try it on.' Then she lifts up her arms and stretches like Marilyn Monroe showing off her titties through her blouse. Oh my God! Oh, my God! I think one of them got *se paró le pitó!*"

"She means a hard-on," Phee explained. Apparently, she had taken Spanish, too.

"Your sister, I like her!" she said to me then turned to Ophelia. "Girl, you got *cajones*!"

Phee couldn't help but smile.

Theresa handed me Peyton's cell phone.

"Those guys are probably still after us," she said excitedly. "You need to Quantum Girl us the fuck out of here."

"Give me your hands," I said.

"What?" Phee asked. "Why?"

Theresa turned to look behind her toward the front of the building.

"Just do it!" she told Phee. "We need to leave!"

I craned my head to look down her line of sight. The same two men in suits were walking briskly toward us. When they saw me they broke into a run. We all linked hands.

"Where and when am I supposed to take us?" I said in sudden panic.

"Anywhere!" Theresa said as the men drew near. "Just no dinosaurs!"

I turned into Quantum Girl. The transformation nearly sent Phee into shock as she turned pale. I pressed my eyelids together as tight as I could. There was a small pop and we were gone from there but to when?[11] Regardless, in an instant, we found ourselves together on an open plain.

---

[11] The pop, for those with scientifically curious minds, is caused by the air that rushes in to fill the instantaneous absence of matter caused by phasing from one place or time to another.

CHAPTER XXII

It was night. The air was warm, filled with the sound of crickets and bison, which strangely enough sounded like the croaking of giant frogs. We could see one herd in the distance, thousands upon thousands of them before the advent of man had brought them to near extinction. Above us was a veil of stars such as I have never seen. I know now why the ancients called the galaxy we live in the Milky Way. With neither pollution nor city lights to hinder their view, the stars shown with a beauty and a radiance as in the distant future could only be witnessed through telescopes that had been flung into orbit. The sheer majesty of it as I breathed it all in was broken at last by Theresa, who sadly bemoaned, "I think I'm standing in buffalo dung."

"Sorry," I said.

"What the hell's going on?" Phee demanded. "Why do you look like that?"

"I told you," Theresa said. Having taken off the offending shoe and perched on one leg, she brought it near her nose, sniffed it, and carved out a sour expression on her face. Glancing at Phee, she went on, "She's Quantum Girl."

Phee took a long step back from the two of us as I reverted to the Payton me. She stared at me and Theresa with both apprehension and fear.

"This is *really* freaking me out," she said. "Where *are* we?"

"Not where," Theresa broke in. "When."

"I didn't ask *you*!" Phee snapped back.

"Roughly one hundred thousand years in the past," I told her. "I wanted to avoid the threat of Indians."

"Why were you wearing that outfit and why was your skin glowing purple like that?" Phee demanded again.

"I'll explain in a bit," I assured her. "But for now we're going to need to build a fire."

"Too bad we didn't bring sleeping bags," Phee lamented.

"Or food," Theresa added.

"We did," came a familiar voice from just a few yards away.

Both Theresa and Phee turned toward the sound of my voice. There, glowing quantumly stood Quantum Girl. Lover and sister alike kept looking back and forth between the two versions of me as though they were both seated dead center at a tennis match. Next to the quantum me stood a wooden pallet, stacked with food and a stockpile of necessities.

"I didn't want to go off and leave you," I explained, "and possibly lose you in the past so I doubled myself and one went off for supplies."

"But we just got here," Phee said. There was no end to how much she was confused by it all.

"I can freeze time," I said. "I can do a lot of things it seems from having read Peyton's diary. The time-stopping thing though I figured out last night when I stayed with Theresa. But I still need to master it all."

With that, my Quantum Girl self merged back into me. I think Phee was starting to hyperventilate. I tried to distract her from all that she had seen.

"Anyone hungry?" I said. "Let's eat and then set up the tent."

Theresa came up to me. "That is so cool," she whispered. "Why didn't you do that when we were in bed?"

"We're not here for any of that," I whispered back.

"Well, it's something to look forward to," she said quietly and smiled.

As we sat around the campfire that we had built, having filled our stomachs with some of the food I had brought back through time, I told Ophelia everything I knew—how Peyton had come to my dimension, how she left, how she came back again only to die in my arms, and how she gave me powers that I barely knew how to use. I told her how I had come here for the first time covered in her sister's blood, how she had reacted, and how I had decided to undo that moment until I could decide how things needed to be told.

Phee rose to her feet, rushed over to a spot a few yards away and then dropped down to her hands and knees and threw up. Then she stood back up and broke into tears.

"This can't be happening!" she sobbed, her back to us. "Peyton wasn't just my sister. She was my very best friend! I can't even bury her! Her body isn't even here. It's lost in some other dimension!"

I got up and went over to her to gently put my hands on her shoulders but she shook them off.

"Don't touch me!" she yelled through her tears, choking on her words. "You're not *her*! Oh, God! Why did this have to happen?"

"Guys..." Theresa interjected. "It's getting dark. We need to make some kind of perimeter. I mean, there are probably wild animals out here."

"I already projected a force field," I assured her. "We have our perimeter. We're totally safe."

"Who's going to protect us from *her*?" Ophelia said, indicating Theresa with a motion of her head.

"She's not so bad once you get to know her," I said quietly.

"And you *love* her?" she questioned, shaking her head.

"I know what she did to your sister," I said. "And I know from the diary what your sister did to Thara-Klo when she was Khattaaara. People can change. That's what makes us…" I searched for the right word, "human I guess. Maybe there's even hope for Thara-Klo."

And then I stopped time again and divided myself into ten of me. Together, we assembled the tents and laid out the sleeping bags and provisions. I had even brought some backup batteries from the present or the future (it got confusing) along with my laptop onto which I had downloaded all the seasons of both Game of Thrones and the first two seasons of House of the Dragon. After I reconsolidated myself, I turned the clock back on. It was like magic to Theresa and Phee. One second there was a pallet stacked with things, the next it was empty and everything had been set up.

Ten minutes later found us comfortably in the tent, which was sixteen by nine feet and tall enough for us to stand up in. I had also purchased three memory foam mattresses for the sleeping bags to be placed on. As for the explanation as to how I got the money for all of this, I noticed an old All Star comic book on Ophelia's desk and held it as I duplicated myself again, which had the effect of duplicating the comic book as well. Then, after replacing the original and, from what Theresa had told me about the Internet, I did a bit of research, dropped it off at a comic book grading firm, phased a week into the future, picked it up, phased over to Sotheby's, consigned it there, phased forward to three weeks after the auction and received a check for something just over 1.2 million dollars, which of course was just *slightly* more than I needed to purchase about a thousand dollars worth of camping equipment and supplies. I had to use Peyton's ID to deposit the check, with the clear intent to give half of the money to Ophelia later on. The hardest part of it all was having to endorse the check backwards as it must be remembered that in this dimension everything is the reverse of the dimension from which I came.

Anyway… There we were, Theresa on one side of me, Ophelia (Phee) on the other, I with Peyton's cell phone in my hand, each of us lying on our stomachs, watching Peyton as she spoke her journal entries.

"Thus far," she said, "I have been able to command five separate powers. I can counteract gravity and make duplicates of myself to a virtually infinite number. I can hurl out blasts of energy, project myself through time, space, and alternate dimensions, and do that X-ray thing. Oh, and I can project any sort of clothing on myself including my costume, so I guess that makes six. All I need to do is clear my mind and think about what I want to have happen. It seems to get easier with every attempt. My biggest threat is Thara-Klo, who ironically was my daughter in a previous existence. Like me, she can project herself through space though not through time or other dimensions as far as I can tell. She can also shapeshift, which I consider a terrible threat as it makes it difficult to determine who's real and who's her. And, like me, she can hurl out blasts of energy. The only friend I have in all of this is Phee. I had to undo time to protect her, but I promised that one day I would give her back all her memories that were lost in the process."

"Well, that didn't…" Phee started to say. "I mean, she died before…" and she broke off again only to finish the sentence with, "I guess I'll never know."

There were other entries that were more personal. I handed her the phone.

"Whether you choose to believe it or not," I said, trying to console the tears I saw welling up in her eyes, "a part of her is me."

"I'd like to think so," she said with those tears now down her cheeks, " but I miss her so much."

"Tomorrow morning," I said, "I'll start trying to figure out what I can do—what Quantum Girl can do. Who knows? Maybe I can bring her back."

For the next month, I did my best to master all of my potential, from floating above the ground to blasting branches off of trees to creating hundreds, sometimes thousands of me, and being able to thunder across the plain like the vast herds of bison we would sometimes see in the distance.

Strange as it may seem, Theresa and Phee began to bond. The anger and animosity that had jailed Phee's heart over Peyton waned somewhat with their continual proximity. Once, too, Theresa killed a rattler that was about to strike Phee by throwing one of the hunting knives that I had brought back through time. Theresa kept the rattle as well as one from another kill and sometimes would dance seductively in the moonlight with them as though they were maracas. Day after day they grew closer, which served to help morale. After thirty days had passed and our supplies were nearing an end, with my having mastered my newfound abilities as best I could imagine, we decided it was time to go home. As I changed back from Quantum

Girl to Payton, Theresa turned to me.

"Girl, you are *una chica vrava!* When we get back you can seriously kick some Thara-Klo ass!"

"The other Peyton wasn't so successful," I said with a frown, "and she had way more experience than me."

"Plus," Phee broke in, "you seem to forget she's wanted by the authorities."

"We'll go back to my universe first to try and sort things out," I said. "Hands please."

We joined hands. I no longer needed to close my eyes for us to phase and with three deep breaths and a pop of the air we were gone from that ancient scene. The transition to my bedroom in my dimension was instantaneous. It was night and the room was dark. As we let go of each other's hands I heard Phee gasp and I turned to see Liam standing in the hallway at the open door. His hand reached inward and turned on the light. Then he stepped into the room. It felt as though we were burglars, caught red-handed by the cops!

CHAPTER XXIII

"Liam!" I exclaimed, breathless at having been taken by surprise. "What are you doing in my room?"

"How are you not dead?" he asked. "We found you in the bathtub, a bullet through your chest. I was at your funeral. We buried you!"

"That wasn't me," I said.

"What the fuck is going on?" he responded, irritated. "And who are *they*?"

Phee took a step toward Liam extending her hand. "I'm Ophelia." She proclaimed. "She's Theresa. We're Payton's friends."

Liam awkwardly accepted the handshake then turned toward Payton again.

"Just tell me one thing," he demanded. "If it wasn't you that we buried, who the hell is in your grave?"

"She was me from a parallel dimension," I told him, apparently unconvincingly.

"And you expect me to believe that?" he said. There was angry frustration on his face.

My tone became scolding. "I expect you to hear me out. Seriously, it's either that or you can believe that I'm some sort of zombie, here to munch on your brains, what little there apparently are! You'd think you'd be happy I'm alive!"

"I am," he said. "It's just..."

"He's confused," Phee interrupted. "Just like I was. The Peyton you buried—that was my sister."

He stared at me; his lips pursed in an attempt to hold back tears. He had come to grips with the *fact* that I was dead and now here I was, standing right in front of him, alive once more. "Liam," I said. I tried to take his hands but he nervously pulled them away. "Let's all sit down and I'll explain."

Thus, we sat, and with the breadth of infinite patience, I began with words that at first were met with disbelief and then with abject wonder as for just a moment I phased into Quantum Girl. Meanwhile, Phee who appeared completely, utterly, and immeasurably taken by Liam and had made sure that she sat next to him, managed to take hold of his hand through it all. Theresa, my Theresa, sat beside me, affectionately rubbing my back with her nearest hand. I spent the next hour relating to Liam all that had occurred, taking care to omit the salacious parts, which even Phee had not been privy to.

"And so here we are," I said in the end.

Liam stood up. "I need to get some fresh air," he said. Then he turned back to Phee, extended his hand down toward her, and asked, "Would you like to come with?"

Phee smiled.

"Dude," Theresa exclaimed. "she's like your trans... dimensional... self."

Both of them, Liam and Phee, appeared so engrossed in each other that they probably didn't even hear the remark.

"Definitely," Phee answered, her eyes mated with his. Then she took his hand and he helped her to her feet.

After they left the room, Theresa said, staring at the door, "I'm sorry but that's just plain weird."

"I think it's sweet," I said and smiled, taking hold of *her* hand.

"I mean, what if they had kids?" she went on.

"The ancient Egyptians married their brothers and sisters," I explained. "It's called a consanguineous marriage."

"Yeah, well, it sounds more like twincest to me."

I said nothing. I just curled my lip. After a moment's silence, Theresa suddenly blurted out, "I am starving. Can we go to the kitchen wherever it is?"

I nodded then added, "It's downstairs."

I decided not to turn on the light once there. I didn't want to call attention to our presence in case either Mom or Dad were to get up. The only light came from the fixture over the sink and from the open freezer door into which Theresa was searching. I sat at the table; my head buried in folded arms that rested on the tabletop.

"Don't you have any microwave food?" she asked.

"What's microwave food?" I sleepily replied.

"How on earth has your universe survived?" she said, continuing to search.

"There should be cold chicken in the fridge," I yawned. "Unless Liam ate it all."

She closed the freezer, opened the refrigerator, and found a chicken leg, which she began to eat even before sitting down next to me. She was chewing as she spoke, and, it seemed, wanting to micromanage my career.

"After all this is over," she said, "you should think about branding yourself."

"What do you mean?" I asked, my eyelids shut.

"You know," she said, as she continued to eat, talking with her mouth full. "Quantum Girl dolls, Quantum Girl T-shirts... Maybe even a movie. The Adventures of Quantum Girl and her sidekick, Barrio Babe with whom she has one hella dope relationship."

"That's all well and fine," I said, lifting up my head a bit to glance at her, "but there's still the matter of Thara-Klo and the cops."

At this point, Liam had entered the kitchen with Ophelia, both of them still holding hands. Meanwhile, Theresa continued to attack the unprotected chicken leg like a hungry jackal To her defense though, none of us had eaten anything all day.

"Just sayin'," she said between bites. Then she looked up at the siblings and commented, under her breath, "Jesus, Mary, and Joseph. It's the Bobbsey Twins, *Oh* feel ya and *I'll* feel ya. Oh, brother!"

"We were just outside," Liam announced.

"Talking," Ophelia, said, finishing his words.

I sat up and then wearily rose to my feet. "We'll go in the morning. Right now, I need some sleep."

I awoke early the next day. My bed felt so comfortable compared to the sleeping bag that I'd slept in for an entire month, and I got to wear my soft nightie, which I hadn't thought to bring back to the past. Theresa was sound asleep on her stomach in a pair of pajamas Liam had kindly lent her. Theresa would always moan while she slept. I never asked what she dreamt of but I hoped it was of me.

I lifted my arms and stretched, squinting from the daylight, as there came a gentle knock on the door. "Come in," I said with a voice that wasn't quite awake. The door opened, and Liam entered the room.

"When are you leaving?" he asked.

"After I get some breakfast," I said.

"What about *her*?" he shot back, with a disparaging emphasis on the *her*.

"*Her* is my girlfriend," I yawned. "And she's coming with me. So is Ophelia."

"You should leave her here—Phee Phee, I mean," he insisted.

I glared at him. "'Phee Phee?' Really? I don't think she's safe with you!"

"Whatever!" He shrugged and then said, "I'll bring some breakfast up."

"You're so sweet," I yawned, this time covering my mouth.

"I was thinking of Mom and Dad," he went on. "I need to break it gradually that you're not really dead." He broke off and then predicted, "They're not going to believe me though."

"Of course, they will," I insisted. I threw my legs over the bed, shook my head to wake up some more, and then divided myself. I watched Liam's amazement as a Quantum Girl self rose from me.

"Fuck me!" he exclaimed under his breath.

"I *don't* think she can hear you from here," I said, ever so smugly.

"Shut *up*!" he said back in his defense.

The Payton me stretched and yawned again.

"I'll be staying here," the Payton me said.

"While I go try and save the world," the Quantum Girl me added and then clarified. "The *other* world."

An hour or so later—after heart-wrenchingly painful goodbyes between Liam and *Phee Phee*—Ophelia, Theresa, and my Quantum Girl self all held hands again as my Payton self and Liam watched. Pop went the air and we were back in Peyton and Ophelia's bedroom in the alternate world.

CHAPTER XXIV

It was nighttime there and the room was dark as coal. Then suddenly I felt cold metal against my left wrist followed by a ratchet sound.

"Gotcha!" I heard Thara-Klo say. "Again!"

It had been just over four weeks since Peyton had died. But that also meant that Khattaaara, reincarnated *as* Peyton, was dead for a second time. How many universes had to be born and then meet oblivion before Khattaaara was brought back to life? Are there gods who control our destiny or can that proverbial monkey, sitting at a keyboard, given a billion eternities, eventually type out the Lord of the Rings? Peyton and I, while different in our souls, were mirror images of each other down to the very rungs of our DNA. And now, much to my regret, I had inherited her immortal foe.

Thara-Klo thought she had me, but Theresa wouldn't let that happen. The fact of the matter is that she still had one of the hunting knives on her from when we went back in time. She had used it on rattlers and rabbits, but this time she used it on Thara-Klo.

"No, got *you*, bitch!" she said. as she stabbed her deep into the left side of the alien's chest. Thara-Klo collapsed instantly and fell, moaning in pain, on the floor. A hunting knife can make a mortal wound, even to someone from Rendenaaar with quantum powers.

"No one messes with my girl!" she spat out at her.

Thara-Klo looked at her and then stared at me, gasping for breath.

"What do we do with her?" Ophelia asked as she turned from Theresa to me.

Theresa stared hard at her victim. "I say we just cut her throat!" Then she dropped to her knees and placed the blade against Thara-Klo's neck.

"We *can't* do that," Ophelia insisted.

"Why the fuck not?" Theresa asked, anger in her throat. "She's the one responsible for your sister being dead!"

"What do you mean?" Thara-Klo moaned. "She's standing right there."

Theresa moved closer and glared into her eyes. "That's not her!" she said, filled with anger. "That's her double from a parallel world!"

"The Peyton you're looking for died in my arms after having been shot by your or because of you," I said. "I don't know which."

Thara-Klo appeared to have had a weight lifted from her. "You have no idea the danger she represented," she replied. She stared at me and then went on. "Even this one. If there's one of *her*, there must have been a Khattaaara."

I shook my head. "There isn't. There's nothing in my mind that remembers anything about Rendenaaar. Maybe in my dimension, your world just didn't exist."

"Let us hope, for your sake, that you're right," Thara-Klo replied.

"What's *that* supposed to mean?" Theresa edged in. She felt she was my protector, even though I was the one with the powers.

"It means, little girl, that Khattaaara Gaaalthaaara was probably the most evil woman who ever inhaled breath." Peyton's presumptive daughter was never one to mince words.

"That's the pot calling the kettle," Ophelia said.

"You were the one who destroyed worlds and civilizations," I added.

"Is *that* what my father told her?" There was an ironic smile on Thara-Klo's face as she said those words.

Ophelia spoke out next. "Peyton would never harm *anyone*!" she said defensively. I think she had defended her sister from the day she was old enough to speak.

"Your sister murdered uncounted billions of people," Thara-Klo insisted. "She destroyed Rendenaaaran and alien civilizations without a second thought. A hundred billion galaxies that once teemed with intelligent life were rendered dead and cold by her hand." The alien's voice showed no compassion.

"That was Khattaaara, not Peyton," I said.

"Just because she looks like her..." Ophelia added and would have said more but Thara-Klo interrupted.

"Do you think that Peyton Herron was the first of Khattaaara's reincarnations? Mother and I have had our run-ins before. Nearly every universe that I have lived through has spawned her rebirth. Each one had been so innocent until some random event would happen to then trigger the beast in her."

"Why should we trust you?" That was Theresa. She was the cat and I was her kitten— at least that's how she seemed to view *our* world.

Thara-Klo ignored her. Her attention was still on Ophelia. "Did your Peyton ever mention any dreams?"

"She always had nightmares," Phee answered. "but one occurred again and again—the same one since we were small."

Thara-Klo interjected. "A bright light. An explosion. Then excruciating pain."

Phee's eyes grew fixed as she took to remembering. "She'd wake up screaming that she was on fire. How did you know?"

"Because that's *how* Khattaaara died"

"Peyton was different," said Ophelia. "She would have fought it off."

"Perhaps, but now we'll never know." Thara-Klo winced from her pain and then went on. "And there's still the matter of Dhraaal."

"What about the man you killed that *I'm* now being blamed for?" My words were accusatory and to the point.

"A Chinese operative who infiltrated into the FBI. He got what he deserved."

I shook my head to myself. "I'm not sure what to believe anymore." I glanced at Theresa and Ophelia and then I looked at Thara-Klo. "I need these handcuffs off of me so I can get my powers back."

"The keys are in my jacket—outer pocket, lower left."

I searched her pocket for the key and found it and then unlocked the cuff from my wrist. Ophelia, meanwhile, went to the light switch on the wall and flicked it on. Thara-Klo, who was on her back, staring up, squinted from the sudden light.

"Ophelia," I started to say and then corrected myself with, "Phee." She turned and looked at me.

"Would you grab me some alcohol and bandages and towels?" I asked her. "I need to stop the bleeding."

Phee went to the bathroom. "I have a towel and bandages," she said, "but no alcohol—only Bactine."

"That'll have to do," I replied.

She returned it a moment later.

"I brought an Ace bandage, too," she said. "I thought we might be able to use it to hold the bandages in place."

"Good thinking," I replied. I was now on my knees beside my alien daughter. Phee squatted down on the other side of her and glared at Thara-Klo.

"You had better be telling the truth," she said and then glanced at me. "Help me get her jacket off."

I helped her, trying to ignore the sounds of Thara-Klo's pain from the ordeal. I unbuttoned her blouse then we turned her onto her back to reveal the stab wound. Both the blouse and the wound were stained with blue, the color of Rendenaaaran blood. I used a part of the towel to wipe the blood from her back and then offered her a corner of it.

"Better bite down hard," I said.

She nodded consent and I placed the bit of the towel in her mouth. Then I pulled back the Bactine cap and squirted some of the contents onto the wound. Thara-Klo screamed as loud as any person could when biting down on a rag.

"Burns like hell, doesn't it?" Phee said. "I can only imagine what my sister felt when she was shot."

But her words were wasted on the air. Thara-Klo had passed out from the pain. Regardless, I clapped a handcuff on one of her wrists. Ophelia and I then stood up. I looked at her and Theresa. I spoke to them in a somber tone.

"I can't be anywhere near here if I want to be Quantum Girl. Besides, this is the first place they'll come look for me."

"You can stay at my house," Theresa offered. "My mom doesn't have to know."

"You need to see Mom and Dad before you go, Ophelia chimed in." Her voice choked. "Just make them think you're her."

"No. That wouldn't be fair *to* her," I said.

Theresa stared down at Thara-Klo. "You two go. I'll stay with the Wicked Witch. I know how to deal with her kind."

Ophelia took my hand and led me to her parents' bedroom. She offered a gentle knock on the door, which was met with a sleepy, "Come in," from her mom.

Once inside the dark room, lit only by the light from the hall behind us, we found her parents who were mirror images of my own, but they were not my own. It was like being Alice Through the Looking Glass. This couple had raised two girls, whereas mine had raised a girl and a boy. In that alone, they had met with different challenges. Phee's father could never throw a ball with his son but rather had to contend to live with three females realizing that there would be no one to carry on his name. Yet in each case, on each world, there still remained that unconditional love that James Herron was capable of regardless of which dimension he was from. How strange though it seemed at the time and still does to this day that he wore the same pajamas that were pinstriped in blue.

"Mom? Dad?" said Phee as her mother yawned out her awakening.

Mrs. Herron was the first to sit up in the bed. She strained her eyes in the dimly lit room.

"Peyton?" Her voice was like a gasp. She nudged her husband. "James, wake up," she said.

Mr. Herron sat up in bed rubbing the sleep from his eyes, "What's going on?" he asked as he caught the outlines of Ophelia and me.

Then he reached over and switched on the lamp on his nightstand, took another look, and dropped his jaw.

"Oh, my God!" he exclaimed.

"We've heard so much on the news," Mrs. Herron said.

"They say you killed a man—a federal agent," James Herron said. He seemed beside himself.

Mrs. Herron rose from the bed and put on her robe. Then she walked over to Payton and seemed about to take her in her arms when Ophelia's voice broke the quiet that had taken hold.

"This isn't Peyton," she said.

The Katherine Herron of this world stared hard at me. "What do you mean?" she replied, "I know my own daughter."

"Yes, it's Payton," Phee said. "It's just not *our* Peyton."

By this time, James Herron had risen from bed and put on his robe and slippers.

"What sort of nonsense is all this?" he exclaimed with a definite edge to his voice. "If this is the story the two of you have concocted to tell the authorities…"

"It's not." Phee insisted. Then she turned to me. "Are you recovered enough to show them?"

"Not quite," I whispered to her.

"Show us what?" said the Katherine Herron of this world as she stared hard at both of us.

"It'll take a few more minutes," I whispered again.

"Well?" said a now grown impatient Mrs. Herron.

"If you want an explanation," Phee commanded, "you'll need to wait a moment or two." She paused, gathering strength. "The story on the news. It's all a lie. Do you remember about a year ago when we were all so concerned about her? I didn't know. You didn't know. It went a lot deeper than that. It got really bad." She glanced at me and then turned back to look at her parents—first her Mom and then her Dad.

"I know this is going to sound… unbelievable… but Peyton, *our*

168

Peyton, took her own life and a being from another time brought her back and put what he called a quantum seed in her head. He claimed that she was the reincarnation of a woman called Khattaaara. The quantum seed gave her powers."

Katherine shook her head. "Look, you two," she said, "this isn't funny."

"It's not meant to be." Phee was more serious than I had ever seen. "Anyway, yesterday... I think it was yesterday for you... Peyton was kidnapped by a woman from the past called Thara-Klo and she got Peyton shot. Fatally. But before she died she phased... teleported... into this Payton's dimension and gave *her* the quantum seed."

"You seriously expect us to believe this?" Mrs. Herron said, glancing at her husband.

"Remember how we found cuts on Peyton's arm?" Phee went on, undaunted. Then she turned to me. "Show them your left arm."

I extended it and pulled up my sleeve. Phee took hold of my arm and showed it to them. There was no evidence of any cuts or scars.

"Scars can heal," Mr. Herron said.

"There aren't any scars," Phee insisted, "because this isn't *our* Peyton."

Then she turned to me. "Are you good to go?" she asked.

I took a deep breath. Enough time had elapsed. I could hear the drop of water that dripped from the faucet in the adjacent bathroom and splashed into the sink. Three other heartbeats thudded rhythmically out of sync in the room I was in and there was a fourth in the distance and a fifth that sounded somehow discordant from the rest. "I think so," I said. My words seemed to echo through the air.

"Show them," Phee said, letting go of my arm.

And so I transformed into Quantum Girl right before their eyes.

"Merciful God in Heaven!" Katherine Herron exclaimed as she stood frozen, staring at me, her eyes fixed, unblinking, as James, his gaze also transfixed, slowly walked up beside her, and took her hand in his.

169

"I think they need a moment," Phee quietly said to me as I became myself again. She stared up at her father who swallowed hard and then gently embraced his wife.

"Come on," she said to me and we quietly left the room.

As we descended the stairs, I could hear the woman who was the image of my own mother crying. How she must have felt. Once when I was six years old I had wandered off. We were in a shopping mall and somehow I became separated from Liam and my Mom. I'd gotten distracted by a toy that we had passed. It was a robot girl that talked to me and asked me my name. But when my mother noticed I was gone she became frantic. She held onto Liam's hand and began rushing through the aisles, calling out my name until at last, she found me. She knelt down and grabbed me in her arms so tight I felt I couldn't breathe. There were tears streaming down her cheeks.

"Don't you ever do that again," she kept saying over and over. Then she loosened her grip, held me by my shoulders, and looked at me through tear-drenched eyes.

"I'm sorry," I said. "I was just talking to the robot girl. Are you okay?"

She wiped her tears with the backs of her hands. "I'm fine," she said, "but you always need to stay with me. Mommy loves you so much!"

"Do you love *me*, too?" Liam asked.

"Of course, I do," she replied as she started to cry again. "I love you both." Her arms reached out and embraced us and both of us began to cry with her.

"I hope she doesn't kill her," Phee said, as she stood at a window staring out. As for me, I was sitting in an overstuffed chair in the living room, my legs hanging over one of the arms and leaning back against the other.

"Theresa?" I replied. "She's gentle as a newborn…"

"Crocodile?" Phee interjected.

"I *was* going to say lamb," I replied.

"Hah!" she uttered under her breath in the dark of the room.

"I thought you two were starting to get along?" I said.

She turned to face me. "Just because I handle a gun," she replied, "doesn't mean I feel safe staring down the barrel." She paused and then added, "They're watching the house."

"I know," I said. "I can hear their radios. I can hear *them*. There are two in one car. One is rubbing his hands together from the cold. The other is sipping coffee."

She stared at me. "How do you do that?" she asked.

"I don't know," I replied. "Enhanced senses. They're just a part of me now." I looked at her. "Does it bother you that she's a lesbian, because *I'm* one, too?" I paused and then added, "I *didn't* choose how I am."

"That doesn't bother me," she replied. "It wouldn't bother me if you were *my* Peyton and if *she* were gay. Right now though, we need to focus on what to do with Thara-Klo." She paused and then admitted, "Theresa's just a bit too streetwise for me. And I like you, Payton. I really do. But I miss my sister so much."

What went on between Theresa and Thara-Klo while they were alone together I didn't learn until much later. Apparently, Thara-Klo brought Theresa to tears, reminding her that her actions caused my mirror image to take her own life. From that came a bit of perspective into a woman, whom I myself at that time did not understand. Thara-Klo it seemed was not the ruthless enemy that Peyton and I had perceived her to be. Despite what she had done to Peyton, her actions had been predicated on wanting to save humanity. Here was a woman who was not only an extraterrestrial but alien to our universe, who wanted to save us all from the demon that had laid dormant in the girl who looked like me.

Now presumably there was an end to all that—at least as far this universe went—but there was still the matter of the threat, not only to me, which was irrelevant as I had a place to go, having another dimension in which to hide, but to Peyton's family members who now all had targets on their backs. Each of them had been questioned after the murder that Thara-Klo had staged in Peyton's likeness. I had an obligation to her—to Peyton—a promise I had made. Somehow, now, her final words took on a grander meaning. Her world was not just the planet she lived on but those three people whom she unconditionally loved. Somehow, looking at them, it was as though they were my family, too. Peyton Elise and Payton Alise might have been two separate people but we were connected in unimaginable ways down to the coding in our cells. Her fight was now my fight. Their lives were now my responsibility and I would protect them with my dying breath.

When Ophelia and I finally led her parents into her bedroom, we found Theresa sitting on the carpet, clutching her knees in an almost fetal position. Thara-Klo still lay bandaged on the floor, her face turned away, the cerulean blood on her blouse that had bled through the dressing now coagulated to the color of night.

"Dear God!" Katherine Herron exclaimed as she saw my mirror's daughter pale as falling snow. "This is not how Christians treat others, no matter what."

She rushed over to Thara-Klo, squatted down, gently turned her head toward her, and gasped.

"Hello, Ladybug," Thara-Klo said so softly that only Katherine and I could hear.

Katherine Herron stood up as though she had seen a ghost then took several steps back.

"What's wrong?" Phee said, concerned.

"How can it be?" Katherine Herron said as she stared at her, her eyes glazed.

Phee took her by the shoulders and looked at her.

"How can *what* be?" she asked.

"She hasn't aged a day," came the frightened reply.

"What do you mean?" Phee asked.

"Aunt Sarah," her mother said.

"No, that's Thara, not Sarah," Phee insisted. "Thara-Klo."

Katherine Herron's gaze turned to her daughter.

"She's my mother's sister, the aunt I've talked about so much. But I thought she had died long ago when I was a little girl. I don't understand. It's been forty years, but she hasn't aged one bit." Then she found her strength and turned to her husband.

"James. Pick her up," she said, "*gently*. Then lay her down on Peyton's bed."

Mr. Herron walked over to Thara-Klo and lifted her in his arms while she entangled her fingers behind his neck. The effect of his act, however, was to cause her open blouse to fall away, revealing her double pair of breasts. It was obvious that he noticed them as he set her down on the bed.

"Thank you, love," she said as she unlocked her fingers and let her arms fall to her sides. There was no modesty in her to be had, but the family man, obviously nonplussed by the revelation, quickly turned his head away.

I went over to her, brushing past him as I did, and brought the two sides of her blouse back together over her, buttoning her up.

"We're trying to help you," I said to her under my breath. "You don't have to return the favor by trying to destroy their marriage."

"Now, now, Quantum Girl," she quietly said back to me and smiled. "He's a universe and a half too young for my taste."

I sneered at her and shook my head. Then I turned to the others in the room.

"We should change her bandages," Katherine Herron said.

"And put one over her mouth." That was from me. Regardless that Thara-Klo appeared to be on our side I still was bothered by how her words seemed to gain her such favor as quickly as they had. I wanted it to have come more slowly. But, then, I was the only one who had seen Peyton die.

The James Herron of this dimension had gone over to his wife and was holding her in his arms to try and allay any anxieties she might have had from having just been reunited with her immortal aunt.

"I just wish there was some way to bring our Peyton back," Ophelia lamented. It wasn't as though she thought it could actually happen, but I suppose being in the presence of two people with superhuman powers can make one believe that the impossible isn't out of reach.

Thara-Klo broke in. "There is," she said.

Katherine looked up from her husband's embrace and stared with blurry eyes at Thara-Klo. "What do you mean?" she asked, as a spark of hope raised within her.

Phee also brightened at Thara-Klo's words, as her imagination took hold and as Thra-Klo went on. "Payton—this Payton—can go back in time and undo it all."

"I've thought about that," I said, "but it would create a paradox."

"What do you mean?" Phee said, staring at me. Then she turned toward Thara-Klo, as the alien woman gave response.

"If she goes back and prevents her from getting shot," she explained, "our Peyton would never have traveled to her dimension and turned her into Quantum Girl, meaning she could never have gone back to save her."

"Worse," I added, "it might even create an irreversible time loop. It's not worth the risk."

"So, how do we do it?" Phee asked.

Thara-Klo provided the answer. "She goes back to her own dimension a split second before Peyton died, just after she had placed the god-stone in this Payton's head. Freezing time, she then merges herself with Peyton, which would heal her, and then phases back out of her into her former self, leaving our Peyton intact and with the god-stone in *her* head." She paused and then went on. "Understand there is a possibility that afterward. you will forget everything that's happened since."

"That means she'll forget everything about me," Theresa said, suddenly upset.

"Wait!" I said. "Why can't I just emerge from Peyton as me? I realize there will then be two of me, but Peyton could bring this me back here."

Thera-Klo shook her head. "You need to remember that the god-stone in your head is the exact same one as the one in *her* head. They are just from two different times. But it exists apart *from* time, so there is really only one. As it is, after she comes into herself, you will barely have enough willpower to phase out. Merging back into your former self is your only option short of you yourself ceasing to exist."

I shrugged. "We need to do this," I said. "It's Peyton's life."

"I suppose," said a saddened Theresa.

"This is all really difficult for me to take in," Katherine Herron said to her husband. "My aunt, who is not really my aunt, is Peyton's daughter from a different life. And Peyton. Oh my God, Peyton!" She pulled back to look at him. "James, I will tell you here and now that if we can't get her back I pray the Lord Jesus will take me from this Earth and bring me to her whether it's in Heaven or Rendenaaar or wherever dead souls go."

"Let's just pray that all of this works," James said. "Besides, you have another daughter who needs you and a husband who loves you. You're just as important a part of *our* lives."

The woman stared back at him and shrugged with half a smile. Then she turned her head toward Phee.

"Ophelia," she said. "We need to take care of this woman, whoever she is, till she recovers. You go get her the Bible on my nightstand. Maybe we can teach her the meaning of a righteous life in this universe."

"Yes, Ma'am," came the reply.

Katherine Herron looked toward Thara-Klo. "I'll call Emma to tend her wound," adding, "She can be trusted."

"Who's Emma?" I asked.

"A doctor," Phee explained. "Mom's best friend,"

"Not on *my* world," I said.

Phee turned to her father.

"What do we do with her after she's healed?" she asked.

"We let her go," Theresa broke in, glancing at the alien being. "She's promised to not harm Peyton—either one. I gave her my word she'd go free."

"She did," said the alien woman. "And *I* gave her mine."

Changing the subject, I announced, "I need to get some sleep."

"We all do," said Phee.

"Theresa and I will head over to her house," I said. "Phee, it's been great having a sister."

"You be well," she replied.

Theresa looked at me. "Come on," she said.

Phee went to the window and stared out. "Guys? There are now five cop cars outside."

"Shit!" Theresa shook her head. "I knew staying here was a bad idea."

"I can't phase through space with those cuffs in the house," I said.

Phee tossed the key to Theresa. "Here," she said as she motioned toward Thara-Klo. "Take them off of her,"

"There's still the question of what to do with them when they're off," I shrugged.

Theresa went over to Thara-Klo. "Don't worry", she said. "I'll take care of them." She then put the key in the lock of the one around Thara-Klo's wrist. I could hear the click as the cuff snapped open. "Just to let you know," she said in a low voice. "you'll have to kill me, too, if you break your word and try to harm my girl."

"Understood," came the alien woman's reply.

"Got 'em," Theresa announced, as she stood up, handcuffs in hand. Then she went over and stood before me, her eyes now wet with tears. With a sudden move, she wrapped her arms around my neck and kissed me passionately. My arms went under hers. My fingers embraced her back as I returned the kiss with equal emotion. All too soon, it seemed, both of us let go. She backed up a step, stared at me one more time, and then turned and went to the door.

"Good luck," Phee said, as Theresa was about to leave.

"Be careful," I added.

"I've got it covered," Theresa responded and then she left the room.

In another minute she was outside the house. In that I had quantum hearing, I could follow the conversation. Apparently, a couple of the cops had stopped her after she went out the front door. "*¿Por qué la policía siempre acosa a mi gente? Tengo derechos, sabes. Necesito ir a casa. Mi madre me espera,*" she said with irritation, meaning, "Why do the cops always harass my people? I have rights, you know. I need to go home. My mother is waiting for me."

One cop then said to the other, "You don't happen to speak Spanish, do you?" at which point the other cop interrupted him, and said, "Look at my name tag. Moretti. *Capisco l'italiano*, not *Español*. Just let her go. She's not our suspect." Then he said to Theresa, "You can go. Vamoose. Amscray." At which point Theresa said back, "*Digan lo que digan, pedazos de mierda,*" which means, "Whatever you say, you fucking pieces of shit." To which the same cop replied, "Yeah, yeah. Just get out of here. We've got work to do."

The next morning found me naked in the middle of the room, with Phee, who had just walked in, staring at me.

"Why are you…"

"Naked?" I finished for her. "Because I'm going back to the moment when I *was* naked. I was in the shower when Peyton phased into my dimension. Besides, I don't know what effect wearing clothes would have on whomever I phase into."

"I guess that makes sense," Phee admitted.

"Smart girl," Thara-Klo replied. "You wouldn't want to phase a second set of clothes onto your host."

"I'm just scared," I said. "If I succeed, I forget everything. If I fail, I have to watch her die all over again."

Phee looked at me and smiled. "You'll do just fine," she replied.

"Gods, I hope so," I said, despite that I had become a nonbeliever.

Thara-Klo stared at me with questions in her eyes. "So which gods do your people worship?"

"The same as here," I said, "only we count them as three."

"How vain your people are," she replied. "First, you believed that the Earth was the center of the universe and when that was disproved, you contended that out of all the length and width and breadth of your universe, man himself is the glorified reflection of the supposéd creator of it all."

"*Some*body's destined for Hell," Phee whispered to me.

"Don't look at *me*," I whispered back, "I'm a Gods-fearing atheist."

"I'm not deaf, you know," said the woman from Rendenaaar. "Just injured."

And with those words, I closed my eyes, focused my thoughts, and sent myself back to my dimension and back in time.

CHAPTER XXV

Over the past six months, having somewhat mastered the abilities I was given, I found myself in the bathtub, standing behind my former self who knelt facing my mortally injured mirror twin. I made certain, however, to arrive out of time-phase from them, which meant that I was actually moving thousands of times faster than they were and appeared in jumps so that neither of them could see me as I found the precise moment to do what I had come for, which was to phase into Peyton to heal her wound.

Having missed my mark at first, I backed up time and then caused it to go forward again, the entire action appearing like some movie where the editor had wreaked havoc in the cutting room. Finally, it came. Peyton, dying, stretched out her arm to implant the quantum seed in my past self's head. I stopped time then as horror gripped my very bones. We had talked about paradoxes. In fact, I had been the one to suggest the possibility. But now, if I prevented myself from becoming Quantum Girl, who would go back to save Peyton? But perhaps this was different. I was affecting the past in a way that she would not need saving again. With that hope, I took a deep breath, restarted time, and phased myself into her.

It was an odd feeling to share a consciousness with someone else. It was odder still to realize that there were two individual minds that I was sharing this body with. I felt her pain from having been shot. I felt the fear from her realizing her own mortality. I felt the anguish that she had suffered before she took her own life. There was the hopelessness of her suicide and there was the loneliness that came from the billions of years she had spent waiting for the universe to re-form and for all the time she had to wade through for her to be born again. And then there was the other—an older Quantum Girl—who had not anticipated such a quick and early death. All of this merged with my consciousness in an instant. But it was her body and not her soul that I had traveled back here to heal. And so, before the quantum seed she had given me phased with the one in her head, I used a command I had learned, which apparently she had not, to reverse time just within those tissues that were injured and bring them back to their original, healthy state. In but an instant, then, she was healed. Quickly, I gave the seed one final command as it merged with *its* former self, and that was to phase me into the Payton who stood kneeling over me, thinking over and over again, *Theresa, Theresa, Theresa* for all the good it would do me, separated from her probably for all time by the irony of quantum dimensions.

I remember wondering what she was doing here in my bathroom in my bathtub with me naked, kneeling before her. I wondered why there was so much blood on both of us and in the tub. I didn't think it was mine and she didn't appear to be wounded in any way. It was then that she opened her eyes, blinking several times as though to clear her head.

Here I was though, naked again with her next to me. I remembered thinking how much of a turn-on it could have been to have actually had sex with her, having hinted it so many times that I lost count, but, alas, she leaned toward straight, and how oxymoronic is that? Yet, so much of a self-fulfilling orgasm it would have been, I thought, to make love to my other dimensional self? I had half-heartedly hoped that she would see the effect these thoughts were having on my breasts. It wasn't as if I were involved with anyone. Nor did I find it morally wrong. This was the excuse I gave myself for having such fantasies.

"I'm not sure what just happened," she said, "but I seem to be okay." She paused, looking down at herself, feeling her chest with her hands.

"I thought this was some sort of joke about how we first met," I said, uncertain.

"No," she insisted, and her eyes glazed in thought. "I distinctly remember trying to escape from Thara-Klo and then being shot and coming here. There's blood everywhere," she went on, " but I don't appear to be injured in any way."

She was staring down at herself and poked her index finger through what appeared to be a bullet hole in the front of her blouse.

"I'm so glad you're okay," I said as I looked into her eyes. Then, without even thinking, I lunged forward and kissed her on the lips. I could sense it was a bit awkward for her as there was no response *from* her. I broke away and took a step back. "I'm sorry," I said, suddenly feeling ashamed.

"Hey," she said back, "you kiss on par with Theresa."

I looked at her questioningly.

"Forget I said that," she went on.

"So if you did get shot," I asked, "what just happened? How are you all healed?"

"I don't know," she replied.

"Maybe it was the god-stone," I said.

Peyton's face turned pale. "Why would you call it that?" she asked.

"Beats me," I replied. "It just popped into my head. Did I say something wrong?"

"No," she said, shrugging it off. "It's nothing. Anyway, I need to get back."

"Of course, you do," I said to her. Then I glanced down at myself and remembered that I was naked. "You know, I'm standing here in my birthday suit," I reminded her.

"Nothing I haven't seen before," she replied.

She stepped out of the shower, grabbed my robe that was hanging on a hook, and tossed it to me.

"Thanks," I said as I began to put it on. Then I stared off into the distance. "You know, it would have been nice to have power coursing through *my* veins, even if just for a day." I took a deep breath and sighed. "Another goodbye and I hope not the last. I've missed you. Don't be a stranger too long."

181

"I won't," she said and smiled. Then she became Quantum Girl again for the umpteenth time and, just like that, with a pop, she was gone.

CHAPTER XXVI

Khattaaara

I was in what looked like a nebula, colored light all around, motionless in a void without sound and yet still able to breathe despite that there was no air. Nothing was familiar. I had no idea how long I had been unconscious but I remembered the quantum force that had engulfed me, as my loathsome daughter smiled while the energy bled through me. I remembered the thoughts of betrayal and the pain—the unbearable, excruciating pain.

But where was Rendenaaar? Where was *I*? The thought crossed my mind that this was neither time nor space but the realm of the god-stones. I could still feel a god-stone in my head but it was different. It was not the mother stone. It was one of the lessers. Of the seven known god-stones, mine had been the most powerful but then why should it not have been? *After all*, I thought to myself, *I am Khattaaara Gaaalthaaara.* I alone with my mother stone had the power of creation and resurrection. Was it not true that when Dhraaal was murdered by our own daughter, his atoms scattered even beyond the galaxies, I alone brought back the very quants that had comprised them and reassembled them back into my husband? Could I not uncreate worlds or civilizations at my whim? Did not vile creatures grovel at my feet, begging me to allow their continued existence as they both feared and worshipped me—petty beings, who drew forth both my anger and my wrath such that I should even waste my time upon the insignificance of their lives? And yet, here I was, alone without my harem of men and women to satisfy my hunger and feed my sexual desires. Could this be the *Gollinkaaar*? Could it be that I had passed beyond life's constraints? But if so, why should I be here alone? The only other explanation was, as brought forth by *Torrlaaagh*, that a paradox had been created, and thus was I trapped between dimensions. Normally, it would have been simple enough

183

for me to reenter any quantum plane but something was wrong. As I stared down at the purple glow that radiated from my arms, I realized that it was Dhraaal's god-stone that was now in my head! How could that be? I wondered. It was I who had purloined the seven, with the six, each subordinate to the one. How foolish I considered myself afterward to not have kept them all. I wondered what could have become of mine and what fate might have befallen Dhraaal that I now possessed his stone. Still, mine must yet exist. Once created, no god-stone can ever be destroyed. It is the only thing that can defy the end of time. *Perhaps*, I thought to myself, *the god-stone in my head might somehow link to at least one of the others to help me find the dimension to which I belonged.* Then, suddenly, I found myself with gravity beneath my feet, standing in a room, unlike anything on Rendenaaar.

Aside from the fact that both the architecture and furnishings were primitive, there were four other people there with me—an adolescent female, an older female, and an older male, and there on one of the beds was my impetuous daughter looking years older than I had ever known her to be. *Dear, Thara,* I thought to myself, *how is it that after all this time we find ourselves together once more?* The girl said something to me in words I did not understand. Looking around, I saw my reflection in what was apparently an image refabricator. I was garbed in some odd-looking costume, similar to those worn by the Zaaaartharians in the Iaanthran galaxy. There was a covering over my head and face and most of the upper portion of my body, though my legs, I noticed, were bare. *How odd*, I thought, *that the fabric appears as though it were some sort of astronomical window.* But strangest of all was that my skin was radiating light from the upper spectrum. Had I somehow become radioactive? Were these pieces of clothing designed to shield others from the radiation or were they created to enhance my own abilities? Also, I appeared about two cycles younger than Thara-Klo; perhaps the same age as the adolescent female that stood several *boraaag* from me. Could some unknown phenomenon have time-phased me into my former self? *But wait*, I thought, as my gaze fell down to my chest. *Where is my lower pair of khalthraaam?*[12] And then as I looked back behind me my heart nearly stopped. My *yaaargh* was gone! How was that possible? What sort of madness was this to reappear disfigured? Rendenaaaran orgasm can only be achieved when a female's *yaaargh* pairs with a male's, as he enters hers with his, or when stimulated orally, male or female, it doesn't matter which. To think that I had been somehow mutilated—to never again be sexually gratified—filled me with rage.

"*Gwaaash ric frum? Gwaaash ric fruuum?*" I said and then I turned to my miserable excuse for a daughter. "*Kaaale nordr niiikk?*" I demanded.

The girl uttered something incomprehensible once more to which my daughter responded with words that were similarly foreign to me. *How dare she interrupt my question!* I thought to myself. *How dare Thara-Klo do the same! The girl must be punished!* As the child took steps toward me. anger fomented in my veins. *How dare the creature approach the empress of the universe without our permission!* None of these vile *straaagaaan* had paid obeisance to me. None had lowered their eyes or laid prostrate upon the ground in my presence. Dare they even choose to breathe the same air as me without acknowledging that I, Khattaaara Gaaalthaaara, am their god! Without another thought, I hurled an energy blast at the girl, threw her against the far wall, and pinned her there, high above the floor so that she squirmed like a *baaathrag* that was caught in a net. Then, as insolent as ever, Thara-Klo, projected an energy field to protect her with one hand and aimed a blast at me with the other, which I countered with a blast of my own; my own daughter—she who had emerged from my *yaaargh*, whom I had loved and tried to teach the ethics of unlimited power. The girl shouted something to the two adults who stood frozen like *zraaagdmms*, when they find themselves about to be attacked. I was about to destroy them all when it occurred

---

[12] Pronounced K'*hal* tah rahm.

to me that these must be my daughter's pets, so I hesitated. The whole situation was alien to me. I needed time to figure out what had happened. Truly, but for the mutilation (which perhaps I could later fix) I did not mind my being in my younger self, but there were other considerations. How did this all happen? Where precisely was I? And what had beset both me and my world since the blast had derailed my conscious train of thought? Thus, did I raise my arms and hurl out a blast of energy that ripped a hole to the sky. I shifted out into it. Looking downward at the primitive structures and upward at the sky that revealed only one great star that shown yellow, not orange with no sign of Rendenaaar's sister planet or its moons. No, this was some other world.

I shifted again and again to various parts of this locality until I found myself standing in what appeared to be an ancient city. There were other beings all around me, some in metal conveyances that rolled along the ground. Such was the case on Rendenaaar in ancient times, a thousand or more cycles ago but this was not my world. Nor had I in all of my encounters seen anything like it. It made me pause and wonder to what far reaches of the universe had I traveled and why of the hundred or so planets that I had left inhabitable was Thara-Klo also here. I needed to know.

As I stood there I noticed many of the inhabitants turn and stare at me. I assumed it was because of the odd clothing that I wore that in no way resembled whatever fashion in which they themselves were attired. In front of me was a window, behind which were statues, dressed similarly to those looking at me. I willed the costume I was wearing out of existence and then replicated attire onto me such as clothed one of the female statues that I might attract less attention. Wherever I was, it was nearly intolerable. There were multitudes of individuals that chattered incoherently and pushed this way and that to get to wherever they were going. The conveyances were noisy and spewed filth into the air. But worst of all were the odors of the inhabitants themselves, each different and each equally offensive to my nostrils. How they could tolerate being around each other mystified me. I tried my best to tamp down the olfactory portion of my brain so that it might lessen the nauseating effects. Regardless, I stood where I was and surveyed my surroundings.

The god-stone in my head allowed me to view through objects many *jaaaruns* in each direction. A short distance away I detected a concentration of radio emissions and so it was that to there that I proceeded to go. My senses led me to a structure with large glass windows, each with a somewhat circular grey emblem on it at its center. I walked inside into a throng of inhabitants gathered around tables with devices that displayed moving images. They, however, did not interest me as much as the devices' connectivity to what these beings called the Internet. Going up to one of them, I was able to mentally link with it and selectively acquire its knowledge.

I learned that I was on a planet called Earth, at least in the language of this region. The human species as they called themselves had existed for approximately one hundred thousand of their planetary cycles, their civilizations for only five thousand, and their electronic technology for only one hundred. They had no conception of how to accomplish faster-than-light speed or time travel. They were ignorant of quantum architecture and were subject to the irrational belief, as had been the case with so many other primitive civilizations that I have encountered, that some supreme being favored them after having created them in its own image, and would eventually reward them with eternal existence if they were faithful to it or else be banished to some realm of endless torture.

Physically, oddly enough, these creatures were similar to Gaaalthaaarans with the exception that the female of the species possessed rounded ears similar to our males and with only a single pair of *khalthraaam*, which they call breasts. The *yaaargh* or tail is conspicuously absent in both sexes. Meanwhile, the equivalent of the male *yaaargh* is anatomically referred to as the penis and presents itself in the lower front of the male groin, while the female equivalent, called the vagina, is recessed *into* her groin. But unlike how Gaaalthaaaran sexual organs are located within their *yaaargh* well behind them, humans have theirs in close proximity to their excretory orifices, which I find rather disgusting. Furthermore, the insertion of the penis into the vagina relies on a continual thrusting action rather than upon the automatic stimulation and expansion of the *fhalthraaa* on the outer surface of the male *yaaargh* within the *afraaadim* that lines the inner surface of the female's.

Politically, the various nations on Earth have for thousands of their cycles existed in an extremely chaotic state, for with more than sixty-five hundred languages spoken, communication between them had often proved difficult if not impractical. Like unto the world of Rendenaaar, however, their species is divided into three major groups, though not as dissimilar as ours. Slavery was also a practice by the authoritarian groups, though oddly enough, for the most part, eventually abandoned.[13] And, as was the case on so many other worlds, one of their greatest *achievements* lay in their ability to wage war against each other and their *inability* to leave their own planet. Each nation, divided from the others, wished to control as much of the planet's land surface as possible while continuing to populate it far beyond its own sustainability.

These were my thoughts as I projected images and sounds at voluminous speed into the air in front of me that only I could hear or see. My attention to all of this was interrupted by one of the male creatures who had approached me.

"May I help you with anything?" he said in that language that the local inhabitants call English.

As he spoke, doing my best to ignore him, I found what I was looking for. There was a news article, which featured a man calling himself Thomas Drall who was the CEO of Quantech Labs in a place called Constance, Arizona. As the man stood there, waiting for my response, I answered, "No, thank you. I'm just looking," and then

---

[13] I say, "for the most part," due to circumstances, which will later be made clear.

shifted back to the room I had first found myself in. I accelerated myself so that I could do what I wanted between instants of time. Once, when I was new to the powers of the god-stones, I had frozen time entirely only to find that light was also at a standstill, which made it impossible to see, while the atoms and molecules of the air became immovable barriers. The room now only held two individuals—my daughter. and the adolescent girl—neither of whom had any awareness of my presence. I scavenged around until I found a red messenger bag that had apparently belonged to me or rather to the girl whose body in which I had awakened. Inside was a wallet with a driver's license and a student ID, each with her—now my— my photograph and with a name that read, "Peyton Elise Herron," whom it revealed had been born fifteen earth years ago. There were also images of her with the girl in the room, as well as the two adults I had seen when I had first arrived. But there were none of her with Thara-Klo. Inside the bag were also various items, such as I had learned were makeup, keys, currency, and coins. Odd, I thought, that there should be no weapons. But considering the fact that this body had all of Dhraaal's powers, she wouldn't have needed them. The question I asked myself, though, was why she should look so much like me when I was her age and how did I wind up, not only *in* her but with dominance over her mind? Even as I had these thoughts, I could feel an onrush of some of her memories. The girl in the room was her sister, Ophelia. The adults were her parents. And she considered Thara-Klo her mortal enemy, which was strange in that my daughter now occupied *her* bed. These were questions that I wanted answers to. It was with that in mind that I decided to shift to where Dhraaal was, with the perplexity that all of us were on this planet in some galaxy that I had neither heard of nor seen, that the denizens of this *nation* called the Milky Way.

Dhraaal was standing at a window with his back toward me as I shifted or, in keeping with the memories of this body's former inhabitant, *phased* into his office. He was dressed in what these people called a suit. The room was furnished with what in retrospect were fine quality antiques but there was nothing of Rendenaaar here and that saddened me. There was so much culture in our society, so much art, so much that represented the lives and worth of our great civilization that rendered it supreme in the universe. But here were only artifacts of a primitive culture that seemed so banal to me.

"Good morning, Husband," I said. I may have said it in Gaaalthaaaran. I don't recall.

Dhraaal wheeled around, somewhat taken aback, but as was his style he kept his cool.

"I wondered how long it would take your consciousness to supplant that of your reincarnation," he said with just a hint of a smile.

"That explains a *few* things," I replied.

"You were very confused I dare say," he said. "Took your own life. I had to go to great pains to resurrect you." He stared hard at me. "You *are* feeling better now, I assume."

"For the most part," I replied. "Only what happened to my *khalthraaam* and my *yaaargh*, not to mention," I went on, as I walked over to a mirror that hung on one wall and ruefully pulled my hair away to one side, "my ear*s*?"

Dhraaal was hesitant in his response. "The creatures here," he said and then paused. "They call themselves human; something to do with their self-perceived compassion toward the world. Their females, sadly, only have one pair of *khalthraaam,* and, as for your ears and *yaaargh*, it all appears to be a bit of an oversight by their allegéd creator. But, as they say, if you eat a bowl of cherries, you need to deal with the pits."

"What's that supposed to mean?" I asked.

"It means you need to be grateful that you're finally alive again," he said then went on. "You were very fragile. But there were things I saw that went beyond physical appearance that assured me that it *was* you reborn."

"And so you gave me your god-stone," I said, somewhat taken

aback by the sacrifice.

"I had to protect you from our willful child," he said and then asked, "How long have you been conscious?"

"About an hour their time," I replied. I then asked him, "Where exactly are we? I don't recall this planet."

"That's because we're not in our universe," came his grave response. "Ours ended almost beyond the reach of memory."

I began to move toward him.

"Really," I pondered with the uttered word. "Is this the next one?"

"Try a trillion," he said with a sigh.

Having reached him, I wrapped my arms around his neck.

"And in all that time," I said with a smile, "you waited for me to be reborn."

"There was always something special between us, you and I," he admitted, "my dear sister."

"No dalliances?" I asked.

"Nothing of any significance," came the stoic response.

"I know I would have done the same," I said with reassurance. And then I kissed him. How many lifetimes, how many eons, how many deaths and births of existence had he waited for that kiss? "Can we go somewhere more conducive to," and I hesitated to repeat the word, "dalliances?"—this after my mouth had lingered long enough against his.

"We can go to my home," he said.

"Lead the way," I responded, taking his hand in mine.

We drove down a road to his home in a transportation device called a Lamborghini. The vehicle or race car, as he called it, had individual seats but was exposed to the open air. Dhraaal caused the vehicle to travel at what I considered a reckless velocity, considering the fact that he no longer possessed a god-stone to protect him. My long hair blew freely in the turbulence created by the air that passed over and around us. Such was the volume of sound it created that we had to shout to each other to compete with the wind—at least I had to shout to him. He needn't have shouted back. I could have heard him in a hurricane with the god-stone in my head.

"Whatever became of the mother stone after Thara-Klo sent me into oblivion?" I shouted against the deafening current of air.

"She took it for herself," Dhraaal shouted back.

"I just saw her!" I shouted.

"Really…" he replied.

"She was in the house I appeared in just after I awakened in the quantum fabric!" I brushed away the hair that had blown across my face. "How long have you been on this planet?" I shouted out.

"Thousands of years," he shouted back. "Since ancient times on this world! I have lived many lives and had many names—Alexander, Caesar, Leonardo, Copernicus, Newton, and on and on! The god-stone led me to this planet but it could not pinpoint the exact time. I just needed to be certain I arrived before and not after you were reborn!"

"And our daughter?" I called back.

"About eighty years as best I can determine! Shrewd one that girl! Took to raising your incarnate's grandmother!"

Suddenly, he slowed down the vehicle. There was a large building before us made of brick and stone, attractive in its own way. He drove the car onto a semicircular driveway and then stopped. I took a deep breath and then let it out.

"Well, my dear," he said. "At long last—home."

"That *ride* was exhilarating," I told him. "But the wind and the noise were a bit much."

Dhraaal just smiled. I have to admit though… the speed, the open air, the illusion of danger all gave me a rush. My heart was pounding in my chest. The memory of a rollercoaster flashed into my mind but that was an Earth experience—one lived through by the girl who was but wasn't me. Dhraaal emerged from his side of the conveyance and then walked around to where I was sitting and opened the door for me. He took my hand to help me out. As we stood there, side by side,

I turned to him.

"What happened to the others?" I asked.

Dhraaal looked at me and shrugged. "I have no idea. For all I know they may have fled to other dimensions."

"I miss Shaaalra," I admitted.

"You and she had quite an affection for each other," he said.

"Purely sexual, but enjoyable nonetheless," I replied, trying my best to remember.

Dhraaal took my hand once more and led me to the entrance, which stood twice our height with a window positioned above the soft-colored wooden double doors with serpentine shapes that appeared to dance across their surfaces. The window was framed in ornately carved wood and was comprised of five tall panels made up of bits of colored glass that displayed a landscape behind flowers and vegetation that he later told me had been made long ago by a man named Louis Comfort Tiffany.

As we stood at the twin doors that guarded the entrance, Dhraaal paused. "We're going to need to capture Thara-Klo," he said, his eyes fixed upon the door in front of him. "Without the stone from her head, I'm doomed to turn into cosmic dust in the course of a few decades."

He unlocked the doors by pressing some numbers that were mounted on a shallow metal square to one side. A small light flickered from red to green. There was a soft click and then the lever on the door gave way, turning clockwise through the movement of his hand. Both doors then swung inward, revealing a large entry hall that led to the rest of the house.

The inside of Dhraaal's home was in a strange way magnificent. It was decorated profusely with furniture and statues that he said were called art nouveau. The shapes were all fluid, with intricate designs and flowing curves.

"So, what are your plans afterward?" I asked, staring down and running my fingers around the rim of a bronze vase.

"If we can retrieve the mother stone," he replied, "we can use it to awaken every one of our race into the bodies of these humans."

"Rendenaaar can be born again," I said, envisioning how magnificent that would be, and yet I thought back to how that world had rebelled against me in the end.

"Yes," Dhraaal said in presumptive triumph. "To hell with these insects that people this world."

"To hell with them!" I echoed. "Now, take me to your bedchamber and make love to me," and I turned and stared at him, my husband, who had stood ever-vigilant, watching for me, waiting like a gluttonous male who's starved and has hungered for that one special delicacy.

CHAPTER XXVII

Payton

It was late at night, as I stood outside Liam's bedroom door and knocked. The door opened, and Liam stood facing me on the other side.

"I guess you're through brooding in your room," he said.

"I've had flashes of things," I said back, "like it was a memory. I had superpowers, and there was this girl. You were there and—I think her name was Ophelia—and she had a crush on you and you on her."

"I'm sure I'd remember that if it had happened," he said with a hint of a smile.

I stared at him, a serious expression painted all over my face. "It's like there's this fog in my head."

"You are one strange double," he said, and his smile broadened.

"What's that supposed to mean?" I asked with growing irritation.

"Double X. Chromosome. That's what the guys call the girls at school. Double X chromos. Double exasperating. Double."

"Y," I said back at him.

"Why what?" he asked.

"No," I replied. "Just Y. The letter Y. In honor of *your* chromosomes. Like, whenever a boy approaches us we just ask Y? Dumbass!"

There wasn't any further crack from him. He just looked at me, frowned, and shut the door in my face.

CHAPTER XXVIII

Khattaaara

Dhraaal let me upstairs to his bedroom. At its center against the far wall stood a bed with elaborate carvings that was made, he told me, long ago in the time of a man named Louis Quince, who was the potentate of some kingdom called France. The headboard had wonderful flourishes at the top, while the footboard offered a representation of a bow that was crossed by a quiver filled with arrows. Meanwhile, the sides were carved with representations of flowers called roses that are I was informed quite beautiful in their living state and give off a fragrant aroma—*perhaps bred,* I mused at the time, *to cancel out the fetid stench of the inhabitants on this planet!*

Dhraaal turned toward me with eager eyes. Although we had known each other since we were children, he being both my half-brother and my husband, he had never seen me naked as an adolescent, nor taken me at so young an age. He stood facing me and began to undress me, a little at a time. The disparity in our physical ages did not seem to matter to him, nor was it a hindrance to me as I had been with him at about the age he now appeared for years before my death. Yet this body was still immature so that when we first made love, I felt a sharp pain before there was any pleasure. Such was normal, Dhraaal reassured me. Human females were different in this way. Apparently, I had been what humans called a virgin. That was the word he used. But a virgin I was no more.

Sex in humans is different from that of Gaaalthaaarans, the pleasure being somewhat localized, rather than pervasive. The *yaaarghig,* so lacking in humans, intertwine when Gaaalthaaarans mate. Regardless, that did not stop us. As the moments elapsed and the two of us became sexually entangled, my breath became labored, my fingers gripped the bedsheets, my back arched, my eyes stared upward, blinded by the sensations that seemed to pulse through my loins, until, at last, I cried out sudden pleasure as a surge of endorphins caused my mind to grow numb. I looked down to see the pinkish *groaaal* drip from my loins as Dhraaal withdrew that small part of his *yaaargh* from me. There was no chance that I would ever become pregnant with child regardless of how fertile this body I was in, for we were two different species, alien to one another.[14] Dhraaal himself having succumbed to similar pleasure fell gently down on the bed beside me and we clung to each other and kissed and repeated our act again and again until the rude light of the dawn began to break through the window panes.

We ate a quiet breakfast and then returned to bed, trying to make up for the time we had been apart. For me, the passage was brief, but for Dhraaal it was a billion eternities. How much did this man love me to search for me for so long? My heart raced at the thought as he penetrated me again and again with both his *yaaargh* and his tongue. At last, we lay motionless, both of us on our backs, covered by a silken sheet. It was then that Dhraaal once more spoke to me of a device he had built to restore our civilization.

"It's not quite finished," he explained, "but it will serve as a conduit for you to invoke the energies within the quantum fabric. The god-stone in your head will enable you to create an entanglement around the entire planet. The device will allow you to superimpose the minds of all of our lost on these humans." He paused for a moment and then went on. "Their brains will be overwritten the same way that yours overwrote the mind of that adolescent Herron girl. To quote some old Earth vernacular, 'They won't know what hit 'em.'"

I turned my head toward him.

"How did you manage all of this?" I asked.

"Let's just say," he said, "I've had a lot of time on my hands."

---

[14] It must be noted that whereas a *yaaargh* is in its extended state just over a meter in length and whereas a vagina is a mere fifteenth of that, he had to take care not to injure me.

197

Then he turned off the lights, kissed me goodnight, and we both fell asleep. But my dreams were not peaceful. I dreamt of the end of my life, attacked by my own daughter while in the palace. She came at me at night and fired an atomic gun at me, incinerating me. It was as though I was reliving the moment it had happened and felt once more the excruciating pain of being burned alive—so much so that it awakened me. I did not need to open my eyes to know that my body was covered in sweat; naked in the air-conditioned room, the nightmare left me shivering. I snuggled up to Dhraaal, who stirred enough to put his arm around me, wrapped his *yaaargh* around one of my legs, and once more placed part of it inside me for that is how Gaaalthaaarans show love in their sleep. It gave me comfort. And a force field around us both gave us warmth for the rest of the night.

After an erotic shower together, we dressed and headed back to Dhraaal's office. We had just entered and were standing talking when I heard a helicopter overhead. Through the ceiling, I could see a cadre of five men, each dressed in black, sliding down ropes to the rooftop. My quantum vision showed that each was armed with a weapon and heading to the door that led down to the interior of the building. When the person in the lead couldn't open it, another placed a small block of white material near the handle. The men then stepped back, and a moment later there came an explosion that left a hole where the handle had previously been. They then opened the door and went inside, one by one, down a corridor that led to the room we were in. Up to that point, Dhraaal had no idea that anything was amiss. Then the invasion came. The men burst through the door as though it were a space-jump portal and their mission was to engage in an act of war. Having entered, all of the men aimed their weapons at me.

"What's going on?" Dhraaal demanded. "What is the meaning of this?"

The man who appeared to be in charge spoke out. "We're here to take her into custody," he said.

I glanced at Dhraaal. "They *are* kidding, aren't they?" I said with derision in my voice.

Another of the men began to approach me, having the temerity to actually touch my person. I focused on him. At once, He became enveloped in purple flames. There was the odor of burning flesh. One could hear his deafening screams as he writhed in his well-deserved agony. In another moment, his body was reduced to a skeleton that fell to pieces onto the floor. It was then that the squad leader gave his command.

"Shoot her!" he ordered. Then he and each of his men fired their weapons at me. Bullets rained in my direction, but before any of them could reach me, I froze them in their path through space, reversed their direction, and fired them back at the men at one hundred times the velocity they had sent them toward me. The bullets ripped through the squad, mortally wounding all but one, whom I left unscathed.

"What *are* you?" the squad leader asked as he lay bleeding out with his companions, staining the elaborately patterned carpet.

"Dare you even speak to me!" I said with godlike indignation. Then, with a wave of my hand, I raised him into the air and hurled him out the window, twelve stories above the ground.

Turning my attention from the broken glass, I stared down at the three dying men. One by one, I caused them to disintegrate—to become one with energy and air. Then I turned to the remaining soldier. He looked at me with abject fear coursing through his veins.

"Tell your people to stay away!" I told him in no uncertain terms. "Tell them that *I* rule this world from now on." I paused and then commanded, "Go!" and so he backed up toward the door. As he turned to leave, I added, "Tell them they need to bow to their new Empress, Khattaaara or their planet will be laid to waste!"

The man left without a backward glance or a single word. I turned to Dhraaal.

"Are you all right?" I asked him with concern.

"I'm fine," he said. "But I feel I must commend you. You're back to your old self again."

CHAPTER XXIX

Theresa

I lived alone with my mother in a small house in Los Angeles, but I went to a private school that she worked very hard to get me into. My father had been out of the picture since before I was born. He lived in Mexico. I was 15 years old and a sophomore. My grades were decent; I was not a straight-A student but I was on the girls' basketball team. Oh, and just to make matters clear, I was and still am only attracted to other girls. I guess that makes me a lesbian but I don't really like the word. When I was small, my uncle, my mother's younger brother, who was twenty-eight years old at the time, used to molest me and it went on for years until I told my third-grade teacher. The police were called. He was arrested and is still in jail. I don't want to go into details but let's just say that it scarred me. Maybe that's why I just like girls—maybe not. I don't know. I'm not a psychologist, though I'd often thought to become one if I managed to live long enough to finish my education. The neighborhood where I lived wasn't the best. My other uncle, whose name is Martin, used to drive for Uber and so he would take me to and from school every day. But there were a lot of gangs where I lived and a lot of violence— even drive-by shootings. The gang in my part of the hood had tried again and again to get me to join. They called me *Flaca,* which means skinny. I tried my best to ignore them and when I couldn't, I'd tell them to leave me alone. I'd gotten jumped by girl members of their gang enough times that I learned to fight back. It made me tough. The problem was that sometimes I myself had been tough on the wrong people, like Peyton. I was tough on her and I bullied her because I thought that she ignored me and I wanted her as my girlfriend. I mean, from *my* point of view, I couldn't see how any girl would not want to be intimate with another girl if she was pretty. Peyton was tall like I was and beautiful but that's where the likenesses ended. I mean, I was—am—Latina with dark hair (and don't give me any of that Lantinx shit!) and she was white with long blonde hair—dishwater blonde, not the stupid Barbie kind, though I wouldn't have sent any of those kind packing as will be clear later on. Peyton was also very erudite. I learned that word in English class. It means well-read in terms of books and shit. As for me, my grades were just so-so, but I had street smarts, which in my part of town kept you alive, staying in survival mode twenty-four-seven, which is to say I'd had my fair share of scraps and black eyes, but whoever I went up against wouldn't ever take me on a second time. As far as Peyton went, I used to bully her a lot and I eventually became sorry about that because she tried to commit suicide as a result. Afterward, I apologized and I did a really stupid thing. I kissed her. I mean like full tongue. The problem was, there was nothing back from her. Not the slightest bit of emotion. It was embarrassing and I ran off so ashamed or embarrassed or I don't know. I didn't even wait for my ride. I walked for miles back to my digs. My mom was beside herself with worry by the time I made it home but I didn't say a word. I just shut myself in my room, threw myself down on my bed, and cried till I fell asleep.

Then Peyton died for real, though I didn't know this at first because I met this girl, who I thought was her but who turned out to be her other-dimensional twin, who as it turned out, like me, only liked girls and in no short time we fell in love and we both knew in our hearts that that would never change but life can take unexpected turns.

The thing was, Payton, my Payton, had to go back to her dimension to try and fix things because, she like her mirror twin turned out to be a superhero called Quantum Girl, which if I had told anyone at the time they would have locked me up as insane or delusional or just batshit crazy. Anyway, just after this happened— after we'd kissed and said goodbye forever, I sat in the dining room at home with my mother with supper in front of me—supper that I really didn't have the stomach for.

"You don't understand, Mama," I said. "I love her and now she's gone."

"I'm sure she'll come back," my mother replied.

"There isn't any way," I told her. "She's in a parallel dimension."

"You talk such nonsense," she said. "You eat your supper before it gets cold." She paused to gather her thoughts. "If she loves you, she'll come back. Things will work out. We are all a part of God's plan."

"That's just it," I said, bemoaning her point. "You always said that loving someone—someone your own sex—is a sin. So why would God help?"

"Because God loves everyone," she replied. "And putting sex aside, God believes in love, which is difficult to come by. Your Papa, rest his soul, loved me with all of his heart until his dying day."

"Papa's in Nogales, Mama," I said. "I know he left you. Uncle Martin told me years ago."

"*Tu tío Martin necesita ocuparse de sus propios asuntos,*" she replied, meaning he needed to mind his own business. But then she put her hands on mine and looked me in the eyes. "If your Payton loves you just one-tenth as much as I love you," she said unphased by the revelation, "then God will find a way to bring her back to you."

"I hope so, Mama," I said. "I hope so."

CHAPTER XXX

Payton

I was in my bedroom lying in my bed, staring up toward the ceiling, thinking how sad it was to be alone in the world. I mean, I knew I had family but there are different kinds of alone. When you're a small child you really don't think about it much. Your family and your playmates are all you truly need. If you get hurt or afraid you can always go to your mother or father for them to try and make things better. But as you grow older your needs change. The hugs or kisses that your parents once gave you are no longer enough. Sometimes you get on their nerves or they get on yours. An adult, or a near adult, needs greater affection than any parent can provide. He or she needs intimacy. Liam used to tease me when I said I just liked girls. This time was no different.

"You'll get over it," he once said to me. "You just need to meet the right guy."

"Would *you* have sex with a guy?" I said back.

"Hell, no," he replied. "That's disgusting."

"Well," I said to him, "that's kind of how I feel. I mean, I'm not disgusted by guys. I once had sex with one. Okay," I went on, "why are you attracted to the girls you're attracted to?"

"Because they're beautiful," he replied

"Not just because they have a place to stick your dick in?" I asked.

"No," he said back.

"Then why?" I persisted.

"Well, I don't know," he answered. "They can be gentle and listen and they sort of fit in and not compete."

"Exactly," I said.

"But you don't have the equipment," he replied.

"You'd be surprised what two girls can accomplish in bed," I laughed.

"Yeah," he sort of conceded. "I've watched girl-girl porn. But they're only together because there're no guys around."

"Oh, my Gods!" I exclaimed. "You are so naïve!"

He just shrugged, and went off to his bedroom, probably to jack off to more of that girl-girl porn, knowing in his heart that any of them would just jump at the chance to have sex with him. In his dreams!

Anyway, there I was an hour later, moping in my bed, and there was a knock on my door.

"Yes?" I replied.

The door opened to reveal brother Liam again.

"You look as though your dog just died," he said.

I craned my head to look at him. "I don't have a dog. You know I don't have a dog."

"Maybe you should get one," he fired back.

"Maybe I should get a wire terrier, so I could ask it every day, 'Why are you so annoying?'" This, as I plopped my head back down on my pillow.

Liam shrugged. "I just came to tell you that dinner's going to be ready in ten."

"Not hungry," I said. "And before you head down, would you please turn off the light and shut the door?"

"Yes, *Ma'am*," he replied and then flicked the switch on the wall to its downward position, swung the door shut, and immersed me in darkness.

I was about to close my eyes and head off to dreamland when I noticed a strange violet light coming from the bathroom. I turned my head to look toward it and then rose from the bed to inspect what it was. As I entered the room, I saw that the glow seemed to emanate from one small point at the line that was made where the bathtub intersected the floor. I squatted down to find that all of the brightness was coming from one small bead less than the size of a pea. Reaching down, I picked it up and brought it up close to examine it. The tiny orb was neither hot nor cold but it gave an odd sensation to my fingers, as though it was vibrating. I stood up, continuing to stare at what seemed an almost hypnotic radiation. Then, all at once, it shot out of my hand toward my face, striking the middle of my forehead. And then it was gone and I was in the dark. And then I wasn't! No longer was the purple light confined to one small spot but it seemed to burst from me! I stared down at my hands, which now glowed. My arms were covered in… something… and it was as though stars shown through the cloth of what I at first believed was my long t-shirt. I walked to the mirror that hung over the sink and looked at myself. There was a cowl on my face—my face that now emanated the same violet iridescence as my hands. I stared and stared and as I did, memory after memory went crashing through my brain.

"Oh, my Gods!" I muttered to myself. "Theresa!"

I reached down and felt for the whistle that Peyton had given me that now had been rendered invisible on its chain by my Quantum Girl costume. I brought it up to my lips for the first time since it had been given to me, took a deep breath, and invoked a sound that could be heard through the dimensions of space.

CHAPTER XXXI

Khattaaara

It was the middle of the night. Dhraaal and I had finished up hours of making love and I had just fallen asleep when a deafening noise invaded my brain. I sat up at once and cupped my hands to my ears, but nothing would make it stop. It bleated and then stopped and then bleated again and on and on. I materialized some clothes on me then directed the god-stone to take me to the source of the din. I appeared in a bathroom that appeared identical to the one adjacent to the room where I had first appeared. The room was dark, but for a girl, my twin, who was dressed in the same costume as I had worn when I had first awakened.

"Who the hell are you?" I demanded of the girl, who held against her lips the object that had made the offending sound.

CHAPTER XXXII

Peyton

The ancient legends of Rendenaaar told that after Khii created the world, two seraphim, identical in form, sprang from her *yaaargh*. One she named Grei and the other Naei. Grei was good and Naei was evil. The legend says that the two fought so hard against each other, their bodies so entangled, that they became one, known as Naeigrai, who was neither good nor bad. Naeigrei became the first woman and from one of her tears shed from loneliness she fashioned the first man whom she named Whuraaaan. Together, Naeigrei and Whuraaaan peopled Rendenaaar and became the mother and father of all Gaaalthaaarans. So, the story goes.

CHAPTER XXXIII

Payton

As I stood there in the dark, having just summoned Peyton, I wondered about Theresa. How devastated she must have been, thinking that we could never be together again, trapped in different dimensions. And then, suddenly, *she* appeared—Peyton—but there was anger written on her face. I had never seen that in her before.

"Who the hell are *you*?" she demanded.

"What's wrong?" I asked as she looked around the room.

"Where *am* I?" she demanded again. "Where *is* this place?"

"Peyton..." I said. The name had barely passed my lips when she interrupted.

"I am *not* Peyton! *Thraaagh, flaaacthral baaagn!* I am Khattaaara Gaaalthaaara, Mistress-of-All-that-Exists! Remove your mask, woman! I command it!"

Khattaaara! The realization suddenly came to me that something must have happened to Peyton after I had saved her from death. Regardless, I caused my cowl to disappear. Peyton, or Khattaaara as she now claimed to be, stared hard at me then reached out, and with the index finger of her right hand, poked my cheek.

"How is this possible?" she said with questions brewing on her face. "You are *not* a projection."

"I'm not," I said back.

"*Sdraaalknaaad!*" she said to herself in astonishment. "*Jraaadraaank iraaaf naaangh!*"

"I don't speak Rendenaaaran!" I said.

"The awakening has left me mad!" she spat out in English.

"Just angry it seems," I replied.

She stared at me with contempt.

"I'm you," I explained, "in *this* universe."

She cocked her head slightly, considering, and then spoke as though she were alone in the room, though why still in English, I wondered? Perhaps there was still some of Peyton left in her. "Interdimensional travel," she muttered as her eyes took on a faraway look. "Dhraaal told me he had never been able to achieve that. And yet your *praaavodaaar* did. Or rather *I* did in my reincarnation. I always *said* I was smarter than that husband of mine! Now, I shall be the god of everything, of infinite worlds and infinite universes." She stared at me again. "But if you have my same powers you stand in my way."

Her eyes began to glow and then bright, violet light radiated from them like the high beams from an oncoming car. Only it wasn't just light. Mixed in were high-energy quants that blasted me across the room, smashing into me, pushing me backward to shatter the wall behind me. It was a new power, one that neither Peyton nor I had learned. This was definitely *not* good. I wondered what other undiscovered abilities might she have.

As I began to try and pull myself out of the wall, Liam, having heard the crash, burst into the room. Khattaaara turned toward him.

"Liam!" I shouted to him. "Run! Get out of here!"

Disregarding my warning, my all too protective brother lunged toward Khattaaara and then froze as he saw her face—a face identical to mine!

"Liam! No!" I shouted again.

One arm and then the other, fighting plaster and wood, I freed myself from the wall and then phased to stand between Liam and Khattaaara as Quantum Girl. Then I split into two so that another of me phased a foot away from Liam, facing him. As he stared at me in a near state of shock, I caused my cowl to disappear. Then, filling the room with twenty other Quantum Girls to try and overwhelm Khattaaara, I looked at him and smiled.

"Hey, Dumbass," I said softly. "You tried to protect me. Love you much." Then I wrapped my arms around him and phased us out of there.

Meanwhile, Khattaaara was quite literally beside herself, looking and turning this way and that, as one by one, I merged my Quantum Girl selves into the me who had fled the room.

I don't know whether it was subconscious or a random act but I had phased us to Peyton's dimension to New York City at 8:40 a.m. on the morning of September 11, 2001. The problem was that we materialized in the middle of one of the lanes on West Street where the driver of a taxicab on a collision course with us slammed on his brakes. The cab stopped mere inches from us.

"Hey!" he yelled like an angry New Yorker. "Watch where's yer goin', morons! An' Halloween ain't for another month!"

I held up both my hands in an apologetic manner. "Sorry," I mouthed in his direction. We stepped aside, avoiding more oncoming traffic, and made it to the sidewalk unscathed. As we did, I phased back into my street clothes.

Liam stared hard at me. "*What* just happened?" he said.

"It's a long story," I replied, and it was.

"Where are we?" he asked. "How the hell did we get here? And why were there so many of you? I mean, this is really, really freaking me out."

"I can explain," I assured him and then my attention suddenly turned toward the street up about a quarter of a mile. The first of what would be two 747s crashed into the North Tower of the World Trade Center.

"Oh, my Gods!" I gasped. I glanced at Liam and then stared back at the tower. "Stay here. Wait for me," I said. I phased into Quantum Girl and vanished right in front of him.

I first phased up to the building near where the plane had entered and then into the plane itself. All of the passengers were screaming in terror as flames engulfed the interior, burning everyone alive. Clothes and hair caught on fire first and then human flesh. One woman had actually gotten up and wedged herself between her little boy and the seatback in front of him, wrapping her arms around him to try and protect him. Regardless, he died in excruciating pain with all the rest, screaming out, "Mommy!" I couldn't allow this to happen. I phased back in time five minutes, duplicated into hundreds of me (not all at the same time), and then phased the passengers and the crews out of harm's way, leaving behind the hijackers to suffer their fate. I did the same with the passengers and crew of the other plane as it was about to crash into Tower 2. Then came the tricky part—rescuing those in the buildings. I had phased out the people on the floors affected by the explosions and all of those on the floors above other than the jumpers whom I rescued just before they would have hit the ground (after nullifying the effect of their acceleration). Saving those on the floors below proved challenging, to say the least. I needed to jump ahead a month or so to learn which of them had been killed and then just rescue those. That done, I phased about two hundred John and Jane Does corpses from various county morgues into the collapsing structures just in case any human remains were supposed to have been found, not wanting to alter the timeline.

But while the entire rescue occurred in only moments as far as anyone who might have been able to watch would have observed, from my perspective, it took days—at least that last part. In fact, it took so much time that twice I had to spend a night in a vacant hotel room, steal some food from the kitchen, get some sleep, time travel back, and then pick up where I had left off. One by one, though, I phased each and every one of them to Central Park at night, but not night in their time. I phased them ahead to mine— to June 28, 2026.

"Please, everyone, stay calm," I said as I hung fifteen feet above them in the air. There were just three of me at that point, backs together, all facing outward, all of me speaking in concert. "I know you're probably all frightened but now you're all safe. You're still in the city, but this is the year 2026. I'm sorry, but I couldn't leave you in the past as it would have changed the way things were meant to be. I'm sure, though, your families will be happy..." I paused and then went on, "and shocked to see you all alive."

As I merged back into one, a man shouted up at me. "Who are you?"

"Quantum Girl!" I shouted back. "Good luck to you all," I said, and then I phased from the scene. All in all, I had rescued two thousand, seven hundred sixty people along with five dogs and one cat in the cargo sections of the planes.

It was times like that, which made me think about my responsibility as a superhero, especially in that I was the only Quantum Girl left. I was not like Phee's Wonder Woman, sculpted from clay by her mother, to be given the powers of Zeus and five other gods. I was Payton Herron, born of her mother's womb, who had her abilities given to her by her alternate self. But in that, I had been endowed with a mastery over time and space, I had a duty to act in ways that were for the good of mankind—at least that is where my own heart chose to direct my better self.

I appeared back beside Liam as he stood watching the South Tower collapse.

"Don't worry," I said. "I got everyone out including those in the planes."

He turned to me. "How?" he said. "I don't understand. *What* is going on? How are you able to do any of this?"

"As I said," I told him. "It's complicated. But more importantly, do you have any cash on you? I'm starved."

Moments later found us sitting opposite each other in a booth at a small local restaurant with breakfast before us. I pushed away the plate that I had emptied of its blueberry crepes. Liam looked up at me from the remains of his hamburger and fries.

"I want to go *with* you," he said.

"It's too dangerous," I replied

"I'm your big brother," he said. "I can handle myself."

"You mean like in the bedroom," I asked. "You'd be dead by now. Besides, you're just fifteen minutes older than me, and only because you pushed me aside to get out first. How rude was *that*?" I offered half a smile.

"I still want to go," he insisted. "I need to be there with you to know you're all right. No fun to be home alone worrying. Mom and Dad are at the conference. But why the big rush to get back? It's not even our universe you're trying to save."

I sipped my drink through the straw in my glass and then raised my eyes to meet his.

"If you must know," I said, "I have a girlfriend there."

"It figures." He moaned out the words.

"And to be perfectly upfront about it all," I went on, "so do you."

"What do you mean?" he asked.

"I mean," I said, and I took a breath, "her name is Ophelia, and it's definitely weird because she's the other Peyton's twin sister. But you two kind of hit it off in a Hardy Boy Nancy Drew sort of way before I reset the timeline."

"So..." he asked, considering, "she's sort of like my sister."

"I dunno," I replied. "I mean the two of you didn't grow up together and you have totally different quantum signatures. Technically different parents, dimensionally speaking." I took another sip of my drink. "Then again, your kids might wind up with three eyes and twelve toes. I'm *not* a geneticist."

I may not have answered his question but I had piqued his interest. "What does she look like?" he asked.

"She looks a lot like me," I said, "only I'm definitely prettier and sexier and half a centimeter taller."

"And obviously more modest," he added as I was sucking up Coke through the straw.

Abruptly, I started to laugh with the Coke going up my nose.

"Obviously," I replied. "Ow!"

Liam joined in the laughter.

"She has pale blonde hair and pale blue eyes and absolutely perfect skin," I went on to say.

"Does she have big boobs?" he asked.

I stared at him wide-eyed. "No, she doesn't have *big* boobs!" I said. "If she did she'd have *three* of them with *you* around. Jesus, Mary, Joseph, and Sam! What is *wrong* with you? She has the absolute sweetest personality and she's smart. And if you must know, she probably has the best legs in any dimension, baring mine, of course."

"So, you'll take me," he concluded. "I mean now I *have* to go if just to *meet* her and have babies with her so that you can be an aunt."

"You are so unselfish," I remarked back. I wiped my mouth and nose with my napkin. "Yes, I'll take you," I relented. "Gods, I needed a good laugh after all I've been through, but I'm dead serious about Ophelia. To be perfectly aboveboard I think she's in love with you and I think you were with her."

I laid down my napkin and then looked at him again. "You done?" I asked.

Liam nodded.

"Then pay the bill, leave a tip, and let's go," I said.

A sudden thought struck me as he reached into his wallet. "Wait a minute," I said. "Let me see your money."

He laid a twenty-dollar bill on the table between us. I looked at it and then waved my hand over it and turned it into its mirror image.

"Everything's backwards here," I said, "if you hadn't already noticed."

Liam breathed out a sigh of relief. "Thank Gods!" he replied. "I thought it was a side effect from your zapping us here."

"Phasing," I corrected him. "It's called phasing."

"Like it makes a difference," he shrugged. I called to the waitress, handed her the tray on which I'd placed the twenty, and then we both rose from the table and left. After finding a secluded spot out of sight from any watchful eyes, I took hold of his hands, became Quantum Girl again, and phased us back to the present. We materialized in Peyton and Ophelia's bedroom. The room was veiled in darkness. The light switch no longer worked. The best I could do was to cause myself to glow a bit more. As I turned just a bit, my foot brushed against something on the floor. When I looked down to see what it was my stomach rose to my throat. There, just in front of me, lay what had once been Ophelia, dead in a heap, partially decapitated, her head tilted off to one side, her eyes staring blindly at nothing, a large hole blasted clear through her chest. To see her lifeless body was more than I could bear. Edges of ribs and blood-drenched lungs were visible through the cavity that had been created in her chest, with her heart gone, probably burned to a cinder. I didn't need to wonder who was responsible. It was Khattaaara, who had murdered her reincarnate's sister. I glanced toward Liam.

"Don't look," I warned him. But he did anyway.

"Oh, my Gods!" he exclaimed. "Is that..."

"Ophelia," I said as my spirit sank to the floor.

We went into the other rooms. Our parents' doppelgangers were also dead, murdered while they slept.

"It's not Mom and Dad," I assured him. "Not *our* Mom, and Dad if that's any comfort."

"It's not," Liam said.

In the guest room on the bed lay the skeletal remains of what had once been Thara-Klo, murdered by her own mother, so like Medea[15]. But while Medea did it to spite her husband, Khattaaara murdered her daughter to spite her own womb or whatever the equivalent of it was on Rendenaaar.

Suddenly, I heard moaning coming from outside and my heart stopped for I knew that voice. Instantly, I phased out to the front lawn. There on the grass lay Theresa, her eyes shut, blood all over her; bloodied, matted hair half-covering her face. Her arms and legs had been blown off her and lay scattered on the ground. I lifted what was

---

[15] As told in Euripides 5th Century BC tragedy, Medea, the title character, who is the mythical daughter of Helios, the niece of Circe, and the one who helped Jason and the Argonauts search for the Golden Fleece, murders her own children as revenge against Jason, who is their father, after he abandons her to marry the daughter of King Creon, whom she also kills.

left of her into my arms. I phased off my cowl and back into my street clothes. I pushed the hair off her face, as tears streamed down my cheeks.

"Oh, my Gods! Oh, my Gods! Oh, my Gods!" I wept.

Theresa opened her eyes. She smiled at me. Her voice was almost a whisper as she spoke.

"You came back," she said. "I knew you would. I must look a mess right now and I can't feel my arms or my legs." She tried to laugh but instead just coughed up blood.

"You're going to be all right," I sobbed.

Theresa stared at me then said in a weak voice, "The other Peyton. She did this. She's not right in the head."

"I'm going to get you to a hospital. They'll fix you up. We're going to spend our whole lives together."

"I'm so cold," she said as she shivered. Then she looked at me. "Do me a favor?" she asked.

"Anything," I said as my tears continued to flow.

She could barely talk. "You find someone else to love you as much as I do," she said and then said something I couldn't make out. Then her body went limp in my arms, and the heart that I had learned to cherish stopped beating in her chest.

"Oh, no!" I wept. "No, no no..." I began to sob uncontrollably. I could feel the entire dimension wavering. Then I heard Liam's voice. He had exited the house and was standing beside me.

"Come on, Sis," he said in his gentlest voice. "We need to go."

I looked up at him with tear-drenched eyes.

"She was everything to me!" I wept out the words.

Liam extended his hand to me.

"I know," he said.

I took hold of him and he helped me to my feet.

I phased us to a lot of places afterward but it was always the same. Monuments, statues, churches, temples—every place that had heralded our civilization now stood in ruins. The last place we went was the Capitol building in Washington, D.C., which was nothing but rubble, amid the bodies of the nation's leaders. I projected a virtual TV on the wall of what was left of the Lincoln Memorial where the two of us watched Tucker Carlson.

"Good evening and welcome to Tucker Carlson." He began. "On October 30, 1938, at precisely eight o'clock at night, legendary actor-director, Orson Welles began a reading of H.G. Wells' War of the Worlds on CBS radio. Because the broadcast was so convincing, those who tuned in late believed that it was real and a nationwide panic began. That was nearly ninety years ago. For centuries, men have speculated about the possibility of other intelligent life in the universe but after today we no longer need to imagine. What appears to be a teenage girl called Peyton Elise Herron, who supposedly grew up in sunny California, has re-identified herself to the world as Khattaaara Gaaalthaaara, Divine Empress of All that Lives and Breathes and who supposedly hales from a planet she calls Rendenaaar which, according to her, existed in a universe long before our own. And, as the Divine Empress of All that Lives and Breathes, she has demanded that she is to be summarily designated as not only the supreme leader of the world but as humanity's new god. Ordinarily, one might consider such a demand laughable and attribute it to either a prank or to a person who is sadly delusional. But Peyton Herron appears to be someone who needs to be taken seriously. She has demonstrated unique powers that would put even Superman to shame. As it stands, she has singlehandedly destroyed most of our cherished landmarks from the Lincoln Memorial to Mount Rushmore, the Statue of Liberty, the Eiffel Tower, and Big Ben. Even the Sphinx and the Taj Mahal have been utterly and completely turned into rubble. I could go on but the pattern is clear. Virtually every symbol of our past has been wiped from the face of the earth as though in doing so we would forget who we are as a people. It's an age-old strategy—remove the glory of the past, erase history, and you will find complicity among people. Remove their leaders, put yourself in authority, and they have no choice but to look to you. And your children will have no knowledge of what once was. Peyton or Khattaaara or whatever name she wants to be called has murdered every member of Congress and the British Parliament, and publicly incinerated the Presidents of the United States, Russia, and China on national television. Thus far, no weapon has been able to touch her; not so much as a scratch requiring even a Band-Aid. She is able to hover in midair, disappear at will, project deadly beams of pure energy from her hands and eyes, and turn herself into a literal army by creating thousands of copies of herself. This does not even begin to resemble the 1938 broadcast. Orson Welles and, I would venture to guess, even *H.G.* Wells, would be trembling in fear at the thought of what is now happening. This is *not* fiction. No speculation is necessary. This is all too real, and no one can predict how it will end."

"Jesus," Liam exclaimed.

"I want to kill her," I said, "but I can't. Peyton's in there somewhere. I just don't know how to get her out."

"So, what are we going to do?" he asked.

"We going to go back in time before all this began," I told him. We are going to go back and we're going to fix this and make things right.

Liam looked at me with hope fleeting from his eyes. "How do we know that we haven't already tried and failed?"

"Because *your* body wasn't at the house with the rest," I said, "nor was mine."

Liam appeared a bit taken aback at the thought of his own death.

"Look at the bright side," I said. "You'll get to meet the love of your life for the first time all over again."

I guess I must have taken on a serious look as Liam stared at me, concerned.

"What's wrong?" he said.

"Hold on," I told him. "I'll be back in a flash."

I phased back to the house. There was one room we didn't go into because we'd assumed that we'd found everyone who was supposed to be there. As I walked into the kitchen—as Quantum Girl walked into the kitchen—he spoke to me.

"I came down here to get Ophelia some soda," Liam said, "when I ran into your interdimensional twin. She threw me into the counter. Must have broken my neck because I can hardly feel past my chin. Ironic, isn't it? I was supposed to find happiness with my heartthrob, and now I can't even feel my heart."

"I'm going back in time to fix this," I said.

"We've tried it thousands of times," he insisted. "It always ends the same way. The only good part of it is, being paralyzed as I am, I can't rush upstairs to see what Khattaaara did to her. I take it this is the first time for you. Back here, I mean."

"I'm not quite sure how..." I started to say.

"How time works?" he interrupted. "You once told me that there are an infinite number of possibilities. Maybe this is just the one where I've gone through it again and again but you haven't—at least not yet. Maybe if you read my mind."

"How?" I asked.

"Merge into me," he said.

"I've never done that," I said. "Not with anyone other than the other Peyton."

"Sure you have or you will. I know because I've seen you do it." His voice was amazingly calm for someone who knew he would never walk again—for someone who had just lost what might have been the most precious love in his life, and I knew how that felt. "You need to learn from past mistakes," he went on, "so maybe this time you'll make the right choices."

I focused on him the same as I had when I had healed Peyton. I thought about trying to heal him as well but it wasn't the same. Peyton and I had identical DNA even if it was reversed. My cells could heal hers but Liam's were different. It wouldn't work. It didn't work. But still, I could read all the images in his mind, all the neurons and dendrites that gave rise to all of his memories. He hadn't lied to me or exaggerated. He and I had literally tried to change things thousands of times without success. How then could this time be different? My mind focused on that as I phased out of him. Then, suddenly, it was clear to me and I knew what had to be done to change all that had occurred. I clenched my fists and set my jaw. Whatever powers Khattaaara had mastery of that I did not, I knew now how to change how things had gone.

"I think I know the way," I said, but he was no longer there. "Liam?" I shouted as my eyes searched the darkened room. But he was gone—gone with those last words—gone with that last thought. Whatever I was about to do would change the course of what had been to the inevitability of what was meant to be. Why had he vanished? Had the knowledge he had imbued in me caused this history to change?

I phased back to the Liam who had yet to be harmed.

"I thought you said you needed to go?" he asked, for to him it appeared that I hadn't even left.

"It doesn't matter," I replied. "I know how to set things right—at least most of them."

CHAPTER XXXIV

Payton

There were hundreds of Quantum Girls in the sky, all me, as Khattaaara burst through the Herron roof, while I simultaneously appeared in the bedroom, *not* as Quantum Girl but as myself. It was yesterday all over again and Liam was with me. Ophelia had her head (thankfully still attached) out the window watching the confrontation, not really knowing what was going on. She had just seen her sister acting batshit crazy and violent and now there were hundreds of what appeared to *be* her surrounding her.

"Khattaaara, Khattaaara, Khattaaara…" each of me began to chant in unison.

Khattaaara appeared confused and disoriented. She tried to push out a force field to keep all of the Quantum Girls that were me away but each time we met her with resistance in the shape of a force field of our own.

"Hey, guys!" Phee said. "You really need to see this. Peyton is battling herself!"

"Not quite," I replied.

Ophelia pulled her head back into the room, turned, and saw me.

"Oh, my God!" she exclaimed.

"Ophelia!" said Katherine Herron.

"Mom, not the time!" Phee insisted then she turned to me. "How did you get back?"

"How do you know it's me and not," and I paused, "*your* Peyton?"

"Am I the only one here that noticed?" she asked, astonished. "Your dimension is a mirror of ours. Everything is backwards. Your moles are on the opposite sides."

It was at that moment that I recognized t how astute Phee actually was. Suddenly, a look of shock came over her face as she saw my brother in the room.

"Liam!" she cried out.

Liam looked at me and then asked me under his breath, "Is that *her*?" knowing I could hear his every word.

"Yes," I mouthed back.

"And we're an item?" he went on.

"Yes," I said again in mouthed-out words.

"I love this dimension," he added with a smile that turned toward Phee as she walked over to me.

"What are you two whispering about," she asked in a low tone.

"You," I explained. "Time paradox. Liam doesn't remember your dalliance. As far as he's concerned this is the first time he's ever met you. I told him you two were an item. He appears to have fallen in love with you... again."

Phee looked at Liam and smiled back.

As for me, I winced in pain, grabbing my right forearm with my left hand.

"What's wrong?" Peyton's mother asked, concerned.

"She bit me," I said.

"Who?" asked Peyton's father.

"Um," I said, "did you forget out there? I'm kind of sort of doing battle with Peyton's former self."

The two of them went to the window where Ophelia was back staring out. Meanwhile, Liam had moved close to her and took the opportunity to gaze at her while she was distracted by the battle in the air.

I could see Khattaaara from all directions. There were more than a hundred of me and we were all about a hundred feet in the air, surrounding her. It would have been a strange sight for anyone watching, and indeed, not only had many of the residents poked their heads out of their windows or doors, but had actually emerged from their homes to more closely observe the melee, oblivious to the potential danger they faced.

The battle went on for what seemed to me like an eternity, but was actually more on the order of less than ten minutes, with me trying to grab Khattaaara to restrain her while struggling with the onset of force fields hurled this way and that. As one of me had taken hold of one of her arms, she bit me quite hard. Quantum teeth versus quantum flesh. It may have one of those irresistible force versus immovable object things but all I know is that it hurt like hell and drew blood. I tried to engulf her. I tried to squeeze the breath from her but when it finally became too much for her she pressed her eyelids tight and phased herself from the scene. Disregarding the crowd, I merged back into the one of me that was inside the house.

CHAPTER XXXV

Khattaaara

Suddenly, I was surrounded by a hundred duplicates of me who began to attack me from all directions. I did my best to fend them off but there were too many of them. Was one of them the girl I had just encountered? This was someone who appeared to possess another god-stone. But how? There were only seven in the universe. I had one and Thara-Klo had another. Could she have stolen one from one of those who had possessed the remaining five? Was it Shaaalra's that she had? If so, I would rip out her heart and feed it to my *goraaag*. Or did she have mine? But that was for later. For the moment, I needed to survive. I was being smothered by that army of teenage girls. I pushed out with the force field I had created around myself but it appeared to be of little use against them. One grabbed hold of one of my arms. In return, I sunk my teeth into hers. Her blood was red and tasted of iron. What sort of creatures *were* these, I wondered, and where in the universe was I? I couldn't defeat so many. I need to get away, if not through space then through a quantum thread. I closed my eyes, focused my thoughts—and escaped.

Immediately, I found myself in the middle of one of their transportation paths. Primitive metal vehicles were all around me, hurtling past me in two directions. Some were coming straight at me. I held out my arms toward them, invoked a burst of quantum radiation, and flung them away from me in every direction.

CHAPTER XXXVI

Payton

We were gathered at night in the Herron living room watching television on what I was told was an 80-inch display. I am still amazed at the difference between the sets on my world and those there. On my world of vacuum and cathode-ray tubes, the images were comparatively small with visible dots making up the pictures. Here, it was like looking through a window. I wondered what would be the result to *my* earth if I were to bring to it *this* world's technology. Would it make things better or worse? It was something I needed to think about after the more pressing issues of the day.

Phee and her Mom and Dad were sitting on the sofa facing the screen. Liam was on one arm next to Phee, awed by the fact that she had taken and was holding his hand. Meanwhile, I stood with Theresa in the background—Theresa who was once more alive and whole, due to my reset of time.

What we were watching—and this was just a short while after the battle—were recordings from someone's cellphone of Khattaaara wreaking havoc in the middle of some freeway, causing so many people to be injured or killed.

"And in the local news," the announcer said, "destruction took on a whole new meaning as a mysterious caped superwoman decimated oncoming traffic during this morning's rush hour, killing seven and injuring countless more. Most tragic of all, an injured, grieving mother, cradling the body of her infant who was catapulted from her car as it was thrown into the guardrail."

"Excuse me," I whispered to Theresa. I'll be right back, and with those words, I became Quantum Girl and was gone.

I went back in time some hours to when Khattaaara first appeared on the freeway. I stood mere inches from her, behind her. Then I grabbed her and phased us both to the moon.

I'm not quite certain why man has always dreamt of going there. Jules Verne wrote two books on it. Edgar Rice Burroughs wrote three. There are, however, no moon maids or little green men. The moon is not made of green cheese and the illusion of the face of a man in its landscape was caused by a formation of ancient craters made by meteors that crashed randomly onto its surface four billion years ago. The truth is that it's airless and desolate and boiling hot or freezing cold depending on whether it's night or day. And then there's the radiation and the blinding light of the sun. But there lay earth in the distance, blue and white and inviting, but beyond the reach of the lifeless rocks that, could they speak, would thirst for the fall of rain. And then I jumped forward through time.

We were gathered at night in the Herron living room, watching television on their kick-ass, ginormous screen. Phee and her Mom and Dad were still sitting on the sofa facing the screen. Liam was again sitting on the arm next to Phee, still awed by the fact that she had taken and was holding his hand. Meanwhile, I again stood with Theresa in the background; Theresa who, thank Gods, was once more alive and whole due to my first reset of time. On the screen was the scene from Coraline where she was at the dinner table with her other father and other mother. There was no interruption—no bulletin with breaking news.

I quietly excused myself to Theresa and then went to the guest room, where Thara-Klo lay in bed, quietly reading from the pages of Sun Tzu's *The Art of War.*

"I left her on the moon," I told her. "She'll get back to the Earth, but won't know how to find us."

Thara-Klo spoke without looking up. "It's her finding Dhraaal that should concern you. You need to erase any mention of him from the Internet."

"How?" I asked.

She looked up at me from her book. "Interface with any connected device," she said then went back to her reading.

"I tried using Ophelia's laptop," I said. "Everything's backwards. At least to me."

"Then get her to help," she said, again without lifting her eyes from the book. "You need to do it before she goes online."

CHAPTER XXXVII

Khattaaara

She left me on what I surmised was the moon of the planet I had found myself on. There was no atmosphere. The temperatures were far beyond the capacity of any living thing to exist. Fortunately, the god-stone protected me until I could use a quantum thread to return to the planet, which I later learned was called Zemlya.[16]

Having focused on a populated area, I materialized in a city on the opposite side of the planet from where I had been. It was evening there with crowds of inhabitants on foot and in conveyances on a busy street. Many of them stopped in their paths and began to stare at me. I was not certain if it was because of how I looked—radiating purple light—or because I had suddenly appeared out of nowhere. A short distance from me stood a young female whose attention was focused on a small rectangular device that she was holding in one hand, from which a narrow beam of microwave light shot out into the distance. Similar beams emanated from nearly every individual within sight and even from those within buildings, creating a crisscross of lines in the air so annoying that I had to inhibit that part of my vision. The female in question, however, appeared to have sensed me appraising her because she looked up at me and cocked her head to one side. My curiosity had peaked. Wanting to examine the device in her hand, I materialized next to her and demanded it.

"*Jaaatragh elli Kothaal,*" I said. "*Jaaatragh elli Kothaal!*" I repeated my command louder the second time. The creature just stared at me like an ignorant *Laaagbiin*. Incensed at her lack of obedience, I grabbed her device. In response, the insufferable thing struggled to hold onto it, uttering words I did not understand. *Imprudent jrataaarg!* I thought to myself. *My needs are far greater than thine!* And with that, I caused her to disappear, leaving both her

---

[16] Zemlya or земля is the Russian word for "earth."

garments and the device to drop to the ground as I sent her back to where I had just been—to this planet's singular moon.

As I caused the device to fly up into the palm of my hand, I willed the costume I was in to vanish. And, despite my naked splendor, wanting to blend in I made the woman's garb form around me, though her shoes with thin, pointed heels would not fit. Angrily, I kicked them away. As I did so, I realized that my skin was still irradiated. Turning to look at my reflection in the glass of the building I stood near, I saw that I appeared different and unnatural from how I had been on Rendenaaar and from those who were all around me. With that thought, I canceled the effect and appeared, once more, oddly enough, as my younger self more or less! *Strange*, I thought as I continued to stare at my reflection, *how all of these females possess hair above their eyes.* Personally, I found it hideous and wondered why the males would choose to mate with them. As for myself, I hoped I would become accustomed to it in time.

My attention turned to the device that I now held. It was rather primitive but through it, I was able to access what these beings, who called themselves русске (meaning Russians), referred to as the Internet. It enabled me to instantly learn their language, their history, and their customs.[17] I found it refreshing to think that there had been those like myself who had chosen to bask in power, though they all showed weakness and each eventually caused their own demise. Still, I wondered how there was no mention of Rendenaaar. How was it possible that even in my absence these people did not know of the glory of our great civilization? But neither was I familiar with *them*. Perhaps their star system lay cloaked within a nebula. No other explanation seemed possible.

As I walked across the street, one of their metal conveyances nearly struck me. Fortunately, I stopped it mere *kaaalatj* away from me. I watched as the fragile machine's front caved in upon impact

---

[17] Editor's note: For the sake of the reader, Khattaaara's entries from this point have been translated into English from Russian.

229

with the force field I had created. A large white bag exploded in the driver's face. The man inside appeared quite angry and caused the machine to make a hideous and loud noise. I walked over to the side of the conveyance where he was. The man lowered the window and began to yell at me, whereupon I reached inside, touched his arm, and sent him to join the woman whose clothes I now wore.

Having crossed the street unscathed, I entered what those there called a restaurant and was seated at a table by a human male, wearing a black apron over a white shirt with a black tie around his neck. I was given a menu, a glass of water, bread rolls, and time to decide what I wanted to eat, though I had little or no idea what any of what was listed actually was or tasted like. When the waiter returned, I asked him to choose *for* me. He returned a short while later with what he had referred to as a Cobb salad and a glass of *milk*, which was a slightly thick drink that was white and opaque. The Cobb salad consisted of a variety of plants and meats as well as something which resembled a *graaang* egg, all of which had a pinkish creamy liquid poured over it. The meal was unusually tasty and served to satisfy the hunger that I had felt.

After I had finished the meal and had drunk the last of the milk, a good-looking adult male approached me.

"Excuse me," he inquired, "May I sit down?"

"Who *are* you?" I asked.

Rudely, he seated himself without invitation and then slid a small card over to me.

"My name is Dmitri Semyenov," he said. "I'm a scout for A-Plus Models." He paused and then went on. "Have you ever considered modeling? It's a good way to make a lot of money."

"Not interested," I said.

"Such a beautiful girl," he went on, undaunted. "It would be a waste."

"I need to find my father," I replied. "Right now, *that* is my concern."

"No parents?" he asked.

"No," I said.

"And your home?" he asked. "You do have a place to live?"

"Not yet," I replied. "I need to find my father first."

"And I need to find a model," he said. "Pretty girl, I will help *you* if you will help *me*. I will assist you to find your father. I will give you a place to stay, and you will make lots of money. There is an old Russian saying—people find money and money finds people." He paused and then asked, "What's your name?"

"Khattaaara," I replied.

"Khattaaara," he repeated. "Such a beautiful name for such a beautiful girl."

I remember smiling at the compliment. It was strange for me because I still had no explanation for how it was that it *was* me, somehow recast in human form. But if it were so, I was in a form that men considered beautiful—at least this one thought so.

I left the restaurant with him and got into his machine, which he called a Maserati. It was comfortable inside with seats made from animal skins. This was the first time I remembered ever being in such a vehicle. The god-stone enabled me to instantly emerge at different points of space but this was different. There was acceleration and it was invigorating. I sat in the front with Dmitri. He glanced at me every now and then, reminding me of how beautiful he thought I was. The sky had turned dark by then. Two beams of light from the Maserati illuminated the road where those lamps that were suspended above by metal poles did not—where they were not. The engine purred each time he pressed down on the lever under his right foot. Finally, he drove into a large building and parked the vehicle between two others. Having emerged, he walked around to the side where I sat, opened the door, and extended his hand for me to take hold of, which I did. Once out of the vehicle, he led me to a small room that lifted us to a level near the roof—an elevator. I realized that was what it was as the word suddenly came into my mind. The doors opened directly into his living quarters. His rooms were more luxurious than those of the house in which I had first found myself. He took me to what he called a spare bedroom that had a room attached for personal hygiene and then showed me another one nearby that was filled with attractive garments, most of which fit me when I later tried them on. He explained that they belonged to the modeling agency for which he worked for use by the girls who were hired. There were beverages in a small cooling box and a large panel on the wall that he called a television that caused images with sounds to appear on it when one pressed the buttons on a small box. I became engrossed in what I saw. *Who were these individuals who called themselves the Avengers and did I need to fear them?* I wondered if any of them owned the five other god-stones. The ones called Vision and Dr. Strange seemed likely candidates. But how, I asked myself, did they come into possession of them and which of my companions had they murdered to make them their own? I resolved to get them back once I located my husband. The days of the Avengers were numbered. They had not met the likes of Khattaaara Gaaalthaaara!

The water in what he told me was called the shower beaded down on me luxuriously. I was sadly reminded, though, looking down at my naked flesh, that I now possessed only one pair of *ghalthraams* and sorely lacked my *yaaargh*, which could sensually engulf my husband's, or for that matter, any of my lovers during sex to induce immeasurable pleasure. But at least I was alive, somehow having survived the quantum fires hurled at me by my insolent child. At last, having succumbed to the energies this day had drained me of, I laid down on the bed and promptly fell into a dreamless sleep.

The next day, I found myself in front of a camera, modeling the fashion of this world. "Hands over your head. Intense stare off toward the right. Good, good. Very good," and on and on until finally, "That's a wrap," and it was all over for the day.

Throughout the shoot, the stylist—the woman who did my make-up and hair and clothes—plied me with a liquid that felt warm as it went down my throat. It seemed to relax me, but by the end of the session, I could barely stand.

I remember sitting in the dressing room with one of the other girls who were models as well. The row of bright lightbulbs hurt my eyes. Strange, the thought occurred to me, that yesterday I could stare into this planet's star and now my mind felt as though it was being splintered by something so small as this. Tatiana, one of the other girls, who appeared several years older than most of us, sat down in the chair next to mine.

"Why are you so interested in finding this daddy of yours?" she asked. "Did he fuck you good or something? Maybe when we find him he can fuck me, too."

"He took care of me," I said.

"You want something that will really take care of you?" she asked and then demanded, "Give me your arm."

My head was still swimming. Obediently, I offered it to her. She picked up a rubber hose that was lying on the table and tied it tightly around my arm just below my elbow. Then she took out a long clear cylinder with a thin sharp needle at the one end and brought it close to the skin of my inner forearm. Instinctively, I pulled away.

"Don't be a fucking scaredy cat," she said. "You won't feel anything like when you fuck Dmitri."

I felt a sudden pain as she plunged the needle into my arm but that quickly went away as the fluid it injected began to course through my veins. I felt wonderful. It was as though I owned the universe. My mind drifted to a million places and then I must have passed out.

When I saw light again I could barely think straight. I couldn't concentrate. My powers were useless. The god-stone requires focused neural activity. All I saw were blurred images and voices that drifted in and out of my head.

I was in bed, the same bed as I had slept in, in Dmitri's apartment, only now I was naked under a sheet that barely covered me. Dmitri and Tatiana were also in the room, talking incoherently, or was it I who just couldn't understand their words in my stupor? Occasionally, I could pick out bits of what they were saying.

"Keep her on the heroin," Dmitri said. "I've arranged for her to be transported in the morning. She'll bring ten million rubles at least."

"And me?" Tatiana asked.

"I told you," Dmitri replied. "I cut you loose after two more girls."

CHAPTER XXXVIII

Payton

I had taken Phee and Liam back to my dimension for protection. Khattaaara had not reappeared but there was no telling if or when she might. I begged Theresa to go with them, as well as Peyton's Mom and Dad, but the three of them adamantly refused. It didn't matter that I had to turn back time to prevent their deaths. Their expressed logic was that I could always do it again. The truth is the Herrons still held hope about getting their daughter back and, as for Theresa, she loved me too much to leave me on my own, though in all three cases, I thought it was a huge mistake.

Anyway, Mom and Dad had returned from the conference when the three of us phased back home. We agreed not to tell them about my abilities. I said that Phee was an exchange student from France and Phee did her best French accent as she does speak the language fairly proficiently with three semesters of it under her belt. Meanwhile, I was supposed to be going *to* France to live with *her* parents, which was only half a lie.

I was in my bedroom when I heard Phee and Liam outside. I didn't mean to eavesdrop, but I couldn't escape the fact that I did have quantum hearing.

"No, I like it, you're calling me Lia," she said. "Lia and Liam. It's cute."

"You don't think it's…" and he hesitated, "strange?"

"Everything that's gone on in our lives of late is strange," she answered. "Super-powered sisters. Different dimensions. The fact that we were hatched from similar eggs needn't ruin the soufflé." She broke off her words and then went on after a bit. "We've known each other for nearly two months now. Well, I've known *you*. I can't control *your* heart but you're the adrenaline to mine that skips a beat every time I look at you or feel you near."

"But..." he started then stopped.

"We're not the same person," Phee said. "We're not brother and sister. We don't even have the same quantum signature. We're two peas from different pods. No need to bring Gregor Mendel into the mix."

There was a long pause but both of their heart rates went up, whatever was going on. Phee was the first to break the silence.

"My mom's pretty cool about my staying over though she armed me with an arsenal of condoms. She's a strong adherent to the Bible but she also recognizes the teenage sex drive."

"'Ophelia Jane Herron,'" she boomed, trying to imitate her mother, "'I will not have you barefoot and pregnant. Not at your age!'"

"'But Mother,' I protested," Ophelia went on, "'I own six pairs of shoes.'"

"And what did she say?" he asked.

"'It's just an expression,' she said, and then came that ever-maternal sigh."

Such love, I thought to myself. *So what if their kids have twelve fingers, twelve toes, and three eyes? Besides, there's no knowing if the backward DNA in her eggs can actually be fertilized by his sperm.*

CHAPTER XXXIX

Khattaaara

I awakened drugged in a long metal box that had padding all around. There was a mask over my nose and mouth from which I saw a plastic tube emerge that led to a small metal cylinder. Even in my half-conscious state, I panicked. "Let me out!" I sobbed, and then I passed out again.

Every so often, falling in and out of consciousness, I would feel bumping or movement this way or that. I must have been in an airship of some sort as I felt the acceleration and the angling, as though whatever I was in was being flown through the atmosphere, and my ears popped a number of times. When, at last, the machine I was in finally settled (presumably to the ground) there was more movement, more bumping, and then motion that felt was horizontal. My thoughts were still heavily clouded and I had held back my urine for far too long, to the point that it became unbearable and I had no choice but to let it out. The warm stream dampened my legs and lower torso and the stench made my prison all the worse. The mask helped somewhat but not entirely—not in such a confined, closed space. Would I ever be released from this nightmare, I wondered, or would I be trapped in there until I died? *No*, I thought. *That last cannot be. If the intent of those who had imprisoned me had been to kill me, they would not have given me a tank of oxygen to breathe.* But even so, that source of breath was running out. The air was becoming thinner. Finally, I pulled the mask off to inhale what atmosphere was left in the box, now putrefied by the odor of my own bodily fluid. How undignified that the god of all existence should endure such humiliation. Is this what was to become of me I wondered—anonymity and death? How sad the universe would feel that its empress should end her reign in such an undignified fashion! And then, all at once, the motion stopped.

The light from outside blinded me when the box was finally opened. I still could not think straight and offered little resistance as two men, strangely dressed, yanked me out and stood me on my feet. We were outdoors and those same men pulled me by my arms to a courtyard where an old, brown-skinned woman, stripped off my clothes and then took me by the hand and led me to a brick wall. There a brown-skinned boy, younger than me, sprayed me with icy water from a very large hose, shouting words at me that I couldn't understand. Finally, he made a circling gesture with his hand, which I took to mean that he wanted me to turn around, so I did. When the water stopped, the boy ran up to me, put the fingers of one hand between my legs, and began rubbing me, while doing the same to himself with the other. The old woman went up to him and slapped him to the ground, yelling more words—angry words—that were all foreign to me.

The woman then took me inside a large, colored tent, mumbling more incomprehensible words. Inside were several young women dressed from head to toe in black with only their hands and eyes exposed. I was dressed similarly a then sat down on a stool, whereupon a middle-aged man entered the room with a small black case that he held in one hand. Pulling over a chair, he sat down next to me, pulled up the sleeve on my left arm, took out a cylinder like the one Tatiana had used, and injected more fluid into my vein. Once again, I felt a surge of ecstasy. I closed my eyes. My flesh quivered and, although I no longer had powers, I felt that I could conquer worlds. I just didn't want to right then.

When the man had gone, one of the women went to the entrance of the tent and called out. A moment later, the boy returned holding his cheek with one hand (where the old woman had struck him) and a coil of rope similar to the one that bound my wrists in the other. A third woman pulled the boy's hand away from his face to see the red mark, and then all three of the women began to laugh, shaking their heads at him. The boy scowled and then stared down at the ground in shame. He walked over to me, started to glance up but then changed his mind and began to tie one end of his rope to the one around my wrists. Then, without so much as a word, he tugged on the rope and virtually dragged me from the tent as though I were some animal on a leash. The boy, whom, even in my stupor, I felt great rancor toward, caused me to swear to myself that should I ever get the chance, his life would meet a slow and painful end.

I was brought or, rather, forcibly yanked to a small stage where had already been gathered the other women I had met. One by one, we were each auctioned off to this or that bearded man with a cloth wrapped around his head. I was the last to be sold. The boy came forward, as he had with the rest, with a wand or stick and used it to lift the hem of my dress, though in my case, the stick traveled to a greater altitude than had been the case with the others, revealing that which he had previously uninvitedly touched. That he shall be torn limb from limb and then roasted over a fire was the one clear thought that expanded into my still narcotized brain. In any event, the bidding became frantic until, finally, I found myself sold to some fat, balding, agéd man who reminded me of a *jaaakirak* with mange. The man, upon winning, gleefully clapped his hands together. When the auctioneer walked over to him, the beast stroked his beard, thought for a moment, and then answered something—I had no idea what—in that I had no command of the language he spoke—not so much as one word.

Thus was I drugged, kidnapped, molested, and then sold, only to then be boarded onto one of their primitive airships again. Once we were aloft, a female in white clothing placed a pill into my mouth that I spat out at her, causing her to slap me across my face. She then forced a second pill down my throat, despite that I tried to bite off her fingers. Whatever it was that I eventually swallowed had the effect of making me even more confused.

"Why am I here?" I asked groggily.

"Because you, like other pretty Russian girls, represent a profit," she said.

"And if I choose not to be some old man's sex slave?" I asked mumbling out the words.

The woman looked at me with arrogance. "Then we cut off the heroin we've addicted you to," she said, "and leave you to drop to your knees and beg him to do whatever he wants just so you can have more drugs."

"Dhraaal will kill you all when he finds me," I replied, the words now barely able to escape my lips.

"No one will ever find you," she replied. "You are lost to the world."

"I have powers," I warned.

The woman picked up a syringe that was lying on a metal tray.

"As do I," she bragged. "Right now they are in liquid form." She paused and then asked, "What's your name?"

"I am Khattaaara Gaaalthaaara," I said, "Daughter of Rhahaaana, *Garayaaad* to the *Vraaadorn*."

CHAPTER XL

Payton

I was with Theresa in her bedroom and on her bed, sitting Indian-style, though I don't think I'm allowed to call it that on *her* world—cultural disparity and all—no more allowing little boys who don't self-identify as little girls to play Cowboys and Indians anymore unless the Indians win. Anyway… (head-rattle for what has gone on in this dimension) so I guess I was sitting *cross-legged*, facing the foot of the bed. Theresa was sitting behind me, pressed up against me, her head buried in the curve of my neck, her arms wrapped around me, her legs cradling mine. Her hands had hiked up my blouse and she was cupping my breasts, causing me sensations of pleasure from both her nearness and the physical stimulation. I was barefoot but clothed. Theresa was in her underwear.

"I keep bouncing back and forth between dimensions," I told her. "I've looked hundreds of places for her but I have no idea where else to search or what to do when I find her. Besides, we're both equally matched. And Gods only know if she's found Dhraaal. She's had enough time."

"You need to relax," she purred, as she withdrew her arms and began to unbutton my blouse. "I can help you. Just a little *us* time first."

"Stop!" I insisted and she did. "If you want to get me naked just ask! I can phase out of my clothes with just a thought! Seriously, there's more to life than making out!"

"Are we having our first argument?" she asked. "Because I'm totally cool with that, only I don't want to argue back."

I took her hands and wrapped her arms around me as I glanced back just a bit.

"Look, I'm sorry," I said apologetically. "I didn't mean to snap. But I need to go. I need to think. I need to be alone—just for a while.

And it's not just Peyton's life. It's all of existence that's at stake."

I became transparent, and then told her, "Please tell your mother I said thank you for dinner. I'll be back when I figure things out." And then I was gone, leaving her with empty arms.

I phased through dimensions to my bedroom, only to find Goldilocks and Brother Bear in my bed making love. This was just not right!

"Oh, my Gods! Is sex all anyone ever thinks about?" I said shaking my head.

Liam suddenly stared at Phee with a curious expression on his face. The male mind tends to be so utterly bewildered when it first comes to learn that females like sex, too. Would that they realized that we like it ten times as much!

"And why are you in my room?" I demanded.

"Have you seen *his* room?" Phee replied.

"Point taken," I said. "But I need the two of you out of here. I have to gather my thoughts." I shook my head to myself adding, "though not on my bed anymore."

I glanced at the clock that was on my nightstand. "How long have you two been here?"

"About an hour," Phee answered. "Why?"

"Because," I announced, "I intend to go back in time, and prevent you two from defiling my sheets."

"But that will undo all of this!" Liam protested. "This was our first time. She even let me go down on her."

Phee smiled with the broadest of smiles.

"Too much information!" I said, adding, "Sorry brother."

"No! Wait!" he exclaimed, and those were his last words before I phased back an hour and a half to ensure that the desecration of my sacred space was decidedly undone. Whether Ophelia Jane Herron would agree to her own undoing, well, that would be up to her, but not in my room, thank you.

It was just shy of an hour earlier. I was lying in my bed, staring up at the ceiling when, lo and behold, who should walk in but my brother and my sort of sister, arms interlocked, fingers intertwined, until *they* saw *me*. Both were startled.

"Sorry," Liam apologized. "We thought you were in the other dimension with Theresa."

"You make it seem as though there are only two dimensions," I replied.

"Sorry, Pay." That was from the Mistress Ophelia.

"I thought I'd explained to you," I said, "that there are an infinite number of parallels, minus one."

Liam, having sufficiently ignored my correction, turned to Phee and said, "We *can* go to my room."

"I guess," she replied with an exasperated sign. "Whatever. I can always shower afterward." She directed his stare toward me. "In *her* shower."

"Please shut the door," I called out as they were about to leave. "And try to keep the ohs and ahs to a whisper. I need to focus." The last part uttered to myself.

"As do I," came a familiar voice—actually, my own. I looked up, and there before me in the middle of the room, stood Peyton, well, to be more accurate, Quantum Girl.

I jumped up to a sitting position, moved back, and was about to phase the hell out of there, when she called out, "Wait! It's me, Peyton!"

I remained in a static mode, half-phased, probably looking like a transparent, wavering version of myself.

"Prove it!" I demanded in a voice that must have sounded to her like a bad radio transmission from outer space.

"I gave you a whistle," she said.

"Khattaaara already knows that," I replied.

"You have a brother named Liam!" she went on.

"Ditto," I replied, "and he's in his bedroom fucking your sister!"

"What?" she exclaimed, glancing toward the door and then staring back at my wavering self. "There's a lot more technology on my world!"

"Closer," I said, "but no cigar."

"Mr. Chatterjee is a total asshole!" she went on.

"That's something she wouldn't know," I replied, and with that remark, I phased back. "Universe after universe, good and bad, but Chatterjee is always an asshole!"

A laugh broke from my lips, as did from hers, and then she started to collapse. I jumped from the bed and caught her.

"I don't understand," I said. "Did you overpower Khattaaara?"

"No," she replied.

I pulled back just a bit to look at her face. She kept squeezing her eyelids shut and shaking her head like someone who's been awake too long and is trying to keep from falling asleep.

"I'm not the Peyton you saved," she went on. "I'm the one who missed getting reabsorbed after the battle with Khattaaara in outer space. I always believed in having backups, but this time it was unintentional. I just regained consciousness a little while ago, but it's taken every ounce of my will not to be drawn into my other self. And now that *she's* slash *I've* been drugged, I don't know how long I can stay separate."

"Drugged?" I asked. "By whom?"

"I or Khattaaara—whatever—wound up in Russia," Peyton explained. "St. Petersburg to be exact. She's now in Bahrain, about to be a concubine to some middle-aged Arab Shaikh. She got caught up as a victim in sex trafficking."

"So, what can we do?" I asked.

"I can lead you there," she said, "but once I'm that close, I won't be able to stay separate anymore. It'll all be up to you."

She started to collapse for a second but then regained herself.

"I'm ready whenever you are," she said.

I extended my hand to her. As she took it, I became Quantum Girl as well. Then we phased together to Bahrain.

We materialized in the harem where Peyton or Khattaaara or whoever she now was, was being held with more than a dozen other girls—some as young as eleven or twelve—the oldest being no more than seventeen. I wondered what they did with them after they became too old to satisfy the pedophilia of their lords and masters. The room was lavishly decorated with silken drapes and large silk pillows that served as beds for the girls who were either in a state of undress or nearly so. Persian carpets lay on the floor or hung on the walls and there was the scent of a sweet, floral perfume that permeated the air. In the center of the room was a marble fountain, at the top of which three life-size gilt bronze nymphs, each facing a different direction, allowed white wine to spew from their vaginas and onto the faces and into the open mouths and of the three gilt bronze men that were lying on their backs with their legs partially submerged and with tall erections that sodomized the bronze nymphs, each of whom had her arms stretched upward, her eyes closed as though in ecstasy while her smallish breasts were thrust outward, tipped with bulletlike golden nipples. No doubt the beverage contained more than alcohol and grapes in order to keep the harem obedient and addicted.

As she had predicted, the straggler Peyton was absorbed into Khattaaara who had been there all this time. She virtually melted into her like some astral spirit being drawn back into its living host. And so, I was again *by* myself to try and save my *mirror* image sister. I went over to her, knelt down, and tried to rouse her from the stupor she was in.

"Peyton," I whispered, as I flashed off my cowl.

She stirred and then opened her eyes just a bit.

"I need to get you out of here," I said. "What is this place? Who are all these girls?"

She mumbled something in what must have been Russian.

"I don't understand," I said. "It's me. Payton." I paused and stared at her. Then I saw the track marks on her arms. "My Gods!" I whispered. "What did they do to you?"

I held her against me and then I phased us out of there.

I brought us back to my bedroom—my dimension—my world. She was incoherent and I was in over my head.

"Liam! Ophelia!" I called out to them for help. I turned back into me before they came.

Liam was first into the room; then came Phee.

"I got her," I said. "Help me get her onto the bed."

"Peyton!" Phee cried out.

Liam came over and lifted Peyton (or Khattaaara or whoever she might wake up to be) into his arms, carried her to the bed, and laid her gently down. Phee went over to her and sat down on the edge, facing her and taking hold of her hands. Then she turned her head toward me.

"What's wrong?" she asked. "Why isn't she responding?"

"She's been drugged," I answered. "And I don't know how much of her is Peyton. When I found her she muttered something in Russian. I think that's where she landed before winding up in some harem in Bahrain."

"Maybe we should get her to a doctor," Liam said.

"Really?" I replied, wondering where his head was at. "In *this* dimension where her organs are all reversed or in hers where she's wanted for murder?"

Phee just stared at her sister. "I'll stay with her," she said.

I looked at Liam. "That's the best we can do for now," I said. "She just needs to get the drugs out of her system. There's going to be withdrawal. It's going to take all of us working together." And, with that, I split off a second version of myself. Then the other me spoke to Liam and Ophelia. "Just in case, for whatever reason, I'm not nearby, there's a whistle on my nightstand. Keep it with you, whoever's awake and by her side. Use it if you need me. In the meantime, there's something I need to do but I'm going to need her clothes."

"Shoo, shoo, shoo," both of you, the Payton me said to Liam and Ophelia, gesturing scattering motions with my hands. Then the two of me undressed her and put her into one of my/our nightgowns. After donning the harem clothes, the Bobbsey twins were invited back in.

"How do I look?" the one of me asked, spinning around. Then a sudden thought occurred to me. "Just one thing, though. I was thinking of phasing to your bedroom and using your laptop to download Russian into my brain, but it's all frigging backwards to me so that's out. I just hope at least one of the girls speaks English. Oh, well," I sighed. "Wish me luck." And, with that, I was off—the one of me. The other me remained.

And so, I went to the harem where Khattaaara had been sold as a sex slave. I phased myself right onto her bed. There were girls on either side of me, neither of whom appeared awake. I nudged one of them.

"Do you speak English?" I whispered.

The girl, who was about sixteen, moaned, mumbled something, and then turned her back toward me as she continued her path toward sleep. I rolled over to stare at the gaudy ceiling.

"Does anyone here speak English?" I said in a low voice.

"I do," whispered a young Russian-sounding voice on the other side of me.

I turned to look. Beside me lay a very pretty girl who appeared to be no older than twelve. She had long, straight dark hair and pale blue eyes.

"My name is Anya," she whispered.

"My name's Payton," I whispered back. "How old are you?"

"Eleven," she said. "My birthday was last week."

"How did you get here?"

"I was walking home from school," she replied, "and a lady—she asked me to help her find her *kushka*, uh, kitty cat, so I did, only a man, he grabbed me from behind and put a cloth over my mouth and nose that smelled like gasoline. Then I passed out. When I woke up,

I was here. The man said that if I did not cooperate, he would have my Mama and Papa and my little sister killed."

"And what did he mean by cooperate?" I asked, already knowing the answer.

"He makes me do bad things to him," she said as an anxious look fell upon her face, "and he does bad things to me, just like with the other girls."

"He won't be doing it anymore," I assured her.

"How can you stop him?" she asked. "You're just like us."

I stood, then, and became Quantum Girl.

"Are you an angel?" she whispered.

"No," I whispered back, "but I'm here to help. Now, wake up all the other girls and have them get dressed. Tell them to be quiet, though, but quick."

Anya went from girl to girl and woke each one, telling them what they needed to do. As each of the girls roused into wakefulness, as each of them saw me, each without fail shook her head in disbelief. Regardless, every one of them got up and quietly dressed. Then they huddled together with continual glances in my direction. Anya, who was near the middle of the now curious group, came over to me.

"They want to know who you are," she said.

"Tell them I'm Quantum Girl and that I'm here to help them escape."

Anya returned to the group and told them. Regardless, there were still curious and apprehensive looks cast in my direction. I motioned to Anya to come back over to me.

"Have them all form a small circle and hold hands," I told her. "You, too, with them," I added. Once done, I walked over and broke the circle where Anya was, taking her hand as well as the hand of the girl who was on my other side. I supposed I could have muttered something like *Klatu barada nikto* or *Abracadabra* or something, but I'm not one for theatrics so, without so much as a word, I phased us to the Sistine Chapel in Vatican City. It was all that I could think of as a safe place to leave them. There we stood amidst a throng of tourists, beneath Michelangelo's great fresco, with its brilliant colors. High above us, were both the saved and the damned, each finding his or her own place in the fabric of eternity. Therein too, perhaps, lay the symbols of the true garment that I was meant to wear, if in spirit at least. Whether there are gods or angels or devils, blessed or cursed, the images reflected a battle between good and evil with the pronouncement that good shall triumph in the end. But would such be the fate of every world, of each universe and dimension and of every echo of mankind or was this just a fable to mark the futile hopes and aspirations of beings who would soon be erased from all memory by passionless time?

For the moment, though, there were larger concerns. I don't know which created a greater stir—the group of teenage girls all dressed like Yvette Mimieux in I Dream of Jeannie or the seemingly radioactive Quantum Girl. Fortunately, I did speak decent Italian from two summer trips with Mom and Dad and Liam, who is fluent in no other language than Pig Latin which he always insisted was "an accomplishment in and of itself."

"*Queste ragazze sono state tutte rapite,*" I told everyone within hearing range in a voice that reverberated through the gallery, "*vittime della tratta sessuale! Hanno tutti bisogno di aiuto! Per favore chiama la polizia!*" all of which basically meant that the girls with me were sex trafficking victims and someone needed to call the police.

That said, I turned to Anya and asked, "Where do you live?"

"452 Ulitsa Krylenko. Apartment 318. Saint Petersburg," she answered.

"I want you to hold onto me really hard," I told her, "and think about your home, just your home."

As she put her arms around me and closed her eyes tight, I allowed the quantum seed to reach into her mind. The seed took us into the kitchen of her parents' apartment. Her mother, who had been carrying plates from the sink, turned and saw us and dropped them all, letting them smash to bits on the floor. Anya's father, who had been sitting calmly drinking coffee at the table, heard the crash and looked up.

"Anuska!" her mother screamed.

Anya rushed up to her mother and hugged her as tightly as she could. "Mama!" she sobbed as tears streamed down her cheeks.

Her mother wept out something I couldn't understand. Then her father rose up and went to them both and he, too, began to cry. The man dropped to his knees as Anya let go of her mother and turned and hugged him. Her father wrapped his arms around his little girl and wept oceans of tears. Then he asked Anya something, to which she replied. But as both of them turned toward me, I phased out of there. The truth of the matter is that I had begun to cry as well.

I returned to the Harem. It had now become apparent that the absence of the girls had been discovered for there were guards armed with what I took to be AK-47s and there in the midst of it all was the old, fat shaikh who had purchased Khattaaara and the rest. Upon seeing me, the guards aimed their weapons in my direction and then began to fire but their bullets dissolved from existence in mid-air as they struck the invisible force field I had created around myself.

Anger swelled within me. I focused on the guards and sent them flying across the room to be thrown into unconsciousness or death as they struck the walls—I didn't care which. Only the shaikh remained standing. The man muttered something incomprehensible. Ignoring him, I held my arms down against my sides, focused on a single thought, and thus the room and the building in which it was contained exploded like it had been hit by a hydrogen bomb. There was no more Shaikh. There was no more palace. That was the end to human trafficking—at least for here.

It was in the midst of the explosion that I heard the shrill whine of the whistle that I had given to Liam and Phee, which Peyton had in turn given to me. When I phased into the bedroom, I was covered in soot; which is what happens when the force field that protects you retains all of the powder that it protected you from. The other me, the

Payton me, phased in at the same time. She glanced at me, and then both of us turned our attention to what was happening on the bed. Liam and Phee were both trying to restrain Khattaaara, who appeared to be having a seizure. Phee cast a fleeting glance at one of me.

"Payton, help us!" she begged.

The two of me merged back together as a smudged Payton.

"It's the heroin," I said as I went over to the bed to help them. "She's going through withdrawal."

"We *need* a doctor!" Phee exclaimed. "I don't want her to die! Not again!"

"I'll be right back," I said and I phased from the room.

I emerged in the Norris Medical Library at USC. I then split into ten of me and began to search at super speed through various books for pharmaceutical information on heroin addiction. After about ten seconds of that, I found what I had been looking for. Merging back, I phased into the medical center in Peyton's dimension, the reason being that the drugs in mine were mirror isomers of the drugs in hers and might not have worked. I entered the pharmacy and retrieved a small bottle of pills labeled, Lucemyra (even though it read backwards for me) and then I phased back to my room.

"We need to give her three tablets four times a day," I said. "I'll get some water. They won't cure her, but they'll help."

I went into the bathroom and filled up a glass from the sink. As I turned off the faucet, I looked at my hands and then glanced at my reflection in the mirror. My face, as were my arms and hands, was covered in a black powder that had resulted from the blast. But there was a greater concern at the moment. I needed to ease Peyton's pain.

"I just hope she can hold them down," I said as I walked back into the room with the water-filled glass.

Phee pulled Khattaaara/Peyton up to a sitting position, pushing a pillow behind her. Then she opened the bottle and placed a pill into her mouth.

"You need to swallow this," she said. "It will help with the pain

251

you're going through."

Khattaaara/Peyton nodded her head. I put the glass to her mouth. Her hands went up and met mine. She drank, swallowed the pill, and then coughed hard, having choked on a bit of the water as it went down. I stepped a foot or so back, as Phee cradled her, patting her gently on the back. Khattaaara/ Peyton looked at me. My eyes met the swollen ones that were hers but they gave no clue as to who was behind them. All I could tell was that this was someone who had been thrown down in defeat. Whatever powers Khattaaara or Peyton had possessed had succumbed to the drugs that still coursed through her veins. The girl who could survive the hostile depths of outer space and blasts of quantum force had been laid waste by a beakerful of drugs.

Phee continued to hold her for several more minutes but then gently eased her back down and kissed her forehead. Then she took her hands, brought them up to her lips, and kissed them. Khattaaara or Peyton just stared at her with thought-filled eyes. As for myself, I was in sore need of a warm shower and some good, strong soap.

The water felt good as it rained down on both of me. I had divided myself into two, in order to be able to scrub off all the dirt, and it felt good to be able to rub my own back without having to reach around to do it. It was odd, though, that when I washed the dirt off of one of me, the dirt vanished off of the other.

Phee walked in and stood on the dry side of the curtain.

"How did you wind up with so much soot on you?" she asked.

"Explosion," both of me said at once.

"Oh my God!" she exclaimed. "Was anyone hurt?"

Again, the two of me said in concert, "No one that mattered."

I turned off the water and then pulled back the curtain. There was only one of me, then, who stood naked, facing Phee. "Towel?" I said.

Phee turned around and grabbed a towel off one hook. As I began to dry myself we both turned toward the door only to see Khattaaara or Peyton rush into the room to the toilet, bend over it, and throw up into the bowl. She then wiped her mouth with the back of her right hand, grabbed the sides of the bowl, and threw up again, finally dropping to her knees before it, as though it had become her sacred altar. After two more dry heaves, she wearily tried to rise to her feet. The towel now wrapped around me, both Phee and I raced over to help her up and then guided her back to the bed. Beads of sweat dotted her flesh her at first and then she began to shiver. Phee covered her with blankets and tucked them around her. Then she stood up, turned away, and at once began to cry. I went over to her and held her.

"It's going to be all right," I whispered. I kept my arms around her until the crying stopped.

Morning came and went and came and went again. Phee stood vigilant at Khattaaara/Peyton's side. There was no sleep for her. There was no rest. There was only love in her heart for her sister and the fear that her sister wouldn't survive. She fed her pills and we gave her soup, encouraging her to drink it, though often in vain. Liam and I were in the kitchen. It was night again. I was standing with my back leaned up against the counter by the sink. Liam was in a chair at the table, a can of soda in one hand that he was imbibing in small sips.

"It's been three days," I said to him. "Supposedly, it can take more than a week. Phee is exhausted. Try and get her to rest. She's pale as a ghost."

"I'll do what I can," he said, putting the soda down and rising up. "Can you spell her for a bit?"

"I'm up in the room right now," I said. I looked at him and shrugged.

Up in my bedroom, as Phee sat watching her sister in a chair that bore the gravity of her soul, I stood behind her, my hands on her shoulders.

"She finally passed out," Phee said.

"It takes time," I said back. "Why don't you get some rest? I'll stay with her."

Phee looked back toward me.

"She's a part of me," she said.

"You're no good to her in pieces," I replied. Then she stood up and faced me. I placed my hands on her arms, which had fallen to her sides.

"I'll fix you something to eat and bring it up to your room," I told her. Mom and Dad had given her the same guest room that Thara-Klo had been given in the other world.

Although I still had a hold of her, Phee glanced back to see me also sitting in the chair by the bed.

"The two of you are so fucking weird," she said, "but I love you both so much."

"The feeling is mutual," I replied.

"What about Theresa?" she went on. "You've spent so much time here, ignoring her. You need a long break, too."

"You forget," I reminded her, "I can be in many places at once."

Phee shook her head to herself. "All this time and I still haven't gotten that part through my brain."

Another one of me, the one with Theresa, leaned back against the wall just outside the open door to the bathroom in her house. Theresa was on the toilet peeing. I could hear the liquid fleeing from her as it splashed down hard onto the water. I could hear the sheet of paper being torn along its perforations. I could hear the ruffling of her skirt, as she began to stand up and the sound of the seat bang down as it briefly clung to her and then let go, having served its purpose for the moment. It was the same as when I was with Ophelia, and yet this time it was as though I was a part of her, there *with* her. Intimacy is a curious beast.

"Assuming she's back to normal, so to speak, what's she gonna do about the cops?" Theresa asked.

And then there was the flush as the adulterated liquid was forced down to the sewer by the water that would replace it.

"I don't know. One step at a time, I guess," I said as she washed her hands at the sink.

"We can all thank Thara-Klo for that," she replied. "Not to mention that she murdered that man."

"And he's the one person whose death I can't undo," I said, lamenting. "The cuffs were less than ten feet away. I'd lose my powers if I went back there again. But she said he was a traitor."

There was the ruffle of terry cloth as she dried her hands,

"She says. All I know is that that woman has one fucked-up sense of morality." Theresa emerged from the bathroom and positioned herself eye-to-eye with me, wrapping her arms around my neck.

"I guess hatred blinds you sometimes," I said.

"You're not defending her, are you?" she asked.

"No," I replied. "If it wasn't for her, Peyton would never have died, Khattaaara would never have emerged, and we wouldn't be *in* this mess."

"Just wanted to hear it from your lips," Theresa said and then she kissed me.

Back in my bedroom as I still sat in the chair, Khattaaara/Peyton opened her eyes.

"Hey there," she said.

"Peyton or Khattaaara?" I questioned.

"Peyton," she replied.

"You're not in pain anymore?" I asked.

"I still hurt," she said, "but it's tolerable."

"What happened to Khattaaara?" I pressed on. "I was worried I'd have to battle her again."

"Well, now you don't," she said, which was accompanied by a weak smile.

"I'll go get Ophelia," I told her. "She's been beside herself with grief."

"I'll be here," she said and then I left her to go find Phee.

CHAPTER XLI

Peyton

In many Eastern faiths, what is called Samsāra describes the reincarnation of the human soul, which, it holds, is eternal. With each resurrection it says, a different path is taken, with karma reconciled at some distant point in time. Thus, while each of us is born in innocence, our steps are oft misguided, and, with each rebirth, our soul is tied to what we once had been. Yet when that bond is cut as happens when a universe ends and another begins, the divided self, should it come together, might find each half at odds. The quantum fabric, however, will not abide half-measures so that, in the end, the parted souls must at last unite and come to grips with all that each had done.

I was trapped inside of her. It was like being in the middle of a nightmare where you try to speak, try to move, but you can't. Khattaaara was in control and she was pretending to be me. She stood in front of the mirror that hung on the closet door—a mirror that wasn't just a mirror to her with her quantum seed but a window to her soul. What she could see, staring in, was me, Peyton, her resurrection, trapped inside her brain as though it were another parallel dimension. And it was the same for me. I could see her standing in the room admiring herself. I wanted out. I screamed at her. I pounded on the glass. She saw. She knew. And a sinister smile twisted her face.

It was then that I saw Phee come up beside her. She was dressed in the same one-piece swimsuit that she used for practice in her swim class and at meets.

"Someone once told me," Phee commented, "that when you look in a mirror you see what you *want* to see."

"And what do *I* want to see?" Khattaaara asked, pretending to be me. It is a curious predicament when one needs to convince one's sister that one is not the previous embodiment of oneself.

"Khattaaara. That's who you're looking for, isn't it?" Phee reasoned, totally taken in by the charade. "Better that she's gone."

"It isn't that," said Khattaaara in her most convincing voice. "I still *am* Khattaaara or at least her reincarnation. So, tell me, dear sister, how did I go from being a goddess to just a girl?"

"*I'm* 'just a girl.'" Phee proclaimed.

"Of course, you are, my darling. And I am *so* sorry for what I did to you as *her*. You were there for me when I was hurting. I will never forget that. If this world were about to be destroyed I would faithfully protect you."

Oddly enough, after all that had come about, I think she meant it.

"I appreciate that," Phee said. "And I'd do the same in return." She paused as though hesitant to frame the question. "But are you sure you're one hundred percent?" she asked.

"*I'm* fine, though Quantum Girl is still not up to speed. Nowhere near it actually." This was just the beginning of Khattaaara's lament.

"Even if you were," Phee replied, "you or she or... this is all so confusing. Even as Quantum Girl you can still be hurt. You can still die. Whatever Quantum Girl is she isn't Wonder Woman."

"And yet I often wonder," Khattaaara answered, apparently not having the slightest idea what Phee's reference meant. "Did you know, Khattaaara had a twin sister, too?" she went on. Her name was Klothaaara and Khattaaara loved her. She was smart and beautiful and the two of them were best friends, always by each other's sides, but then Klothaaara died and Khattaaara was never the same.

"So you remember being her," Phee said.

Khattaaara looked at Phee's reflection.

"All too well," she replied. "And I remember the hatred it filled me with. She could have been saved. There must have been a way. But no one tried—at least not hard enough."

Phee reacted with uncertainty, as Khattaaara turned and went to the window to stare through the curtains, down at the police car that sat parked on the street just outside the house.

"Are they still there?" Phee asked.

"Of course they are," Khattaaara replied.

"They won't be there forever," Phee said. "Eventually, they'll get tired and go away."

"At then what?" Khattaaara said. She turned toward Phee, scowling with indignation. "There's still nowhere I can freely go with just a fraction of my powers—no way to protect myself."

"Peypey," Phee said softly, trying to calm her. "You were happy before you could do any of that. As for the rest, we'll figure something out. As for your powers, you'll get them back, I'm sure of it," Phee insisted. "Then there can be a Quantum Girl again."

"Who is Quantum Girl?" Khattaaara spat out at her. "Where can I find her?"

"Find her? What do you mean? She's... Oh my God!" Phee exclaimed. "You're not Peyton! You're still Khattaaara!"

"And now I'm out of here," she announced and then tried to phase away. Still affected by the drugs, it took moments of concentration, disappearing and reappearing again and again until it finally worked and she was gone from the house with me still inside her brain.

CHAPTER XLII

Payton

She didn't know I was there, watching her. Every dimension has a unique signature but there is also an in-between. One might describe it as a pocket in space and time that underpins the reality of this universe and all the rest. I was *in* one of those as I watched her, my sort of sister, Ophelia. She was outside the Herron home, her Herron home, not mine. She was barefoot, wearing a pink, one-piece bathing suit, and there was that sheer, pink swimsuit coverup that was open in the front, the back of which landed just halfway down her butt, the whole of it looking like a shot of Sue Lyon in Lolita. In her left hand she held two plastic cups and in the other, a thermos, stainless steel tinged a shade of blue that would have complimented her eyes were they not hidden by the red-framed heart-shaped sunglasses. She sauntered over to the squad car that was parked outside the house and rapped on the passenger window with the thermos. The electric panel rolled down, revealing a uniformed cop on the other side.

"I thought, since you're parked out here, you might like some coffee."

"Thanks," said the cop, as he accepted the gift. Phee's right hand reached up to her sunglasses and lowered them on her nose so that her eyes laid waste to the man.

"You don't have to worry," she said. "Our family just shoots their victims. We hardly ever resort to poison." She paused, as the cop handed the thermos and one of the cups to his partner who sat behind the steering wheel.

"You boys gonna be here long?" Phee asked. "It certainly is warm outside."

"Long as it takes," said the cop.

"There's a gas station about half a mile up," she said glancing down the road, "and around four blocks north on Edgemont, if either of you needs to, well, you know."

"I'll keep that in mind," said the cop.

"You can leave the Thermos near the door when you're done," Phee said. Then she turned around and retraced her steps back to the house. Both cops watched the slowly retreating form of her legs as they rose their way up to the somewhat immodest bikini briefs.

The cop let out a sigh. "They sure didn't make 'em like that when I went to school."

"Of course, they did," said his partner. "You were just too busy holding onto your mother's apron strings to care."

I revealed myself in the backyard just a bit later. Phee stood on the diving board with goggles over her eyes, and a white bathing cap covering her hair. Three bounces, followed by a reverse dive with an inward twist, then into the water with a minimal splash. Seconds later she resurfaced, caught a glimpse of me, and swam over to the edge where I stood, viewing me through the water-stained glass of her goggles.

"I came when I heard," I said. "What's wrong?"

"The quantum bird has flown the coup," she announced. "I'm almost positive she's still Khattaaara."

"Get dressed," I told her, "and put on something warm."

CHAPTER XLIII

Khattaaara

She was inside of me, a voice that wouldn't stop screaming in my brain. I tried to ignore her but she kept me from focusing. *Let me out! Let me out!* she kept screaming inside my head. I had to find Dhraaal. I needed his guidance. I needed to make this stop. And then there were the memories. Being violated again and again by those disgusting men. Придурки![18] *Chaaadkaaagh*![19] How dare they defile the goddess of everything! *They will pay!* I reminded myself. *I will keep them alive after I peel off their skins! They will know immortality—a billion years of pain! Then there is the girl—the sister. She had been there for me all the time—always at my side until the drugs got out of me. She was what Thara-Klo should have been. Whatever happens to this world, I will protect her.* As I had this thought, the voice inside me calmed just a bit—just for a moment—and then it started up again, screaming, unrelenting, the sound of my own voice within my head, but I dared not let her out. Would that I could have multiplied like her, a thousand of *me* could have destroyed the one of *her*, but I could not focus. My head was on fire. I had to find Dhraaal!

A part of me held her memories. Would that I had had her parents and her life back on Rendenaaar. And yet this was me, reborn into a different universe with a different set of norms, a different code of conduct, indoctrinated from childhood to cherish every life, baptized to a god who promised hope and salvation in some imaginary realm. The screaming in my head began again. How could he have abandoned me? It was he who put his god-stone in my head, but where was he now? He must have left a way for me to find him. I had tapped into the Internet at the house but there was nothing—at least nothing I could find, even when I *became* the Internet. I thought to go

---

[18] Pre dur' ky! Assholes! In Russian.
[19] Excrement! in Gaaalthaaaran.

to the library, but Peyton was wanted for murder by the government and, for all intents and purposes, I was Peyton.

I phased to a border town in Mexico. I could speak their language now. I could speak all languages now. No one would know me there. No one would recognize me. But the voice, the voice! It wouldn't stop! *She* wouldn't stop! I wound up in the middle of its downtown section. There were people there, alone or together or with children, going about their daily lives. I had made it despite the constant yelling in my head but now there was a sudden pain in my left arm, an intense hard pressure such as I had never felt before. And then, as I started to walk off to find what I had come for I realized that my left arm had merged with the lamppost I had phased next to. It took every ounce of my will to get it free as I tried to focus amid the noise that no one else could hear. I couldn't take it anymore. I beat at my head with my fists. What was the significance of her counting some numbers of beer on some wall, singing it again and again? I screamed out, "Stop!" as tears flowed from my eyes and down my cheeks. People around me began to stare and so, despite my newfound insanity, I chose to walk away and immerse myself in a different crowd. But truth be told, none of those who had witnessed my outburst had really paid me much concern. To them, my actions were just a momentary annoyance, for I was just an out-of-place American, a *gringa*, of little interest when weighed against their personal lives.

After questioning several people, I found what I was looking for—a beauty supply shop with a sign that read, "*Productos Cosméticos.*" As I entered, a small bell that hung over the door jingled, announcing me to whoever was there. Once inside I noticed a middle-aged woman seated behind the counter to my right, her skin brown, her face lined with age. There was a somewhat vacant look in her eyes as though she had sat at that same counter for a thousand years, waiting endlessly to be ferried off to some better place. She looked up at me with tired dark eyes. I spoke to her in her native tongue. I asked if she sold any wigs. She directed me to a section toward the middle of the store in an adjacent aisle. I thanked her and followed her directions.

I picked out a straight black wig that curved inward just below my chin. Colored contacts at an optical store gave me hazel-colored eyes. Added to that were eye makeup, red lipstick, and very fashionable clothes from a New York Fifth Avenue boutique. No one would recognize me unless they knew me and looked closely. So long as I stayed away from where Peyton had grown up, I felt that I would be safe. Gathering my strength, against the endless singing in my head, I phased to the steps of the New York Public Library, unfortunate for the pigeon that had stood where my right foot had appeared. I phased out of it, gladdened by the thought that I had not materialized in another human or, worse, inside one of the two stone lions that guarded the front doors.

Having ascended the marble stairs, I made my way inside and to the reference desk where I enlisted the services of one of the librarians—a man in his late twenties who began the conversation by undressing me with his eyes.

"May I help you?" the man asked.

"I'm looking for information on someone," I replied.

"Have you checked online?" he asked.

"I'm afraid I came up empty," I replied.

"There are directories we can check," he said. "What is the person's name?" His attention was now drawn to his computer screen.

"Dhraaal," I answered. "That's all I know."

CHAPTER XLIV

Ophelia

She had brought me to Titan, one of Saturn's moons. I stood with her, taking in the marvels of the ancient land. It was the most incredible experience I have ever had other than the first time I had sex, which was with Liam just a few short days before. The entire landscape was orange and there were mountains in every direction, though the two of us were the only living things there. Above us hung Saturn's rings that were like nothing anyone could ever imagine. It was as though we were seeing stardust circling the giant planet with its swirling, colored bands of hydrogen, contaminated with sulfur and ammonia, ever-changing their patterns from its cyclonic winds. The rings, Payton told me, were made of ice and rock, separated from each other by tiny shepherd moons. And then there were the *other* moons—the larger ones—those not obscured by the planet—Dione and Hyperion and dozens of others that can barely be seen from the Earth, even with the best of telescopes. How breathtaking it was as we watched, protected from the void of space by a force field that Payton, as Quantum Girl, had surrounded us with. The light was such that even the violet she radiated was tinged with the colors all around.

"Where's the earth?" I asked.

She pointed up with her left arm toward a section of the sky just north of Saturn's rings.

"Over there to the right of the sun," she said.

I stared in that direction. I saw the sun, now less than half the size of a pea.

"I can't make it out," I said, squinting my eyes.

She waved her hand and caused a map of the stars and the planets to appear. Then she brought up her other arm, pulled her hands apart, and enlarged that portion of the sky where Mother Earth and her daughter, the moon, circled their burning star.

"How are you able to do that?" I inquired.

"Everything in the universe is simply a construct of the quantum fabric," she explained. "I just manipulate what is into what I want it to be."

"You're starting to talk like Peyton," I said.

"I *am* Peyton," she replied. "Just a different version of her."

She was now on the ground with her legs bent, leaning back on her arms while I sat beside her, having gathered my knees up to my chest. My left cheek rested on them as I looked at her, my sort of other twin.

"Are you able to make anything out of thin air?" I asked her.

"It's incredibly draining," she replied, "and dangerous for me. But I can manipulate matter and light." She paused and sighed. "And sometimes Theresa, but don't you dare tell her I said so."

"I won't," I said, lulled by the visual atmosphere.

"It's like my costume," she went on. "It's just an illusion to brave all levels of decency, I'm actually naked right now. But I could make my street clothes look like this if I wanted. It's just less confining this way."

"You and Peypey are two totally different people," I said. "I miss her so much. I mean..." and I broke off.

"I know," she said as she gazed up toward our distant home.

CHAPTER XLV

Khattaaara

The librarian, after some short research, handed me a spool of microfiche on which (using the reader) I was able to find a newspaper article from several years ago entitled, "New Head of Quantech," revealing that a Thomas Drall had been installed as CEO.

I couldn't risk long jumps; at least not where I might phase my head or heart into solid matter. There would be no return from that. Instead, I phased into the sky above the lab, visually scouted out the terrain from that vantage point, and then phased down to the surface where I would be close, but unobserved. After that, I entered the building. As I stood in the middle of the lobby, looking around, a guard in a dark suit walked up to me.

"May I help you?" he asked.

"I'm looking for Thomas Drall," I replied.

"Are you expected?" in inquired.

"No," I replied, and then explained, "I'm his daughter. Katara."

"Wait just a moment," he said. Then he walked to one side and spoke into a microphone that was connected to a coiled wire, that reached up to a small device in his ear. He returned a moment later. "Follow me," he ordered, and he turned and walked to a bank of elevators, waved a card over a small panel in the wall, and waited for the doors to open.

I went into the elevator alone and traveled up to the penthouse suite. When the doors opened again, Dhraaal was seated at a large desk that faced me. He looked up and then rose and walked over to me as I entered the room. Then he took my hands in his.

"You look amazing," he said.

I shrugged. "The authorities are looking for me," I replied. Despite my disguise, I was still filled with anxiety over the prospect of having to do battle against an entire planet with my powers as they were.

"So I heard," he said, "but you have the stone," and then he looked at me, at once both curious and concerned. "I don't understand why you didn't just teleport into my office. Why announce yourself?"

"Long story," I replied. "Plus, she's still inside of me," I said.

"Who?" he asked.

I leaned into him, pressing my cheek against his chest. He responded by putting his arms around me and pulling me close to him and for the briefest of moments I felt safe.

"My infernal reincarnation," I said back. "She learned how to duplicate herself before I emerged and then one of her duplicates merged into me afterward."

"My poor Khattaaara," Dhraaal said, rubbing my back.

I pulled away just enough to look up at him.

"She won't stop screaming and singing in my head," I wept. "She demands that I let her out, but if I do I know she'll try to destroy me."

"This wasn't how it was supposed to be," he said in a serious tone. "The other times it was never like this."

"Other times?" I asked, my voice weakened even more than it had been by the thoughts that had arisen in my mind.

"You've been reincarnated thousands of times in thousands of universes," he explained, "and each time our daughter has managed to defeat us and destroy *you*."

"But how?" I asked.

"She has your god-stone in her head," he said.

"What are we going to do?" I asked as I stared into his eyes.

"We need to end this eternal battle once and for all," he said profoundly.

I barely heard his words. I grabbed my head.

"It just doesn't stop!" I wept. "It never ends!"

"I'll phone my physician," Dhraaal replied. His voice was reassuring. "Perhaps he can prescribe some medication."

He walked over to the wet bar that stood against one wall and then poured a golden liquid from a crystal decanter into a small glass.

"In the meantime," he said, "perhaps some brandy will help."

He returned to me with the glass. I stared at him.

"Why didn't you take me when you put the god-stone in my head? You can't imagine what I've been put through."

He gently placed the glass in my hand.

"I couldn't very well kidnap a fifteen-year-old girl," he explained. "I needed to wait until your personality reemerged. I would have preferred for your reincarnate to have aged a bit more but you took it upon yourself to commit suicide so I didn't have much choice."

I sniffed the liquid and then drank it. It felt warm going down my throat.

"I'm glad I found you," I said.

"It's been a long time," Dhraaal lamented.

I went to the window and stared out. "*How* long?" I asked.

"Since Rendenaaar?" he said with a note of nostalgia in his voice. "A billion, billion universes come and gone."

"Surely you haven't lived through them all?" I pressed on.

"I would like to have said so," he replied, "but the truth is that I've cheated. I jumped across many of them until I eventually came *here* roughly five millennia ago when the stone was in *my* head."

"Why so far from now?" I asked. The brandy had taken effect. The voice was quieter now though not entirely gone.

"The god-stone couldn't predict when you would be reborn," he explained. "Only where. Anyway, I'm glad you're here now." He paused and then stared at me. "By the way," he asked, "how *did* you find me?"

"Sheer luck," I replied. "Your name came up on something called Google." I brought the glass to my lips again then swallowed what was left. "What have you been up to all this time?"

"Amassing wealth," he said. "Bit of a problem having had to reinvent myself every few decades or so. These humans don't take well to immortality when it isn't for them. I've been experimenting with a device to tap into quantum fabric in order to resurrect Rendenaaar though it has been difficult working with this world's somewhat primitive technology."

"You always found a way," I said with encouragement.

Dhraaal looked at me with grave seriousness. "I don't think Thara's aware how different the god-stone is that she has. That does go in our favor."

"I don't know if it's from my revival or from the drugs that I was given, but my brain is all scrambled. Even with the mother stone back in my head, there is so much I need to relearn."

"I will help you," Dhraaal reassured me. "We will resurrect our planet then you and I shall once more rule all that exists."

CHAPTER XLVI

Payton

I was lying back on the bed in Theresa's room as she lay on her side facing me gently stroking my hair. I was wearing my pink nightgown or what appeared to be my pink nightie in that I was actually naked. Theresa was in a long T-shirt that fell down to her knees.

"Do you think we can trust Thara-Klo?" I asked her.

"Why?" she said. "What's up?"

"Khattaaara and I are too evenly matched for me to defeat her," I said, "But with Thara-Klo..."

"Two against one," she said as she gently kissed my mouth. "I don't know," she went on continuing to peck at my lips between breaths, "I'd like to say yes, but then she *is* a product of that other world. How about we sleep on it?"

"Fine," I replied, "only don't make those sounds."

"What sounds?" she asked.

"The whimpering sounds," I replied. "In your sleep."

"I can't control what I do in my sleep," she said.

"Then I'll wake you up," I replied.

"Well, *then*," she said, pecking kisses with every other word, "if I'm awake there are things I'll make you do to me."

"Right now, I need to talk to Thara-Klo," I said from a few feet away where I had duplicated and phased.

She laid down, and snuggled into me then noticed the other one—the Quantum Girl one—standing near the foot of the bed.

"Fuck," she muttered, momentarily confused. "God, I hate when you do that!"

"Would you rather that *all* of me went away?" the Payton me asked, already knowing her answer as my quantum self phased from the room.

"No," she said, "I'm good. We're good."

I glanced toward her. "We need to get some sleep," I told her.

"And?" she asked.

"You need to take your hand away from there," I replied.

"From where?" came her feigned innocent remark.

"You *know* where," I said.

"Don't you like it?" she asked.

"This isn't the time," I said.

"When *is* the right time?" she asked.

"Anytime but now," I replied.

Theresa lifted her arm and wrapped it around my waist then snuggled herself into me.

"I'll hold you to that," she softly said and then both of us closed our eyes and drifted off. "Anytime."

Sleep is one of the greatest enemies of mankind. It robs us of one-third of our existence. The average life expectancy in industrialized nations is roughly eighty years. That means that the average person sleeps for more than two and one-half decades—six years longer than Rip Van Winkle. Granted, we are not entirely unconscious during sleep but although we dream, many of our dreams are unpleasant and most are quickly forgotten upon waking. I only bring this up because dividing into more than one of myself necessitates that only one of me sacrifice that portion of my life so that as I slept next to Theresa, I could still engage in a conversation with Thara-Klo.

She had been recuperating rather well from her injury when I came to the guest room where she lay quietly in bed reading a copy of *Thus Spoke Zarathustra* by Friedrich Nietzsche, the Nineteenth Century German philosopher and writer. In the book, the protagonist, Zarathustra (whom Nietzsche patterned after Zarathustra's namesake, who founded Zoroastrianism), imagined an eternal struggle between good and evil, believing that beneath man is "an inexhaustible well of truth to which no pail descends without coming up again filled with gold and goodness." He spoke of both the *Übermensch* or superman and the eternal return. He admonished those who put their hopes in some future unproven existence rather than focusing their energies on their lives on this Earth.

Thara-Klo looked up from the book and stared at me in my Quantum Girl presence.

"Is it still Halloween?" she asked facetiously.

"The costume affords me protection," I shot back.

"Still don't trust me?" she said. It was more of an observation than a question.

"Trust takes time," I replied. "You've yet to apologize for getting Peyton shot."

Thara-Klo laid the book down on her lap.

"I am sorry in retrospect," she admitted, "but you've now seen what I'd feared. Peyton Herron, the other Peyton Herron, may have been the kindest, most gentle creature to have ever walked the Earth but there was a beast that lived inside her, so deadly that she could destroy an entire universe with just a single thought and often did." She paused and then went on. "But tell me, why are you here now?"

"I want to know why you care," came my response. "This isn't your planet. It's not even your universe."

"Nor yours," she replied. She rose from the bed and put on a robe. "You want answers? I want to show you something."

Her gaze seemed to go blank for a moment. Then her eyes glowed blue and the room disappeared to be replaced by an outdoor mall, only not like anything I had ever seen. The buildings were futuristic in appearance. There were vehicles of sorts that popped in and out of the sky and then floated off to land on one platform or another from which people got off or got on. But it was the people up close that made me realize what I was seeing. The females were all like Thara-Klo with pointed ears and two pairs of breasts, one beneath the other, which was apparent from the tight-fitting clothing that appeared to be in style. And every one of them had a tail. Those on the adults were proportionally longer than those on any child, which were little more than stubs, presumably eventually growing in length as they matured. The female tail was smooth, with an arrow-like tip that appeared to be covered in hair, which matched that on her head. Meanwhile, those of the males had bumps all over them and the hair at the tip was rounded rather than coming to a point, which may have been a male sex trait as the male ears were also rounded, resembling our own. As Thara-Klo explained, the Rendenaaaran people do not possess sexual organs like humans. Rather, the end of the female's tail opens whenever there is a desire to mate and the male inserts his into hers. This may be done by the male facing the female or from behind her. But even more unlike humans, the tails are proudly displayed by Gaaalthaaarans of both sexes (Gaaalthaaaran was the word for her species, she said), such being considered the most important part for the continuation of their race.

"How did we get here?" I asked as a man on his way to somewhere walked right through me. "I didn't feel us phase."

"We didn't phase, as you call it," she explained. "I folded space and time. We're in what you might call a pocket dimension. We can see *them* but they can't see *us*. Our quantum thread right now lies an infinitesimal bit over theirs, a hair's breadth into their future."

"If you're thinking this is Rendenaaar," she went on, "it's not. This is Earth's future if left unchecked, where humans have all been transformed into my kind."

"But how is that possible?" I asked.

"A virus," she explained, "will be spread among them that will alter their genetic code to change them. They will live as we lived, mate through their *yaaarghs*—what you think of as a tail—and revive our long-dead race. Khattaaara will bring Rendenaaar back into existence only to destroy all of its life again. This is your Earth just twenty years from now unless she's stopped. She's done this before on other worlds—transformed their races just to murder them as if to exact her revenge on the ghosts of her people again and again."

There was a brilliant flash of light, so bright that I covered my

273

eyes. There were no sounds in this view of days to come but all of them, as far as I could see, suddenly screamed out in agony as a quantum blast burned the flesh from their bones and reduced them to ashes so that in the end all that remained was a desolate, scorched world and Khattaaara, who hovered above it in the dismal sky.

"Rendenaaar existed trillions of universes ago," I said. "Why would she even care?"

The scene then vanished and I found myself back in the guest room with Thara-Klo and no one else around.

"She's insane," she replied, "and drunk with power. She may have been a good person once. I remember her when I was very young as being loving and caring but something happened to her once the god-stone went into her head. Something went wrong. Perhaps it triggered a mental imbalance. I don't know. But she became different— dispassionate, filled with venom, sexually insatiable, and, more than that, cruel. Her life was ended once. It needs to end again."

"But you'll be killing Peyton as well," I protested.

"A small sacrifice for the billions of lives she threatens to end just here on *this* world."

"What about the future?" I asked.

She walked to the window and stared out. "Everything is irreconcilable," she said. "The future where Dhraaal and Khattaaara have succeeded in conquering humanity will happen because it already has happened. But we can change the future that we ourselves go to."

"How?" I asked. "By murdering Peyton? There must be another way."

Thara-Klo thought for a moment. "Perhaps," she said, "if we can help your dimensional twin defeat her other self."

CHAPTER XLVII

Khattaaara

We were in Dhraaal's bedroom. The long day had at last come to an end and we lay in bed together, naked under a sheet—he on his back and I on my side facing him. My long blonde hair fell upon his shoulder. The fingers of my left hand gently stroked his forehead and then moved under the sheet to rub up and down his *yaaargh*, which began to throb at my caress.

"How will this be different?" I asked.

"Because this time," he said with somewhat labored breath, "from whatever dimension, Quantum Woman does not yet exist." He paused to moan then went on. "There is just that inexperienced child."

"And when Rendenaaar is reborn?" I pressed on, tightening my grip on his *yaaargh*. Dhraaal closed his eyes as his body stiffened, and then relaxed once again as did my grasp, which became gentle again. He breathed out a great sigh.

"We will all rule like gods," he quietly proclaimed.

I rose up and knelt, straddling him, my naked legs pressing hard against his hips. It was then that his *yaaargh* entered me. In that he was Gaaalthaaaran and not human, that was how it had to be. How different it was from before, but pleasurable nevertheless. Then, all at once, after he was done in me, our bodies dripping in his azure *graaam*, I began to cause him to slowly phase away—slow enough for him to realize that something was wrong.

"Khattaaara!" he gasped. "What are you doing?" His face was riddled with panic and fear.

"There is only room for one god in the universe," I said.

He screamed out, "No!" And then he was gone; gone to the lady in the moon; gone like the driver of that car. I fell down onto the bed, onto my back, laughed villainously to myself, and then stretched out my arms, closed my eyes, and dreamt of Rendenaaar.

CHAPTER XLVIII

Payton

Thara-Klo then caused us to once more become like ghosts, but this time in the bedroom where Ophelia lay asleep, her head turned toward the far wall. But this was here and now, what was and not what would or what might be.

"Can she hear us?" I asked

"No," Thara-Klo said. "It's like before,"

"How long have you known about Peyton?" I asked.

"Since the day she was born," she replied and her voice sounded almost wistful. "I held her in the hospital that night." She paused for a moment as a thoughtful look appeared in her eyes. "Imagine holding your own mother as an infant in your arms—having the power of life and death over one so helpless and small. I had my opportunity there and then but I could not take the life of a newborn child."

"I loved Margaret, Peyton's grandmother. Magpie—that's what I used to call her. I stayed as close as I could. When Peyton was small, when she was alone, sometimes I would come to her as Willem, a wisp of what might have been a boy her own age. We would play together when Ophelia wasn't around. I can't count the number of times I prayed that Khattaaara would never emerge and that this sweet little girl would remain Peyton forever. But I knew in my heart that it never could be. The quantum threads would not ever show mercy for either the Gaaalthaaaran or the human soul."

"And so the time came when she needed to die. And my emotions, my hatred of my mother, what she had done to me and to countless others, got the better of me. I put the thought of suicide in her head, but then Dhraaal resurrected her and then she had the god-stone and I knew I had played my hand too late."

"Am I bound to my own Khattaaara?" I asked, the question ever-present in my brain.

"In your dimension," she said, "Rendenaaar did not exist." She took a deep breath. "Now, Quantum Girl. Are you prepared for the ultimate battle between evil and good?"

"What choice do I have?" I asked. "*You* tell *me*."

CHAPTER XLIX

Khattaaara

I had never felt so free. The brandy had been helping with the voice in my head and soon with the medication it would be gone—*she* would be gone. How was it that I could have been reborn to have lived such a mundane life? How the thought that I might have grown up to become subservient to some pompous male made me sick to the depths of my entrails, like food that has been swallowed where there is no stomach to contain it for long. To have waited a billion, billion years only to awaken a slave to a brutish sex—better never to have been born at all. Thank the gods of Rendenaaar that I came to my senses!

The brunette I now was walked into the Quantech lobby on stilettos that would have pierced holes in the granite floor if I chose—such was the sense of power that now coursed through my veins. The same security guard approached me with, "Good morning, Miss Drall."

I did not return the greeting. Those empowered by wealth or rank need not. Rather, I stopped in my tracks, turned my head just a bit in his direction, and spoke. "My father's physician will be arriving within the hour. Please show him up."

"Yes, Miss Drall," the guard said respectfully. "Will there be anything else?"

"Yes," I said. "I'll need a key card."

"I'll have one made," came the creature's obedient reply.

"My father left on a business trip last night," I went on. "He placed me in charge of his affairs while he's gone." I paused as I felt a pang of hunger. "And order me some lunch," I went on. "Find the best restaurant and send someone to pick it up."

"Yes, Ma'am," he replied once more.

I went to the elevator, the dog at my heels to use his card to open the doors so that I might ascend to my new throne.

CHAPTER L

Payton

I was in Theresa's bedroom, my legs hanging over the edge of her bed as she sat on it with hers folded, viewing her laptop.

"I get how the two of you can find her," Theresa said. "Even how you can capture her. But how do you plan on getting Peyton back?"

"It's not a question of how," I replied. "It's a question of if."

"What if it isn't really Khattaaara?" she asked.

I looked at her with a lack of understanding. "Meaning?" *I* asked.

"She had this near-death experience," she went on. "What if that just made her believe she's this evil woman from the past? What if it's all psychological?"

"Either way," I answered, "she's a force to be reckoned with."

Then, suddenly, there was Khattaaara in the room with an entirely new look. She had chin-length straight dark hair, twenty-something make-up, and was wearing a dress and heels that looked like they had just been pulled off a window mannequin on Rodeo Drive.

"I most certainly am," she announced.

"Fuck me!" Theresa muttered, half to herself.

Khattaaara glanced at Theresa.

"Maybe a different time," she said and then turned toward me. "Right now," she went on, "I want the god-stone in your head. Surrender it this very instant or I'll end her." She waited around five seconds then shrugged. "Too much time," she proclaimed and with that, she extended one arm toward Theresa. As for me, I threw myself between them to protect her. I screamed out, "No!" but the energy went right through me, striking her.

I turned and grabbed her and held her in my arms.

"No, no, oh no!" I cried.

Gently, I laid her back down on the bed and then turned and stood and faced Khattaaara. Rage rose within me.

"I don't care who's inside of you!" I spat at her. "You're dead!"

Within an instant, there were *twenty* rage-filled Quantum Girls that had surrounded Khattaaara as I lifted Theresa into my arms and phased us both to the hospital ER. Meanwhile, Khattaaara, for whatever reason, didn't duplicate herself to fight me off. Instead, she muttered, "Shit!" and with that, she was gone.

I left Theresa with the nurses, and then, finding someplace private, I phased back to her bedroom, merged all of me back into one. and then broke the news to her mother.

"*¡Mi bebé! ¡Mi bebé! ¡Dios la ayude! ¡Mi bebé!*" her mother wept as she fell into my arms and into tears.

CHAPTER LI

Peyton

Khattaaara! I could hear her every thought. I had tried screaming and singing and even begging for her to let me out but all to no avail. And then Dhraaal had given her alcohol which caused my consciousness to fade in and out. It was like some lucid nightmare that I could not awaken from.

When I felt Dhraaal inside her, I went into hysterics. It was bad enough that because of her I had been drugged and raped, but to be defied by some alien being went beyond the pale! I wept without tears as I unwillingly shared the orgasm that she felt. It just wasn't fair! I wanted my first time to be with someone I loved—not with the man who had raped me and definitely not with a creature with a zebra-like tail that doubled as a sexual appendage!

She was in Dhraaal's office in her now permanent disguise. The physician had come and gone and the pharmacy had filled a prescription for some antipsychotic drug. She took one pill as she stood once more at the wet bar and washed it down with brandy. Then she looked at the clock and waited till half an hour had passed, sitting at what once was Dhraaal's desk, passing time with a Newton's cradle and its metal balls, held up by strings that carried the motion of the one that was dropped to all the rest. Rising from the tufted leather chair, she walked to the middle of the room, closed her eyes, and made a second one of her appear, then a third and a fourth, until there was barely enough space (or oxygen for that matter) in the room. Unbeknownst to her, one of the duplicates was me. I quickly took the opportunity to phase out of the room, out to the desert, where I stood and screamed out the insanity I had fled.

When I had somewhat calmed myself, I phased back home to the kitchen where Phee stood at the island counter drinking the milk she had just poured from a carton into a glass.

"Phee?" I said from behind her.

Phee instantly turned, caught sight of me, and dropped the glass, which shattered and spilled on the floor. Her body stiffened as noticeable fear gripped her every cell. Terror shone like a beacon in her eyes.

"Stay away from me!" she said, as her voice trembled. "I know who you are! I know what you did to Theresa!"

I raised my hands, my palms out toward her in a gesture that I thought would convey that I didn't want to do her harm.

"No," I said, "it's me. It's Peyton. At least a part of me. Of her. I'm one of the multiples from before Khattaaara's mind took over." I paused and then swore to her, "Really."

Phee stared at me, looking for some truth in what I had just said.

"Peyton?" she said, her voice breaking as she did, tears coming to her eyes. "I don't understand any of this—how all of this could have gone so wrong?"

"I know," I said, trying to assuage any doubts. "Life was all so much simpler before I tried to kill myself and Dhraaal put the seed in my head."

Suddenly, a serious look took over her face.

"What's done is done," she said.

"It still feels like I'm responsible," I replied. "I didn't ask for any of this," I said and began to cry, "and I don't know what to do. I'm not the superhero everyone makes me out to be."

"Wonder Woman isn't real," Phee said. "You are."

I wiped mine from my eyes with the back of my hand.

"Sometimes I wish I weren't," I said.

"Don't ever say that!" Phee replied. "I can't imagine what it'd be like without you!"

"You can't imagine what it was like being in Khattaaara's body," I said, "and being forced to watch her, to *be* her and have sex with that disgusting old man or whatever he was!"

"I'm so sorry, Peypey," Phee said and then added, "Look, Payton

283

and Thara-Klo are trying to figure out a plan to get you back in control."

"Thara-Klo?" I exclaimed. "Thara-Klo who tried to blast me out of existence? *That* Thara-Klo?"

"It's a long story," Phee said, "but as it turns out, Killer Klo is on *our* side."

We gathered in the living room later that night after all the tears had been shed. I was lying on the sofa in my mother's arms as the rest sat around—except for Dad who was too restless to sit. Liam and Phee were on the loveseat. Payton and Thara-Klo each sat in overstuffed chairs facing each other. Thara-Klo acted as though nothing had ever happened between us. After some casual banter, she turned to me.

"The problem, as I see it," she said, "is not in destroying Khattaaara—something that would please me to no end—but to preserve the young innocent who represents nothing but kindness and good. The reality, however, is that Khattaaara and Peyton are one and the same, a single soul severed by the end of one universe and the beginning of another but still connected by a single quantum thread."

"So, what do we do?" I asked. "What do *I* do?"

"You need to become one with her," she said. "You need to accept who you were and assimilate that with who you now are and decide who you want to be. That's a lot to handle, especially for a teenage girl."

"When I was inside her, I tried. There was nothing I could do."

"No," she insisted. "You resisted becoming a part of her. Right now, you are the only remaining remnant of Peyton Herron. You must be willing to accept who you were, merge your consciousness with hers, accept the evils that you've done, and be the hero you were meant to be. Be the mother I always wanted. There is strength in who you are. Khattaaara is weak. All that is in her is depravity and hate. You just need to come to grips with the fact that you are her and that she is you and that the Peyton half is the stronger of the two."

CHAPTER LII

Khattaaara

It was the first time I had ever been to a nightclub. Actually, it was probably more of a rave. Overall, the place was dark, lit by black and neon lights. Those in attendance were, for the most part, in their twenties or early thirties with a few stragglers on either end of the spectrum. Not one of the security guards letting those waiting outside in line had asked for any ID from me. They just wanted to assume that I was legal and let me through the door ahead of the throngs of those desperately trying to get in. Humans appear to seek status. Even Dhraaal in his pretense at *being* human, had succumbed to that need.

After mulling through a lot of sequins and silk, I sat down at the bar and ordered some green-colored drink with fruit, in a cone-shaped glass, in which was plunged a red plastic straw and a miniature umbrella. As I sipped the tart concoction, a good-looking man who appeared somewhat older than me approached me. He was dressed in an open white shirt over which was a black sport coat. He looked at me and then at the unoccupied stool to my left.

"Mind if I sit?" he asked with a Texas drawl. I glanced at the stool and then at him.

"Why should I care?" I replied as I glanced around the room. "There are a lot of chairs all around." Then I took on an expression of sudden but feigned realization. "Oh," I said, "What you're asking is if I mind if you sit *next* to me. Be my guest." And so he sat down on the stool.

"I haven't seen you here before?" he said, unphased. "You new here? You are definitely the hottest girl in the room."

"May I ask *you* a question?" I said back.

"Go ahead," came the all-smiles reply.

I sipped the drink through my straw and then paused, pulling my lips away. "I'd like to know," I said, "do you want to fuck me or do you want to just hit me up with every bullshit cliche in the book?"

We went into the ladies' room (which was one hell of a lot cleaner than the men's) and locked the door. He pushed me up against the wall, kissed me passionately, and began to unbutton my blouse. I wrapped my arms around his neck. Then he put his hands under my skirt and grabbed my butt. I could feel the force of his fingers as he turned us both around so that my derriere landed on the dressing table. Then we fucked, throughout the course (or intercourse) of which came a lot of moaning, heavy breathing, and screams of ecstasy from me. When it was over he started to zip up his pants.

"Come on, Baby," I said. "Let's go at it again."

The man shook his head. "Darlin'," he said, "I only got so much in me."

I reached out and laced my fingers behind his neck. "But I want more," I pouted.

"There are a lot of guys out there that'd love to take you on," he said. "I'm sure you can get a ride from any one of them."

"But I want *you*," I said "We *both* do."

The man suddenly noticed that there was another one of me behind him. The other me pressed up against his back and moved her hand down to his crotch. The act stimulated him but he seemed unnerved by the other's presence.

"What's going on?" he said. "She your twin? Under normal circumstances, I'd love to do you both but the truth is I've had a lot to drink and the car can only go so many miles before runnin' outta gas."

Then a third one of me appeared and then a fourth.

"What the hell!" the man exclaimed, now filled with anxiety.

Twenty more and then thirty and then more and more of me, popping into existence in the room, pawing at him, crushing him, driving him to the floor then stomping him with our pointed heels that bled the life out of him as he screamed out cries of agony, until, at last, he lay there without motion in a pool of crimson blood like the corpse that he now was. *So odd, the color of these humans' blood* I remember thinking to myself as my legions recombined into one.

"Oh, that felt so good," I said out loud. And it had. So very, very good. I closed my eyes, as I stretched out my arms. I smiled to myself and then I vanished from the room.

CHAPTER LIII

Payton

Theresa lay unconscious on a hospital bed. Her brain had stopped functioning from the quantum energy blast. She was on life-support with a breathing tube down her throat. The doctors gave her no hope of recovery. It was night when I phased into the hospital in an empty corridor. I couldn't go through the entrance, which had security guards, concerned that my face was now all too well-known. Despite the fact that I am not Peyton Herron, the mirror resemblance was something I couldn't explain away. Peyton Herron only had one sister who was *not* her identical twin.

As I stood in the doorway to her room, I saw Theresa's mother sitting in a chair beside her bed. *"Dios del cielo, ayuda a mi hija Theresa Maria a recuperarse. Ella es una buena chica y la quiero mucho. Ella es todo lo que tengo en el mundo. Por favor, Dios, ayúdala,"* she said as she wept out the words; words, which meant, "God in Heaven, help my daughter, Theresa Maria, to be well again. She is a good girl and I love her so much. She is all that I have in the world. Please, God, help her."

I decided not to interrupt. Theresa was all but gone from this earth and there was nothing I could do. More than her being my lover, here was her mother, spending what moments she could with her dying little girl. I glanced around to see that no one was watching and then I phased from the corridor I was in.

I could have said that the morning came without incident but that was the furthest thing. I had spent the night at Peyton's home. So odd that I'd shared the bed with Peyton, while Ophelia slept in hers on the other side of the room. Liam, sadly, had to make due on the couch. Rightfully so, Peyton's mom refused to let him bunk with Ophelia despite their remonstrations to the contrary.

Morning broke with grave ferocity. A black and white was still outside as had been the case since the death of the federal officer. What made it different and decidedly deadly, was the appearance of a scarlet costumed Quantum Girl, namely Khattaaara. There was not just one of her, however, but a virtually uncountable number peopling the sky over the Herron home.

"Come out, Quantum Girl," they all said at once. "We know you're in there." The sound was deafening. Peyton and I both peered past the bedroom curtains and out through the window at the eerie scene. It was then that I became Quantum Girl once more.

"There are hundreds of her," I said, turning to the others who had all gathered in the room.

"It's taking every ounce of strength to keep my mind out of hers." That was Peyton who spoke.

Thara-Klo turned to her. "You stay here for now," she said and then she turned to me. "Quantum Girl, you and I need to go out there."

Ophelia looked at her. "Why don't you have a costume?" she asked.

"Because I don't need one," came the curt reply.

Within seconds, hundreds of me had phased into the sky to do battle with the woman from another time. Quantum blasts hurled back and forth between us with little effect. Meanwhile, Thara-Klo had morphed back into her dragon form, breathing out blasts of quantum ice at the crimson force. One by one, the Quantum Khattaaaras turned into vapor, screaming like banshees as they did.

As a crowd of onlookers began to gather on the ground, three Apache helicopters flew in from the north, firing machine guns at the dragon. Then, as the dragon, which was Thara-Klo, began to be hit, it turned its head toward them and exhaled a blast of white quantum flames, striking one of the choppers head-on and crippling it. The machine began spinning out of control, about to crash into one house. Both the pilot and the gunner were screaming as they were being burned alive. Meanwhile, the house lay in its trajectory.

As I saw what was about to happen, some of me phased down into the house and rescued the couple that lived there, along with their two small children and their dog. An instant later, the helicopter crashed through the roof of the house, exploding into a fireball.

But the dragon wasn't through with the military onslaught. Flapping its giant wings, it soared high into the sky and then dove down like a missile, breathing out cold flames as it went, melting the main propellers of the two remaining machines, which then collided into each other and blew up in the sky.

By now a huge crowd had assembled beneath to observe the spectacle, all of its members now endangered by the falling debris. Dividing into more of me as the battle with Khattaaara continued, I turned into a blur of Quantum Girls in order to rescue each and every person who stood in harm's way. As I did, I could hear one of the officers talking on his radio.

"It's like a war zone here!" he said into the mic.

"What are you seeing?" the dispatcher responded.

"Helicopters, flying women, and a dragon!" the cop proclaimed.

"Please repeat," the dispatcher said. "Did you say flying women and a dragon?"

"That's an affirmative," he replied. "Flying women and a *white* dragon to be precise. And I would suggest you send backup. As many as you can."

The dragon continued to flap its massive wings and breathe out its flames at the red-outfitted Quantum Girls, turning them, again and again, into shrieking sprays of crimson dust, while others of them hurled red fireballs at it, punching large holes in its wings, and, finally, one through its heart. With a dying surge of strength, the dragon that was Thara-Klo, breathed out a tremendous blast of cold fire and disintegrated all but one of Khattaaara who had shielded herself behind me.

The pain of their destruction as felt by the common mind must have been enormous, for that one remaining red-garbed Apollyon fell into unconsciousness and hung aloft midair. As she did, the dragon breathed its last and plummeted to the ground, ripping a crater into the asphalt, concrete, and soil.

It was then that Peyton phased beside us and then that Khattaaara began to open her eyes. I drew my arm back, clenched my fist, and dealt her an uppercut to the jaw, knocking her out again.

"That's for Theresa!" I said. Then I turned to Peyton and reminded her, "It's now all up to you."

Peyton took in a deep breath, exhaled, and then merged into Khattaaara.

There were changes in her face—in Khattaaara's face—not physical but from emotions. The crimson costume turned to silver, and then she opened her eyes.

"Peyton?" I said, uncertain whom I would find.

"Yes," she said. "Peyton. And Khattaaara. But the anger that was there is gone."

CHAPTER LIV

Peyton

I had just merged with Khattaaara only it was different from before. I accepted her as part of me—an ancient, hideous relic of a long-forgotten civilization—but I also needed to accept what I had done and balance that against who I now was. There is good and bad in each of us but our salvation can only come from the realization that we are, each of us, the product of our experiences and the result of whom we were taught to be. That I am Khattaaara is an irrevocable given, but I am also Peyton, who was raised with a sense of morality and shown the difference between right and wrong. And, whether I am Peyton or Khattaaara, I am also Quantum Girl, a symbol of what is fair and just and good, for this is my chosen path.

Payton smiled at me and I smiled back. Then I gazed downward, and saw Thara-Klo on the ground, dying, lying in the crater she had caused to exist when she, as the dragon, fell to earth like a meteor. I phased to the ground beside her and then squatted down next to where she lay.

"She did good," she said with a voice that coughed out words. I took away my cowl and tried to smile.

"You both did," I said as I choked on my tears, "but I let you down so much. I should have protected you. You were my little girl."

"It took a long time," my Thara said, "but I'm so proud, Mother, of who you are today."

Then her eyes went blank as she died. A moment later, the woman who had been borne of my tail in that forgotten time, withered into an old woman, turned into a skeleton, and then into dust. I knelt down beside what had been my perfect child and screamed out "No!" It was a scream to deafen the world.

Payton appeared beside me, still garbed as Quantum Girl. She offered me her hand, and, with her help, I stood up beside her, facing her. I hugged her so tight, as tears began to flow from my eyes.

"It's going to be all right," she said, gently rubbing my back.

I pulled away just enough to look at her and tried to wipe my tears.

"I don't know how it ever can be," I said.

She looked at me the same as Phee so often did.

"There are three people inside that house who love you very much. Go to them," she said.

I nodded and then phased back to the bedroom where everyone else stood in wait.

CHAPTER LV

Payton

The battle was over. The war had been won. But what of the rest? As I had these thoughts, standing in the crater alone, as a gust of wind blew the last remains of Thara-Klo into the vacant air, my eyes caught sight of a glowing silver bead. I squatted down and picked it up and recognized it for what it was—a god-stone—a quantum seed.

CHAPTER LVI

Peyton

I hugged my father, as I rested my cheek against his chest, tears flowing down like rain. His arms were wrapped around me, there to protect not Quantum Girl, but Peyton Elise Herron, the child who was his favorite, that one who was me.

"I remember it all," I said to him. "I remember Rendenaaar. I remember giving birth to Thara-Klo. And I remember hurting so many people! I was such a horrible person! Why was I ever born?"

"I don't know why *Khattaaara* was born," he said in a soft and comforting voice, "but I know that we raised you to be caring and kind. No matter what memories you have, you're who we taught you to be."

I looked up at him. It was then that Phee came to my side.

"You're not a horrible person," she said. "You're filled with compassion and love and whatever you were in the before, that was a billion, trillion years ago. You were given a second chance and you turned yourself into something special and good. Whoever you were as Khattaaara, that's not who you are anymore. You're Quantum Girl. You care about people. You are the very *definition* of a hero."

I smiled at her through my tears.

EPILOGUE

Payton

I stood in a quantum pocket in the hospital room as the doctor hung over Theresa like a harbinger of death.

"I'm afraid we're going to have to take her off life support," he told her grieving mother.

"What do you mean?" Mrs. Martinez wept out. "She's breathing! She's alive!"

"She's in a coma that she'll never recover from," the doctor said. "I'm sorry, but there's no hope that she'll ever wake up."

I phased a few hours forward. Theresa still lay in her bed. Her official death was not scheduled until morning. I walked up next to her, the god-stone in my hand. It lit up the darkness with its brilliant white light. I phased out the breathing tube and then placed the seed, the god-stone—whatever it was—on her forehead. It began to spin violently, shrank in size, melted through her flesh, and went into her brain. The heart monitor flatlined and then began to spike again. And then it happened. She opened her eyes and sat up.

"Where the hell *am* I?" she demanded to know. "And what the fuck are *you* doing here?"

"Theresa. It's me. Payton," I said.

"I know who you are!" she spat back. "You're the slut I hit in the head with the basketball. Get the fuck away from me!"

A burst of white energy shot out of her eyes and I was hurled across the room.

As I pulled myself up again I pleaded, "Theresa, please! You love me!"

"I could never love anything as disgusting as you!" she spat out. "Go away! Go back where you came from!" And then she screamed out, "Now!"

Suddenly, the room was filled with a blinding light that drowned out everything else.

When the light subsided I was no longer in the room. It was day again and I was standing amidst a crowd of oddly dressed people, with bright blue or violet eyes. The females had pointed ears and all of them had tails! I felt something behind me and looked back in horror to find that I had a tail as well!

"What the fuck!" was all I could think to say, but I spoke it in Gaaalthaaaran words.

AFTERWORD

The Quantum Girl Saga deals with a lot more than aliens and superpowers. They touch upon bullying, self-harm, and suicide. These are issues faced by young people today. As a teenager myself, I strongly encourage anyone twenty-five or younger, who is facing those issues or others such as sexual assault or date rape, substance abuse, child abuse, sexual trafficking, anxiety or depression, or if things are bad at home and you are considering running away, please call the Thursday's Child hotline at 1 (800) USA KIDS from a landline, or (818) 831-1234 internationally or from a cellphone. Phone lines are open 24/7 and are confidential and free. They care. I care. I'm Peyton Herron, Quantum Girl, and spokesperson for Thursday's Child. Their website is www.thursdayschild.org, where you can also get help.

www.ingramcontent.com/pod-product-compliance
Lightning Source LLC
Chambersburg PA
CBHW072121020726
47501CB00003B/919